ABOUT *WRITTEN IN FIRE*

The explosive conclusion to the bestselling Brilliance Trilogy

For thirty years humanity struggled to cope with the brilliants, the one percent of people born with remarkable gifts. For thirty years we tried to avoid a devastating civil war.

We failed.

The White House is a smoking ruin. Madison Square Garden is an internment camp. In Wyoming, an armed militia of thousands marches toward a final, apocalyptic battle.

Nick Cooper has spent his life fighting for his children and his country. Now, as the world staggers on the edge of ruin, he must risk everything he loves to face his oldest enemy—a brilliant terrorist so driven by his ideals that he will sacrifice humanity's future to achieve them.

From "one of our best storytellers" (Michael Connelly) comes the blistering conclusion to the acclaimed series that is a "forget-to-pick-up-milk, forget-to-water-the-plants, forget-to-eat total immersion experience" (Gillian Flynn).

WRITTEN IN FIRE

WRITTEN IN FIRE

MARCUS SAKEY

THOMAS & MERCER

Published by Thomas & Mercer, Seattle

www.apub.com

Amazon, the Amazon logo, and Thomas & Mercer are trademarks of Amazon.com, Inc., or its affiliates.

ISBN-13: 9781477827642
ISBN-10: 1477827641

Cover design by Shasti O'Leary-Soudant

Printed in the United States of America

For Joss, who burns so very bright.

Some say the world will end in fire,
Some say in ice.
From what I've tasted of desire
I hold with those who favor fire.

—Robert Frost

This must be what God feels.

A single glance at my outstretched hand and I know the number of hair follicles covering the back of it, can differentiate and quantify the darker androgenic strands from the barely discernible vellus hairs.

Vellus, from the Latin, meaning fleece.

I summon the page in *Gray's Anatomy* on which I learned the word and examine the diagram of a hair follicle. But also: The texture and weave of the paper. The attenuation of light from the banker's lamp that illuminates it. The sandalwood scent of the girl three chairs down. I can evoke these details with perfect clarity, this utterly forgettable and forgotten moment that nonetheless was imprinted in a cluster of brain cells in my hippocampus, as every other moment and experience of my life has been. At a whim I can activate those neurons and scrub forward or backward to relive the day with full sensual clarity.

An unimportant day at Harvard thirty-eight years ago.

To be precise, thirty-eight years, four months, fifteen hours, five minutes, and forty-two seconds ago. Forty-three. Forty-four.

I lower my hand, feeling the extension and contraction of each individual muscle.

The world rushes in.

Manhattan, the corner of 42nd and Lexington. Cars and construction noises and throngs of lemming-people and cold December air and a snatch of Bing Crosby singing "Silver Bells" from the opening door of a café and the smells of exhaust and falafel and urine. An assault of sensation, unfiltered, overwhelming.

Like descending a staircase and forgetting the last step, empty air where solid floor was expected.

Like sitting in a chair, then noticing it's the cockpit of a fighter jet going three times the speed of sound.

Like lifting an abandoned hat, only to discover it rests on a severed head.

Panic drenches my skin, panic envelops my body. My endocrine system dumps adrenaline, my pupils widen my sphincter tightens my fingers clench—

Control.

Balance.

Breath.

Mantra: *You are Dr. Abraham Couzen. You are the first person in history to transcend the boundary between normal and abnormal. Your serum of non-coding RNA has radically altered your gene expression. A genius by any measure, you are now more.*

You are brilliant.

People flow around me as I stand on the corner, and I can see the vector of each, can predict the moments they will cross and bump, the slowed step, the itched elbow, before they happen. I can, if I wish, screen everything down to lines of motion and force, an interactive map, like a fabric weaving itself.

A man jostles my shoulder, and I entertain a brief whim of breaking his neck, picturing instantly the steps to do so: a palm on his chin, a handful of his hair, a foot planted for leverage, a fast, sharp swivel building from the hips for maximum force.

I let him live.

A woman passes and I read her secrets from her sloped shoulders and the hair falling to screen her peripheral vision, the jump of her eyes at the taxi's horn, the baggy jacket and ringless finger and comfortable shoes. The hairs on her pant legs are from three different cats, and I can picture the apartment she lives in alone, the train ride in from Brooklyn, perhaps, though not the fashionable part. I can see the abuse as a child—an uncle or family friend, not her father—that framed her isolation. The slight pallor and trembling hands reveal she drinks at night, most likely wine, judging by the teeth. The haircut indicates she makes at least sixty thousand dollars a year, the handbag assures she makes no more than eighty. An office job with little human interaction, something with numbers. Accounting, probably in a major corporation.

This must be what God feels.

Then I realize two things. I've got a nosebleed. And I'm being watched.

It manifests as a tingle, the kind fools attribute to notions of "the collective unconscious." In truth it's simply indicators gathered by the senses but not processed by the frontal lobe: a tremor of shadow, a partial reflection in a glass, the almost-but-not-quite undetectable warmth and sound of another body in the room.

For me, the original stimuli are easily examined, focused like a blurry image in a microscope. I call up my sense memory of the last moments, the texture of the crowd, the smell of humanity, the movement of vehicles. The lines of force tell a tale, much like ripples in water reveal rocks beneath the surface. I am not mistaken.

They are many, they are armed, and they are here for me.

I roll my neck and crack my fingers.

This should be interesting.

CHAPTER 1

They were running out of time, but even so, Cooper couldn't stop staring.

There was nothing unusual about the rope, which was the kind of bright yellow synthetic cord used to lash down a tarp. What was unusual was that it had been tied in a noose and flung over a Manhattan streetlight.

What was unusual was that a corpse hung from it.

He'd been maybe seventeen. A good-looking kid, lean with strong features. He wore a McDonald's uniform, and across the bright yellow shirt, whoever murdered him had markered the word TWIST. Not random, then. Lynched by neighbors, coworkers, maybe even friends. Somewhere along the line he'd lost a shoe, and that was what Cooper couldn't stop staring at, the thin white sock, so exposed in the December wind.

"Jesus Christ." Ethan Park panted the words; they'd been sprinting until they hit the crowd gathered around the body.

It had been two weeks since seventy-five thousand troops were massacred by their own equipment in the Wyoming desert, the result of a computer virus designed and implemented by abnorms. Humanity never took well to the exceptional. And liked it even less when the exceptional fought back.

He was just a boy, Cooper thought. The sky was pewter and pregnant with snow, and the body spun slowly in the wind. Scuffed tennis shoe, shock of white sock, scuffed tennis shoe.

"Jesus Christ," Ethan repeated. "I never thought I'd see something like this."

My whole life, I've been afraid of seeing exactly this. It's why I've done all the things I've done: hunted my own kind, gone undercover as a terrorist, killed more times than I can recall. Taken a knife to the heart. Seen my daughter marked for the academy and my son in a coma.

And I still couldn't stop it.

"Let's go."

"But—"

"Now." Without waiting for a response, Cooper resumed his sprint. They'd covered half a Manhattan mile in the five minutes since the video hit had come in. Not bad, but not good enough. Not with Dr. Abraham Couzen only a few blocks away.

Ten in the morning and cold, the wind whipping down the avenue, channeled by redbrick buildings and construction barricades. The pedestrians Cooper shoved past carried coffee cups and purses, checked watches or spoke on phones, but to his eyes, they all had the edgy uncertainty of hostages told to act normal. In a deli window, a newspaper taped to the glass held a full-page photo of the smoking ruin that had once been the White House, the marble columns tossed like toys around the impact crater, beneath the words NEVER FORGET.

Not a problem, Cooper thought, and blitzed across 3rd, ignoring the scream of car horns. The tip had come from Valerie West, his old teammate at the DAR. Whispering like she was afraid of being overheard, she'd told him that a cluster of security cameras had face-matched Couzen. "Just standing there like he's taking the air. The prick."

An appraisal he shared. Dr. Couzen was the last hope of preventing full-scale war. All of the horrors of the last years—the academies where brilliant children were brainwashed, the rise of John Smith and his terrorist movement, the legislation to microchip abnorms, the devastation of three cities, the massacre of soldiers attacking the New Canaan Holdfast, all of it—they were just symptoms. The root cause was the inequity between normals and brilliants.

Abe Couzen and Ethan had found the cure. They had managed to replicate brilliance. To give normal people gifts. Once that was public, there would be no motive for war. No need for the majority to fear the abilities of a tiny minority, and consequently, no need for the few to fear the wrath of the many. No reason for the world to burn.

Except that instead of sharing their discovery, Abraham Couzen had packed it up and vanished. And the world had caught fire.

It might not be too late. If you can get to him first.

Pouring on extra speed, Cooper hit the corner and spun south, Ethan panting along behind. Valerie had done them a massive favor, but the same camera scan that had alerted her would have pinged others at the Department of Analysis and Response, not to mention moles in the DAR whose real allegiance was to the New Canaan Holdfast, or worse, to John Smith's terrorist organization. No doubt a shadow army was converging on 42nd and Lex.

Under the circumstances, there hadn't been time to come up with anything as refined as a plan. What he had barely qualified as an intention: get to Couzen first, and hope that Ethan would be able to convince his old mentor to see reason. If that didn't work, option B was to knock him out and drag him. Which would be fun in midtown Manhattan.

Lexington was five lanes here, southbound, a moving mass of taxis and buses. He sprinted past a Duane Reade, shoved between a couple of tourists with cameras, leapt into the street and back to avoid a pack of schoolgirls. The sidewalks held enough people that it took all of Cooper's attention to screen his moves. His gift afforded him an enormous advantage one-on-one, but was jammed by crowds; subconsciously, he kept trying to calculate the intention of every individual at the same time. Cooper gritted his teeth and kept pushing until suddenly he was free.

Too suddenly. And too late.

Fifteen feet away, a group stood in an edgy cluster. The one in the center was stoop shouldered and frail, with the jerky mannerisms of a bird. For all his accomplishments, Dr. Abraham Couzen looked like the kind of cranky homeless man who yelled at ATMs.

The four men surrounding him had broad shoulders and an air of intense alertness. Their suits were decent but not high end, and tailored to conceal shoulder holsters. Field agents. And, surprise surprise, the man in charge was Bobby Quinn, his old partner. Which meant the Department of Analysis and Response had beaten them here. Not by much, but life could change in—

Making Couzen's work public is the last hope for preventing a war.

Bobby Quinn could be convinced, but it might not be his call.

So what, then? Attack four DAR agents, including your buddy?

Well, they are focused on arresting Couzen. If you—

Holy shit!

—seconds.

It happened as fast as Cooper had ever seen. One instant the doctor's heartbeat was seventy-five beats a minute, slightly elevated but in line with the circumstances. The next it had leapt to a hundred and fifty.

Cooper started to shout a warning, but before he could, the scientist stiffened the first two fingers of each hand and jammed them knuckle-deep in an agent's eyes, flowed into simultaneous flat-hand chops to the tracheas of two others, then slammed his knee into Bobby Quinn's groin, twice. Before it had begun, the fight was over. The agents fell away, gasping and groaning.

Abe Couzen took a deep breath. His fingers trembled, and a trickle of blood ran from one nostril. Even so, Cooper sensed a stillness to him. Somehow, after having taken down four armed professionals in less than two seconds, the scientist was calm.

Until Ethan arrived, staggering to a halt beside Cooper. At the sight of his former protégé, emotions flashed in quick succession across Abe's face: pleasure, puzzlement, suspicion, anger. "You're with them?"

"What?" Ethan panted furiously. "No, I'm ... this is ... he's ..."

"I'm not with anyone, Dr. Couzen." Cooper kept his hands low and out. "But I'm here to help."

Around them, the world was catching on to the fight. Most people started to move away. A few pushed forward to see what was happening. Somewhere a woman gasped. Cooper ignored it all, just watched his target. He wasn't a reader, couldn't pick up deep secrets from body language. But what Abe was thinking was no secret. He was weighing the idea of killing them. All of them: the agents, Cooper, even Ethan. A pure and viper-cold calculation, laced with certainty. He believed he could do it

Instead, he turned and ran.

Horns screamed and tires squealed as the man leapt into traffic. A cabbie stomped his brakes, the car a yellow blur slewing sideways, colliding with a Honda. Abe didn't even slow, just shot past the accident in progress, the cars missing him by less than a foot. Cooper leapt into pursuit, but his angle was bad, and by the time he'd made the opposite sidewalk, his quarry had put thirty yards between them. He leaned into the run, not taking his eyes off the man's back as he dodged through foot traffic grown suddenly heavy, a stream of people exiting from—

Shit. Grand Central. Abe shoved in the doors, sending a woman sprawling in the process. By the time Cooper had reached the door, she was rising, saying, "What's your problem, asshole?" just before he knocked her back down. He sprinted the length of the hallway, past displays for d-pads and the new Lucy Veronica line of suits, and into the sweating cool of the concourse.

A roar overwhelmed him, the echoed overlapping of thousands of conversations. Over the loudspeaker a strained voice pleaded, "People! There are no more seats on the Metro-North

Hudson Line. I repeat, there *are no more* seats on the Hudson Line. Please, *please*, stop rushing the platform—"

Everyone in Manhattan appeared to be trying to leave. Beneath the starry dome of the main concourse, ticket lines had degenerated into formless throngs, the peace barely kept by uniformed soldiers slinging assault rifles. Every outbound train on the board was listed as sold out, but the voice on the loudspeaker did nothing to stop people from pushing toward the platforms, ticket or no. It wasn't a crowd, it was a mob, a howling, throbbing, reeking mob, everyone shoving and yelling, luggage slung over shoulders, children clutched in arms.

Bad enough for anyone, but Cooper *hated* crowds, felt dizzy and lost in them. His gift, never under his control, read the impulses and intentions of everyone at the same time. It was like trying to focus while the dog howled and the baby shrieked and the phone rang and the radio blared, only there were a thousand dogs and babies and phones and radios all going at once.

He took a breath, clenched and unclenched his fists. There was a trash can near one wall, and he climbed atop it, staring at the crowd, trying to sort faces, to spot one needle in a needlestack. A nearby soldier yelled to get down, but Cooper ignored him, kept scanning—

Saw him. Abe had glanced over his shoulder to check the pursuit, and in that moment Cooper caught a glimpse of his face. Despite the crowd, the scientist had doubled the gap between them.

Impossible. The mass of people was a living wall, packed shoulder to shoulder. No one would be able to get through them.

That's not quite true. Shannon would.

Before he'd known her name, before they'd saved each other's lives, before they'd become lovers, Cooper had called her the Girl Who Walks Through Walls. Shannon read people as vectors, could anticipate where a sudden hole would open, predict the spot others would avoid, sense which people would collide and slow everyone around them. "Shifting," she called it, and where he hated crowds, she thrived in them, could move untouched and unseen.

Abe Couzen was moving the same way.

The scientist sidestepped a falling man, flowed like mercury through the hole, turned left, stopped completely until a space miraculously opened between two shoving women. He slipped through, ducked under the arm of a guard, and pushed toward the far edge of the chaos.

Cooper stared, looking for a—

If you can't catch him, you have to guess his destination.

Trains leaving the city are sold out, but the subway can take him pretty much anywhere in town.

There must be a hundred places to hide effectively, especially given this chaos.

He took down four agents in a second, but he's running from you. Got it.

—solution. He jumped off the trash can and raced back the way he'd come. Once out of the main concourse, the crowd thinned, and he was back on the street in no time, nearly colliding with Ethan, who said, "Did you—"

Cooper shook his head and sprinted west, then north on Vanderbilt. If he'd read the situation right, Abe would have assumed that he was with the DAR. After all, they'd arrived just as Bobby Quinn tried to arrest him. He must have presumed Cooper was backup, probably one of many.

Abe Couzen was a genius. If he was running from the DAR, he would know that the first order of business was mobility. Hide, and the department could shut down Grand Central, access the security cameras, search room to room if they had to. Board a subway, and that train could be stopped remotely, transformed into a cage. Fight, and there would always be another agent. No, if Cooper was right, Abe would want to get back out on the street as soon as possible, and the closest door was—

Right there, where the scientist was stepping out. Cooper smiled, then strode forward. "As I was saying—"

"That's him! That's the man with the gun!" Abe was pale and shaking, pointing a finger in his direction.

For the benefit, Cooper realized, of the soldiers who stepped out behind him. Three of them, young, on edge, fingers on the triggers of their assault rifles.

It only took thirty seconds and his old DAR badge to clear things up.

But by then, Abraham Couzen had vanished.

CHAPTER 2

"I don't understand," Ethan said, for about the ninth time. They were in a cab, crawling westward. "*Abe* beat up those guys?"

"What'd you think, they slipped on banana peels?"

"I figured you did it. Those were DAR agents, right? Abe is in his sixties. And not a ninja."

Cooper snorted. He was used to people running—mostly that's what happened when he chased them—but this was different. He'd miscalculated, and the stakes were too high. He thought of the moment when he saw the doctor's pulse literally double from one beat to the next. *Control of the endocrine system to manipulate his own adrenaline level. Probably norepinephrine too, for focus, maybe even cortisol and oxytocin. Enough of those and anyone is a ninja.* "We should have guessed. Damn it."

"Guessed what? Cooper, what's going on?"

"Your old pal has gone and turned himself brilliant."

"*What?*"

"The little lab project you two whipped up, the magic potion that turns normals into abnorms? He must have taken it."

Ethan's mouth fell open. For a moment he just sat there, his eyes unfocused. "Holy shit." A grin split his face. "It works. I mean, the test results were off the charts, I knew it would, but we hadn't gotten to clinical trials."

"Looks like Abe skipped that step."

"What can you tell me about symptom manifestations? I wonder what physical effects he's feeling. How did his gift distinguish itself? Did you notice any—"

"Doc."

Ethan caught himself, laughed. "Yeah, sorry. I'm just . . . I'm having a sciencegasm."

"Try to breathe." Cooper sighed, rubbed at his eyes. "One way that his gift distinguished itself is that he had a bunch of them."

"You mean corollary abilities?"

"Nope. I mean distinct gifts."

"That's impossible. I mean, in children, sure. That's why the Treffert-Down Spectrum isn't administered until age eight. Before then, gifts are a free-floating proclivity toward patterning, manifesting mathematically one day, spatially the next. But as their brains continue to develop—"

"You're not hearing me." Cooper turned from the window. "I watched Abe's pulse double. Instantly. That's conscious endocrine control."

"So what? Something like 13 percent of brilliants have some level of CEC."

"12.2 percent. But more important, he took down four agents. You think those guys aren't trained for a tweaked-out brilliant? Plus, one of them was Bobby Quinn. I know you and he don't get along, but trust me, he's good at his job. Hormonal control alone isn't the answer. But if Abe were also physiolinguistic, he might be able to read their body language and tailor a series of attacks based on their positions."

"Those could coexist," Ethan said. "Your patterning is more than just physical. Souped-up intuition, right?"

"But then, in Grand Central, he was able to move like Shannon. He read the motions of the crowd before they happened."

"Maybe he just found a hole."

"There wasn't a hole. There wasn't room to inhale. And yet he barely slowed down. As icing, at the same time he worked out a diversion. That's like solving a quadratic equation while juggling and running a marathon."

Ethan was quiet for a moment. "If you're right . . ."

"This is what I do." Cooper blew a breath. "I'm right. And it's not just multiple gifts. It's the strength of them. I'm tier one and thirty years younger, and after what I saw this morning, I'm not sure I could take him. Which means that for all purposes, the good doctor Abraham Couzen is tier zero. And I'd like to know *how.*"

Ethan hesitated. "I need a minute to think."

"I bet." Out the window, the city scrolled past. The same New York he'd visited countless times, and yet, not the same at all. There was an uneasy tension to everything, a nervous twitchiness. America could take a punch, but the last year had been a series of haymakers. The stock exchange bombing in March, resulting in more than a thousand dead. Abnorm terrorists seizing control of Tulsa, Fresno, and Cleveland, the last of which burned to the ground in the ensuing riots. The destruction of the White House and the massacre of seventy-five thousand soldiers. Not to mention the erosion of the social order: shuttered financial markets, basic services falling apart, growing mistrust of the government, increasingly violent tribalism.

America could take more than one punch, but it was reeling, and the evidence was everywhere. Trash bags were piled on street corners, black plastic stretching at the seams. Private military contractors with automatic weapons guarded luxury apartments. Billboards advertised Madison Square Garden as a haven for "those feeling threatened." The rows of buildings seemed almost to be watching them, and it took a moment to realize that it was because so many had broken windows. A block of small businesses had been burned out, the glass gone, brick blackened, nothing but crusted ruins within. Graffiti on a scorched metal roll-door read, WE ARE BETTER THAN THIS.

Cooper thought of a flash of white sock, and wondered.

"Okay," Ethan said. "This is just a theory, right? Without data, I can't say for sure."

"Roll the dice."

"People have been searching for the genetic basis of brilliance for three decades. They couldn't find it because it wasn't there, not in the code. Our breakthrough was discovering the epigenetic basis of it. That's why the answer was so slippery, because epigenetics is about the way DNA expresses, not the genes themselves. DNA is the raw ingredients, but you can make very different dishes from the same ingredients, and human DNA has twenty-one thousand genes. That's a lot of ingredients. The trick is locating the specific cause. Abe called it the three-potato theory."

"Right, you told me," Cooper said. "If the cause of the gifts was eating three potatoes in a row, figuring that out is hard, because it's a big world. But once you know, all you have to do is eat three potatoes."

"Here's the thing, though. Nature is messy. Evolution is about random errors—mutations—that end up conferring a survival advantage and get passed on. But so does a lot of other junk, stuff that doesn't really do much but hitch a ride. So while you end up with three potatoes, they're ugly potatoes. Lumpy, deformed potatoes. But what we developed was different. We reverse engineered it, developing a gene theory that was carefully targeted."

Cooper got it. "You created a perfect potato. The Platonic ideal of a potato."

Ethan shrugged. "It's just a guess."

"But if you're right, then Abe isn't just gifted. He's the ultimate expression of brilliance. He can move like Shannon, analyze like Erik Epstein, plan like John Smith."

"I . . . it's possible."

Cooper took a deep breath. Exhaled. "Well. I guess we better find him then, huh?"

■

The apartment building was in Hell's Kitchen, a five-story walk-up on a street of weathered red brick and haggard trees. As they walked to the front door, Ethan said, "I don't know who this guy is to Abe. Isn't this a long shot?"

"When a long shot is all you have, you shoot long. Unless you can think of someone else?"

Ethan shook his head. "He's private to the point of paranoia. Vincent is about the only person I ever heard him mention from his personal life."

The front door was locked. Cooper found LUCE, VINCENT on the directory and rang the buzzer. No answer.

Well, you could always break the glass with an elbow, then kick in the hallway door. Noisy, though. Or you could—

Ethan Park leaned forward and pressed five call buttons at once. After a moment, a voice said, "Hello?"

Pressing the TALK button, Ethan said, "UPS, got a package for you."

"You've got to be kidding. There's no way that—"

The buzzer sounded and the door clicked open.

"What's the point in a lock," Cooper asked, "if you open it for the first disembodied voice?"

"Manhattan factor. You put a chain and three deadbolts on your apartment, and then start to get lonely. I used to live here, remember? A package isn't quite a friend coming up, but it's the next best thing."

They passed a bank of mailboxes and found the stairs. Halfway up, they were passed by a dude hustling downward, no doubt to meet UPS. The fifth floor was dimly lit and grungily carpeted. One of the doors hung half ajar, the frame splintered.

"Shit." Cooper motioned Ethan behind him and pushed the door open. The room beyond was typical Manhattan, in that a tall man could have cooked dinner from the futon. The walls were painted tasteful shades, and neatly framed posters of musicians had once hung on the walls. Once.

Now, the floor was covered with broken glass and smashed wood fragments. Stuffing gaped from slashes in the furniture. Shelves had been swept clean, drawers upended, curtains torn. A stand-up piano was lying down; the bow of a violin pierced a lamp shade. Debris crunched beneath Cooper's feet as he stepped in.

"Oh, man," Ethan said. "You think Abe did this?"

Cooper spun slowly, putting together the pieces. The shattered dishes, torn curtains, broken mirror. He stepped to the futon and knelt down. The fabric reeked of urine. There was a bloodstain on the pillow, fairly broad but centered in a specific spot, like someone had lain still as they bled. *Or been held down. Forced to watch.*

"You little shit," a man said, "we told you not to come—" In the doorway stood a man whose chest bulged beneath a Yankees jersey. Behind him stood two other guys, one with the same bland good looks, the other smaller but thicker. Yankees said, "Who are you?"

Cooper rose. Very consciously, he looked at the destruction, then snapped his eyes up to the man's face. Caught the quick dart of the eyes, the slight flush, the pulse kicking up, and knew the whole story. He forced himself to smile. "It's okay." He showed his badge. "We're looking for Vincent Luce. You know him?"

"Vincent?" The man scowled. "Thought I did. Heard him playing piano all the time. Weird music, kinda pretty. But it turns out he's an abnorm. Never said a word about that. Just been living right here without telling anyone."

"How do you know?"

"Walls are thin. He and some old guy were in here yelling at each other. The old guy said it, and Vincent tried to hush him up. Said it was real important no one find out."

Cooper nodded, took his d-pad from his pocket, and uncrumpled it with a flick of his wrist. He called up a picture of Abraham Couzen. "This guy?"

"Yeah, that's him."

"Okay, listen. I'm not here about a busted door or broken dishes. I mean, we're all normals here, right?"

Yankees nodded.

"So. You're a neighbor, and the walls are thin. I figure you probably *overheard* this going down."

The man stared at him, smiled slightly. "I got you. Sure."

"Tell me about the fight."

Yankees grinned. "Wouldn't call it a fight."

"They kicked in Vincent's door," Cooper said. "Broke his nose. Held him down while they smashed everything. Then what?"

"We—one of them told him to leave and never come back."

"You think he did?"

"When it was all done." Yankees gripped his crotch, mimed a firehose. "He got the message."

Cooper was overwhelmed by a sudden flash of memory. A bathroom stall, white porcelain stained crimson. His eyes blackened, nose broken, two fingers snapped, spleen ruptured. Twelve years old, back in California, one of his father's military postings. A bully and his posse standing above.

The worst angle in the world: prone, prey, broken, looking up at others looking down and laughing. Slowly, he nodded. "You've been very helpful."

"Hey, anything. Hope you find the freak."

Cooper let them take a step toward the hall before he said, "By the way, I lied."

"Huh?"

"We're not all normals." He rolled his shoulders and shook out his hands. "The three of you humiliated and beat the shit out of one brilliant. Let's see if you can do it again."

Cooper let that sink in, then turned to Ethan. "Doc, do me a favor, would you?" He smiled. "Shut the door."

. . . and we're back, I don't have to hope you stayed with us, I know you did, because here is where you find the truth. Not the liberal drivel the No-News Networks pass off, but the straight dope. Hundred-and-fifty-proof truth, uncut and uncolored, a coast-to-coast broadcast of nothing but the good stuff. Get ready to drink deep, because El Swifto is fired up this morning.

It's been two weeks since the tragic events of December 1st, when enemies rose up in the heart of our nation and used our own weapons against us.

And in response, America has done . . . diddly squat is what we've done, my friends, and that's just the polite term I'm using, because the one I have in mind is not radio friendly.

This country was founded by men who acted. Men of vision and strength who faced everything thrown at them head-on. That's the America I love. And in that America, we would already have rained death on Wyoming. We would have glassed the New Canaan Holdfast and mounted Erik Epstein's head on a spike. We would have blasted the whole collection of cowards and deviants back to the Stone Age.

But instead our politicians wring their hands and talk, and talk, and talk. A bunch of bureaucrats, that's what we've got instead of a government. Not leaders, not commanders, not world builders. Frightened little boys and girls without the stones to act.

This is America today, my friends. This is the American Nightmare.

Let's go to the phones. Dave from Flint, it's great to have you on the program.

"Swift, sir, it's an absolute pleasure. Thank you for telling it how it is."

Just doing my duty, Dave.

"What I want to know is, what can regular people do? I agree with everything you're saying, I'm ready to do something about the abnorm situation, but I don't know what."

Well, let me be clear here. The leftist media likes to accuse me of racism. They call me intolerant, a fearmonger. They fling similar insults at any patriot who dares stand up.

But they can't stop me from telling the truth, and the truth is that the New Canaan Holdfast in Wyoming—which slaughtered our soldiers, assassinated our president, and destroyed the seat of our government—is an abnorm group. Founded by abnorms, financed by abnorms, ruled by abnorms.

The Children of Darwin—who starved three cities and burned one to the ground—are an abnorm group.

John Smith—oh, I know, the liberals like to say he was framed, but you heard it from Swift, he's a terrorist—is an abnorm.

Some people say that not all abnorms are evil. Maybe. But this is a time of war, and while not every abnorm is an enemy, all our enemies are abnorms.

If there are good ones out there, patriotic ones who stand by their country, by our country, yours, Dave, and mine, then I say, fine, they're my brothers.

But my feeling is that there are ninety-nine decent, honest, normal people for every one of the twists—oops, the FCC will ding me for that—and it's time we remembered. So if our government is too weak, too soft, too tangled in gridlock, and too fat on pork to do anything, well, maybe it's time we acted ourselves.

Thanks for calling, Dave. Next up we've got Anne-Marie from Lubbock, Texas . . .

CHAPTER 3

"You can go in now, sir," the assistant said. "Can I get—" The rip-ping whine of a circular saw cut him off. When it died, he said, "Can I get you—" Again the saw screamed through lumber. The moment it stopped, the man opened his mouth to try again.

"I'm fine." Secretary of Defense Owen Leahy rose and walked into what had been the Speaker's office.

From behind a desk of heavy wood, Gabriela Ramirez nod-ded at him, held up one finger, and continued talking on the phone. "I understand. Yes. I'm trying to get you that assistance now." A pause. "Well, Governor, perhaps if you had declared a state of emergency when the Children of Darwin first attacked, you wouldn't be in this position. Yes. You're welcome." She tugged the headset from her ear and tossed it on the desk.

Leahy said, "Madam President."

"Owen," she said. Out in the hallway, a pneumatic nail gun went *thunk, thunk, thunk*, the sound only slightly more muffled here. "Sorry about the racket. You'd think that the Speaker's office would have been pretty secure in the first place, but evidently the Secret Service disagrees."

In 1947, Congress had codified the line of presidential suc-cession to seventeen places, although in the decades since, there had never been a need to go beyond the VP. Then in a span of three months one president was impeached and his successor murdered, and now Gabriela Ramirez, the Speaker of the House of Representatives, had become the president of the United States.

"I think the Secret Service is right," Leahy said. "You should relocate to Camp David for now."

"America needs to know their government is still functioning."

"America needs you to stay alive."

"What do you think about the yahoos in the desert?"

"Seriously, ma'am, Camp David is a fortress—"

"Wyoming, outside Rawlins. This morning's security briefing said there are a couple of thousand now?"

"About five thousand," Leahy said. "With more arriving every day. They're chartering buses, coming in pickup trucks with gun racks in the back. The camp is a mile from the New Canaan Holdfast fence line. Tri-d news picking up the story hasn't helped. May as well be running advertisements."

"All civilians?"

"Depends what you mean. They're survivalists, right-wingers, that sort of thing. Plenty are former soldiers. But there's no structure. Just disparate groups keeping to their own. Drinking beer and yelling anti-abnorm slurs. Firing guns in the air."

"You're not concerned."

"I wouldn't say that."

"What would you say?"

"That I'm monitoring the situation."

"Fine. Mind if we walk and talk? I've got an AFL-CIO thing." Gabriela Ramirez stood, took a charcoal suit jacket from her chair back, and slid into it. "What's the status on the military retrograde?"

"On schedule. All nuclear warheads were secured following December 1st. As of this morning, all ground-based missiles have been deactivated. Those carried by—"

"I'm sorry, but when you say 'deactivated'—there's no way that Erik Epstein can reactivate them?"

"No, ma'am."

"You're sure? His computer virus launched a missile that destroyed the White House, and no one thought he could do that."

Leahy fought the urge to grit his teeth, said, "They've been physically disabled. Like removing the spark plugs from a car. Nothing a computer can do about that."

The president took a final slug of coffee, set the mug on her desk, and started for the door. Leahy held it open. To her assistant, Ramirez said, "Geoff, tell them I'm coming down." Out in the hallway, the cacophony of construction noise bounced off the polished marble. Sawdust hazed the air. Two Secret Service agents fell into step in front of them, another two behind.

"What about naval vessels?"

"Long-range ordnance has been disabled on ships and submarines both. Which leaves us vulnerable to enemies abroad—"

"The air force?"

Leahy sighed. "All but mission-critical flights have been grounded, and those planes are flying disarmed. Throughout the entire military, distributed communications are being replaced with hard networks, computer-aided navigation and vehicle support are being taken offline, front-line technology is being gutted . . . look, ma'am, my office sent over a detailed report, but the short answer is that we are well on our way to turning the clock back to 1910."

"Are you on board with this, Owen?" Ramirez glanced sideways at him. "Speak your mind."

"I'm the secretary of defense of the United States. I've spent my whole life strengthening America's military, and I don't enjoy tearing it apart."

"I understand," she said. "But for whatever reason, on December 1st, Erik Epstein limited his attack to the White House and the soldiers threatening the New Canaan Holdfast. His computer virus resulted in almost eighty thousand deaths, but it could have killed tens of millions. Epstein had complete operational control. He could have annihilated our military and vaporized our cities with our own weapons. He claims he didn't because he was only acting in self-defense, but I won't leave him the opportunity to change his mind."

Acting in self-defense, Leahy thought. *She doesn't know it, but what that really means is, responding to my order to attack. My illegal order.*

Since 1986, when the existence of the abnorms was first discovered, America had been heading toward open conflict. The gifted were simply too powerful. Though they accounted for only one percent of the population, they were explicitly better than the other 99 percent. Demigods in a world of mortals. Unchecked, they would make regular Americans obsolete—or slaves.

Along with a few like-minded individuals, Leahy had fought to contain them. Public dissent and fear had been sowed. Special academies had been developed to reeducate the most powerful. And after John Smith planted bombs that destroyed the stock exchange and killed more than a thousand people, legislation had been passed to implant microchips in every abnorm in America. In the months leading up to the December 1st attacks, Leahy thought they had things under control. They had been so close.

But then President Walker's role in the plan had been uncovered, and he'd been impeached and brought up on charges. Vice President Lionel Clay was a good man but too weak for the big chair; he'd only been put on the ticket for electoral math reasons. As further terrorist attacks rocked America and an abnorm splinter group known as the Children of Darwin isolated three cities, Clay had dithered and hesitated. He'd even been on the verge of allowing the New Canaan Holdfast, Erik Epstein's abnorm enclave, to secede.

There had been no choice but to force his hand. So Leahy had ordered an attack on the NCH.

He hadn't made the decision alone. He owed his career and allegiance to Terence Mitchum, officially the number three man at the NSA. In reality, Mitchum had been the leader of their shadow government, a clear-eyed patriot who had understood that protecting a nation required firm action. Unfortunately, Mitchum had been in the White House when the missile struck. *One more casualty in a war the rest of the nation is only just acknowledging.*

Leahy said, "Self-defense or no, once we've successfully retrograded the military to boots and bayonets, we're going to have to invade."

"I haven't made that decision."

"Madam President, the public—"

"I know that everybody wants payback. But at some point we're committing to an ugly path. There has to be a solution besides genocide."

They stepped outside Longworth onto South Capitol. The Secret Service had commandeered the narrow street and built heavy gates and guard posts at either end. The only vehicles allowed were the presidential motorcade, today four armored Escalades, six motorcycles, and the limo itself. The morning was cold, exhaust steaming from the running vehicles, low clouds roiling above.

"I agree," Leahy said. "I don't want to wipe out the gifted. But we have to dismantle the New Canaan Holdfast. And we have to implement the Monitoring Oversight Initiative. Sign it into law and we can have 95 percent of abnorms microchipped within three months. I know it sounds old-fashioned, but it will work."

"What if they don't comply? What if they'd rather fight to the death?"

"In that case—"

A blast of sound and force tossed him into the air.

Swirling sky, gray marble, then concrete rushing toward him, falling, he was falling, and he put his hands out as he slammed into the street, a shrieking hum in his ears like an endless scream, and all around smoke and fire and bodies and people staggering, bleeding, an agent staring at her left shoulder where her arm no longer hung, her face lit by the burning ruin of the limousine.

Leahy gasped, coughed, saw blood spatter the street along with flesh—he'd bitten part of his tongue off. There it was, part of his tongue, lying on the concrete.

Hands seized him roughly, hauled him up, and he flailed, threw an elbow that was blocked, his arms were pinned as two men dragged him, and he tried to tell the agents to wait, that he needed his tongue, but then one of the Escalades was in front of him, agents leaning against the hood with sidearms out, firing gunshots he could barely hear, aiming in different directions—it wasn't just a bomb, it was an assault—and then the agents hurled him in the open door of the SUV where he collided with someone, the president, both of them landing in a tangle, the door slamming shut, someone thumping on it, and before either he or Ramirez could move, the driver jammed on the gas and the truck lurched, tossing them against the backseat, more gunfire, he could hear it more clearly now, fast *pop-pop-pops*, then a shivering crunch and they were flung again, the Escalade clipping something, out the window an inferno, the limousine, and then a burst of speed as the driver cleared it.

Leahy looked down, realized he was on top of the president. He started to move, then caught himself and shielded her body with his, lying on her like a lover, their faces inches apart, her eyes dilated and cheek torn. He could smell smoke and her perfume as his mouth filled with blood and the truck gained speed and the driver said something he couldn't hear through the hum in his ears and the thought that kept repeating: a voice in his head saying, over and over, that this was on him.

CHAPTER 4

Luke Hammond woke screaming without making a sound.

The screaming: watching his sons burn alive.

Joshua burning in the sky as his Wyvern came apart around him, jet fuel exploding in a wash of light sucked into his lungs to scorch him from the inside out as he fell, endlessly. Zack burning in his tank, trapped in twisted metal, hair on fire and skin bubbling as thick black polymer smoke choked the world.

Every time he'd closed his eyes for the last two weeks, he watched them die.

The silence: forty years of service beginning on long-range recon patrol in Viet Nam. LRRP, meaning way the hell out of bounds, so at nineteen he'd learned to wake fully aware and in control, because those who woke foggy died.

Wan sunlight beat down from a white Wyoming sky. Ninety-three million miles away, the sun was, and since his sons had died that number somehow seemed to mean something. Not the digits, the distance, the way something that means everything can also be forever out of reach.

"He's here."

Luke sat up, leaned against the frame of the pickup bed. December, and chilly, though thankfully not much snow. Snow might have done them in. He'd retired from the army two years ago, but he still did an immediate situational assessment, just like every time he woke, even though until recently the sitrep went something like: 0317 HOURS, AWAKENED BY STRONG NEED TO URINATE.

Today, though—lately, though.

Situation report: The beautiful boys who used to run at you, arms wide, saying, "Up! Up!" are dead. The sun-stained hours pushing them on swings and dabbing hydrogen peroxide on skinned knees did not protect them. The moments they fell asleep in your arms and you, bone-tired and sore, stayed where you were because you knew that this transient sweetness needed to be drunk deep—those moments did not keep them safe. The thousands of times you told them you loved them provided no shelter.

Your sons are dead. Burned alive. They are ninety-three million miles away.

What is left of you is fifty-nine years old. Washboard belly and pincushion feet. You were sleeping in the cold metal bed of your pickup truck, five miles outside Rawlins, Wyoming, a town built for passing through. Surrounded by thousands of similarly wounded men and women, all gathered for a purpose none of you can quite name.

"He's here."

Luke pushed the blankets aside and slid out of the truck. To the soldier who'd woken him, he said, "They still coming in?"

"Yes, sir. Faster than ever."

He nodded. Drew a deep breath, the air cold in his lungs—*Josh's lungs were scorched by a fire that burned at a thousand degrees*—and went to meet his old boss.

Major General Samuel Miller, retired, wore the weatherbeaten features Luke associated with cowboys, but his eyes had a city-savvy that weighed, measured, and collated the world. He wore fatigues with rank insignia, two stars on center chest, and looked more comfortable in the ACUs than in the slacks-and-polo combo he'd worn the last time they'd been together.

"Luke," the general said, shaking his hand and then pulling him into a hug. "I'm so sorry. Josh and Zack were good men. Good soldiers."

"Thank you."

His old friend studied him. "How are you holding up?"

"I don't know how to answer that."

The general nodded. "Stupid question. I'm sorry."

"Let me show you around."

They climbed into his truck, the interior as spotless as the body. He'd once taken pride in such things. Had once thought they mattered. Luke turned up the heat and then started moving, the dry ground crunching beneath his tires. "More than eight thousand people here now, and more arriving every hour."

The encampment was without order, tents flung up wherever people had stopped. They stood in loose groups, leaning against vehicles and talking, or warming their hands over smoldering campfires. Most had rifles slung over one shoulder or sidearms in hip holsters. They passed a motorcycle club, fifty bikes parked at precise angles, hard men drinking Budweiser beside a growing mountain of crumpled empties. The bikers nodded at Luke, and he nodded back.

"You've made the rounds."

"Yeah. Ever since you said you were coming out. Softening the ground."

"What are they like?"

"The stories are all different, and exactly the same."

Luke gave the general a casual tour, letting him take in the whole through its parts:

A militia out of Michigan practicing maneuvers in forest-green camouflage that popped against the brown scrub. The bus they'd arrived on had once been for schoolchildren, but it was now painted with the name THE NEW SONS OF LIBERTY, the letters five feet tall and gripped in the talons of a screaming eagle.

A bonfire burning, a circle of rednecks wasting a week's worth of wood in one afternoon, Credence Clearwater blaring like this was the mother of all tailgates.

A man field-stripping a Kalashnikov while a woman smoked and watched.

A circle of soldiers, gone AWOL but still in uniform, exchanging a sort of rough laughter Luke recognized. It was the kind that stood in for tears.

General Miller said, "They're a mess."

"They are. But more keep coming. All they need is leadership." He turned the truck around. "Show you something else."

Five minutes threading through campsites took them to the northern edge of the encampment. Beyond was nothing but rocky desert and gray sky—and, a mile away, a twenty-foot fence topped with concertina wire. The boundary of the New Canaan Holdfast. Twenty-three thousand square miles of land, 24 percent of the state of Wyoming, all owned by Erik Epstein, who had turned it into a sort of abnorm Israel. Luke shut off the engine. "Looks different in person, doesn't it?"

With the engine off, they could hear the wind, a low, mournful whistle that sounded like it had come from far away. Miller said, "I'm not going to insult you by saying that this won't bring your sons back. But I need to know if that's the only reason."

"Why?"

"It's reason enough to follow. But I want you to help lead."

Luke stared out the window. One finger at a time, he cracked the knuckles of his left hand. When he was done, he moved to the right. "Last week, I woke up on my couch. I'd gotten drunk the night before, thought it might help me with the dreams. All that happened was that I had a hangover to deal with too. I'd fallen asleep with the tri-d on, and it was some Sunday morning news program. One of those yappy debate shows. And there was this kid. Nice hair, bright shirt, Rolex. He was talking about how maybe the best thing to do was just let the NCH secede. Give them sovereignty, get on with things." For a moment he was back there, head cracked in a vise, teeth feeling furry, Zack's screams ringing in his ears, and this kid on his tri-d. "And this wave of something came over me. It wasn't anger, or hatred. It was . . . sadness. I felt sad for this kid, so ready to walk away from everything, and then it occurred to me how many others there must be like that. Next thing I knew I was in my truck, and then I was here, staring at that fence. And I wasn't alone."

Luke turned to his old boss. "Am I furious? Of course. Do I want revenge? Shit yeah. But it's more than that. That land out there, past the fence, it's still America. And I've spent my life defending America. I'm not ready to just let Erik Epstein destroy it, no matter how many billions he has or how much of Wyoming he owns."

For a long moment, General Miller said nothing. Just stared at the desert and the fence with those eyes, those ever-appraising eyes.

Then he said, "Good answer."

Elvis played here.
Led Zeppelin played here.
The Rolling Stones played here.
Now it's your rock stars' turn.

You just want to them to be safe. In these uncertain times, wouldn't it be nice to have a place your family was protected and cared for? Somewhere you could lay down your burdens and focus on the things that matter.

We're all hoping for the best. But if someone you love is gifted and feeling threatened, it's time to seek HAVEN.

HAVEN
@ Madison Square Garden

CHAPTER 5

Natalie's face filled the screen. "Shoot," she said. "I was really hoping to get you. Umm. Well, there's someone who wants to say hi."

Cooper had watched the video message three times already, but even so, his chest hollowed out with joy as the image twisted in a flash of colors that resolved itself into Todd's grinning face. "Hi, Dad!"

His boy, his beautiful ten-year-old son, not only alive, but awake, in a hospital bed, with a bad haircut from the surgery.

"I'm doing okay," Todd said. "It doesn't hurt much. And the doctors say I can run and even play soccer—"

"They said *soon*, honey—"

"And Mom told me you got him, you got the guy! That's awesome, Dad." His son bit his lip. "I'm sorry I got in your way. I know I screwed it up for you."

No, Todd, buddy, you didn't screw anything up. You were a ten-year-old trying to protect his father against a monster. The last thing you did was screw up—

"Everybody is really nice, but I miss home. I hope we can go back soon. I love you!"

The screen shifted back to Natalie. His ex looked tired. "Things here are okay. Erik is being good to us. He arranged this call—I guess the lines are . . . Well. We're safe." She took a breath, and he saw all of the things she wanted to say but couldn't. It was partly a matter of privacy; his family was still in the New Canaan Holdfast, and communications would be monitored. But there was more to it than that, he knew. The last time he'd seen her had been just after a killer named Soren Johansen had buried a dagger in his heart and put his son in a coma, the same day Erik Epstein destroyed the White House and killed seventy-five thousand soldiers. America had tumbled over the edge of a precipice that day, and he knew that Natalie was wondering what that meant. For him, and for them, and for their children.

In the end, she settled on, "Be careful, Nick," and then the video froze on a distorted image of her hand as she turned off the recording.

The call had come in while he chased Abe Couzen through Grand Central. *One more reason to backhand the good doctor.* It had been two weeks since Cooper had spoken to his family, and though he'd tried every day, he'd never been able to get through. The news blamed the NCH, said that Epstein had severed communication with the rest of America, but Cooper suspected it was the other way around. If the government planned to attack the Holdfast, isolating them would be an important step in the hearts-and-minds campaign.

Just in case, he tried calling them back. "We're sorry," the recording announced, "the network is experiencing technical difficulties. Your call cannot be connected at this time. Please try again later."

Redial.

"We're sorry, the network—"

Redial.

"We're sorry—"

Cooper hung up, pocketed the phone, and pictured Abe Couzen dying in a fire. It was a soothing image.

"That your ex?" Ethan asked around a mouthful of gyro.

"Yeah. Natalie."

"She and Shannon get along?"

"What do you mean?"

"You know, ex-wife, current girlfriend."

Current girlfriend. Cooper pictured the last time he'd seen Shannon, two weeks ago. He'd been about to lose a gunfight, one of John Smith's soldiers had him cold, and when Cooper heard shots, he'd expected to feel the bullets. Instead, he'd turned to find that Shannon had appeared out of nowhere, a submachine gun braced at her shoulder. She'd flashed him that one-sided grin and said, "Hi."

Problem is, half an hour later, you were saying good-bye. That was the way it was with them. They were soldiers in a shadow war, both living on the ragged edge of life. In theory that sounded romantic, but in reality it was hell on relationships. She was smart and sexy and incredibly capable, and together they made a formidable team. But they hadn't actually spent much time together. There was always some reason one of them had to go, some secret mission or desperate struggle. And the way things were going, it was hard to imagine that changing.

"It's complicated," he said.

"I bet."

Wanting to change the subject, he said, "You hear from Amy?"

Ethan wiped his lips, nodded, a weary sadness in the motion. "She's still with her mom in Chicago. Says that things are weird there too, but that they're okay. Sent a picture of Violet." He held out his phone, and Cooper took it. The little girl was cute in that shapeless way of young babies, and he had a sense memory of his own daughter at that age, Kate so small and light he could drape her across his forearm, and often did, chattering at her while he made breakfast in the sunlit kitchen he'd once shared with Natalie. A "surprise," they'd called Kate, never an accident. Her arrival had made them try extra hard for a while, but things had started to wear out between them, and it had been around Kate's first birthday that he and Nat had agreed it was better to part warmly than stay together and ruin it.

"She's beautiful." Cooper returned the phone and flexed his fingers. His joints had that bruised feeling, coupled with a line of fire where his hand had been split to the palm. It had been tissue-melded in the same underground clinic that had repaired his heart after Soren killed him, and while it hurt like a mother right now, and his heart still slip-skipped an occasional beat, his recovery had been near miraculous. *Gotta give Erik Epstein that much.*

"How you feeling?"

"Good enough for government work."

"Funny." Ethan crumpled the tinfoil from his sandwich, winged it at a trash can. "You were pretty rough on them. The guys in Vincent's apartment."

"They beat him, smashed everything he owned, and then pissed on him, all because he's an abnorm." Cooper shook his head. "I don't like bullies, Doc."

The cold of the stoop was creeping through his jacket, and his coffee was weak and acrid. In the window of a greystone opposite them, Christmas lights blinked in sequence, making paper snowflakes glow red and green. It was funny to think that someone had made the effort, had dug out decorations from a hall closet, found Scotch tape and push pins. The world kept turning even as it fell apart.

"How do you do this?" Ethan's question had the sound of words he'd debated not speaking.

"Do what?"

"This." Ethan made an *everything* sort of gesture. "I've been away from Amy and Vi for two weeks, and I'm going crazy I miss them so much. I want to hug my girls. I want to get back to work, I want to cook an awesome meal, I want to sleep in my own bed. How do you live this way?"

"Somebody has to save the world."

"You keep saying that." Ethan paused. "What if we can't find Abe?"

"We have to."

"Yeah, but, it can't all be on us, right? Things will work out. Like always."

Cooper understood. A year ago, he would have said the same. That while there were tensions and concerns, there was hope, too—systems in place, and civilization itself, which had a mass and momentum, an inertia that would protect it. That while the world needed defending, it wasn't so fragile that it might shatter.

A year ago he would have said all those things. Now, he just met Ethan's gaze and said nothing at all.

"All right," Ethan said. "So. We know Abe is here. And that he's tier zero. And that the DAR is after him."

"That last is the rub." Cooper sipped his lousy coffee. "There's a reason the logo for the DAR is an eye. Even with resources stretched thin, Bobby Quinn will be able to tap into surveillance cameras, news drones, traffic cams. There are hundreds of lenses in every square block. Manhattan is a hard place to hide from the DAR."

"Can we use that? Reach out to your friend, the one who told you about Abe this morning?"

"No. Valerie kept us in the game, but I can't ask her to play against her own team. Besides, even if she did, that would put us on the same footing as the DAR. We need to get ahead of them."

"How?"

"The personal angle. You know Abe, they don't. They won't know about Vincent. We find him."

Ethan considered it, as cloud shadows slid across high-rises and the rattle of the subway rose a block away and beneath them. "I don't see him going back to his apartment. Would he try to leave the city?"

"Maybe. It wouldn't be easy, though." Commercial flights had been shut down since Epstein demonstrated he could crash anything with a computer. That was part of the reason there had been such a rush on the trains. That, and the looming sense that an open conflict was coming, and that when it did, cities would be a dangerous place to be.

"He could have a car—"

"Nah," Cooper said. "Professional piano players, even brilliants, don't make enough to keep a car in this city." It felt good to work the problem. Though it seemed a lifetime ago, it had been less than a year since he'd hunted his own kind for the DAR's most clandestine division. Slipping back into that way of thinking was easy.

Vincent's racist asshole neighbors wouldn't have let him pack a bag, or maybe even grab a wallet. He might well be on the streets with nothing.

A friend? Possibly. But right now, Vincent won't be in a trusting frame of mind.

He's scared, broke, and trapped. Looking for . . .

Sanctuary.

Cooper stood, finished the last of his coffee, then crumpled the cup and dropped it in the trash. "Let's go."

■

He'd been to Madison Square Garden only once, for a Knicks game a few years ago, and had come in through the bright glass lobby, along with about twenty thousand other people. This time they headed for a side entrance, what had once probably been for employees, a set of grungy metal doors on the undecorated side of the massive building. A mobile sign on a parked trailer read, MADISON SQUARE GARDEN REFUGEE HAVEN, and below that, ALL GIFTED WELCOME. Two soldiers in active camouflage chatted by the door, the digital patterns of their BDUs flexing and shifting as they gestured.

"Gentlemen," one of them said as he opened the door. "Please have your identification ready."

The room was a cramped security antechamber. Cameras monitored every angle, and more soldiers manned a walkthrough scanner and an X-ray conveyor. A weary mother carried a girl of six while her husband argued with a pretty woman in civilian clothes.

"But I don't understand," he said. "I thought families could come."

"They can," the woman said. "But for your safety, we're quartering the gifted members of the family separately."

"I'm not leaving my wife and daughter."

"It's just a matter of bunk assignment. You'll still be together."

"If we're staying separately, then how are we—"

"Honey." The man's wife touched his shoulder. "We don't have a choice. Unless you want to wait for someone to break down our door and drag you away?"

The little girl startled at that, said, "Who's taking Daddy?"

"Nobody, baby," the man said. "Nobody." He stroked her hair. To Cooper's eyes, the man's rage and helplessness burned a dangerous shade of red, but he said, "Okay."

"Please step this way." The pretty woman turned to Cooper. "Welcome to Haven. Are you requesting admission?"

"No." He flipped open his wallet. The picture was of a wildly different man. A man filled with certainty, who didn't *hope* he was doing the right thing, he *knew* it. Fighting the good fight. Making hard choices for the greater good. Embodying the tropes that made him tear up at the heroic moments of movies—the swell of music, the bold self-sacrifice, the faith that the cause was worth dying for—all the soldierly clichés he'd bought into since he was a kid, they had belonged to:

COOPER, NICHOLAS J.
SPECIAL AGENT
DEPARTMENT OF ANALYSIS AND RESPONSE
EQUITABLE SERVICES DIVISION

Beside the ID was a badge, the logo in the center the all-seeing eye of the DAR. While he wasn't on active duty, technically, he was still a government agent on extended leave. He'd thought about formally resigning from the department when he'd accepted the job as special advisor to President Clay, but he'd been uncertain he'd stay in politics.

There's a wild understatement for you

The woman examined the identification. "Welcome, sir." She handed them plastic badges. "Please keep these on your person at all time; they grant full access to Haven. If you're armed, we'll need you to leave your weapons here."

"Why?"

"Just a precaution. We have several thousand residents and can't risk an incident."

Cooper wondered what that meant. "We're not armed. But maybe you can help me find a . . . resident. Vincent Luce."

She typed on hidden keys. "Section C, row six, room eight. Elevator to the fifth floor and follow the hallway out to the mid-court entrance."

Badges in hand, they bypassed the security station, where soldiers waved wands over the family's three sad bags. Packing them must have been hard. How did you decide which parts of your life to abandon? The father stared at him, and Cooper nodded. The man didn't.

They stepped into the waiting elevator. When the doors closed, Ethan said, "I do not get it."

"What?"

"No *way* I'd bring my family here."

"No?" Cooper pressed the button for five. "You tried to sneak out of Cleveland in the middle of the night past a military quarantine. You telling me that if there'd been a warm, safe place to go to, you wouldn't have considered it?"

"We didn't 'try.' We did it. And all prisons start out warm and safe."

"Prison? Come on."

"Look how quickly this came together. Just days after the attack they had sleeping arrangements, security, even an ad campaign. Someone planned it in advance."

"So?"

"So what are the odds they did it out of the goodness of their hearts?"

The elevator doors opened, and they stepped out into a bare concrete hallway. Soldiers and civilians moved through the unpolished guts of the arena: electrical conduit above, forklifts parked in alcoves, a faint tang of stale urine to the air.

"Speaking of residents and best interests," Cooper said. "Vincent is literally our only lead, and we're going to be asking him to betray Abe. Depending what your old boss means to him, he may not want to do that."

"I got ya," Ethan hammed in a bad film noir accent, "you're saying we might needs to get rough, show him the wrong end of a pair a pliers."

"I'm saying that he is going to help us, period."

"Wait. You're not kidding?" Ethan stopped walking. "Come on, man. That's Gestapo crap."

Maybe it was the leftover frustration from this morning, or the way the world seemed desperate to destroy itself, or the urine smell of the corridor. Maybe he was just tired and sore and hadn't seen his kids in too damn long. Whatever the reason, the rage surged snake-quick, and without consciously planning the move, he spun and put Ethan up against the wall. The scientist yelped in surprise.

"I am sick," Cooper enunciated carefully, "of being compared to the Gestapo." A voice in his head said, *Easy, easy,* but another pointed out that he'd had two chances to kill John Smith, that he had brought down one president and failed another, that hard as he had tried to make a better world for his children, all that had happened was that he'd hastened the end of it. "America is at war because I didn't act like the Gestapo. Seventy-five thousand soldiers died because I didn't act like the Gestapo. That boy was lynched because I didn't act like the Gestapo."

It was only as he said it that he realized that was what was haunting him. A dead teenager missing a shoe. That was the real reason he'd beaten three men senseless this morning. And why just now his muscles had moved ahead of his mind. He made himself take a deep breath, and saw the fear in Ethan's eyes, and his own rage drained away as swiftly as it had arrived.

"I'm sorry." He let go of the doc. "I'm just tired of people who never have to make these decisions telling me that I'm a monster."

Ethan stared at him. Opened his mouth, closed it. "Soren would have killed my whole family. You saved my wife and daughter. We may not always agree, but I will never think you're a monster."

Cooper nodded. Started away.

"A wee bit temperamental, maybe."

■

Cooper had anticipated a crowd of milling thousands, had envisioned loud conversations and the yells of children and maybe even some laughter. Instead, there were about a hundred people listlessly wandering the floor of the arena, speaking in whispers, their eyes carefully downcast. Dozens of armed soldiers watched them. The feeling was of a prison yard, or a zoo.

Beyond the floor, the seats had been removed, and the slope built out in tiers of prefab rooms like LEGO blocks, row upon row rising into darkness. The cavernous stadium was hauntingly quiet, the murmur of voices from the floor faint against the weight of all that space.

Someone planned it in advance. Cooper heard Ethan's voice in his head. *What are the odds they did it out of the goodness of their hearts?*

The soldier at the base of the Section C stairwell had a spray of pimples across his chin. He scanned their badges, then said, "Need me to unlock one, sir?"

"They're kept locked?"

"Yes, sir. For safety."

Cooper stared at him, said, "C-6-8."

The guard started up, and Cooper followed, one hand tracing the rail, smelling old beer and counting. *Seven to a row, twenty rows to a section, twenty sections, just shy of three thousand of them. Three thousand cages.*

Cages for people like you.

When they reached Vincent's, the guard swiped his ID card, then readied his rifle and said, "C-6-8! Coming in." He reached for the handle. Cooper stopped him. "I've got it."

"Are you sure?"

"I'm sure." He waited for the guard to walk away, then opened the door.

The prefab was maybe eight feet by four, the size of a walk-in closet or a sheet of plywood. A windowless box with just enough room for a bunk and a chemical toilet, the reek of which filled the air. The man lying down had the fine features of actors in scotch ads, although the black eye and broken nose diminished the impact of his good looks. Without shifting his gaze from the fluorescent, Vincent Luce said, "You're not a guard."

"My name is Nick Cooper. We need to talk."

"About?"

Cooper gestured at the door. "Want to get some air?"

■

The quietest space they'd been able to find was the old press box, where tri-d cameras would once have recorded Knicks games. Vincent leaned against the exterior wall, his eyes staring out at the arena-turned-prison, battered face reflected in the glass. "Is this where you do the waterboarding? I should tell you, I don't know any secret abnorm plans."

"I want to talk about Dr. Abraham Couzen."

"Are you kidding me?" The abnorm spun, fire in his eyes. "Unbelievable."

Cooper had been about to explain, but stopped himself. *That's not defensiveness.*

"First he outs me to my fascist asshole neighbors, who . . ." He caught himself, bit off the sentence. "And when I make the scared, stupid decision to come here, he wants to save the day? Screw Abe. I'd rather stay than have him be the one who gets me out."

"I thought . . ." Cooper paused. There was something he was missing here, something obvious.

"What, is this his idea of a romantic gesture?"

Oh. Cooper glanced sideways at Ethan, who gave a *hey, news to me* shrug. "So you and Abe are a couple?"

"We broke up a year ago. If you could call us a couple anyway. To be together you have to respect each other. He never saw me as a person. More like a fetish."

"What do you mean?" Cooper pulled out a rolling chair and sat down.

"He likes twists," Vincent said. "It was never me that turned him on, it was my gift. Look at his work. He could've cured cancer, and he spends all his energy figuring out how to make normal people brilliant."

"Wait," Ethan interjected. "He told you about our research?"

Vincent cocked his head. His fingers, long and slender, tapped out a rhythm on the glass. "You're Ethan Park."

"Umm. Yeah."

"I've heard a lot about you. So much that I almost used to be jealous."

"I . . . me too. You."

Vincent smiled coldly. "I doubt that. Abe didn't talk about things he didn't care about. But you were his bright boy. He said your work on telomere sequences was crucial. Part of the reason he now knew what God felt like. Asshole."

"When was this?"

"The day before yesterday, when he was showing me around his lab."

"What?" Cooper said at the same time Ethan said, *"His lab?"*

"Huh." Vincent looked back and forth between them. "I just figured it out. Abe didn't send you. You're chasing him."

Cooper thought about lying, decided against it. "Can you tell me about his lab?"

"That's why you're after him? Because of his work?"

"Yes."

"Are you going to hurt him?"

"No."

"If I tell you," the man said, slowly, "will you get me out of here?"

"You got my word."

Vincent turned to Ethan. "Can I trust him?"

"Yes," the scientist said without hesitation, and despite everything, Cooper had to admit that made him feel good.

A buzzer sounded, dull through the glass. The people wandering the arena floor reacted as if they'd been kicked, hurriedly forming lines, their eyes down and hands at their sides as they filed back to their cages. Staring out the glass, Vincent said, "My music is too advanced for most listeners, but Abe loved to watch me play. He'd always ask me to dual-solo. Play a separate solo with each hand, at the same time." The man shook his head. "I thought he liked the sound. But that wasn't it. He just wanted to watch my gift."

He turned to face them. "His lab's in the South Bronx, on Bay Avenue. He made a big deal out of what a secret it was, how he'd funneled money to build it, how even Ethan didn't know about it. I don't remember the address, but it's a one-story brick building, no windows, across from a salvage yard."

Cooper took his d-pad from his pocket, uncrumpled it with a flick, then called up a map. The street was near the river, and only half a mile long. He felt that old flush of certainty, the sense that he was right behind a target.

"What are you going to do to him?"

Still looking at the map, Cooper said, "You've seen how bad things are getting. We're headed toward a war or worse. Abe's work could prevent that."

"How?"

"By leveling the playing field."

"You're not concerned about the side effects?"

Cooper looked at Ethan, then back again. "Side effects?"

"Senator, respectfully, it's not a matter of grounding airplanes and taking missiles offline. The system that brings fresh water into your house is controlled by computer. Same with the system that manages sewage. The electrical grid is dependent on computers. Local, regional, national, and global communications. Oil wells. Televisions. Traffic lights. Vending machines. Food transportation and refrigeration. Automatic locks. Medical care. The limousine you arrived in. The watch you're glancing at now. There isn't a facet of modern life that doesn't rely on computer control at some level.

"So when you ask what is required to guarantee our safety from another December 1st, the only answer I can give is this: buy a rifle and move to a cave."

—FBI "Cyber Czar" Gisela Bracq, to the United States Senate

CHAPTER 6

Normally she liked the train. It was something about the dissonance between the seeming stillness of the ride and the dizzy blur of the outside world. The juxtaposition was comforting—symbolic, perhaps, of the way she chose to live. But today all of Shannon's focus was on one of her oldest friends, and whether she would be able to kill him.

She'd been back in the Holdfast for more than a week, watering her fake plant and staring out the windows of her unlived-in apartment, when Erik had asked her to come see him. Her studio was in Newton and he lived in Tesla, but when the world's richest man called, one hopped, and so she'd gotten on a glider and met him that afternoon.

His idea had been intriguing.

No, sweetie. Learning a favorite author has a new book is intriguing. A restaurant you've never tried is intriguing. Nick's smile when you shot the guard who had the drop on him was intriguing.

This is something else.

"Statistically poor," Epstein had said. "83.7 percent chance of failure to capture John Smith alive. 77.3 percent chance of failure to kill him. 65.1 percent chance of situation reversal, possibly resulting in your death."

"You know, you and John are a lot alike," Shannon had said.

"Negative. We comprise dramatically different personality matrices—"

"Maybe," Shannon said. "But one thing you have in common. You both really suck at pitching me jobs." It was only the second time she'd met Erik, the real Erik, not his brother Jakob, who was the public face of the man. The first time had been nine days ago, when she delivered a drugged and broken Soren Johansen to him. Cooper had asked her to, believing that Soren might give them leverage or information against Smith; at the time, Shannon wasn't so sure of that, but now she wondered.

Regardless, Erik didn't react to her jab, just slouched there, his face lit in flickers from the holographs that hung in the air around them: a topographical chart of the price of pork bellies plotted against incidents of terrorism, images of a rainstorm in the South China Sea, vector maps of bullets fired from various weapons, a time-lapse of moss creeping up a tree, news footage of a limo burning—the new president's, Ramirez, and wasn't it just the way that the first female prez in history nearly gets blown up two weeks after swearing the oath? This inner sanctum was a sub-terranean space more akin to a planetarium than an office, and while she had tried to play cool, it was hard not to be overwhelmed by the sheer lunatic volume of information. "Why would I agree to do something that is almost certainly going to get me killed?"

"The situation is increasingly fluid," Epstein had said in a voice whiny with frustration. "Patterns rely on data, but data is shifting too quickly. Impossible to sort it, parse it, specify it. But statistically, an attack upon the Holdfast is a near certainty."

"And you think handing over John Smith to the government will prevent that?"

"Prevent, no. Delay."

She'd sucked air through her teeth, looked at the schematics of the light rail train that hung in front of her. "John will know I'm not with him anymore. Why would he agree to meet?"

"Temptation. Significant stakes offered."

"What stakes?"

"Joining. Me. You. All of us, together."

That would be a temptation. John was his own revolution, and based on the shit state of the world, doing quite well. But how much more effective could he be with Epstein behind him?

"I'm not sure I'm willing. It's one thing to cross him, another to try to kill him."

"Preferably capture."

"In order to turn him over to people who will kill him."

"Previous subtleties of situation are now irrelevant. There are only two positions. For war, against war. Not choosing is choosing."

It was a fact she hadn't been able to dispute, which was how she'd ended up here, on the LRT that circled Tesla, a magnetic train without sound or vibration, the only evidence of motion the city blowing by outside. Shannon looked out the window and considered what it meant that John wanted a war. He was the greatest strategic mind alive, a man who thought not five steps but five *years* ahead, and if he wanted a war, it was because he believed he could win it.

That was a very sobering thought indeed. Brilliants were outnumbered 99 to 1. Any victory would involve oceans of blood.

Focus, Shan. You're already outmatched. Don't be distracted, too.

You don't know if your ace in the hole is actually an ace—or even if it's in the hole.

And John is supposed to board at the next stop.

Normally, being on a job made the colors of the day a little brighter and the taste of the air a little sweeter. But now all she felt was nervous.

The train glided into the Ashbury station without a sound. A handful of passengers got off, others climbed on. Midday, and the car was nearing capacity. Shannon had one boot propped up on the opposite seat, gave tiny headshakes to the people who eyed it. She scanned the people boarding, those navigating the rows. Two teens flirted. A young woman hummed softly to a newborn. An old lady dozed, her head rocked back at an awkward angle. A man in a cowboy hat moved down the aisle. The brim was pulled low to hide his face, but he had John's physique. Shannon flexed her fingers, ready to slide into character, only the man walked right past her. Shit.

When she looked back at the opposite seat, someone was sitting in it. A boy, probably sixteen, staring right at her. Shannon's boot was still on the seat, his legs on either side of it.

Well, aren't you slick.

"Listen, I'm flattered, but I'm waiting for someone," she said.

The boy said nothing. But now there was a d-pad in his hand that hadn't been there a moment before. Without a word, he held it out to her.

Her heart fell. Of course. Well, it had been a long shot. She took the pad, which glowed to life.

"Hello, Shannon," John Smith said on the screen. "I have to say, I'm disappointed."

"*You're* disappointed? At least I showed up. I'm here. Where are you?"

"I'm not in New Canaan right now," he said. "Which is probably for the best, since I see you have some new friends. I count six of Epstein's best tactical assets, including the fellow in the hat you thought was me. I suppose they're just commuting?"

"They're here for protection," she said. "We didn't know what to expect—"

"Stop," he said. "This is me."

She took a deep breath, let it out. "Okay."

"We're going to chat for a minute. But first you need to see something. Colin?"

The boy opposite moved in a blur, his hand flying into and out of his pocket. When he opened it, she saw a small cylinder topped with a button. Her stomach twisted.

"In the interest of time, let me dispense with your thoughts. No, you cannot move faster than Colin, nor can you shift without him noticing. He's gifted and very, very good. And yes, LRT station scanners are attuned to conventional explosives, so no, Colin couldn't have boarded with any. Which is why half an hour ago he injected himself with radio-triggered explosive nanites. Individually they're not much, but when they self-organize into a lattice in a host body, they pack a punch. The blast will take out most of this car."

She stared at Colin, took in his sunken cheeks, his fervent eyes, the sweat at his temples and throat. "Why?"

"I'd ask you the same question. We go back a long way."

"It wasn't easy. But I don't want a war, and you do."

"I don't *want* a war, Shannon; I *have* one."

"So why waste time talking to me?"

On the screen, John sighed. "On the off chance you were telling the truth about Epstein's offer. I thought there was a chance that he'd come around and realized we're on the same side. There are only two, after all, brilliants and straights. All the rest is window dressing, and sooner or later the whole world is going to come around to my point of view."

"You mean you're going to force it to."

"No one knows for sure why the Neanderthals went extinct," John said. "Some scientists say climate, some think it was direct conflict with *Homo sapiens*, others believe it was finite resources. Whatever the reason, the fact is that there was a species on the planet that was better able to survive. Simple as that. The gifted are the new order, Shannon. Conflict is inevitable. I'm just speeding things up a bit. And guaranteeing victory."

"Nice history lesson," she said. "But all you've done is turn the rest of the world against us. We're going to get creamed, John."

He laughed. "I don't think so."

She stared at her friend and longtime compatriot. A man she had fought and killed for, back when she believed all he wanted was equality. A man who had evaded capture for years, despite being the most wanted man in America, and who had built up a revolutionary army while he did it. *A man who beat three chess grandmasters at the same time when he was fourteen.*

She'd been nervous all along. Suddenly she was afraid. And not for herself.

"Anyway, I'm sorry it's happening this way. I hate killing brilliants, and I consider you a friend. But you're on the other side, and you're dangerous."

Shannon felt her pulse kick up, her hand start to shake. She looked at Colin. "Don't do this. You're just a boy, don't—"

"He's a holy warrior," Smith said, "ready to sacrifice himself for the greater good."

Colin didn't quite smile, but the words filled him with light, a feverish glow that strained at his pores and spilled out his eyes and made his thumb quiver on the trigger. He wanted to do it, she saw. He believed he was following a prophet, believed it with teenage certainty.

"John, there are civilians," she said, careful to keep her voice low. If anyone overheard and started to panic, Colin would undoubtedly press the button. "Innocents. Across the aisle there's a woman with a baby."

"I keep telling you. This is war. There will be blood. How can you not get that?"

He's not bluffing.

Time to see if that ace is worth anything.

"I do, John. And I have something to show you." Very slowly, hyperconscious of Colin's twitching thumb, she took out her own d-pad and activated it. Turned it so that he could see the video.

A plain white room, surgical and too bright.

A tray lined with glittering instruments: scalpels, pliers, wires.

A table with a man strapped on it.

"Soren?" John said incredulously.

"Thought he was dead, huh? I'm told he has a T-naught of 11.2. A second of pain to us is more than eleven to him. Can you imagine?"

There was a long moment of silence. When John spoke again, his voice was thick. "I was wrong. I'm not disappointed. I'm disgusted. This is beneath you."

"I agree. It's not me doing this. It's you."

Shannon sat perfectly still. Every cell in her body screamed. She could smell her own sweat. The lives of everyone in the train car depended on two things: how much John really cared for his friends—and how valuable he believed killing her was.

"You'll let him go?"

She laughed. "Not a chance. But you'll notice that he hasn't been touched, not a mark on him—apart from Nick kicking his ass, of course. But Epstein patched him up, and they've kept him humanely. So how about Colin puts away his remote, gets off the train, and we all go on with our lives?"

Smith's face revealed nothing, but she could imagine the calculations behind it. Weighing costs and benefits. She had no doubt that he would sacrifice Soren to agony and burn everyone on this train if he believed it was worthwhile. Out the windows, the scenery began to slow. They were coming into the next station. *If he triggers the bomb there, even more people will die.*

"John," she said. "I'm not that important."

Across the aisle, the baby let loose a squeal.

"Fine. Colin, you did well. Get off. If anyone tries to stop you, blow the train."

The boy seemed almost disappointed, but he put his hand back in his pocket and rose swiftly. As the train glided to a stop, he vanished in the crowd at the door.

"I misjudged you, Shannon. How does it feel to get dirty?"

"Lousy," she said. "But I'll just have to comfort myself with the thought that I saved all these people's lives." She clicked disconnect before he could reply.

And buried her head in her hands.

"I have no information on that. We only investigate crimes."

—Birmingham Police Commissioner Jarrett Evans
on allegations that off-duty police officers
kidnapped and executed three abnorms in Alabama

CHAPTER 7

Bay Avenue was a collection of bleak warehouses, light industrial buildings, and garages. The palette ran from brown to gray, and the air smelled faintly of fish. When the winter sun flared through a narrow slit in the clouds, dull glints fired off broken windshields in the auto salvage yard.

Abe Couzen's building was squat and ugly. No sign, no mail box, and in place of a traditional lock, a thumbprint scanner. Just as Vincent had described.

The only problem was that the door stood open.

"Get behind me," Cooper said, and Ethan moved with alacrity.

Other than a delivery truck rumbling in a loading dock fifty yards away, the block was quiet. Still, it was hard to imagine positive circumstances in which the good doctor had left his secret lab open to the public.

One way to find out.

Cooper pushed the door the rest of the way. The sunlight was weak tea, and what illumination spilled in didn't reveal much. Stepping lightly, he eased inside.

There was a faint hum in the background and an antiseptic smell. A bank of switches was on the wall. He debated for a moment, decided sight was better than surprise, and flipped them on. Fluorescent tubes clicked and buzzed to life.

The tables were lined with centrifuges and sensors and apparatuses whose function he could only guess at. A row of contamination suits hung like limp corpses. In the center of the room, one of the benches had been knocked over, the shiny equipment left where it had fallen. Broken glass sparkled. Glossy crimson was splashed in a line across one bench, onto the floor, then up the near wall, as though by the flick of a giant paintbrush. A bloodstained shirt and hoodie lay on the floor by a stainless steel refrigerator.

Dr. Abraham Couzen was nowhere to be seen.

Cooper put a finger to his lips, then gestured to Ethan to stay put. He moved to the far wall. The first door led to a small bathroom. There was half a roll of toilet paper on the tank, and the sink held toothpaste and a brush, a disposable razor and a can of shaving cream. The other room was a makeshift bedroom, little more than a supply closet with an army cot in it. No one inside, and nowhere to hide.

Shit.

In the center of the room, Ethan dipped a finger into the blood spray, held it up red and shining. Still wet. Cooper moved to the discarded clothing. Beside the hoodie lay most of a ham-and-cheese sandwich on cheap white bread. Several bites were missing. He was starting for a bank of servers when he heard the rumble of a truck engine.

Idiot. How did you miss that?

He turned to Ethan, just had time to say, "Doc, don't do anything stupid," before men burst in the door yelling.

They wore full body armor and headgear like motorcycle helmets. Their assault rifles swept the room in lethal arcs, a dance of clockwork precision, and Cooper knew that was partly a matter of endless training and partly because those helmets had a HUD that showed the position of every other teammate, as well as video feed, heat vision, weapon assessment protocols . . .

"Hands on your head! Do it, do it now!"

Very deliberately, he raised his hands and knit the fingers.

"On your knees! Down, down, down!"

He complied, thinking, *That delivery truck was running, and the driver in it was too fit and too alert.*

Thinking, *A squad of Faceless. The most elite tactical units of the DAR. I wonder if they killed Abe?*

Thinking, *I wonder if you're next?*

The commanding officer wore the same gear, but carried a sidearm, rather than an assault rifle. He stepped in front of Cooper and stared down, his visor reflecting the room. "Surprise."

Even modulated by the helmet's speaker system, the voice was familiar. Cooper shook his head, said, "Hey, partner."

Lifting one hand to his ear, Bobby Quinn pressed a button that retracted the shield, revealing a wolfish grin. "Hiya, Coop. Still trying to save the world?"

"Same as always."

"How's it going?"

"Same as always."

Quinn glanced at a kneeling and very pale Ethan Park, then turned to his squad. "They're friendlies. Secure the area."

The Faceless shifted into action smoothly, each commando moving to a task. Cooper took Bobby's hand and let the other man pull him up. "How are the nuts feeling?"

"Cracked." Quinn took in the fight scene. "You do this?"

"Huh-uh. How we found it. How long have you been watching the place?"

"We haven't."

"So then how . . ." He paused, caught Quinn's cat-with-a-canary grin. "Oh, you shit. You've been tracking us."

"Just since this morning. Didn't know you were in town before then. But when I saw you take off after Couzen, I thought to myself, 'Well, Bobby old son, you can run around chasing ghosts, or you can lie here clutching your yarbles and let Coop do the work for you.' PLR, baby. PLR."

"Path of least resistance," Cooper said automatically. "It's good to see you."

"You too. Doesn't mean I'm not going to kick your ass, though. Dr. Park, you can stand up now."

Ethan rose, walked over hesitantly. "Agent Quinn."

"Your ass I'm definitely going to kick."

"I'm sorry about running. I was protecting my family."

"Stow it. Where's your boss?"

Ethan shrugged.

One of the Faceless approached, said, "The building and surrounding areas are clear, sir. No sign of target."

Quinn nodded. "Close the door and clear the street. If Couzen comes back, let's not spook him. Meanwhile, secure and confiscate. Pack it all, every terminal, every piece of equipment, every cocktail napkin."

"Wait, you can't do that—"

"Dr. Park, you are *really* going to want to watch that tone."

Ethan took a breath, held his palms up and out. "Sorry. I just meant, you don't want to move the equipment yet. Some of it will lose settings if you power it down, and we need to know what they were."

Quinn sucked air through his teeth. "Okay. You've just been deputized. Help the team secure everything."

Ethan looked at Cooper. He nodded. The scientist hurried off, saying, "Wait, don't touch that, please . . ."

Quinn removed his helmet and tucked it under one arm. "How's Todd?"

"Awake. The doctors say no permanent damage."

"Man, that is *great* news. Where are they?"

"In Tesla."

Quinn's face darkened. "They're in the Holdfast? What are you doing here, then?"

"No choice. Couzen's work is the best hope to stop a war."

"Sir." The soldier who interrupted had his visor up, and Cooper was reminded just how young most of them were. "Everything's been cleared out. The server drives are gone, machine settings wiped out."

"What about physical notes?"

"No, sir. But we were able to access the security system." The man hesitated. "I don't think the target will be coming back."

Quinn paused at that, then turned and walked to the man's terminal. Cooper followed.

In the security footage, the lab was neat, the bench still standing, equipment unbroken. The time stamp read just half an hour previous. Dr. Couzen stumbled in, stripping off his blood-soaked clothes. The man looked ragged, and he was too involved in the act of getting a sandwich from the refrigerator to notice that he wasn't alone.

Not that it would have made much of a difference.

"Ho-lee shit." Quinn stared. "That's—"

John Smith stepped out of the bedroom, flanked by a man and a woman Cooper recognized. He should; he'd maintained active kill orders on both of them when he was with the DAR. Haruto Yamato and Charly Herr. Tier ones wanted on a long list of terror and assassination charges.

Abe must have heard something, because he spun. For a fraction of a second, the four stared at one another. Then Abe dropped the sandwich and sprinted toward the door. He'd made it halfway there when a muscular man stepped out to block the entryway.

"I don't know that one."

"Paul York," Quinn said, eyes on the screen. "Bombed the recruiting centers in Cali."

Three notorious terrorists, not to mention Smith himself. That's a lot of force for one scientist.

Then, on the heels of that, *Smith never does anything without calculation.*

The three fighters closed in. Against them, Abe looked frail, his chest sunken and spotted with age.

Right up to the moment that he tipped one of the heavy lab benches over, the force of the move actually lifting it a few inches off the ground to slam into Herr, as in the same motion the scientist caught a scalpel out of the air, whirled, and sliced a deep gash across York's chest. A rope of crimson splashed out across a bench, onto the floor, and up the nearest wall. The muscleman staggered back, and Abe turned to face Yamato, who had sidestepped the falling equipment and assumed a fight stance. Yamato's eyes were closed, but his hands flew in a dizzying array of blocks and counters against the storm of blows the doctor unleashed—

John Smith raised a slender pistol and pulled the trigger. Abe's hands snapped to his neck and touched the tiny dart protruding there.

Then he fell over.

On the video, everyone got to work without instruction. York spray-foamed his chest wound while Yamato bound Abe Couzen. After pulling her hair back, Charly Herr went to town on the computers, field-stripping them fast and yanking their storage units. John Smith stood in the center of the lab, turning in a slow circle. When he spotted the security cameras, a tiny smile bloomed on his lips. Through a distance of time but not space, he and Cooper stared at one another.

Then John Smith blew him a kiss.

For a moment, Cooper couldn't speak, couldn't breathe. His hands shook and he heard a roaring in his ears that seemed louder than blood. He was barely aware he'd moved when Quinn said, "Where are you—"

"There's a bar on the next block."

■

Cooper didn't really think the bourbon would help. So far he was right, but he figured persistence was a virtue. Beside him, Quinn sipped a club soda and eyed his glass with unabashed envy. "Now what?"

"Now I'm going to have another." Cooper slammed the drink, then gestured with the glass.

"I meant—"

"I know what you meant." Neon light fell on dusty bottles. He rubbed his eyes. "Three weeks ago we had John Smith in a burnout with a gun to his head, and decided to do the 'right thing.' Should have killed him."

"Three weeks ago everything was different. Funny world, huh?"

"Hilarious." They went silent as the bartender filled the glass. Cooper waited for him to step away before he sipped at the bourbon. "What's your play for Smith?"

"No play."

"You're going to let him get away?"

"The whole world is on fire, and there's a shortage of water." Quinn shrugged. "Smith has avoided capture for seven years. No reason to believe that's gonna change. Besides, he's not the priority he was."

"What do you mean?"

Quinn gave him a funny look. "Maybe you saw the news? A big white building blew up?"

"Erik Epstein isn't the problem, and neither is the New Canaan Holdfast."

"A lot of corpses would argue with you."

"That was self-defense," Cooper said. "If the schoolyard bully is coming after you, it isn't enough to trade punches. You lay him flat and you kick him hard. Show everybody that attacking you has consequences."

"So in this analogy," Quinn said stiffly, "America is the bully?"

"I'm just saying, Epstein *stopped*. He didn't have to. He could have ordered missile strikes on every military base, rained nukes on the country. Instead, he showed restraint."

Quinn's knuckles went white on his glass. For a long moment, he said nothing. When he did finally speak, his voice was brittle. "I can't see that particular shade of gray. And my old partner couldn't have either."

It was true. The man he had been would have wanted to knock the teeth out of the man who sat here today. *What a difference a year makes.*

"You haven't been to the NCH," he said softly. "Everybody is talking like it's an army of slavering rapists. But they're just kids, Bobby. A bunch of brilliant kids out in the desert trying to build a new world because they're scared of the old one. Rightfully scared. Remember?"

Quinn had been ready to retort, but that last word caught him off guard, and Cooper could see him considering the things they had learned together, the abuse of power by those who were supposed to wield it to protect. The president ordering the murder of his own citizens; someone in the government triggering the explosion at the stock exchange and blaming it on John Smith; the plan to implant microchips in every abnorm; the academies where children were brainwashed. All of the things normal people had done not because they were evil, but because they too were frightened.

"Maybe you're right," Quinn said. "But they attacked us. They killed our president and our soldiers."

"Despite what the last fifty years of American policy would suggest, 'They hit us so we're hitting back' is not a military strategy. I was taught that successful wars are waged for measurable goals. What's the goal here? I'd really like to know. What does victory look like? Leveling Wyoming? Killing all the gifted?"

His partner sighed. Reached for his soda, then said, "Screw it." He waved over the bartender. "Set me up with one of those, would you?" As the man poured, Quinn said, "All right, I'll bite. Tell me why I should keep after Smith."

"Because of Couzen. You know he took his own medicine, right? Made himself into a brilliant."

"Figured that this morning," Quinn said. "Only way to explain how he fought. But so what?"

"Ethan's theory is that the serum doesn't just make people brilliant. It makes them the ultimate brilliant, with a full spectrum of gifts."

"So you're thinking Smith wants it for himself. Drink the magic potion, buy a cape, turn into a supervillain?"

"No," Cooper said. "Ethan says their work would have no effect on brilliants. Something about the existing epigenetic structure of abnorms. He tried to explain, but my eyes kept glazing over. Point is, this would only affect normals."

"So what's the angle?" Quinn shook his head. "The agency interpretation is that removing the barrier to brilliance would lessen tensions, not raise them. If anybody can be gifted, there's less reason for fear. That doesn't play to Smith's agenda. Unless he just wanted to take it off the table?"

"No way. He came personally. There's only one reason he would ever expose himself like that—if he sees victory. Couzen's work is crucial to his goal."

"How?"

Cooper sighed and rubbed at his eyes. "I don't know."

"You don't know."

"I don't know *yet*. But I'm right. This is John Smith. He doesn't gamble, he plans. The strategic equivalent of Einstein, remember?"

"I don't know, buddy. I think you've lost perspective. John Smith is an asshole, but he's got what, maybe, *maybe* a couple of thousand dedicated followers? I just don't see how that matches up to three hundred million Americans."

"It's not about meeting on the battlefield. Look at what the Children of Darwin accomplished. A tiny offshoot of his organization, maybe thirty people in total. And yet they managed to seal off three cities, shut down the grid, and turn normal people against each other. Civilization is *fragile*. They're just now getting food into Tulsa and Fresno, and Cleveland burned to the ground. And that was just a stage in Smith's master plan."

Quinn finished his whiskey, set the glass on the bar. For a moment they sat in silence punctuated only by the clacking of pool balls and the mutter of the tri-d. The man had always been Cooper's planner, the strategist to his tactician, and Cooper let him think.

Finally, Quinn said, "It wouldn't take very much right now. People are hoarding food, fleeing the cities. And we're heading into winter."

"Whatever Smith has planned is going to make that all worse. Confusion and disarray are his favorite weapons. He wants America to slide into chaos. Wants every neighborhood to become its own nation-state. He can't face us directly, but if things get bad enough, if there's looting, riots, tribalism, local warlords, mass starvation, rampant disease . . ."

"Then he doesn't have to. He can pick off one target at a time." Quinn made a sound that wasn't a laugh. "Even if you're right, there's nothing the DAR can do about it. We'll happily take a shot at Smith if he wanders into our sights, but the department—hell, the country—is focused on the Holdfast. Like I said, the whole world's on fire."

"I know," Cooper said. "But I may ask you for some help."

"Doing what?"

"Finishing what I started." He set his drink on the bar and stood up. "I'm going to find John Smith. And I'm going to kill him."

Dear comrades!

As we continue to demonstrate the spirit and might of the great Democratic People's Republic of Korea in our eternal advance to the confident light of glorious victory, we offer a message of hope to the oppressed supermen of the world.

In the darkness of the failed systems in which you were born, your gifts are held against you, as always when dogs govern tigers. And so it is in the corrupt nations that the mighty of soul and purpose are mistreated, shamed, scorned.

Thus I extend an invitation overflowing with love for those who wish only to dwell in the sunlight of revolution. Come to us, our gifted friends, come to us, our brilliant compatriots. Come home and join your people, who live pure in purpose and clear in mind.

For the moment has come to reveal a secret long held—the Democratic People's Republic of Korea is composed entirely of gifted. Every man, woman, and child here is brilliant. Indeed, it was through the wise, benevolent, and self-sacrificing struggle of the Party that so-called "abnorms" came into being, developed by our scientists, who lead the world and are one of many reasons our magnificent land shines as a beacon.

Thus we invite all our brothers and sisters to renounce the failed ways of their corrupt hosts and return home to join the forward march along the road of destiny. The glorious present of our people can be the bright prosperous future of all as we extend our immortal nation on the path of eternity . . .

—Excerpted from the December 3rd speech of Supreme Leader Kim Jong Un, First Secretary of the Workers' Party of Korea, First Chairman of the National Defense Commission of the Democratic People's Republic of Korea, and Supreme Commander of the Korean People's Army

CHAPTER 8

Owen Leahy had come up through intelligence, but he'd never been a field agent, and the cloak-and-dagger stuff was starting to wear.

He'd left Camp David at oh-dark-hundred, the lone passenger on a transport flight packed with crates of medical supplies. After landing in Denver, he'd climbed in the back of a civilian Honda. While Secret Service agents drove, Leahy spent the next hours reading under a blanket like a kid after bedtime. In Cheyenne the agents stopped in the middle of a car wash, then directed him past the dripping hoses and into a precleared waiting room. He sipped burned coffee as an efficient young woman spent half an hour applying makeup: some sort of crackly rubber cement stuff that made him look fifteen years older, shading to deepen his eyes, powder to darken his skin, and a trim fake mustache. She finished it with a ball cap, and stepped back to gauge her handiwork.

"How do I look?" Talking hurt, but he supposed he should be grateful; he'd bitten off the front half inch of his tongue in the attack on President Ramirez. It was a testament to the wizardry of the presidential medical team that he could talk at all.

The woman said, "Forgettable. Your double is coming in now, sir."

They were hardly twins, but the man had the same build, wore the same clothes. Leahy took his keys and strolled out to the waiting pickup truck. The woman in the passenger seat appeared to be in her sixties, but her movements belied that; she had the grace of a professional athlete and a submachine gun tucked at her feet. She also had no personality at all, and he was glad the drive to Rawlins, Wyoming, was only an hour.

As wearying as the precautions might be, they were critical. God only knew what would happen if Erik Epstein discovered that the United States secretary of defense was meeting with the civilian militia camped at his door.

It was nearing dusk when they arrived. He knew that Miller had begun to organize the militia, uniting and inspiring them, but it was one thing to scan satellite images and another to drive through the encampment. It was a full-fledged tent city, thousands upon thousands of residents. Hand-painted plywood signs indicated the housing, mess, and training areas. A bed sheet stretched between two pickups read New Arrivals, with an arrow beneath it pointing to the east, where a large open-air tent had been set up. A teeming mass of people camping, talking, and training, with more arriving every hour of every day. Almost all men, of course, but they spanned the gamut from leather-clad hard cases to suburbanites in ski jackets. Everyone had a gun.

Epstein sowed the wind, and now he'll reap the whirlwind.

And on the heels of that thought, another: *The same could be said of you.*

When he'd given the order to attack Epstein's compound, his intentions had been simple—to force the president to act to respond to the growing threat of the gifted. He'd wanted a nice, small war, one that was easily contained, and out of which could rise a more stable world. A world in which the gifted were valued but also kept very much in check. It wasn't that he hated them. He just loved his own grandchildren more.

Of course, things hadn't worked out as planned. The goal was to manage the gifted, not annihilate them. But after the massacre in the desert and the destruction of the White House, well. His nice little war now threatened to engulf the whole country.

The bulk of the public wanted the army to fix bayonets and start marching.

Which would be a disaster. There were a lot of complicated reasons and one simple one: abnorms were responsible for most of the breakthroughs of the last ten years. If the bulk of American brilliants were wiped out, the nation would be shooting itself in the head.

There's still time. You've got a chance to turn this around.

And this ragtag army is going to help you.

Idly, Leahy wondered what they were doing about sanitation.

After all, fifteen thousand men generated a lot of shit.

■

"Mr. Secretary. This is a surprise." The general wore dusty fatigues. There was dirt under his nails and a pair of reading glasses tucked in his shirt pocket. Behind him walked another soldier, maybe fifty, lean with a killer's eyes.

"We don't need to stand on ceremony, Sam. Owen is fine." Leahy held out a hand.

Miller took it, his grip as firm as ever. "This is Luke Hammond. My number two."

Hammond nodded, said nothing. He moved through the tent without making a sound and took up a position against the far wall. The tent was active camouflage, and the pattern of the nanite-embedded fabric twisted behind him.

"Saw the assassination attempt on tri-d," Miller said. "A coordinated attack?"

Leahy nodded. "Three men, all brilliants. Two assault rifles and an RPG. Secret Service took them down."

"You okay?"

"Bit half my tongue off. They replaced it with a tissue graft. Newtech, some sort of vat-grown muscle generated off stem cells. Hurts like hell. Doc said I was lucky not to have a speech impediment." Leahy paused. "That would have been a career-ending wound. No one has any use for a secretary of defense with a lisp."

Miller smiled slightly but didn't laugh. "And the president?"

"Cuts, bruises, and a new respect for advice on issues of security. She's moved her office to Camp David."

"Good." Samuel Miller still carried himself with the air of a two-star general. A man used to being in charge of any room. "So. I presume this conversation never took place."

"I appreciate that."

"And I appreciate your courtesy in coming here personally. But you should know that we're committed." Before Leahy could respond, Miller held up a hand. "This is a civilian organization on privately held land. More to the point, there are almost fifteen thousand of us, with more arriving every day. Regular men and women who are willing to fight for their country—even if that means defying their president. We're not going to quietly stand down. If you want to get rid of us, you'll need to send soldiers."

"You've got the wrong idea, Sam. I'm not here to ask you to disband your army." The canvas of the tent billowed and snapped in the teeth of the west wind. "I'm here to ask you to use it."

■

"We could talk democratic morality and use-of-force doctrine all day," Leahy said. "The political climate, media impact, the costs and benefits of undeclared wars. But the bottom line is that sometimes to protect America, things have to be done that the government can't be seen to be involved with. This is one of those times. No matter anyone's feelings on the gifted or Erik Epstein, the New Canaan Holdfast represents a direct threat to the security of the country."

"I see." Miller nodded slowly. "You need a cat's paw."

"Just like always," Leahy said, "America needs soldiers who will do what is necessary to defend her."

"While providing plausible deniability," Luke Hammond said.

Leahy had almost forgotten the man was there, he'd been so still. "This isn't a political maneuver. It's a practical one. If the United States military attacks directly, Erik Epstein will use every means at his disposal to strike back. We're taking measures to limit the damage, but over the last fifty years, the nation has become so reliant on technology that protecting ourselves against the NCH is impossible. There are hardwired computers in everything down to our *sewers*. Any victory would be Pyrrhic. Unless we're willing to go back to a horse-driven agrarian society, abnorms can simply do too much damage. But a civilian militia acting without official sanction might be able to succeed without raising the stakes to that level."

Miller said, "What kind of support are you offering?"

"None."

"None?"

"No equipment, no troops, no advisors, no intel, no air support. There can be no trail between us. In fact, I suspect that the president will condemn any attack on New Canaan and order you to lay down arms. And when you refuse, she will order the army to stop you."

Hammond and Miller exchanged glances. The general said, "In that case—"

"But they won't." Leahy paused, let that sink in. The sound of gunfire drifted in from the distance, the steady organized cracks of a firing range. "The military will not intrude. That's what I'm offering you."

Miller stroked his chin. Hammond just stared with those dead eyes. Finally, the general said, "Owen, what you're proposing sounds like a coup d'état."

MARCUS SAKEY

"No. The military won't be seizing power, and neither will I. That's the heart of this. We won't stop you *because we won't be able to.*"

"The retrograde," Miller said.

Leahy nodded. "President Ramirez has ordered that domestic armed forces be reset to a non-technological level, essentially back to boots and bayonets. I'm managing that. And I can guarantee you that we will be able to demonstrate that despite our desire to do what our president wants, we simply won't be able to. Not without giving Epstein the same control he exploited two weeks ago."

"Which obviously can't be risked." Miller nodded. "But that situation won't hold."

"No. This is all based on you moving fast, Sam. If things evolve quickly enough, the military can credibly claim there's nothing we can do. That despite the president's righteous indignation, Epstein's previous attack proves that we don't dare get involved."

"What's to keep him from launching last-ditch strikes anyway?" Luke Hammond leaned forward. "If he sees that the Holdfast is going to be destroyed, why not take the rest of the nation down with it?"

"Two reasons. First, it would take a first-order sociopath to attack innocent civilians across the country if they're not attacking him—if they are, in fact, trying to support him. Epstein is many things, but he's not a monster. Second, the NCH as a whole isn't going to be destroyed. Your army won't be able to get past the Vogler Ring, not without military support, and Epstein will know that."

"Then what's the point? You're asking us to fight a war you know we can't win."

"Genocide isn't winning," Leahy said. "My God, man, do you think I want you to destroy the entire New Canaan Holdfast? The goal is to bring Epstein to heel."

"That's your goal," Hammond said. "Not ours. What's in this for us?"

"Payback. Your army wreaks the vengeance we all desperately want. You beat the shit out of the Holdfast, show the brilliants that actions have consequences. And in the process, you protect America. Isn't that what you've spent a lifetime doing?"

Hammond started to respond, but Miller held up a hand to stop him. "And the end game?"

A nice, small war. And a future for my grandchildren.

"Peace," Leahy said. "What else?"

CHAPTER 9

"—and I say that they cannot murder our brothers and have it go unanswered. They cannot murder our leaders and have it go unanswered. Because *we* will answer it." With ramrod posture and fire in his eyes, the man paced atop a bus painted with an eagle and the words THE NEW SONS OF LIBERTY. The bus was parked amidst a sea of people packed past the limits of the screen. At the lower third, a crawl identified the speaker as Major General Sam Miller, US Army, retired.

"Two hundred and fifty years ago, a group rose up against tyranny. Though they faced the greatest military power of the time, they were not professional soldiers; they were farmers, and shopkeeps, and bankers. They were ordinary men and women who said, 'Enough. This ends now.' They stood together, and they changed the world.

"Today, our enemies are not separated from us by wide seas; they are not communists or foreign kings. The modern enemies of America have grown up in our homes. They have eaten our food, attended our schools, worshiped in our churches. And then when it suited them, they attacked us in the most cowardly way. They didn't even have the courage to face us. They killed with a computer." Distaste dripped from the word, and the crowd matched it in boos and jeers.

"No," he said when they'd quieted, "the modern enemies of America are not on the other side of the world. They are in the heart of our great nation. They are just eighty-seven miles"—he pointed behind—"that way, in the city of Tesla. From there, terrorists launched an attack that murdered our sons and daughters in front of our eyes.

"Those in power tell us to ignore the blow. To turn the other cheek. To forgive those who stole not just our land, but our future.

"And so we are faced with a choice. Will we lie down and watch the dream that is America wither and die? Or will we, like those patriots of old, rise up?

"Make no mistake. Stand with me, and the weaklings in power will condemn you. Stand with me, and you may bleed. Stand with me, and you may be called upon to make the ultimate sacrifice.

"But in the histories studied by our children's children's *children*, this moment will live forever. It will live forever as the moment that America collapsed into darkness—or as the shining moment when a group of ordinary people, farmers and shopkeeps and bankers, rose up and said, 'Enough. This ends now.'"

Miller lowered the microphone and waited.

From the front rows, the cheer started. "This ends now."

Quickly the crowd began to pick it up. "This ends now!"

Until with one voice, twenty thousand people cried, "This! Ends! Now!"

"This! Ends! NOW!"

"THIS! ENDS! NOW!"

Miller stood rigid in the swaying waves of sound, staring out at his army—then snapped a picture-perfect salute.

The footage cut to a reporter wearing camping gear and an earnest expression. "Retired two-star general Samuel Miller, addressing a crowd outside the New Canaan Holdfast that has grown to more than twenty thousand people in the last two weeks. Support for the New Sons of Liberty has poured in, with sources ranging from grassroots donors to billionaire Ryan Fine, founder and CEO of Finest Supplies, the nationwide grocery chain—"

Cooper crumpled the d-pad and rubbed at his eyes. The chopper was civilian, quieter and smoother than he was used to, but in the seat next to his, Ethan Park still looked distinctly uncomfortable. "That's what we're flying into?"

"That's what we're flying *over*. What Miller neglected to mention is that those eighty-seven miles are occupied, defended, and surrounded by a big-ass fence."

It had taken longer than Cooper would've liked to get to the NCH. There had been a time when Epstein would have arranged a jet. Circumstances being what they were, the trip had taken two days, two cars, a train, and now this helicopter.

"Still. Are you sure this is the safest place?"

"Honestly, Doc, I don't even know what that question means these days."

"It means, asshole, that you convinced me to bring my family here. It means that right now my wife and our four-month-old daughter are on another helicopter heading for what's looking like a war zone."

"Would you feel safer in Manhattan?" Cooper gazed at him. "Convincing Bobby Quinn to let you come with me cost every favor he owed, and if he knew where I was taking you, he wouldn't have. Would you prefer the DAR chasing you? Not to mention John Smith?"

"No." Ethan blew a breath. "It's just . . . I never signed up to fight a war."

"That doesn't keep you safe when the bombs fall." The helicopter banked, and out the window he could see the mirrored city that was Tesla, the solar glass shining in the midday sun. "The only way out is through. You helped Abe figure out how to make people gifted once. Re-create that work, and General Miller and his posse won't be a problem."

Out the window, Tesla grew larger. The city was a neat grid arrayed around a cluster of shiny rectangular buildings that were the corporate heart of Erik Epstein's power. More than $300 billion in assets, spread across every industry. Wealth as a living entity, wealth that grew and morphed and shifted, that fed on smaller companies and spread its tentacles to every facet of American life. It was hard to overvalue that much money; larger than the combined market capitalizations of McDonald's and Coca-Cola, it had given rise to this new Israel in the heart of the American desert. A place where brilliants could live and work without fear.

Or at least that had been the idea. Cooper imagined the mood had changed some.

The airstrip was familiar. He had landed here twice before—once in a glider with Shannon, when he was undercover and they were both deceiving each other; once again a few weeks ago, aboard a US diplomatic jet, as an ambassador and special advisor to the president of the United States.

And now here you are again. Neither agent nor politician, but something different.

The moment the struts touched earth, Cooper began to undo his seat belt. He wasn't sure his message had gotten through, but if it had, they'd be waiting for him—

"Is this it, then? For you and me?"

Still staring out the window, Cooper said, "For now, at least."

"Then. Well. I never really thanked you." The somber tone brought Cooper back to the moment, and he turned to see Ethan holding out his hand. "For saving my family. I owe you one."

"No problem."

"Actually, I get the feeling the whole world owes you."

The sentiment, unexpected and probably overblown, nonetheless touched something in his chest. "Thanks, Doc." He reached out and shook Ethan's hand. "You did good."

They stayed like that for a moment, hands gripping, and it filled him with that warmth he'd always gotten from fidelity and camaraderie, the same feeling that had made him proud to be a soldier all those years ago.

Then the hatch was opening, and through it Cooper saw three figures running his way, and he was out of his seat and on the tarmac and sprinting to meet them, sweeping his son and daughter into his arms, hoisting them up to his chest and all of them laughing and crying and smiling like they'd found the last safe place on earth. He squeezed until he thought their spines might pop, Kate clinging to him, Todd saying, "Dad, Dad, Dad!" and pounding his back.

When he opened his eyes, he saw Natalie standing there, a smile on her lips despite the fear he could read in her posture. "Hey, you," she said.

"Hey, you." He set down his children and embraced his exwife, neither of them holding back as the kids hugged their waists and the cold gray of the afternoon swept away.

"Mr. Cooper," said a voice behind him.

He turned, saw a tall woman with the airy beauty of a runway model. It took him a moment to place her; Epstein's communications director, her name was—

"Patricia Ariel," she said. "I've got a car. Mr. Epstein is waiting for you."

He still had one arm around Natalie's back, and he felt her muscles tense. Todd and Kate both stared with identical heartbroken expressions. Cooper looked at them, then back at Ariel.

"Mr. Epstein," he said, "is going to have to wait a little while longer."

"Sir, he was very clear—"

"I think I've earned a day with my family. If Erik disagrees, he can send soldiers to get me." He gave her a lazy smile. "But he better send a lot of them."

■

Natalie and the kids were still in the diplomatic quarters, a tasteful three-story apartment on a public square. It was messy in a way he'd missed, that lived-in look that accompanied children— toys and books and blankets strewn about, plates in the sink, the smell of processed food in the air.

Todd and Kate chattered nonstop, talking over each other, telling stories and asking questions he answered as fast as he could: where had he been, was he okay, would he look at this drawing, did he see that somersault, had he met the new president, had he been back to their house, did he want to play soccer?

Yes. Yes, he did.

Wyoming was cold in December, the temperature in the midtwenties—negative two, the thermometer in the window read, the NCH of course having converted to the metric system—but he hardly needed a jacket to keep warm. Just standing in the quad playing with his family did the job.

Cooper tipped the ball up with his foot, bounced it off either knee, then toe-popped it to Todd. "How you feeling, kiddo?"

"I'm okay," his son said. "It doesn't hurt. I hate my hair, though." The surgeons had shaved part of his head, and the stubbled portion stood out like a scar.

"Neat thing about hair," Natalie said, "it grows."

"Slowly."

"I think it's cool," Cooper said. "You look tough."

"You look like a dweeb," Kate said, and giggled. Todd stuck his tongue out at her, then kicked the ball gently in her direction. He was a good kid, a good older brother. Cooper and Natalie shared a quick look of private pleasure, and one of those moments of psychic communication that came of years together. *Look what we made.*

"What have you guys been up to? Any new friends?"

Todd shrugged. "It's okay. I want to go home."

"I still like it here," Kate said. "But it's different than before."

"How's that?"

"The grown-ups are all scared."

Intellectually, he knew that his daughter was gifted, almost certainly tier one. But that didn't make it easier to hear his five-year-old announce that all her guardians were frightened. "Are you scared, honey?"

"No," Kate said. "You'll protect us." She spoke with the faith of a child, the simple certainty that her parents would keep the world at bay. That they would always catch her before she fell, always put themselves between her and harm. Which was good; that was what she was supposed to feel. And yet her words filled him with a mix of pride and terror more profound and powerful than anything he'd ever known.

"Right?"

"Of course, baby," he said, but because she could read him, the only way to make the words meaningful was to *mean* them. To commit wholeheartedly to everything that came along with them. In that moment, he knew that he would burn down the whole world if that would keep his daughter not just safe, but secure in the knowledge of her safety.

"Dad," Todd said, his expression at once steady and yet uncertain, like someone looking down at a long drop and standing very still, "how come this is happening? All of it?"

"I don't know, buddy." He paused. "I mean, we've talked before about how people are different, right?"

"Yeah, but . . . Mom told us that the president and a lot of other people died. That wasn't just because they were different, right?"

He looked at Natalie, caught her tiny shrug, and in another burst of that psychic communication, he could almost hear her saying, *Good luck with that one, Dad.*

There was the temptation to lie. But with the world in the state it was . . .

Kate kicked the ball to him. He pinned it beneath one foot. "There's not an easy answer to your question. Are you up to a complicated one?"

"Yeah."

Cooper looked at Kate, who nodded somberly.

"Okay. Life isn't like the movies—you know, how the bad guys just want to be bad guys, villains. In real life, there aren't very many villains. Mostly, people believe they're doing the right thing.

Even the ones who are doing bad things usually believe they're heroes, that whatever terrible thing they're doing is to prevent something worse. They're scared."

"But if there aren't real villains, what are they scared of?"

"It's kind of a circle. When people are scared, it's easy for them to decide anything different is evil. To forget that everyone is basically the same, that we all love our families and want regular lives. And what makes it worse is that some people use that. They make others scared on purpose, because they know if they do, everyone will start acting stupid."

"But why would they want that?"

"It's a way to control people. A way to get what they want."

"What about the guy at the restaurant who tried to kill you? Is he a villain?"

"Yes," Cooper said. "He is. He's broken. Most real life villains are. Usually it's not their fault. But that doesn't matter. They're broken, and they do things that can't be forgiven. Like hurting you."

Todd pondered that, chewing his lip. "Do the bad guys ever win?"

Wow. Cooper hesitated. Finally, he said, "Only if the good people let them. And there are a lot more good people." He bent and picked up the soccer ball. "Now. My turn to ask an important question."

"What?"

"You guys have been here for a couple of weeks." He cocked his head. "Have you figured out where to get decent pizza yet?"

They had.

■

After Cooper whispered his final goodnights and closed the bedroom door, he found Natalie in the kitchen with a bottle of wine and two glasses. She poured without asking, and he took the glass, clinked it with hers, then settled into the opposite chair. For a long moment they just looked at each other. Like coming home from a long vacation and walking the rooms, opening curtains, running fingers over tabletops. Reclaiming space.

"I was proud of you today," she said. "The way you talked to them."

"Christ. Why can't they ask where babies come from, like normal kids?"

"They haven't had a normal life."

One of the things he had always loved about Natalie was that her words and actions and feelings were more aligned than those of most anyone he knew. She didn't have a passive-aggressive gene in her DNA. If she was pissed, she told him.

So he understood that she was just stating a fact, not making an accusation. *But still. You're the reason for that. Your job, your crusade, your mission to save the world. If you'd just been a regular father, they would have had regular lives.*

Of course, if he'd been a regular father, Kate would be in an academy right now, her identity taken away, her strength and independence shattered, her fears cultivated. He'd seen firsthand what those places looked like, and he'd sworn his abnorm daughter would never end up in one.

Fine, but instead an assassin put your normal son in a coma. And you've brought both your children to the center of a war zone. So don't pull a muscle slapping yourself on the back.

Natalie sipped her wine. "How long are you staying?"

"Just tonight."

She sighed and reached across the table. Their hands met, fingers threading with easy habit. "It's important?"

"I'm going after John Smith."

Her fingers tightened. "It's too much. Why does it all depend on you?"

"I don't know, Nat. Believe me, I wouldn't mind a break."

"Are you sure you can't take one?"

He considered. Thought about a boy lynched in Manhattan. About soldiers burning in the desert. About the way Abe Couzen had moved this morning, the scientist's certainty he could kill them all. About John Smith smiling into the security camera and blowing him a kiss.

"Yeah," he said. "I'm sure."

She stared for a long moment, and he could read the struggle in her, the tension. He'd known her so long; they'd been little more than kids when they first got together, and he'd had her patterned in the most intimate ways for a decade. It had been one of the things that came between them, the fact that he knew her so well that he could often tell what she was about to say before she said it.

Like now.

"Okay," she said.

He nodded and squeezed her hand once more. Then disentangled his fingers from hers to pick up the wine glass and—

"Take me to bed."

—swallowed it down the wrong pipe. He coughed, spat what was left of the wine into the glass. When he could breathe again, he said, "Pardon?"

"Take me to bed."

He flashed back to a month ago, the two of them in a fort they'd made with the kids, and the kiss they'd shared. He'd realized at that moment that something had shifted in both of them. They had reawakened to the possibilities of a shared life. But the weeks since hadn't afforded them time to explore those feelings.

"Nat . . ." He stared at her, wanting very much to take her up on the offer. It wasn't just solace or desire, it was a longing for Natalie personally. She was as strong and sexy a woman as he'd ever known, and though they had made love a thousand times, it had been years, and the notion of that combination of experience and novelty rode his system like a drug hit.

But this was the mother of his children, not someone to trifle with. Not casual comfort. Besides, there was Shannon. They'd only been together a handful of times, but they'd also saved each other's lives, brought down a president, and fought side by side to stop a war. Their relationship hadn't been conventional, and there'd been no time to discuss whether they were exclusive, or even where they were going, but still—

"Nick, stop." She set down her glass and leaned in, hand on chin, other arm crossed at the elbow, her eyes bright and deep, hair falling tousled down one shoulder, smelling of red wine and cold air. "I'm not suggesting we get remarried. But you're about to go off on your own again, chasing the most dangerous man in the world, and I hate it, but I get it, and I know you're doing it for us. So before you do . . ." She stared at him for a moment that stretched electric.

Then she rose and gave a husky laugh.

"Before you do, come to the bedroom and fuck me."

DO YOU KNOW WHO YOUR NEIGHBORS ARE?

The DAR does. They've got a list of every abnorm in these Disunited States. Ask for it, though, and they say things like, "disclosing said information is not in the interests of public safety," because it could "jeopardize the well-being, both commercially and personally, of American citizens."

Igor, bring out the Debullshitization Device. Yes, good, my freaky little friend. Punch it in, let's see the translation.

What? Are you sure, you rancid cripple?

Huh. Igor says that translates to, "We care more about not panty-twisting the twists than about the lives of your children."

Luckily, there are still a few heroes-not-zeros in our drugs-not-hugs world, and more than one of them are members of our little hacker community.

And so, hot from the DAR systems, lifted like a goth girl's skirt on free razor blade night, is a list of 1,073,904 abnorms—and their addresses. You're welcome.

You better be grateful, bitches, because this looks to be the swan song. The Governot is already huffing and puffing to blow our house down. Payback's on you—make a little chaos for k0S, will you?

So take it. No seriously, take it. Download it, share it, spread it around like corporate PAC money.

Here's the whole list.
Here it is by state.
By city.
By zip code, you lazy twat.

This act of civil disobedience brought to you by the merry pranksters and puckish rogues of Konstant k0S. All rights raped.

CHAPTER 10

The room was the size of a large planetarium, only instead of stars, holographic data floated in the air, charts and graphs and video and three-dimensional topographies and scrolling news tickers, a dizzying array of information glowing against subterranean darkness. To the average person—to Cooper—it made little sense. There was just too much of it, too many unrelated notions overlaid against each other.

But to Erik Epstein, who absorbed data the way others took in a feedcast, it held all the secrets of the world. The abnorm had made his billions by finding patterns in the stock market, eventually forcing the global financial markets to shut down and reinvent themselves.

"Yesterday," Erik said. "Your delay was inappropriate. Time is a factor."

"Time is always a factor." Cooper looked around, his eyes adjusting to the gloom. Wearing a hoodie and Chuck Taylors, Erik stood in the center of the room, pale ringmaster to this digital circus. His eyes seemed more sunken that usual, as though he hadn't slept in a week. Beside him, his brother Jakob was the picture of refined cool in a five-thousand-dollar Lucy Veronica suit. The two couldn't have seemed less alike, Erik's extreme geek set beside Jakob's air of easy command, but in truth, they functioned as a team; Erik was the brains, the money, the visionary, and Jakob was the face and voice, the man who dined with presidents and tycoons. "And I don't work for you."

"No," Jakob said, "you've made that abundantly clear. In fact, you've failed to do everything we've asked of you."

"That's not quite true. I did convince President Clay to let you secede. Of course, that was before you murdered him." It probably wasn't a good idea to be so flip, given that he was talking to two of the most powerful men in the world. But Cooper just couldn't make himself care. Part of it was that flippancy let him tamp down his seething fury; no matter what he'd said to Quinn, no matter that he understood their actions philosophically, they had still murdered soldiers, and that he could never forgive.

The other part might have to do with last night. There were reasons he and Natalie had divorced, good ones, but they had nothing to do with the bedroom. A fact that had been demonstrated rather thoroughly last night, leaving Cooper with a loose-limbed jauntiness.

They hadn't discussed it this morning. The kids were up, and neither of them wanted to confuse Kate and Todd. But while last night had been rooted in the past, he knew now that Natalie was interested in the future. And she wasn't the only one. It wasn't just the sex, or even Natalie herself. They were good together. Easy. There had been a moment, as he took a break from cooking pancakes to hand her a mug of coffee, that felt as comfortable as slipping on an old pair of jeans and a favorite T-shirt. It felt like home.

"You're different," a small voice said. Cooper squinted, then saw the girl huddled in a chair, her knees tucked up in front of her, a screen of purple bangs hiding her downturned face. Millicent, Erik Epstein's near-constant companion and one of the most powerful readers Cooper had ever met. She sensed the inner fears and secret darknesses of everyone around her, had intuited Daddy's weaknesses and Mommy's cruelties before she could speak. A ten-year-old girl whose insight shaped billion-dollar deals and resulted in murders. As always, Cooper felt a flush of pity for her; too much, too much.

"Hi, Millie. How are you?"

"You're different. Did something happen?" She lifted her head, stared at him with ancient eyes set in a little girl's face.

Natalie astride you, her thighs clamped around your hips, her head thrown back . . .

"Oh," she said. "Sex. But I thought you and Shannon were doing it."

For the first time in a decade, Cooper found himself blushing. To cover it, he turned to the Epsteins. "You've taken care of Ethan Park?"

"Yes," Jakob said. "We've given him a facility that exceeds anything he's known, along with a staff, all brilliant. With his knowledge of Dr. Couzen's process, rediscovering the gene therapy to create gifts is just a matter of time."

"Which you don't have."

"Uncertain," Erik said. "The data is unclear. Disparate factors, personality matrices under exceeding stress, unexplored variables. Predictions are below threshold of utility."

"Yeah?" Cooper pointed at a video feed hanging between graphs, a high-angle perspective on the rocky ground outside New Canaan's southern border. The camp was a hive of activity, twenty thousand people preparing for war. "They seem pretty certain."

"Unimportant."

"An army is about to breach your border, and you say it's unimportant?"

"No. The term *army*, no. Militia. Statistically far less effective."

"Yeah," Cooper said. "But this is the part you've never gotten, Erik. Data only goes so far. Not all emotions can be quantified. You murdered thousands of people, did it on national tri-d. You want a prediction?" He put his hands in his pockets. "I predict they're coming for you."

"You sound almost happy about it," Jakob said.

You're goddamn right, you slick shit. That was my country you attacked, my soldiers you killed, my president you murdered—

He took a moment and a breath. "I'm just tired of everybody making things worse."

"Cooper," Erik said, his voice hesitant. "I . . . I didn't want to do it. They made me." The billionaire looked around the room as if seeking support, someone to tell him it was okay. "It wasn't easy. Isn't. I'm—I hear them, the explosions, and I see them dying. I didn't want to hurt them, but they wanted to hurt us. Were going to. I had to. They made me."

The dark circles under his eyes, the extreme twitchiness, the shoulders slumped farther than usual. He's suffering. The realization brought no compassion. "I understand why you did what you did." Cooper kept his voice level and cold. "But the people you killed were not monsters. They were public servants. Leaders. Soldiers. If you're looking for sympathy, I'm the wrong guy."

Epstein's mouth fell open like he'd been slapped. He stared for a moment, then turned away, pawing at his eyes with the back of his hand. Behind him the data whirled and spun, sharp holograms floating in nothing. Jakob looked at him disdainfully, then went to his brother, put a hand on his shoulder.

His back still to Cooper, Erik said, "The militia is not a factor. No sophisticated weaponry, no air support. Not a factor."

"You're underestimating emotion again. Especially hatred."

"And you," Jakob snapped, "are underestimating us. Again. The Holdfast is a long way from defenseless."

"Even so—"

"Others tried to hurt us. They died. If these people try, they will too." Erik turned to face him. "They will burn in the desert."

Burn in the desert? That phrasing can't be accidental. Cooper said, "It's true, then. The rumor about your little defensive perimeter. The Great Wall of Tesla."

"If by 'little defensive perimeter,'" Jakob replied, "you mean a redundant network of ten thousand microwave emplacements generating targeted radiation that can reduce flesh to ash and bones to powder, then, yeah. It's true."

"I don't want that," Erik said. "I like people."

Cooper wanted to hurt him again. Wanted to lash out and make the man feel what he had done, make him suffer for it. He checked himself. Despite Erik's actions, the sincerity in his voice was hard to question. *He's never made an aggressive move, only defensive. Brutal ones, certainly, but they were to protect his people.*

Besides. Like it or not, you're going to need his help.

"John Smith," Millie said. She was staring at him again, her eyes aglow with reflected data.

Cooper sighed. "Yeah. As bad as things are right now, he's about to make them worse." He told them about tracking Abe Couzen, about the fight on the street and the chase through the train station, the way Abe's gifts had manifested, and he walked them through his kidnapping. "Now, it's possible that Smith just wants to keep the serum from us."

"No," Erik said. "That would be the maneuver of a journeyman. Smith is a grandmaster. Every move functioning to highest efficiency on multiple levels."

"I agree."

"Which is why I asked you to kill him three months ago."

My God. Three months. Is that all it's been? Cooper flashed back to that conversation, when he'd first met the real Erik Epstein. The man telling him stories of ancient history, the early terrorists in first-century Judea who killed Romans and collaborators. How that had provoked a reaction that punished not just the killers but all the Jews. Comparing them to John Smith. Saying that if he were allowed to live, the US military would attack the NCH within three years.

Only, because you spared Smith—hell, you exonerated him—it happened in three months, instead.

You did what you thought was right, what your father taught you. And the world is suffering for it.

In a very real way, this is your fault.

"Yes," Millie said.

He fought the urge to glare, to snap at them, to say that he'd done the best he could. Forced it down, and his temper with it, until he could speak in steady, level tones.

"We've been over my mistakes. And yours. For now, we have to put that aside and focus on ending this. Because John Smith certainly is."

For a moment, the brothers just stared at each other. Finally, Erik turned to him. "What do you propose?"

"First we've got to find Smith. I don't suppose you know where he is?"

"No."

"You did before."

"That was before."

Right. Well, so much for the easy way.

"Then I need to talk to someone who does." Cooper took a deep breath, let it out slowly. "I need to sit down with the man who killed me."

"I just wanted to see if it would work."

—ERNIE ITO, 11, ON WHY HE RELEASED A HOMEGROWN STRAIN OF
BOTULISM IN HIS MIDDLE SCHOOL CAFETERIA, RESULTING IN THE
HOSPITALIZATION OF MORE THAN FOUR HUNDRED CHILDREN AND
THREE DEATHS TO DATE. ITO, A TIER-TWO BRILLIANT, DEVELOPED
THE BACTERIAL STRAIN AS A SCIENCE FAIR PROJECT.

CHAPTER 11

As the chain drew taut, Luke Hammond felt something bloom in his chest. A raw feeling he'd known a few times before.

At nineteen, huddled in the bush in Laos, watching a village burn, black smoke blotting out a sweating sky.

On a ruined rooftop in Beirut as an ancient mosque collapsed in a cloud of dust.

Staring at the computer monitor tracking operators terminating a training camp in El Salvador.

It wasn't a feeling he'd sought out. Not one he was proud of, per se. Not something he'd tried to pass to his sons, but though they'd never discussed it, he'd suspected each had known it as well.

A furious, terrible joy in destruction. The triumphant howl of victory—*no, not quite*—of . . . power. Power that you possessed and your enemy did not.

He downshifted the truck, looked to his left and right, to the dozens of others, pickups and jeeps and semis, all tethered by cold steel chains to the fence behind which hid the people who had murdered his children.

Then he hit the horn, held it for a long blast. A second time.

On the third, he floored the gas, heard the roar from all the other engines as their drivers did the same.

A strained scream filled the air as steel stretched to the breaking point, and he let up, put the truck in reverse, bounced back ten feet, then threw it forward again, the others doing the same, and the collective force rippled back through the chains to the fence, the metal bending, earth popping, razor wire twining and singing, and the post ripped right out of the ground, along with nineteen of its brothers. In his rearview mirror, he saw a hundred-yard span of the New Canaan Holdfast's border ripple and collapse.

Then, from the crowd, the cheer.

"This. Ends. Now!"

Thousands of voices yelling as one.

"This. Ends! Now!"

Pounding through his chest, pumping through his veins, howling through his lungs.

"This! Ends! Now!"

■

The past days had been a blur of activity. There seemed always to be fifty things that needed doing, a hundred urgent tasks. They'd established a command hierarchy, not a formal rank structure so much as a loose delegation of effort. Miller was at the top and Luke his number two, but beneath them were ten other former soldiers who formed the primary team. After that, leaders were chosen by the groups they represented. Miller had been adamant about that, insisting the leadership be shallow and wide. They were analysts and ad men, the presidents of motorcycle clubs and backwater militia commanders, neighborhood watch organizers alongside scoutmasters. Those who had come as a group tended to stay with it; others paired off like pickup teams for a basketball game, resulting in ragtag squads ranging from ten to two hundred.

Thus far, the system worked. For all the differences, everyone was united by anger and pain and loss. There had been squabbles, but fewer than Luke would have guessed.

"As long as we keep moving," Miller had said, "we'll hold together."

"At least until the dying starts. This isn't an army."

The general had smiled grimly. "The dying is what will turn us into one."

Time would tell, Luke supposed, but over the years he'd known Miller, he'd learned not to bet against him. Besides, there had been so much to do.

What had started as an impromptu gathering had grown to a massive endeavor. People divided according to rough experience, accountants managing logistics, history professors teaching tactics, line cooks feeding thousands. But it was the private support that really made the difference.

"Check it out, boss—we've got corporate sponsorship," Ronnie Delgado had joked when the trucks from Finest Supplies started arriving. Eighteen-wheelers packed with canned goods, bottled water, blankets, rifles, ammunition, all of it donated by Ryan Fine, the CEO the news kept referring to as an "eccentric billionaire."

"That's the great thing about being a billionaire," Delgado said. "Poor people they just call crazy."

Delgado was a ranch hand and former national guardsman, a twenty-eight-year-old kid who'd turned out to be a godsend. He worked tirelessly and maintained a steady stream of quips that lightened the mood, but more than anything it was his way with horses.

When General Miller had first announced that he'd convinced Ryan Fine to empty his stables for them—*Delgado: "What is it about corporate dudes that as soon as they get rich they want to put on cowboy boots?"*—Luke had been less than excited. A thousand horses following in their wake seemed a noisy, smelly irritation. While Luke had never been of the new breed of soldier, those more like hackers than warriors, this took low tech to the extreme.

"Horses don't break down," Miller had said. "Computer viruses don't hurt them, and they don't need gasoline."

"And when we run out of food for them?"

"Then we've got fresh meat."

■

Now, after a blur of constant effort and rapid decision-making, of bleary-eyed labor and bad coffee, it was time. The hundred-yard hole they'd ripped in the New Canaan fence was the first strike.

The trucks led the way. Each had a driver and another man riding shotgun; the rest of the space was packed with supplies, every spare inch filled. It was an inversion of traditional tactics, sending the supply train ahead of the army, but they didn't expect the vehicles to get far.

Behind them, the rest of the New Sons of Liberty streamed in on foot. They slung packs and rifles, moved in loose groups. Twenty thousand people filing over the torn and broken fence, boots grinding it into the dirt. The day was just below freezing, but the sky was clear, and the men—women too, though not many— moved with a nervous energy, talking and shouting and singing as if they were heading into a football stadium, not marching off to war.

"Here we go," Delgado said. "The charge of the world's largest lynch mob."

"Hey," Luke said sharply. "Police that."

"I'm just kidding, boss—"

"Not even as a joke. We may not be the Continental army, but we're not the KKK, either. This isn't about hatred."

Delgado said, "My brother was the first to go to college. Princeton, full scholarship. He beat out five hundred candidates to get a job as a White House intern. Mostly he fetched coffee and answered phones, and that's probably what he was doing when Erik Epstein blew him up. So don't—"

"My sons," Luke said, fighting to keep the quaver from his voice, "burned alive. One was a fighter pilot, the other a tank gunner. We've all lost somebody, Ronnie." He took a breath. "Check the horses, will you?" He paused. "Hey. I'm sorry about your brother."

Delgado nodded. "You too. Your boys."

Luke moved through the crowd, shaking hands, answering questions. Everyone knew who he was, and more than one of them said, "This ends now." He returned it, the meaning of the words already lost to him, transformed into mere sounds.

It took him an hour to catch up to Miller. The general was near the front of the ragged column, on foot. He smiled when he saw Luke. "'And Crispin Crispian shall ne'er go by, from this day to the ending of the world, but we in it shall be remembered.'"

"'We few, we happy few, we band of brothers,'" Luke replied. "'For he today that sheds his blood with me shall be my brother.' *Henry the Fifth*. You think the bleeding is gonna start this afternoon?"

Miller shrugged. "Soon enough."

"We could have spared a jeep, you know. You didn't need to walk."

"MacArthur didn't need to wade ashore in the Philippines, either. Army engineers had put out pontoons for him. But old Douglas knew what he was doing." The general checked his watch, glanced at the horizon. There was nothing to see but dusty scrub leading to distant mountains beneath grim skies. Very grim; when the destruction started, it would come from above.

That will be the moment, Luke thought. *We'll either win in that moment, or we'll break, and the New Sons of Liberty won't be even a footnote in the histories.* "Ask you something? Secretary Leahy. You trust him?"

"Not particularly," Miller said. "Owen's a politician. But he'll do what he said, and hold off the military. It serves his ends. He figures if we drive deep enough into the Holdfast, Epstein will come to the government with his hat in hand. Trade his people's freedom for their lives."

"That was my read too. But if he's just using us—"

"Why go along? First, it serves our ends. But more than that, by the time he realizes we've got other plans, it will be too late."

Luke glanced over sharply. "You don't mean to stop?"

"You were in Viet Nam. What did you learn about partial measures?"

"They don't work."

Miller nodded. "We go all the way. Burn the NCH to the ground."

"But . . . the Vogler Ring. If even half of the rumors are true . . ."

"They're true. I called an old friend in the DAR, got the agency report. Ten thousand microwave emplacements with overlapping fields of fire. It'll feel like heat at first, then a bad sunburn, then your eyeballs pop and your blood boils."

"The government let him build that?" Luke shook his head. "Politicians."

"Indeed. No doubt Epstein made a lot of generous donations. Mostly, though, I suspect he got away with it because it's purely defensive, and useless against American military forces."

"Bombardment could clear a path in ten minutes." Luke sucked air through his teeth. "But we don't have artillery or air support. Can we go around?"

"They designed it to turn Tesla into a final refuge. The entire population of the Holdfast can fall back into the capitol. The network surrounds the city with a perfect, unbroken ring of death."

"So then how are we going to get through?"

Miller smiled.

*"I'm your neighbor, for Christ's sake.
Why are you doing this?"*

—LEE PARKER, 32, TO THE MASKED ASSAILANTS WHO ALLEGEDLY
HELD HIM AT GUNPOINT AND SET HIS PORTLAND HOME ON FIRE.
THE ATTACKERS HAD MISTAKEN HIM FOR LEIGH PARKER, 25, A TIER-
THREE GIFTED—AND A WOMAN—WHOSE NAME APPEARED ON THE
LIST OF ABNORMS LEAKED BY THE HACKER GROUP KONSTANT kOS.

CHAPTER 12

The lobby was broad and tall, with big metal ventilation tubes that flexed and hummed as air whistled through. Three feet above was the concrete ceiling, the wiring for the rooftop solar panels bursting through in colorful bundles that reminded him of the ribbon his mom used to wrap around Christmas presents, the edge of her scissors ripping them into tight curls. Between the ventilation system and the roof were open struts, and it was from there that Hawk kept watch, perched out of sight in the crook of a metal elbow. He'd always liked to climb, and he'd been delighted to discover that if he planted his feet on the wall, he could scurry up a pipe, then swing his legs over and do a sit-up into the struts. Hawk would spend hours here, mostly in the lobby, but sometimes creeping across to other rooms in the building, following people as they moved below.

The others made fun of his habit, but mostly not in a mean sort of way. Once Tabitha had even said, "Leave him alone. Aaron is keeping a vigil." She was nineteen, and went on missions, and when she'd said it she'd smiled at him in a way that he liked to pretend meant things he knew it didn't.

You'll go on missions too, Aaron Hakowski thought to himself. *Maybe you and Tabitha together.*

He'd wanted to tell her to call him Hawk, but he'd been afraid she'd laugh. Still, there was the comfort of her word, *vigil*. Like he was a knight. A holy warrior. The Hawk, keeping his vigil with silent dedication. After all, they were behind enemy lines.

Or, maybe not really enemy, because the Holdfast was for gifted, but still, Erik Epstein's security forces could discover them at any moment, everybody said so. Aaron didn't exactly want that to happen, but if it did, and he was on watch, maybe he could warn the others. Or even help. Drop down behind the intruders and steal one of their guns.

Idiot. They'd be brilliants. What would a fourteen-year-old normal be able to do against them?

Still. They wouldn't be expecting it. And if he took down the one inside the door, he could sneak up on the others. He was a good shot, had practiced until his trigger finger bled. If he had a rifle and was behind the soldiers, they would be dressed in black and have helmets that made them look like insects, and they'd be pointing their guns at Tabitha, who for some reason was wearing a torn white teddy—

Fast footsteps snapped him to attention. Two scientists were hurrying down the hall, carrying a gurney between them. As Hawk watched, a fist of cold wind punched open the front door. Haruto Yamato, who they all called sensei when he taught hand-to-hand classes, staggered in along with Ms. Herr, who scared Aaron. Between them they slung an old guy to the gurney and dumped him. Next through the door was a big man who moved gingerly, like something hurt pretty bad.

John was last, but like always, it seemed like he was first. Aaron had put a lot of thought into why that was, and he suspected it had something to do with the way everyone looked at him. Like they were all compasses and he was the North Pole. John spoke to the scientists, who quickly strapped down the old man's wrists and ankles.

"Charly, Haruto, handle security. You've seen what Couzen is capable of. I don't want any surprises. Paul, go with them, get that wound looked at."

"No, I'll stay with—"

"Paul." John put a hand on the big man's shoulder. "I'm going to need you."

Aaron felt a stab of jealousy, imagined John doing that to him, putting a hand on his shoulder and looking in his eyes and saying, "I'm going to need you, Hawk."

Don't be dumb.

The old guy on the gurney was directly beneath him, and Aaron took a careful look, mindful of what Mom had always said, how most people wandered through life with their eyes closed. That led to a flash of memory, in a car, golden sun, a couple of years ago, coming back from McDonald's, both of them munching fries from an open bag while she quizzed him, asked him what the nametag of the cashier had read, how much the order was for, the colors of the cars that had been parked next to theirs when they'd left, and the way she had glanced over with a grin when he'd known all the answers, that smile where she showed her teeth, not the polite one she did in pictures but the real one when he made her laugh—

Stop.

The old man was thin, with a big nose and a bald head. He was unconscious, but still looked angry. There were vicious scratches all over his face, which was weird, because Aaron couldn't imagine Sensei Haruto scratching like a little girl, and Ms. Herr *definitely* wouldn't have, not even when she'd been a little girl, if she ever had, and so Aaron looked closer, and that's when he noticed the stains under the old guy's fingernails.

"One, two, three," said one of the scientists, and on three he and the other guy stood up, raising the gurney with them. Sensei and Ms. Herr and the muscular guy followed. They were headed toward the lab, and he thought about following. But John wasn't going; he stood by the wall until they were out of sight, and then he sagged, like a lot of weight had landed on his shoulders. He sat down on a bench, elbows on his knees, staring at nothing.

Without looking up, he said, "Heya, Hawk."

Aaron felt a flush of something he couldn't quite name, similar to but different from the feeling he'd gotten when Tabitha smiled at him. He thought about working his way back to the electrical pipe, but instead he grabbed the bottom of the strut and lowered himself to dangle. He regretted the move immediately, the floor seeming somehow to get farther away instead of closer, but the only option was to wriggle and kick his way back up, and no *way* was he doing that in front of John, so he just took a breath and made his fingers open before he could think too much. The fall was about ten feet, and landing hurt, but he was proud that he didn't show it. "Hi, Mr. Smith."

"John."

That flush again. "Hi, John. Who was that?"

"A scientist named Abraham Couzen."

"A brilliant?"

"No. Just a genius."

"He's going to help us?"

"You could say."

Aaron thought about that. "So he's not one of us, but he knows something."

The smile that crossed John's lips was brief but pleased. "That's right. He developed something very important. Maybe the most important thing in the last couple of thousand years."

"Wow." Aaron paused. "Will he tell us?"

"He doesn't need to. I already have it."

"Then why do we need him?"

"Partly so he can't tell anyone else. And partly because I want to see what happens to him."

"What's going to happen?"

"He's going to die."

"Oh."

John looked up then. He was different from most grown-ups, who only really looked at the kids when they were mad. That was one of the things Aaron loved about him, that John *saw* him, looked at him and talked to him like he mattered, not like he was just another kid, another war orphan whose mom had—

Stop.

"You okay?"

Aaron shifted his weight from foot to foot. "Why is he going to die?"

"He's too old."

"He didn't look *that* old."

John seemed to be about to say something, then didn't. Instead he patted the bench beside him. Aaron sat down.

"You know, your mom was very proud of you."

I know, was what he wanted to say, but when he opened his mouth he realized he couldn't trust himself, and so he didn't say anything, just looked at his boots. *Don't cry, don't cry, you little pussy, don't you cry.*

There was the sound of a lighter, and then the sharp smell of smoke. John said, "Wanna know a secret?"

Hawk looked up, nodded, faster than he meant to.

"We're about to win."

"We are? Because of Dr. Couzen?"

John Smith took a deep drag off his cigarette. "Partly. He's the last piece of a plan I've been working on for a very long time. A plan that changes everything."

"What is it?"

"It's complicated."

"I'm pretty smart."

"I know, Hawk." John's voice sounded almost hurt. "I know that."

"I mean, of course I'm just a normal. I wish I weren't, but there's nothing I can do about it. But I'd do anything for . . ." Aaron caught himself just before he said *you,* amended it to ". . . the cause." Then he wondered if he'd caught himself in time after all, because the way his friend was looking at him had changed. "What?"

For a long moment, John just stared at him, the cigarette held almost to his lips but not quite.

As if he'd forgotten it was there.

CHAPTER 13

Soren stared.

His cage was made of metal tiles eighteen inches across. Six squares high, six wide, and ten long. The floor was concrete. A metal door replaced exactly ten tiles.

Each tile was enameled glossy white and pierced by a lattice of pinholes, which were the only source of light. A constant pale illumination glowed behind them, never dimming or brightening. The only change occurred when gas flowed through the holes from all directions at once, and he would find himself in a sudden swirling mist, like flying through a sunlit cloud.

When that happened there was little choice but to breathe steadily and wait.

Twice each day a tray with a sludgy soup of proteins and amino acids slid through a slot in the door. The tray was attached, and the only eating utensil was a wide paper straw. A plastic toilet fixed to the floor took his waste. Doubtless he was being watched, his vitals recorded by sensitive instruments hidden behind the metal tiles.

The first occasion the gas had flowed was after he had refused food several times in succession. He'd awakened on his bunk (two tiles wide by four long), still naked, a raped feeling in his throat from the scrape of the tube they must have used to feed him. In several other instances, he had clearly been bathed. On one memorable recent occasion, slight chafing around wrists and ankles suggested that he had been strapped down while unconscious, and so perhaps taken somewhere, although there was no way to be sure.

Soren had sought nothingness most of his life. But a blank and unchanging cage was not nothingness. It was his curse made physical. An ocean of time to drown in. No books, no window, no visitors, not even a spider that he might become. His memories were largely not a place to retreat. There had been a few moments of true contentment or even happiness, and he treasured them, striving to recall every detail of a chess game with John, or the way sunlight shadowed the soft hollow of Samantha's neck. But the mental movies had been screened so many times the colors were fading, and he feared losing them altogether. He could exercise, and meditate, and masturbate, but that left the bulk of the hours untouched.

So he counted.

The sum could be calculated: the pinholes were in offset rows of 48, totaling 2,304 holes per tile. 182 tiles meant 419,328 holes. Minus the 3,456 blocked by his bunk, that left 415,872 holes.

The number itself held no meaning. Its purpose was to provide a benchmark. A way to recognize that he had erred, had missed a pinhole or double-counted one. At which point it was time to return to the beginning. Like Sisyphus, endlessly rolling his boulder up a mountain in Tartarus, endlessly losing it, endlessly beginning again.

Camus had written that one must imagine Sisyphus happy, for his absurd struggle mirrored the efforts of humanity to find meaning in a world devoid of it, and thus the struggle itself must be enough. But Camus had never been in this cage. Neither the physical one nor the one in Soren's head, where his curse made one second into eleven. With nothing to separate one day from another, it was difficult to say exactly how long he had been here, but perhaps two weeks of "real" time.

Almost six months to him. Six months spent counting pinholes.

So when the door began to move, he did not believe it. Hallucinations had come before. But when he turned his head to look, the door did not snap soundlessly shut. Instead, it crept farther open. It took nearly twenty of his seconds to reveal the man standing behind it. For a full minute of his time they simply looked at one another.

Nick Cooper said, "Hi."

■

Cooper had tried to prepare himself.

When civilians said that, they meant taking a deep breath and clenching their fists. But the trick was to go much farther. To imagine the possibilities, good and bad, in detail. To visualize them the way astronauts prepare for a space walk, spending weeks considering what to do if this gasket leaked or that valve failed. It was a method that had served him well in the past, a way to walk into a room already knowing what he might face and how to respond to it.

But no visualization exercise could have prepared him.

The first surge was fear. Raw, primal, deep-chest fear. On some level far below his control, his subconscious mind, his very cells, recognized Soren as the man who had killed him, had slid a carbon-fiber blade into his heart. Even having survived, even having fought back, even having won, the initial fear had a horrifying purity to it.

Quickly, though, other emotions swirled in. Fury at this monster who had attacked his son, had nearly killed his beautiful boy, one of exactly two things Cooper had created that he knew beyond a doubt improved the world. A dirty sense of power which tickled the lizard part of his brain that wanted to root and relish and dominate. A certainty that Soren knew something that could help him, and a voice in his head reminding him of the stakes.

Least expected and least welcome, pity. Something in him was sorry for the shell that stood naked and trembling.

"Hi." He closed the door and set down the chair. It was just a simple ladder-back, but it looked wildly out of place in this pale prison. Which was part of the reason he'd brought it, of course. A scuffed wooden chair, the kind of furniture no one noticed, and yet here it seemed almost to have its own gravity. He trailed a hand along the slats, then sat down.

"I bet," Cooper said, "you never expected to see me again, huh?"

Soren just stared. His whole manner had a reptilian blankness to it. It was how he'd beaten Cooper in the first place. Everyone else's body betrayed their intentions, but Soren's perception of time meant that he essentially had no intentions.

Remember the restaurant. One second you're having breakfast with your kids, the next there's screaming and a rain of blood, and this man showing the same lack of expression as he analyzes the motion of a second bodyguard and puts his knife where it will do the most damage.

He killed two guards, bisected your hand, and stabbed you in the heart, and the only time you knew what he was going to do was when he put Todd in a coma.

"Do you know where you are?"

Nothing.

"I realize that you're not exactly a people person," Cooper said, "but the whole interaction thing works better if you use your words."

Nothing.

Cooper leaned back and crossed a leg at the knee. He studied the man. Skin pale and pulse steady, though elevated from the readings he'd noticed on the monitor outside. No tremor in the hands. No widening in the pupils.

Could he have lost track of reality? This place would be enough to drive a normal man mad, much less Soren.

There was a scar on his left shin, healing but still shiny. No surprise; the last time they'd met, Cooper had stomped the leg with enough force to snap the tibia and drive it through muscle and skin. Adopting a smug smile, he gestured at the scar. "I see they fixed you up."

The muscles around Soren's eyes contracted, and his nostrils flared. Just the tiniest flicker, but enough for Cooper to catch, and he pushed his advantage. "How about the hand? Jerking off lefty since I broke all the fingers on your right?"

Again, the quick flash, there and then gone.

"I know you understand me," Cooper said. "The lights might be off, but you're home. So let's make this easier. Take a seat."

For a moment, the man stood still. Then he moved to the edge of the bunk and sat down. Each play of muscle was precise, each motion graceful.

Sure they are. He's got eleven times longer to make them.

"So. Where to begin." Cooper laced his hands behind his head. "You're in New Canaan, and I have to tell you, every day since I kicked your ass has been better than the one before. First, the Holdfast and the United States came to an agreement, and the army left without firing a shot. Then, as a display of good faith, Erik Epstein put his rather formidable resources to work. Last Thursday John Smith was shot and killed."

Though he'd been projecting cocky ease, Cooper's eyes never left Soren's face. He saw the pulse jump, saw the intake of breath, saw the faint flush in his cheeks and the sheen of his eyes. For a moment, he looked almost human. *Gotcha.*

It had been one thing to know that Smith and Soren had gone to the same academy, to hear Shannon describe them as friends. But there was no telling what that actually meant in Soren's case. Finding out was the main point of this exercise.

And now you have. Turns out, this stone-eyed psychopath does care about someone.

Let him sit with the loss of that for a while.

"There's more, a lot more, but you're getting the general trend. Crisis averted, revolution over, much rejoicing. At this point, we're basically mopping up. I tell you so that you can consider your position." There was the temptation to keep pushing, but basic interrogation technique said to let the guy stew, and that would only be more powerful here. Cooper stood and stretched. "We'll talk more. When we do, you can help me or not. Honestly, I don't much care—but then, I'm not the one in a cage." He scooped up the chair and stepped toward the door.

"Wait."

The voice came from behind, and it was only in that moment that Cooper realized he'd never actually heard the man speak before. He turned. "Yeah?"

"Do you know what I do in my cage?"

"Not much, from what I've seen."

"I relive moments. Again and again. Moments like you dying." Soren's voice was flat. He stared with blank eyes. "Beside the broken son you couldn't protect."

Cooper smiled.

Then he spun from the hips, bringing the chair up as he did, the legs of it cracking into Soren's face. The force knocked the man sideways, his hands whipping back in a failed attempt to catch himself. He tumbled off the bunk and hit the ground hard as Cooper stepped forward, bracing the chair in both hands and raising it high, already visualizing the maneuver, a brutal downward stab, and another, and another, the solid wooden legs tearing the skin of Soren's neck open and crushing his trachea, spasms and panic soon fading to nothing but the twitches of a—

Soren has a T-naught of 11.2.

It took you maybe half a second to swing that chair. Which would have felt like six seconds to him.

That's an eternity in a fight. But he didn't move.

And he's not moving now.

—dead man.

"No." Fingers clenching, teeth aching, Cooper made himself take a breath. He stepped back. Slowly, without turning away, he moved toward the door. "It won't be that easy."

On the ground, Soren rocked up on an elbow. Spat blood.

And staring right into Cooper's eyes, began to laugh.

∎

As the door locked behind him, pneumatic bolts thunking into place, somehow Cooper found himself face-to-face with Soren.

The monster had escaped.

Cooper slid into a fighting stance, readying the chair for a blow—

It was a hologram. A high-resolution tri-d projection captured by the hundreds of tiny cameras mounted behind the cell's walls In it, Soren laughed soundlessly as he wiped blood from his nose.

The control room was typical of the new-world thinking that defined the Holdfast. No bars, no windows, no need for guards. Banks of monitors displayed the vital statistics of not only Soren, but the half dozen other men and women held here. Each facet of the octagonal room held a door to another cell, and outside it, a detailed holographic projection of the person within. They paced, did pushups, stared. One wall of the room was glass, and beyond it lay a fully stocked medical bay, including a robotic surgery prosthetic, a dozen clenched arms hanging from the ceiling like a spider on a line. The whole thing was run remotely—food trays filled and delivered, environment controlled, gas administered, surgery undertaken, all by entering commands in a computer.

As Cooper watched, Soren returned to his bunk and lay back down, his expression indecipherable. Beyond the image, there was a flash of purple.

"Go ahead and hit the holo," Millie said, brushing vivid bangs to cover one eye. "If you want to."

Cooper took a breath, let it out. "I'll pass."

"You could go to my game room. Erik had it designed. It's the same resolution, but the characters are controlled by a predictive network. You move and the system makes the holos react. He'll fall, bleed, scream. You won't actually feel the chair hit, though."

"Haven't figured out how to do that yet, huh?"

"They have," she said. "But it takes a brain implant. You run a cable into it, and it makes you see and feel everything like it's real. It's pretty cool, but I don't like the idea of something in my brain."

"Me either." *And I shouldn't have let Soren into mine.* Cooper set down the chair, dropped into it, and rubbed his eyes. "Sorry about that."

"It's okay," she said. "I liked it."

He looked up, surprised. Superficially, she looked like an average eleven-year-old girl. Four and a half feet tall, baby cheeks, rounded shoulders, coltish legs with knees together. The purple hair was unusual, but it was clearly a distraction—look at my hair, not at me—and the bangs gave her cover to retreat behind.

Her eyes, though, were something else. Something older. It was in the way she examined things. There was none of the self-conscious diffidence of a little girl.

And that's a tragedy, Cooper thought. *Because no matter what she's seen, no matter that her insights help the world's richest man shape the future, she is still a little girl who should be playing with toys, not diagnosing monsters.* He saw a flicker of a smile on her lips, and got the sense she was picking up on his thoughts. To change the subject, he said, "You liked it?"

"Yes."

"I don't understand, why would you—"

"Because you're pure."

He laughed before he could stop himself. "Sorry, Mills, but pure is about the last thing I am."

She sat down on the opposite chair, pulled her knees up, and wrapped her arms around them. A little girl's posture, but like her eyes, the smile she gave him belonged to an older woman. It was a look that said, *Aww, aren't you adorable. I'm going to bat you around for a while.* "Why did you hit him?"

"I lost control."

"No, then you would have killed him."

"I almost did. Until I realized he was trying to goad me into it."

"Of course he was," she said, "but you still want to. It wasn't just anger. I could see it. You want to kill him because he hurt your son. Because he's hurt a lot of people. But also because you feel sorry for him."

"You were here to read him," Cooper said drily, "not me."

"I can't. The way he sees the world, I don't . . . it's like looking at someone through a kaleidoscope. What I see isn't right. It's warped and blurry and just wrong." She shrugged. "So I read you instead."

That was a sobering thought. A reader of Millie's ability observing him in an emotionally charged scene like that one, well, she'd have all of his true secrets: the impulses he knew he should hate himself for having, the urges that dwelt in the dark places, even the part of him that relished the role he'd just inhabited.

The thought, a voice from his subconscious, shocked him. *Is that true? Are you comfortable with being a torturer?*

Because you shouldn't kid yourself. That's what happens next. Soren knows something that will help you find John Smith. You're as certain of it as you are of the fact that he won't willingly tell you.

"It's okay," she said.

"Is it?" He shook his head. "I didn't enjoy being the person I was in there. Most of me didn't, anyway. I know why it's important, and I'll do worse if I have to. But I don't know that it's okay."

"Why?"

Her question didn't sound entirely sincere; it had a leading tone, like it was meant to instruct. Coming from an eleven-year-old, that should have been irritating, but Millie wasn't just any kid, and he decided to answer honestly.

"Because it's not his fault. He didn't chose to be born a freak. He never really had a chance. Everything he is, it's because of his gift. It put him outside the rest of us, forever."

As he said it, he realized that the same thing applied to her. And then he saw her reading him thinking that. "I'm sorry."

"It's okay," she said.

"It's not. I hate this for you. You deserve a normal life."

For a long moment, neither said anything, then Millie ran a hand through her bangs, let a purple curtain fall between them. From behind it, she said, "I come here sometimes. To watch him."

"Soren? Why?"

"Because I can't read him. Sometimes the voices from everyone else, even the people who care about me . . ." She blew a breath. "It's quiet here. Quiet, but I'm not alone."

He let that lie amidst the hum of computer fans and the motion of holograms. Finally, he checked the time. "I'm sorry, Millie. I have to go."

"Oh?" She looked at him. "Going to see Shannon, huh?"

He nodded.

"Are you going to tell her you had sex with Natalie?"

Cooper opened his mouth, closed it. Screened a dozen responses. "You think that's a mistake?"

"How would I know? I'm eleven."

He laughed, stood up. Put a hand out as if to touch her, a tentative move, not sure she'd welcome it. When she didn't flinch, he gave her shoulder a squeeze. "Don't stay too long, okay?"

"Sure."

"By the way, you were right. I do feel sorry for Soren."

"Even though he hurt your son."

"Yes." He shrugged. "It won't stop me. But it doesn't make what I have to do okay."

"You see?" she said. "Pure."

CHAPTER 14

The New Sons of Liberty made it nearly five miles before they heard the voice of God.

Those five miles took seven hours. "There's a reason," Ronnie Delgado had said, "Epstein was able to buy half of Wyoming, and it boils down to, 'It's a shit heap.'"

Luke Hammond couldn't disagree, at least not about the part they were walking through. He knew there was purple mountain majesty somewhere, but the landscape here was ugly, rugged, and cold. The uneven ground was easily enough navigated by men on foot, but eighteen-wheelers were built for interstates. It seemed like every couple of hundred yards a truck got stuck, lost a tire to a sinkhole, snapped an axle.

What few roads had existed before New Canaan was built generally cut straight across the state, with hard-pack paths branching off to ranches and mines. Since then Epstein had laid a system of smooth highways, but they all tapered to fortified entrance points. Nothing that the Sons couldn't have swept aside, but General Miller believed, and Luke concurred, that a direct attack risked unnecessary consequences. There would be plenty of fighting later. Better to make what distance they could bloodlessly, jam the knifepoint of the militia into the body of the Holdfast before they had to fight for every step.

When they heard the voice of God, Luke was walking beside Delgado and dictating a mental e-mail to Josh and Zack. An old habit from when he was overseas frequently. Being career special operations meant he couldn't be the kind of father who never missed a ball game. But he compensated for it as best he could by spending time with them, speaking honestly and directly, and sharing his experience of the world as if the three of them were adventuring in it together. Through his e-mails to them, the three of them had together reconnoitered a Moroccan bazaar, rare silks sold beside Chinese radios, body odor layered beneath wafts of cumin and sandalwood. Via e-mail, together they'd been stricken dumb by the night sounds of the Salvadoran jungle, a symphony of insects, the mating calls of writhing things, the endless dance of predator and prey lit green by night vision goggles.

How can I describe for you, my fine sons, what it is to march into Wyoming? With rhetoric and speeches? With our grim sense of duty and righteousness?

Better to tell you about aching feet and the hot burn of developing blisters.

About the cacophony that is twenty thousand men picking their way across this crusted moonscape. Conversation, footsteps, and rock skitter, laughter. The steady tap of a rifle stock against a man's belt. The rumble-chutter of semis crawling at a mile an hour punctuated by the hiss of air brakes. Crisp air, and the smells of dirt and coffee and fart.

My image of the Holdfast was formed by the media, most of which focused on the cities, especially Tesla. You've no doubt seen the same documentaries: how a plan and $300 billion turned a desert plain into an abnorm Disneyland, filled with broad avenues and public squares, electric cars and genetically engineered trees, water condensers and solar fields, all radiating out from the mirrored castle of Epstein Industries. Even though I knew better, some part of me imagined that not far past the fence line, we would march into this bizarre world.

Instead, I've spent most of the morning putting my back to a truck, along with thirty other men, intent on pushing it over a rut—

Which was as far as he'd gotten when they heard the voice of God.

It was sourceless, coming from every direction at once; in front, behind, above, it seemed even to vibrate up through his boots, booming so loud men covered their ears. A crisp female voice reciting a short message that made his bones ache with each reverberating syllable.

ATTENTION.

YOU ARE ON PRIVATE LAND.

YOU ARE NOT LIBERATORS. YOU HAVE NOT BEEN INVITED. YOU HAVE BROKEN INTO OUR HOME TO DO US HARM.

WE WILL DEFEND OURSELVES.

LEAVE THE NEW CANAAN HOLDFAST IMMEDIATELY.

THIS IS YOUR ONLY WARNING.

As abruptly as it had started, the voice was gone, leaving no trace but the last word echoing across the plain to the distant mountains.

Everything stopped. The carnival atmosphere evaporated. Men looked at one another, uncertainty in darting eyes. Sheepishly, they took hands from their ears; those who had dropped rose to their feet.

For a moment, Luke found himself wondering how the abnorms had done it. Whether there was some sort of buried audio system that they'd crossed, or planes high above them, or if the Holdfast had found a way to simply beam sound. Then he realized that all of the nearby men were looking at him. A hundred or more, and beyond them, thousands, all waiting to be inspired.

He didn't have Miller's gift for speeches. So he did the only thing he could think of. He started walking again.

Ronnie Delgado quickly fell into step, and then others beside him, and then there was a ragged cheer, and someone started yelling, "This! Ends! Now!" They were all picking it up, him included, and the words meant something, one voice shared by a hundred throats, and then a thousand, and then all. They stomped forward, everyone's step quickening. Vehicles jammed on their horns, blowing a raspberry to Erik Epstein and the abnorms and the new world that had usurped their old one. Luke felt a swelling in his chest and a howl in his heart, and Shakespeare's words bounced around his brain, *We few, we happy few, we band of brothers,* all of it backed by the howl of a thousand truck horns—

—which stopped.

All at once. As if a switch had been flipped.

Luke paused. Looked at his watch. The face was blank.

Something caught his eye, a bright spot falling from above. A sort of bird, only it was made of metal and plastic. It was tumbling end over end, and on it he caught the letters CNN just before it collided with the ground.

A newsdrone just fell out of the sky. Which means an EMP. Just like Miller predicted. Which will be followed by—

The world exploded.

Something spattered him, hard and cold, dirt, the sound of the missile strike hitting just after the debris and a wave of heat that tossed him sideways. Luke smacked the ground, the impact ringing through his knees and skinning his palms. He scrambled to stand, reflex taking over, shouting to take cover, to get away from the trucks, not that anyone could hear him, not that there was any cover to take. He couldn't even hear himself over the screaming whistle-and-boom of finger missiles raining into the earth, each bomb tossing bodies silhouetted against ragged fireballs, and then a missile caught the nearest eighteen-wheeler, the gas tank bursting with a shocking violence that threw him down again, backward this time, the heat blistering his skin, sound fading to a ringing hum underlying the whistles-and-booms and whistles-and-booms, earth showering upward in clouds against the greasy black smoke of gasoline fires, the trucks going one at a time, bucking and jumping like rodeo bulls with broken backs, supplies bursting from them, a rain of canned food and blanket scraps and burning paper. He made it to his feet only to have something heavy hit him and drive him down again, smashing the wind from his lungs, the thing heavy and wet, and he went to shove it off and found one of his hands inside Ronnie Delgado's remaining half of a head, what he could see of the man's expression a strange sort of surprise, like he finally got the big joke that had been out there all along, and then Luke was crawling, someone's boot trampling his back, another on his hand, the faint pop of gunfire all around. Men were aiming at the sky, trying to take down the drones, a ridiculous waste of ammunition given the altitude and speed they'd be flying, not to mention the fact that they'd been shielded against the EMP and so were unlikely to be damaged by bullets, and then smoke and swirling dust hid the world, and he squinted and closed his mouth and shoved out from underneath what was left of Delgado, the former national guardsman and ranch hand and comedian whose brother had been the first in their family to go to college, and he was on his feet, cough-choking, waiting for more whistle-screams and the deep ground shake that followed them, the fire and blood and smoke.

None came.

None came.

None came.

He straightened, look around. His head throbbed and vision pulsed, his hand was torn and bleeding, his back clenched, and standing took effort. In the sudden absence of explosions, mostly what he heard was the ringing in his ears, and past that, the crackle of flames from the trucks and the screams of men torn apart.

And then the voice of God, booming again across the desert:

FIRING WILL RECOMMENCE SHORTLY.

WALK AWAY.

BETTER STILL: RUN.

Luke broke into a smile. *Goddamn, but Miller was right.*

Something ran into his eye, and he wiped the blood away. He had to find the general. If Miller had died in the bombardment, everything would fall apart. The whole plan. Luke had proposed a hundred strategies to protect him: keeping him in the rearguard, choosing men as decoys, a team of bodyguards to throw themselves atop him. Miller had refused them all.

"When it comes," the general had said, "I'll take my chances like everyone else. We'll just have to ride it out."

"And then what?" Luke had replied.

"Then we'll show that the emperor is naked."

Luke pushed through men scattered and rising, past smoldering craters and burning trucks. He had to find Miller, had to, because otherwise the abnorms' bluff would win the day—

"EPSTEIN!"

The voice wasn't nearly so loud as God's. But the bullhorn, backed by the full force of General Sam Miller's lungs, still punched right through the ringing in his ears.

Luke turned, saw his old friend. The crazy sonuvabitch had climbed on top of a semi, one of those that wasn't burning, though the trailer had taken a hit, the SUPPLIES part gone, leaving just FINEST, and a gaping hole with packaged food spilling out.

"I'M RIGHT HERE, EPSTEIN!"

Move, Luke told his legs, and they did. First a stagger-walk, then a trot, and finally a run that took him to the semi's front bumper.

"YOU WANT A TARGET? WANT TO END THIS?"

Luke scrabbled up the hood, gripped a chrome exhaust pipe that singed his fingers, held on long enough to pull himself atop the shipping container. Miller saw him, flashed him a grim smile.

It was the same look he'd worn two days ago, when they'd made the plan. Sitting in Miller's tent, the never-ending wind tugging at the canvas, the general had said, "Okay, strategic analysis. You command a technologically superior force with significant defensive capabilities. However, your *offensive* matériel is limited. You're attacked by a large and determined enemy, and you don't have the armaments to wear them down slowly. Simply put, you've only got so many bombs, because you weren't supposed to have any at all. What do you do?"

"Simple," Luke had replied. "You throw it all at them at once. Everything you've got. You hit as hard as you can as fast as you can, and count on fear to do the rest. Same reason we nuked both Hiroshima *and* Nagasaki, using our entire atomic arsenal." Luke had paused. "We're going to take a hell of a beating."

"Once you factor in wounded and fled, probably 20 percent. But those who remain will become an army, instead of a militia."

"Of course, if we're wrong, it will be over."

"If we're wrong, it's over already."

Time to test that logic. Atop the shipping container, Luke felt naked, every instinct screaming to find cover, but he thought of his burning boys, and stood at attention.

"WE ARE THE LEADERS OF THE NEW SONS OF LIBERTY," Miller shouted. "YOU WANT TO END THIS RIGHT NOW? GO AHEAD AND RECOMMENCE FIRING."

Then he lowered the bullhorn, tilted his head back, and spread his arms cruciform. There was blood on his cheek and dirt on his uniform, and against the smoke and rising fire he looked like some primitive war god.

Standing beside him, Luke did the same. He kept his eyes open, staring at the cold and swirling skies, where somewhere above them drones circled invisibly.

Flames crackled. Men groaned. Somewhere, a bird shrieked.

Then he heard the first voice.

"This ends now!"

And a second, and a third, and a thousandth, drowning out the screams and the fire and whatever might have held them back.

CHAPTER 15

The tingle started at the airfield, as Cooper negotiated with one of the pickup pilots who hung out in the lounge.

"Newton, huh?" The woman cocked her head, slid her hands in the pockets of her jacket. "You're in luck. It's a clear night, good thermals. I can get you there in two hours. Four hundred."

"Two hundred."

"Costs four hundred."

"Three hundred in cash—if you get me there in an hour."

"Cash?" She raised an eyebrow. "All right. But you better not puke in my wings."

"I don't get airsick."

"You might, kind of flying I'm gonna have to do to make it in an hour."

Two minutes later he was helping her push a glider onto the runway. Made of carbon-fiber about the thickness of a napkin, the thing didn't weigh more than a couple hundred pounds. The pilot hitched it to a thick metal cable and was checking instruments and talking to ground control before he'd even gotten settled.

The cable jerked tight, then yanked a mile in thirty seconds, slingshotting them into the sky fast enough to leave his stomach behind.

It was his second trip in a glider, and he didn't love it any more than the first, when Shannon had been at the stick. Cooper had no problem with planes, but not having an engine didn't agree with him. It wasn't exactly mitigated by the pilot, who took him at his word and rode hard, bouncing hundreds of feet up on thermals before tilting into velocity-building dives, the cracked landscape of the desert hurtling toward them. After one particularly gnarly cycle, he said, "What happens if you time that wrong?"

"Then we get to see how well the safety foam works," she said. "Supposed to fill the cockpit in a tenth of a second, solidify with impact, then dissolve. Anyway, you were the one said you were in a hurry."

"At least I'm not hungover this time."

"What?"

"Nothing."

The trip ended up taking a bit more than an hour, but he paid the full three hundred, then hopped in one of the electric cabs waiting at the Newton airfield. It started to snow on the ride, thin flurries that haloed the streetlights, and it was still going fifteen minutes later, when he climbed out in the midst of a row of two-story buildings, apartments over businesses. He walked past a bar and hustled up the steps two at a time. Cooper took a moment to smooth his hair and check his breath, then knocked on the door.

He waited, conscious of his heart, and a warmth that wasn't entirely contained to his stomach.

The door swung open.

Shannon clearly hadn't been expecting company. She wore what passed for pajamas—fitted black yoga pants and a thin cotton top that slipped low on one shoulder, revealing her collarbone. Her hair was loosely tucked behind her ears, and though he couldn't see her right hand, the angle of her arm told him she held a pistol in it.

"Hi," he said.

She stared at him. Quirked her lopsided grin. Moving with perfect economy, she set the gun on the entryway table, then reached forward, grabbed his shirt with two hands, and yanked him inside.

Her body was hot and tight against his, all dancer's muscles and humming skin, and her smell enveloped him, woman and a whiff of shampoo. She took a handful of his hair and pressed his mouth to hers, her tongue flickering sweetly as he hoisted her up, legs wrapping his hips, his hands gripping her ass. He kicked the door closed as they staggered into a wall, and she laughed in her throat. "Miss me?"

"Guess," he said, and kissed her again, softer, sucking her lower lip between his own. She moaned and ground against him, and that pulled a moan from him. Her hands slid down his chest, starting for his belt, and, *Yes,* he thought, *God yes,* he wanted it, both of them wanted it, fast this time, a reckless reclaiming of each other, and then later they could take their time, could spend the whole night taking their—

Reclaiming. Unbidden, an image of Natalie astride him flashed through his mind. Shannon's fingers tugged at his pants, pulling them away from his belly as her other hand slid inside the—

"Wait."

Shannon laughed. "Yeah." She kept moving south, and God did it feel good, right—

No. He caught her wrist.

Something sparked in her eyes then. "What's wrong?"

He set her down and ran a hand through his hair.

"Nick?"

"I need to tell you something."

■

Shannon stood at the kitchen counter, not looking at him. Her fingers spun an untouched glass of bourbon. Her tri-d entertained itself, tuned to the Holdfast's pirate news station, the volume muted.

"It wasn't planned. It just happened. I'm—"

"Don't," she said sharply. "Don't say you're sorry."

"I wasn't going to."

"She deserves better than that."

"I agree."

"I get it," she said. "You guys have history. And you and me, we never talked about . . ."

No, he thought. *No, we never did. I was busy taking down one president and serving another, trying to protect the world. You were fighting a revolution and freeing children from slavery, not to mention saving my life.*

"I wish we had," he said. "Talked about it."

Shannon shrugged noncommittally, still not looking at him. "It's almost funny. I didn't know until Natalie came to see me."

"Didn't know—wait. Came to see you? When was this?"

"Couple of weeks ago. After you died."

"Ah." He hadn't known that. When Todd was hurt, and Cooper was beaten and ready to quit, it was Natalie who had propped him up. She had cleared his head, kicked his ass, and sent him off to fight for their children's future. It must have been afterward that she visited Shannon. He could picture it easily. Another woman might have come to insult or threaten, to warn her off. But Natalie would just have felt Shannon deserved to know he'd survived.

At which point, Shannon had split from John Smith, then boarded a plane and arrived just in time to save his life.

The women in his life were amazing.

When the gods really want to mess with you, they give you too much of a good thing.

"I understood you cared about each other," Shannon continued. "But until Natalie showed up at my hotel room, I didn't know that she's still in love with you."

He hesitated. "I'm not sure that's true."

"It is," she said, the same way she might tell him it was snowing.

"I didn't mislead you. We've been done since the divorce. But I think everything that's happened, it's maybe changed the way she feels. Made her wonder if we deserve another shot."

"What about you?"

"I . . . she's the mother of my children. I'll always love her."

"Like I said, I get it." Shannon sipped the whiskey. "I'm a grown woman, Cooper. Not some schoolgirl with a crush."

And there it was. She'd called him Cooper.

"Shannon, I—"

"I'm sure it's confusing."

He wanted very badly to agree, but he'd been with women enough to know how very bad an idea that was. Somehow he kept himself from nodding.

"I'll tell you what, though. You better not toy with her. She's a good one." Shannon took a breath, then another sip of whiskey. "Want a drink?"

He stared at her, feeling a tearing in his chest. Everything had taken on momentum, a slippery sort of velocity that seemed out of his control and headed for a wall. He knew that he could stop the crash. All he needed to do was say, firmly and clearly, that he chose Shannon. That he would always love Natalie, and didn't regret last night, but that it was a farewell. That what he wanted was Shannon, period.

Seconds ticked by. On the tri-d, the image shifted, the footage of President Ramirez replaced by a sea of marching men.

"You see this?" Shannon asked, her voice tightly controlled. She opened a cabinet, took down a glass, and splashed bourbon in it, the bottle shaking only slightly. "They keep replaying the same loop, but I can't seem to turn it off."

"Shannon—"

"Here." She pushed the drink to him, tapped it with her glass. "To the New Sons of Liberty. Tough bastards, I'll give them that. Audio on."

Cooper started to protest, but caught himself when he saw her look. *There's only one way to end this, and that's making your decision, right now, and meaning it.*

God help him, he just couldn't. Feeling a little dizzy, he picked up the drink, swallowed half of it in a go.

The tri-d had reacted to Shannon's voice command, the pirate announcer picking up mid-sentence: "—crew of wankers about five miles past the Rawlins fence line." The shot was a high-angle, but even so, it was packed edge to edge, a living carpet of tiny figures trudging across Wyoming scrubland. A voice he recognized as Patricia Ariel's, Epstein's communications director, boomed out a warning, telling the militia that they were not welcome, that the Holdfast would defend itself. For a moment, everyone on the ground hesitated, and then a cry went up, the New Sons' cheer, "This ends now! This ends now! This ends . . ."

"Attaboy, guys," the announcer continued, "very catchy. Maybe in next week's lesson we can work on words with more than one syllable. Oh, good, truck horns, add those too, nothing quite as scary as tooting. But then, wait for it, wait for it . . ."

The image cut off in an instant. An electromagnetic pulse, Cooper knew, to fry the electronics. He'd read details of the battle on the way to the airfield.

When the footage returned, it was clearly an hour or two later, after whichever news organization was closest had managed to scramble another camera drone. In this one, the landscape was devastated, the trucks torn and toppled, the scrubland turned into a ruined battlefield littered with corpses.

"Oh, da-yam! Well, you know what they say," the announcer continued. "It's all fun and games until someone launches a drone strike. Sorry about that, kids, so much for the Charge of the Dumb Brigade . . ."

Nice try, Cooper thought. *But what you're seeing, my smug friend, is an army setting up base camp.*

"Audio mute." Shannon shook her head. "What I don't get is why Epstein stopped hitting them. News says about a thousand killed, another couple thousand wounded or fled. Which isn't bad, I guess, but the Proteus virus took down like fifty times that. What's the angle in mercy at this point?"

Apparently the romantic discussion had been tabled. He thought about raising it again, but didn't really see what he could add. Better to let things cool off. "It wasn't mercy. He just ran out of bombs."

"You think?"

"The government wouldn't allow the NCH to have offensive weapons. Erik bought some on the black market, built some on the sly, but he couldn't risk having many. I'm not theorizing, I know it. I was DAR, remember?"

"You never let me forget."

Don't rise to it. She's got a right to be pissed. "Anyway, he's not worried about the New Sons. No matter how many men they have, they won't get past the Vogler Ring. It was built to protect the Holdfast from villagers with pitchforks." He shook his head. "It's Smith that concerns me."

Before, even as they watched the aftermath of a battle, her attention had been split. She'd put up a good front, but it was easy for Cooper to see that a front was all it was. But now all thoughts of their romantic future were cleared away. "Tell me."

"He beat us to Abe Couzen."

"That's not good."

"It gets worse." He filled her in, starting at their separation. She listened attentively, asked pointed questions. It was a safe space for them, analyzing a situation and figuring out how to respond. It was what they'd done instead of dating. About the time he got to Abe's lab, she finished her drink and poured another; as he filled her in on his conversation with Soren, he emptied his own, and she slid the bottle his way with unconscious ease. "By the way," he said, "thanks for bringing Soren here. That couldn't have been fun."

"He wasn't much company. Spent the last two days in the trunk of the car." She flashed her half smile. "You really think he can help you?"

"I'm sure of it."

"John is his best friend. He's not going to give him up easily. Are you going to . . ."

"I don't see much choice. Smith has been maneuvering the whole world to this moment. I still don't know why, but I know he doesn't start fights he can't win."

"Is there something you can offer Soren? A carrot instead of a stick?"

"Like what?"

She moved to the window and stared out. Flurries chased each other in a gust of wind. "You could talk to Samantha."

"Who?" The name was familiar in a vague sort of way.

"Don't tell me you don't remember her."

Why are you looking at me that—oh. He remembered, all right. Shannon's friend, pale cream and spun gold and dripping sex appeal. She was tier one, a sort of reader, only with a bent empathy that meant she could pick up on anyone's desires, and then emulate them. "She and Soren know each other?"

"Biblically. Since Hawkesdown Academy." Shannon grimaced. "One messed-up relationship."

You ain't kidding. He'd only met Samantha once, but it had been easy to see that her addiction to painkillers was actually the lesser of her compulsions. Between her gift and her past—seduced by an academy mentor at thirteen, then turned out as a prostitute—she drew her entire self-worth from being needed.

Who could need her more than a temporal abnorm who lived every second as eleven? The intensity of his attention must have felt like heroin to her. And her ability to sense what he wanted without requiring all the social trappings he was incapable of must have made her unique amongst women.

"Can you imagine," Shannon continued, "how the world feels to him? He can't have a conversation. Can't watch a movie. He gets drunk, the hangover lasts for like a week. Hell, sex has to be one of the only things that does work for him. Especially with Sam."

"Does she love him?"

Shannon nodded. "Almost as much as she loves John."

"Ah." He'd had some notion of playing to her feelings, convincing her that she could save Soren. But he'd forgotten that Smith was the thread that united them. It was Smith who had killed her mentor and pimp. There was no way she'd betray him.

"What are you going to do?"

"I don't know." Cooper sighed. "I saw Millie today. Remember her?"

"The little girl with green hair."

"It's purple now. Anyway, she told me she couldn't read Soren, that his perception of time screws things up. I thought maybe stress would change that, but instead, she ended up reading me."

"Poor kid."

He made a face at her. "Actually, she said I was pure."

"She doesn't know you like I do."

"Ha-ha. Afterward, we were talking, and I screwed up, said the dumbest thing: that Soren was a freak, his gift had ruined him, put him outside society. And I no sooner said it than I thought about how the same could be said of her."

Shannon winced. "And of course she read you thinking that."

"Yeah. I feel so sorry for her. There's way too much pressure for a little girl. She tries to cope, hiding behind her hair and her video games, but—" A thought struck him with almost physical force. He had that behind-the-eyeballs feeling of an idea, the tuning out of the world to examine it.

Was it possible?

Millie seemed to think so. And this was the Holdfast. The most technically advanced place on the planet, a closed society where brilliants worked with enormous funding and little restriction. They'd brought him back from the dead here.

"Cooper?" Shannon looked at him with both concern and curiosity. "You okay?"

He picked up his bourbon and swallowed the rest, barely tasting it. Then he turned his face to her.

"Carrot."

TIME Magazine
10 Questions for Sherman VanMeter

Dr. Sherman VanMeter has made a career of
unpacking the densest areas of scientific endeavor
in accessible—if not polite—terms.

**You've written books on everything from
astrophysics to zoology. How are you able to
achieve expertise in so many disparate fields?**

There's a perception that scientific disciplines are
separate countries, when in fact science is a universal
passport. It's about exploring and thinking critically,
not memorization. A question mark, not a period.

Can you give me an example?

Sure. Kids learn about the solar system by memorizing
the names of planets. That's a period. It's also
scientifically useless, because names have no value.

The question mark would be to say instead, "There are
hundreds of thousands of sizable bodies orbiting the
sun. Which ones are exceptional? What makes them
so? Are there similarities? What do they reveal?"

But how do you teach a child to grasp that complexity?

You teach them to grasp the style of thinking. There are no
answers, only questions that shape your understanding,
and which in turn reveal more questions.

**Sounds more like mysticism than science.
How do you draw the line?**

That's where the critical thinking comes in.

**I can see how that applies to the categorization of solar
objects. But what about more abstract questions?**

It works there too. Take love, for example. Artists
would tell you that love is a mysterious force. Priests
claim it's a manifestation of the divine.

Biochemists, on the other hand, will tell you that
love is a feedback loop of dopamine, testosterone,
phenylethylamine, norepinephrine, and feel-my-pee-
pee. The difference is, we can show our work.

So you're not a romantic, then?

We're who we are as a species because of evolution.
And at the essence, evolution is the steady production
of increasingly efficient killing machines.

Isn't it more accurate to say "surviving machines"?

The two go hand in hand. But the killing is the prime mover;
without that, the surviving doesn't come into play.

Kind of a cold way to look at the world, isn't it?

No, it's actually an optimistic one. There's a quote I love from the anthropologist Robert Ardrey: "We were born of risen apes, not fallen angels, and the apes were armed killers besides. And so what shall we wonder at? Our murders and massacres and missiles, and our irreconcilable regiments? Or our treaties whatever they may be worth; our symphonies however seldom they may be played; our peaceful acres, however frequently they may be converted to battlefields; our dreams however rarely they may be accomplished. The miracle of man is not how far he has sunk but how magnificently he has risen."

You used that as the epigraph to your new book, *God Is an Abnorm*. But I noticed you left out the last line, "We are known among the stars by our poems, not our corpses." Why?

That's where Ardrey's poetic license gets the better of his science, which is a perilous mistake. We aren't "known among the stars" at all. The sun isn't pondering human nature, the galaxy isn't sitting in judgment. The universe doesn't care about us. We've evolved into what we are because humanity's current model survived and previous iterations didn't. Simple as that.

Why is a little artistic enthusiasm a perilous mistake?

Because artists are more dangerous than murderers. The most prolific serial killer might have dozens of victims, but poets can lay low entire generations.

CHAPTER 16

Soren dreamed.

He strolled a foreign city, ancient cobblestones beneath his feet. Weathered buildings of white stone, tall doors painted deep green, curtains flickering through open second-story windows, old men watching the world go by. Rome? He'd never been to Rome. A direct flight would have taken eight or nine hours of "normal" time, close to a hundred hours in his perception, but the hours weren't the problem. Time was the sea he swam, and alone he could spend that in meditation, in pursuit of nothingness.

It was the time trapped in a cramped space with other people.

The agony of watching them move as though paralyzed, each expression warping and deforming, their worm lips twisting into tortured syllables, drops of spit arcing lazily from their disgusting mouths. Fat bodies and patchy skulls. The simple, horrible energy of their being, just being, and so loud about it, so garish and cheap. Even asleep their snores filled the world, their farts scented it. The only grace existed where they were not.

That was how he knew this was a dream. On rare occasions his curse was lifted in dreams. He wouldn't have to endure the slow descending footfall of every step, wouldn't wait in the prison behind his eyes while the world caught up to him. He could walk amidst human beings and not hate them.

The cruelest dreams were the lucid ones, where he had control. He could pause outside a restaurant and savor the rich scents of basil and garlic wafting through the open doors. Could scratch an itch on the back of his neck and feel his fingernails. Could note the small chapel ahead and admire the way its every line was in proportion, every stone tested by weather and time. As Soren approached the chapel, he heard sounds coming from within. Automatically, he winced. Sounds were unpleasant. Voices, sighs, laughter, all drew out to grate like metal against teeth.

Only.

These sounds.

He'd never heard anything like them.

A layered swelling, a soar of textures and moods. They had a rhythm that built like love, like when he moved inside Samantha and each slow stroke was an ecstasy to lose himself in, each tingle of sensation a world in its own right. The rhythm seemed almost to have a theme, as though someone had found a way to represent the brightening of dawn after a night so cold and long it seemed it might never end. The lower tones were the inky darkness, the loss and fear, but against them higher notes were insistent, swelling, moving together in a way that made his chest hurt.

He stepped in the door of the chapel, marveling at the way the sound echoed off ancient stone. The interior was lit by thick white tapers with flames that danced, fast, so fast, it was jarring but somehow liberating, and the smell was rich and safe, wax and fire and incense. At the front of the room, a choir sang.

People? *People* made these sounds?

He moved down the aisle, found a dark pew, and sat. As the choir moved their lips, noises came out like he'd never heard before. A calculated tangle of voices, pure and sweet and strong. It took him, shook him, lifted him. His hands twitched in his lap, and his chest heaved. He was crying.

This would be the cruelest dream of all, he could tell, but for now he was in it, and if he must pay the price, he would at least relish this, soak in it, let the sound wash over him like a warm sea, this purity, this essence, this holy . . .

Music.

This was music, he realized. The way others heard it. To him, it had never been anything but endless, horrible grinding, tones that rang through his bones. People liked it, he knew that, but he was not of people.

Too soon the voices began to wind down. When the music drifted to an end, it felt like the vanishing of a physical force propping him up. Then he heard something else. Beside him. Another noise he had never known. A voice as it sounded to the speaker.

"It's something, isn't it?"

Soren knew the dream was about to end, then. He wanted nothing more than to stay a little longer, a little longer, forever. But it was the way of dreams that he turned anyway. On the pew beside him sat Nick Cooper. A man he had killed, and who had returned from the dead to trick him and break his bones and send him to a purgatory of white and counting.

"Music," the monster said. "I thought that might be the best way to show you. You've never heard it before, have you?"

The dream would end soon. Soren turned away, faced the choir again. Perhaps they would sing again.

"You have a T-naught of 11.2. If I say 'one Mississippi,' it takes me about a second. But you've never heard that before, have you? You've heard, 'Oooooooooooooooooooonnnnnnnnnnnnnnnnnnnne Mmmmmmmmmmiiiiiiiiiiiiiiiiiiiiiiiiiiiissssssssssssssssssssssssss . . .'" Cooper broke off. "You've never known life. Not really."

The back of Soren's neck itched again, and he scratched it. Most dreams he merely experienced, but ones this clear were usually under some level of conscious control. He decided to banish Nick Cooper from the chapel, and to focus all his attention on the music until the dream grew threadbare.

"Let me guess," Cooper said. "You think this is a dream."

Despite himself, Soren spun.

"It's like the parable about a man who dreamed he was a butterfly. When he woke, he couldn't be sure that he wasn't a butterfly dreaming he was a man. And other exercises in dorm room philosophy." Cooper's smile did not reach his eyes. "Well, let me end the mystery. You're not dreaming."

"What, then?"

"It's lovely, isn't it? The chance to walk and talk and think without having to watch the rest of the world drag along. Imagine how things might have turned out if you hadn't been born the way you were. You could have had a life. Friends, relationships. You could listen to music or stroll on the beach or have a conversation. All the things everyone else takes for granted. All the things you've always been denied."

"What is this?"

"You know," Cooper said, "you don't have to stick to the whole three-words-at-a-time thing. Stretch your wings. Try a whole sentence."

Soren stared at him. Waited.

Cooper sighed. "It's the possibility of a real life."

"Real?" He glanced around, at the chapel, the choir, the Roman street through the open doors.

"You of all people should know that 'real' is a flexible term. The rest of the world experiences one thing, and you experience another. Which is real? Ours? Yours? Neither?" Cooper shrugged. "Perception is just a matter of electrical signals in the brain. Philosophers and poets and priests say there's more, and maybe they're right. But that doesn't change the fact that consciousness is a matter of current. There is no objective truth, only the subjective experience our minds perceive. After all, when you thought this was a dream, didn't you want to stay in it?"

More than anything, and for the rest of my life. But he just repeated, "What is this?"

"It's a simulation. Designed by the best and brightest in the Holdfast. Really puts the *new* in newtech, huh? It's basically a cutting-edge game, powered by predictive networks that stay one step ahead. I'm not a bioengineer, but the way it was explained to me, it directly stimulates the parts of your brain that process sensory information. The occipital, temporal, frontal, and parietal lobes, neurons in the brain stem, who knows what else. Point is, it's as real as anything else in your head. And because it's generated, here we can nullify your perception of time."

"How?"

"We sedated you while you slept, and Erik's surgical team implanted a small interface device."

"Why?"

"I think what you mean is 'thank you.'" Cooper flashed another cold smile. "For a guy whose idea of entertainment is counting holes in the wall, whose dearest hope is that I'll kill him, this is basically Christmas."

He understood then. "An offer."

Cooper nodded. "And this is just version one-point-oh. With time, Epstein can create a permanent interface, a sort of mental translator that would allow you to experience the world the way the rest of us do."

Scratching at the back of his neck, he said, "What price?"

"Information."

"About John."

"Yes."

Soren paused.

When he had been a child, overwhelmed by every second, unable even to explain to the people around him what was wrong, there had been a voice in his head that promised one day he would be cured. Someone would find a way to nullify this hell he carried behind his eyes. Someday he would be able to experience the world as others did. Simple joy in simple things.

It was the only reason he'd stayed alive. And though he eventually stopped believing the voice, it had left a deep enough mark that surviving had become a habit, one he had never broken, despite daily consideration of it.

Now it turned out he'd been right. There was a cure for him.

The choir began to sing again. Tremulous whispers that bounced and echoed around the chapel. It was the most beautiful thing he had ever known, as lovely as the times with Samantha, but instead of a fading memory, it was here, real enough, and right in front of him.

All your life you have tried to be a leaf and let the current carry you away.

What if instead you became an eagle and soared on the breeze?

"I know you think he's your friend, but Smith used you. He sent you out to kill for him, and when you failed, he abandoned you. He felt no more love for you than a chess player feels toward a powerful piece, knowing full well that he'll sacrifice it to win."

A memory came to him then. John, saying to him, "You'retherook. Overlookedonthebackrow." Speaking in their old way, running the words together to make it easier for Soren. It had been in the apartment in Tesla, the one filled with books, the one where John had reunited him with Samantha.

The itch struck again.

Soren looked at the graceful chapel lit by candles, rich with the scent of wax and furniture polish, ringing with song, the beauty of which he had never known. Then he reached behind his neck with both hands.

Cooper cocked his head. "What are you doing?"

Soren ignored him. His neck felt normal, but he knew there was more to it, and he focused, applied all of his effort. Like trying to wake from a dream, that moment when both worlds seem real, when the boundary between them is pliable, and as he thought that, his hands touched something cold and hard. Looking Cooper straight in the eyes, he wrapped his fingers around it and tugged.

The world froze, twitched, shifted like a video call with poor reception, and vanished.

The chapel, the candles, the choir, gone.

All but Cooper, sitting opposite him in the bright cell of white tiles pierced by holes, 415,872 of them. The man stared at him with an expression of mingled confusion and horror.

Slowly—so, so slowly—Soren slid his right hand out from behind his head and looked at the cable that had been jacked into his neck. The voice inside him raged and screamed, told him to put it back, that it wasn't too late, that this was what he had always dreamed of.

He opened his fingers and let it fall. "No."

But it sounded like, "Nnnnnnnnnnooooooooooooooooooo . . ."

CHAPTER 17

The ground was cold and hard as cast iron taken from the freezer. Luke Hammond felt the chill leaching into his chest, the stones digging into his legs, the dull ache in his muscles. Then he packed the discomfort away. A trick he'd learned at nineteen, as a long-range recon scout in Laos. Catalog the conditions, but don't feel them. Focus on the mission.

The night vision function of the binoculars had been destroyed along with all the other electronics when they'd been hit with the electromagnetic pulse. But the clear Wyoming sky glowed with starlight, and he could see the outpost easily. A cluster of trailers and prefab units surrounding an inflatable structure a hundred yards across and bumpy with rooms and hallways. The hum of generators rose and fell with the wind. A handful of cars and four large buses formed a makeshift parking lot. The outpost had no sign, no fence, no permanent structures of any kind. The whole facility looked like it had been thrown together a week ago—which it had.

There was only one guard, stamping his feet as he lit a cigarette. No serious soldier would have made that mistake on watch, but no one here expected an attack. That was part of the point, and why Luke and his team had traveled almost fifty miles perpendicular to the path of the New Sons to reach this place. In this otherwise unoccupied wasteland, "security" was mostly to protect from coyotes.

He lowered the binoculars and glanced sideways. Eleven men, all prone, all silent, looked back. They were dressed as he was, in layers of black clothing and woven hats. The most visible parts of them were their eyes and their weapons.

Miller had argued for more men, but Luke wanted to keep the squad small. Epstein might be out of bombs, but there were no doubt eyes in the sky tracking every motion of the army. "We'll look like deserters. You know there will be plenty of them. It's one thing to chant slogans and another to suffer drone fire. Epstein can't track every group."

"No," General Miller had said. "But this is critical to our success. Will a dozen men be able to control the situation?"

"Yes," Luke had replied. "Our targets are used to following orders."

His team wasn't the kind of elite unit he was used to, but people who drove across the country to join a militia tended to be of a breed, and he'd selected men with significant combat experience. The nature of it varied dramatically: Gorecki was an ex-marine who worked as a bodyguard for hip-hop superstars, Decker was the master-at-arms for a San Diego motorcycle club, Reynolds had commanded a police rapid response team in Tennessee.

"I'll take the guard outside," Luke whispered. "There are probably a couple more awake in the dorms. Reynolds, that's your team. Do it quietly. Gorecki, take your three and secure the perimeter. Staff will be in the trailers; Decker and I will go door to door. Understood?"

His unit leaders gave him the thumbs-up. Luke started to rise, then paused. "Remember to check your targets. Nobody hurts a kid." He waited to see nods from all eleven men, took one last look through the binos—the guard was still leaning against the hood of a car, his back to them—and handed them to Gorecki.

Luke stayed low, duckwalking toward the parking lot. It felt good to be moving after half an hour on cold ground. The on-mission clarity bloomed, that heightened awareness and sharpened focus. How many times had he done something like this? Dozens? Scores? He'd lost count of the nations he'd fought in. There had been times in his life when he felt that he was only alive when he was operating.

At least, he'd felt that way until he had sons.

The noise of the generators would cover any sound he might make, but he stepped lightly anyway. When he reached the nearest bus, he dropped to his belly, peered under the vehicle. All he could see of the guard were the back of his legs. Luke considered circling, decided to take the less expected route, and army-crawled beneath the bus. More of the guard was revealed with each careful movement. Judging by the number of butts at his feet, he'd been here awhile. The graveyard shift was boring, and it was easy for the mind to wander.

Luke rose, a ghost in shadows. He left his sidearm in its holster and slid a length of cord from his pocket, wrapping it around each gloved palm four times. One step, two, three, and then he was behind the man, close enough to smell the acrid tobacco reek and hear the raspy sound of his breath. Luke waited for him to take a last drag on the cigarette and exhale. Then he crossed his arms to make a loop, snapped it over the guard's head and jerked back and out with both arms at the same moment he kicked out his knee.

In less than a second, the man's entire body weight and all of Luke's strength came to bear on the slender cord against his throat, shutting his windpipe and the carotid artery. His hands flew to his neck, scratching futilely as his legs kicked spasms in the dirt. His strength was gone in three seconds; after eight, he stopped moving entirely. Luke counted another twenty, unwound the cord, and confirmed the job with his knife.

Then he rose and waved his team forward.

They came quickly, automatic weapons ready. Led by Reynolds, six of them moved to the inflatable dome. Gorecki's team spread out to surround the compound. Decker was of the amphetamine-thin variety of biker, a tattooed scarecrow with long hair bound back by his hat. His eyes didn't widen as he took in the dead guard and the blood steaming against the cold ground.

Luke pointed to the nearest trailer. He'd hoped the door might not be locked—they were miles from the nearest town—but a gentle twist gave nothing. The fourth key on the guard's ring did the trick. Luke opened the door and slid inside, Decker behind.

Night glow through the windows revealed a tiny living area. The kitchen was to the left, and on the wall to the right an open door led to what had to be the bedroom. Luke slid to it, footfalls silent on the carpet, then peered in. Pitch-black. He took the flashlight from his pocket, covered it with his palm, and let the blood-warm light trickle in. A desk, the door to a bathroom, a twin mattress with one figure in it. Six steps brought him alongside the bed.

In one move, Luke straddled the sleeper, covering his mouth with his right hand and using the left to aim the flashlight in his eyes. The man woke with a jerk and a gasp against Luke's palm.

"Don't fight."

The man froze, his face pale and eyes wide, pupils constricting visibly in the sudden light.

"I'm going to take my hand off your mouth. Try to scream, you die. Understand?"

A trembling nod.

"What's your role?"

"Wh . . . what?" Voice cracking.

"Your job. What is it?"

"I'm a counselor."

"What's your name?"

"Gary."

"How many children are here, Gary?"

"Umm." It was the first time the man had consciously hesitated.

Decker pulled a long bowie knife from a leg sheath, twisted the blade to catch the light, then slid it across the man's throat, painting a thin line of blood. The counselor jumped, started to yelp, but Luke had his hand down before he could make a sound.

"We got one warning before Epstein tried to kill us. You get the same. Hold back again, or try to lie, and we'll gut you." Luke took his hand away. "Now—"

"Six hundred and four!"

For a moment, Luke almost ordered Decker to kill him, but the fear in the counselor's eyes was pure and uncalculated. "That doesn't make sense."

"I swear—"

"Lower your voice."

"I swear, it's true, I swear."

"This is where Epstein brought the kids who escaped from Davis Academy two weeks ago. There were only about three hundred students in the whole school."

"We p-p-paired them. With other children."

"Why?"

"The academies—these kids were taken from their parents, brainwashed. Taught to hate each other. For years. They need care, help. That's why we're all the way out here, the middle of nowhere. Please, don't cut me again."

"What other children?"

"Huh?"

"You said you paired them with other children."

"Oh. Holdfast kids. V-v-volunteers."

Luke weighed that. It made sense; it wasn't that different from the kind of counseling veterans with PTSD had access to. *It's a gift. It'll make Miller's plan twice as effective.* "You an abnorm?"

"Yes. I'm a tier-four reader, with a master's from—"

"I'm going to ask you a question, and I want you to read me and think very carefully before you answer." He leaned forward. "How badly do you want to live?"

The man stared at him. For a long moment, Luke could see him wrestling to hold on to notions of honor and duty. But abstract concepts were slippery, especially in the middle of the night with a bowie knife resting on your throat.

"What do you want me to do?"

"How many therapists are on staff?"

"Uhhh . . . about ten professionals, plus administrators."

"If you could pick two others to survive the night, who would they be—and where do they sleep?"

Twenty minutes later, Luke and Decker had recruited a couple more therapists.

It would have been quicker, but two of them didn't want to live as badly as Gary.

■

Considering how packed it was, the big dome of the gymnasium was eerily calm. The children sat on the floor, some in pairs, most alone. The ones from Davis Academy had simply lined up and held out their arms to be zip-tied, one at a time. Gary and the other two counselors had been useful; when the children saw adult faces they recognized, they'd just mutely done what they were told.

The only ones who had argued or offered resistance were the Holdfast kids. But the sight of commandos with automatic rifles had kept them in line.

"There's nothing to be afraid of," Gary said, his voice trembling. "These men have promised that no one will be hurt." He stood in the center of the gym, spinning slowly as he talked, trying not to look directly at the armed men surrounding them.

Luke walked the perimeter, taking a headcount and wondering what the academies must be like to have so cowed these kids. He remembered assemblies from his grade school days as noisy affairs, no matter how loudly the staff yelled. And those had been regular kids; these were gifted, mostly tier ones. It wasn't just that they could do things straights couldn't, it was that they would have *known* that. He'd expected them to be cocky, sure that their abilities allowed them special privilege. And even though they were young, there were more than six hundred of them against a dozen soldiers.

Of course, they didn't know that he had no intention of hurting a child. Whatever the academies were like, the people who ran them must not have operated under the same principle. Ugly, but useful. As he'd told General Miller, they were accustomed to taking orders.

500, 502, 504.

Decker and two of the others came in from the outside in a wash of loud, cold wind. The biker nodded to Luke. Good. It was done, then. The rest of the staff had been neutralized, leaving just Gary and his fellow therapists.

The facility belonged to the New Sons of Liberty.

A wave of exhaustion rolled across Luke. No doubt the rest of the team was in the same boat; it was nearing dawn after a long day. They'd left in the middle of the night following the drone attack, and marched hard to get here, covering almost fifty miles in twenty-four hours, breaking only briefly for meals, lying in thorny scrub as they waited for traffic to clear on the roads they'd crossed, nervously eyeing gliders soaring high above them. Add to it the adrenaline of action, even action without resistance, and what he wanted more than anything was to snatch a couple of hours of rack time.

You've still got a long day ahead.

580, 582, 584.

They'd managed the raid because no one in the Holdfast had expected it. General Miller had estimated as many as two thousand people would desert after the drone strikes, and while many would go back the way they'd come, groups would scatter in all directions, too many to track and intercept, especially with the New Sons pushing on toward Tesla.

At least his team wouldn't be walking back. The buses he'd seen in the parking lot, no doubt the same ones that had brought the children here, would return them to the militia quickly enough.

"I know you're scared," Gary said. "We all are. But it's going to be okay. Everyone stay with your buddy and do what you're told, and we'll all get through this."

598, 600, 602 . . . 603.

Luke frowned. On the first headcount, he'd assumed that someone had swapped places, or that his own tired mind had made a mistake. But either Gary had lied to him, or else a kid was hiding somewhere.

On one hand, it didn't matter. A single child wouldn't make a difference. But if the kid was bright enough to try to reach a phone, they'd lose their advantage. The only way they were going to be able to return to the militia was if the powers that be in New Canaan didn't realize what had happened.

As Gary droned on, Luke moved to Reynolds, the former tactical cop. He'd done well, his team taking down the guards inside the facility without alerting anyone. "We're missing one."

Reynolds cursed. "Want me to search?"

"No. Stay here, and stay sharp." Luke cut around the perimeter, trying to ignore the stares of frightened children. The dome was modular, with the gymnasium being the largest section, and inflated halls led to group dorms and classrooms. The good news was that there couldn't be too many places to hide. Doubtless he'd find the missing one under a bed.

At the door, a thought struck him, and he turned around and did another quick headcount. 2, 4, 6, 8 . . . 9. Ten counting himself.

Something in him went icy, and he unsnapped the strap on his sidearm.

The hallway beyond the gym was quiet, just the moaning of the wind against the fabric, and, faint, the sound of a voice and something that might have been a whimper. Luke started out as swiftly as silence would allow, then decided screw silence, and ran.

He found them in one of the classrooms, the sound of pleading coming through a zippered canvas door. The girl was blonde and crying, stretched face-first over a desk. She flopped and yanked, but she was probably sixteen, and thin. Gorecki was behind her tugging at her jeans, while one of the others, a guy out of Michigan named Healy, held both her arms in beefy hands.

When Luke ripped the door open, Healy straightened, an *oh shit* look on his face. Gorecki turned awkwardly, his pants around his ankles to expose his weapon.

For a moment they all stared, Luke and his teammates and the girl too, her head turned sideways and tears streaking her face.

Gorecki said, "She's just a twist, man."

Luke thought of his boys, his fine sons, burning alive. Josh burning in the sky, Zack burning in his tank. Soldiers, both of them. Both murdered by abnorms, by the work of a tier-one computer programmer. A tier one like this girl.

He drew his sidearm, braced it in both hands, and shot Gorecki twice through center mass and once in the head, swiveled, and did the same to Healy.

Then he holstered the weapon and went to look for a blanket for her.

CHAPTER 18

Cooper died again.

The knife was a Fairbairn-Sykes, a slender dagger useful only for killing. Made of carbon-fiber sharpened to a point a molecule thick, it slid through clothes and flesh and muscle to skewer the left ventricle of the heart. Death was almost instant.

Soren withdrew the blade and started away, his face expressionless.

"Repeat," Cooper said.

The projection jumped back ten seconds. Breakfast out for him and Natalie and the kids, a couple of weeks ago. It was security footage, but taken in the Holdfast, so both the coverage and resolution were extraordinary. He could remember the conversation perfectly, Todd talking about soccer here, how the rules were different because of the brilliants, and Cooper was listening and joking around, and then on the edge of the screen Soren slit the throat of one bodyguard, then took three steps and opened the brachial artery of a second. Blood spray lashed nearby tables.

In the footage, Cooper didn't hesitate. He stood and hurled a chair as he charged. The fight was brief and pitiful: the chair missed, his jab missed, and his hook was blocked by the edge of the dagger, which split his hand in half. And that was as good as it got.

What came next was a nightmare. Todd, seeing his dad hurt, ran to help. Soren cocked an arm and spun with terrible force, his elbow colliding with Todd's temple, snapping the boy's head sideways. In the footage, Cooper screamed, then launched himself at Soren, who positioned the dagger precisely to slide through clothes and flesh and muscle to skewer the left ventricle of the heart.

Cooper died again.

Even now, knowing that Todd was going to be okay, that Soren had failed—that Cooper had later beaten him—it still tore shreds from his sanity to watch that elbow whistle through the air, to see his son's eyes go glassy.

That's the point of this exercise, right? Remind yourself what you're facing.

He'd been so pleased with himself for thinking of the carrot for Soren. He'd hated it, too, the notion of presenting comfort to the monster who had attacked his son. But sitting in the virtual chapel beside the assassin, he had again felt an emotion he didn't want: pity.

It was the wetness in Soren's eyes. Tears prompted by hearing music for the first time. *Imagine the strength it must have taken to yank himself from that dream. To possess what he had always wanted but never believed possible . . . and to refuse it.*

Cooper was still reeling. Soren's will had inspired something like awe in him, and he couldn't afford that. Which was why he'd found this quiet conference room to relive the worst moment of his life again and again.

He was about to tell the terminal to repeat the video when his phone pinged. Funny, his phone used to be practically a living thing, always buzzing with a message, an e-mail, an alert, a status update. But in the last months, he'd dropped out of that world. Out of the world at large, really. Now it was something of a novelty to get a message.

QUINN: NEED TO TALK. ASA-F'ING-P.

Cooper started to type a reply, then remembered he was in a conference room. "System. Begin video call." He rattled off Bobby's number.

"All communications with locations outside the Holdfast are temporarily—"

"Override."

"Enter authorization code, please."

"Ask Epstein." He waited, imagining a message popping up in Erik's subterranean lair, one more point of data amidst a river of them. His head throbbed, one of those killer headaches right behind the eyeballs, and he rubbed at them as he waited.

A moment later the air shimmered, the footage of his death replaced by the view of a bright office, white walls with picture frames leaning against them, moving boxes stacked beside a desk. Cooper smiled. "Bobby. Scored an office in the new building, huh? I like it, a window and everything. All your ring-kissing paid off."

Quinn wore a trim suit and an amused expression. "That took, what, forty seconds? You know, the boys will like you better if you play hard to get."

"Just can't help it when you're involved."

"Got some friends who want to say hello." Quinn leaned forward to tap a button, and the video feed split into two.

"Jesus, boss," Luisa Abrahams said, "you look like you spent the night blowing homeless dudes at the bus station." Beside her, Valerie West strangled a laugh.

Not so long ago, the four of them had been a team, the most decorated in Equitable Services. They'd tracked terrorists and assassins, planned operations that spanned the country, served as the long strong arm of the United States. Years of hunting bad guys together, of late nights and delivery food and twanging nerves and last-second saves. Seeing them all now, he realized how much he'd missed that. Missed them. "Weezy," he said, and ran a hand through his hair. "Poetic as ever. This better?"

"Oh yeah, I'm ready to switch jerseys. Sorry, babe," she said as she nudged Val, "but I just can't resist him any longer."

"Enough," Quinn said. "Is this line secure?"

"Not even a little bit. I'm in the Holdfast."

"What? Why?"

"Pursuing my lifelong dream to become a cowboy." Cooper shrugged. "What do you think? I'm hunting John Smith."

"Ah. On that note, after our last chat, I got to thinking," Quinn said. "Most of the department's resources are focused on Epstein these days, but I was curious what our old playmate was up to. I asked Val to do a little pattern scanning."

"Yeah, um." The data analyst shifted in her chair. She had the pallid skin of someone who received most of her light from a computer monitor. Which was true, and part of why she was so great at what she did. It was Val who had tipped him and Ethan off to Abe Couzen in Manhattan. "Look, this is just a theory."

"I rate your theories over other people's facts. What have you got?"

"I think John Smith is about to attack. Like, immediately." She paused. "You play chess, boss?"

"I know how the pieces move."

"Okay, well, there's basically three phases. In the opening, both sides are positioning their forces. So for Smith, that was his time on the run, building a network, recruiting followers. Then comes the midgame, which is a lot of testing weaknesses, trading pieces. It can be bloody, but it's not the real conflict. Like the last few years: assassinations, the explosion at the stock exchange—"

"The Children of Darwin?"

"No," she said. "They were the beginning of the endgame. Nothing is safe in the endgame—your most powerful pieces, the positions you've spent the whole game building, all of it can be sacrificed. All that matters is winning."

Sounds like John Smith in a nutshell. "So what's his play?"

"I don't know. But it's big, and it's imminent."

"Tell me."

"So, first warning is that Smith's lieutenants have fallen off the radar. They all ran pretty deep anyway, but we'd always get ripples: a face-match arriving too late, some credit activity, coded messages in online havens, that sort of thing. Over the last days, that's all stopped. I mean, gone. Then there's the financials. You remember his smurfed bank accounts in the Caymans and Dubai?"

He nodded. The phrase "follow the money" may have been made famous by a movie, but it was standard procedure in intelligence and antiterrorism work. The DAR had a huge staff of forensic accountants dedicated to freezing illegal money. In Smith's case, they'd never been able to prove accounts belonged to him. But there was a difference between proof and certainty, and for years, a number of suspicious offshore accounts had been closely monitored.

"In the last forty-eight hours," Valerie said, "fourteen have gone empty."

"How much in total?"

"North of a hundred million dollars."

"*Holy*—can you trace it?"

She shook her head. "Our hottest coders had backchannel routines to prevent any withdrawal. I mean gray-hat stuff, quasi-legal hacks that could provoke international incidents. But the money is still gone. Worse, no alarm bells were tripped. If Quinn hadn't asked me to look, we wouldn't even have known."

His stomach had a sour feeling like he'd eaten raw chicken. Cooper stared, processing. "So he's going all in. Any guess as to his intentions?"

"Not specifically. But this is John Smith we're talking about, right? You called him the strategic equivalent of Einstein." Valerie shrugged. "Whatever he's planning, it won't be what we expect."

And it will be devastating. Cooper said, "Bobby, you have to take this to the director."

"You think?" Quinn shook his head. "I love you, man, but my paychecks read DAR. I talked to her before I texted you. But remember what I said in that dive bar?"

"Yeah, that the whole world is on fire."

"And that there's a shortage of water." Quinn shrugged. "The director understands the threat. But across the country we've got brilliants being persecuted, burned out, lynched. There are massive food shortages. Riots in a dozen cities. A militia rampaging through Wyoming. Three assassination attempts on the president in the last two weeks. The metric for threat is a moving target."

Cooper's headache hadn't been improved by any of this, and he leaned his elbows on the table, dug his fingers in just above his eyes. "Did you share my theory about the tier zeroes?"

"Sure," Quinn said. "Had to explain to the powers that be how an egghead kicked my butt."

"Any response?"

"They agree it would be bad."

"Terrific." Cooper sighed, straightened. "Listen, I know you all took a risk sharing this with me. I appreciate it."

"Oh, don't be an asshole," Luisa said. "Just wish you were here, boss. This is getting grim."

"Don't worry," Cooper said. "I'm still fighting."

Quinn said, "All right, partner. We need to go earn our paychecks."

"Yeah. Thanks again."

"No sweat. Just remember, beer is on you."

"Forever, buddy. Forever."

His old friend smiled and opened his mouth to reply. Before he could, everything went white, and his office window exploded in a rain of fire and sparkling glass.

The video connection failed.

But in the fraction of a second before it did, Cooper heard screaming.

CHAPTER 19

Owen Leahy was in the shower when the man came for him.

December didn't often mean snow in northern Maryland, but somehow that was how he always thought of Camp David: bare trees brittle with frost, and a swirl of faint snowflakes. The image stuck in his head even in summer, and he'd find himself feeling chilly, craving extra blankets and hot showers. He'd been standing in the billowing steam for half an hour, thinking, idly tracing the pattern of liver spots on his forearms with water-wrinkled fingers.

Then suddenly there was an officer in a naval uniform in his private bathroom. "Mr. Secretary? There's been an attack."

Six minutes later, they were jogging past bare trees and frosted greenery, Leahy's hair dripping on his suit, tie flapping behind him like a tail. Agents and soldiers were everywhere. Although officially a "country retreat," Camp David was in effect a fortress, with antimissile batteries positioned in the woods and a nuclear-safe bunker deep underground.

When the president was in residence, the Laurel Lodge conference room served as the Situation Room. Leahy entered, quick-scanning the assembled team: representatives from the armed forces, the intelligence services, the cabinet. Many were new to their posts, replacing men and women who'd been killed in the missile strike on the White House, but he knew them all.

"Madam President." To the room at large he said, "What's happened?"

Sharon Hamilton, the national security advisor, said, "A wave of terrorist attacks across the country."

"How many?"

"It's hard to say."

"Why?"

"They're still taking place." Hamilton gestured to the bank of tri-ds.

After the last year, Leahy would have bet he couldn't be shaken by footage of disaster. He'd watched the stock exchange fall, seen Cleveland burn, watched American troops massacre each other. And in a way, what was onscreen now was no different. It was just that there was so much of it. The screens were a grid of chaos and fire. Buildings smashed, infernos raging, people running in terror. Civilians spattered in blood, walking hollow-eyed. Children crying in the streets. And on the incident map, red dots glowed across the breadth of the country.

"Jesus. Any pattern to the targets?"

"Mostly military and political. Shooters in city hall in Los Angeles. A suicide bomber in a mess hall in Fort Dix. Two trucks forced the governor of Illinois's limo into the Chicago River. There was a bomb outside the Federal Reserve—that one was stopped. The safety controls on the natural gas lines to the Centers for Disease Control in Atlanta were subverted, and the bulk of the complex is on fire. Most devastating so far is a massive explosion at the DAR, bombs apparently planted during the expansion of the facility. The newest building was flattened."

"Casualties?" He looked to Marjorie May. The DAR director's cheerful name belied her icy blend of political savvy and ruthless efficiency. But now her voice trembled as she said, "It's the middle of the workday. A thousand people, maybe more."

The world wobbled, and for a moment, Leahy thought he might fall down. He gripped the edge of the table so hard his knuckles went white. "The abnorms?"

"I've spoken to Erik Epstein," the president said without looking away from the screen. "He offers condolences and assures us that the Holdfast was not involved."

"Bullshit."

Ramirez glanced over, cocked her head. Leahy said, "Sorry, ma'am, but that seems unlikely."

"Respectfully, I disagree," Marjorie May said. "I think John Smith is likelier. It's his MO, and we've got a pattern of indicators suggesting he was about to attack."

"Even so, Epstein is facing invasion. That makes him the real threat."

"Mr. Secretary, I assure you, Smith represents—"

"I understand," Leahy said. "I'm suggesting they've joined forces. Smith could be functioning as Epstein's fixer, allowing him deniability. Alternately, maybe Smith fears Epstein capitulating in order to protect New Canaan." He paused. "Regardless, this provides the political cover we would need to attack."

"Enough." Gabriela Ramirez had turned from the screens.

"Madam President—"

"Sit down."

Leahy pulled out a chair. He opened his mouth to take up the argument again, but the president cut him off. "Listen to me, all of you. 'Who' is not important. There are attacks on America *happening right now*. Our people are dying. The first order of business isn't assigning blame, and it's not gearing up for war. Our job is to stop any further attacks. To save lives. Am I understood?"

"Yes, ma'am."

"Now. DAR. I'm sorry for your losses, but I need you to work through it. Can your people do that?"

"Yes, ma'am."

"Good. As of this moment, the national priority is stopping more attacks. I want all resources tasked to threat analysis and prevention."

"I understand." Director May hesitated. "We're going to be stretched pretty thin. Many of the people killed today were agents and operators. Plus, on any given day, we have indicators of hundreds of threats. If we're investigating all of them, we won't be able to do much else. Including finding the instigator of today's attacks."

"I want this situation under control first. Secretary Leahy." Ramirez turned to him. "What's your plan for halting the militia attack on the Holdfast?"

Leahy sat quietly. It was a trick he'd developed over the years: fingers on the table, eyes steady but slightly unfocused, like he was performing complex mental calculations. Make them wait. It was particularly effective at managing people who were used to immediate answers to their questions—like presidents. Just before the silence grew uncomfortable, he spoke. "Madam President, I don't think we should."

"Explain."

"Sometimes the best defense is keeping your opponent off-balance. NSOL represents an opportunity to do that."

"*If* I make the decision to attack the Holdfast, it will be with United States soldiers."

"The public is already vocal in their desire for a response. After today's tragedy, they will *demand* we strike back. The New Sons allow us to do that without limiting our options."

"Mob rule is not our way."

"Stopping the militia will be seen as a demonstration of weakness." Before she could respond, he added, "There's also the fact that we can't."

President Ramirez raised one eyebrow.

Choose your words carefully. "The retrograde of military forces leaves us in an awkward position." Looks danced around the room, everyone catching the subtle jab. Ramirez had ordered the retrograde, and though Leahy hadn't said as much, the hint of blame wasn't hard to catch.

"Are you saying that our military isn't currently capable of stopping a crowd of civilians?"

"I'm saying, ma'am, that any incursion into the Holdfast has a good chance of being perceived as an attack. Even if our only purpose is to turn back the militia, there is no way Epstein can be sure of that. Not only that, but the retrograde isn't complete. There are still numerous vulnerabilities in our armed forces." Leahy gestured to the tri-d where live footage of the DAR complex ran. The ruined building looked like God had stomped on it. Choking smoke rose from a hundred places, and bodies were strewn everywhere. "Today is a reminder of what abnorms are capable of. If we corner Epstein, there's no guarantee that he won't launch an all-out attack."

He thought about adding more, decided against it. After a long moment, Ramirez turned back to the screens.

Leahy didn't let himself smile. He wouldn't have wished for the events of the day, but he could use them. The terrorists continued to miss the point. The more damage they wrought, the more they strengthened the position of men like him. Ramirez had basically ordered the DAR to chase their tails playing defense, and in the meantime, left the field open to those who could see that no game was ever won on defense alone.

Even now, the New Sons of Liberty were pushing deeper into the Holdfast. The drone bombardment hadn't stopped them; Epstein's bluff had failed. What came next wouldn't be pretty, but it would be effective.

You're going to have your war. The war America needs. Focused, contained, and crucial.

And when it's over, you'll still be standing—atop the heap.

CHAPTER 20

Cooper couldn't remember how he'd gotten here.

At first he'd tried to convince himself that the dropped call was just that. A digital glitch. But even as he'd frantically redialed, he was remembering the explosion of glass, the fist of smoke.

The screams.

A video call might freeze. The image might distort. But this . . .

After five failed retries, he'd started running. His head was packed with thoughts of his team: The time Luisa had taken three rounds in her vest on a raid, how at the bar that night they couldn't get her to keep her shirt on, she just kept hiking it up to display the bruises, saying, "Would you look at my tit!" Valerie's voice in his ear, only weeks ago, saying that she had outplanned John Smith's security team, beaten them with their own system, the quiet pride in herself.

And Bobby. His partner. Cooper had never had a flesh-and-blood brother, but a cop's partner was his brother. They'd been drunk together, hungover together, worked through both of their divorces together. Kicked in doors together. Taken down a corrupt president together.

An explosion and a fist of smoke. And screaming. In true pain or true panic, socialization fell away, and men and women shrieked the same. Could have been any of them. Could have been all of them.

He'd found himself in Epstein's subterranean sanctuary, dark and cool, smelling of processed food and lit by images of horror.

Video feeds from all over the country showed a nation consumed by madness. A limousine facedown in a black river. A police station with a half-overturned semitrailer sticking out of it. A raging fire consuming a complex of offices. SWAT teams firing tear gas rounds through the shattered windows of a government building.

The Department of Analysis and Response in ruins. Torn open as if a giant had scooped it wide, exposing the interior floors, row on row of naked desks and debris-choked halls and shattered toilets. The new building had collapsed entirely, reduced to a mountain of rubble half-obscured by billowing black smoke.

The new building. He remembered the video of Bobby's office, the white walls with pictures leaning against them, no time yet to hang them.

And no time to come.

Cooper's knees hit the ground and a sound came from his lungs.

Someone hugged him. Slender arms twining around his neck, and the smell of hairspray. "I'm so sorry," Millie said into his shoulder.

He leaned into the embrace, squeezed back with both arms. It wasn't Millie he was holding, it was Natalie, and Shannon, and his children, and his father, and Bobby and Luisa and Val. For a long moment he held them all, his face buried in Millie's hair.

Then, slowly, he released her. She stepped back, her eyes on his. All around him, the apocalyptic images continued.

Val's voice rang in his head. *This is John Smith we're talking about. Whatever he's planning, it won't be what we expect.*

Words spoken when she was alive.

Words spoken moments ago.

Slowly, he rose to his feet.

"I'm, umm, I'm sorry." Erik's features were carved in deep pockets by flickering video. His hands were in his pockets. "About your friends."

"Are they . . ." His voice cracked, and he paused. Coughed. "Are they dead?"

"Statistically—"

"Fuck your statistics!" The words came unbidden. He made himself breathe. After a moment, he said, "Sorry."

"It's . . . I'm sorry." Erik paused. "Yes."

"You're sure."

"The call originated from the west corner of the . . . yes. They're gone. Estimated fatalities in the DAR between twelve hundred and two thousand."

Cooper nodded. "Okay."

"No," Millie started, "it's not—"

"How many attacks were there?"

"Fifteen so far. They were synchronized."

"John Smith."

Epstein nodded. "Your friend Valerie's analysis was correct."

"You were listening in?"

"Of course," Erik said as though that were normal. "However, she was suffering from institutional bias. John Smith wasn't acting against the DAR. And though we are in his endgame, this is not the master stroke."

"No," Cooper said. "He thinks bigger than this."

"Agreed. Statistically—" He caught himself nervously. "Umm, I mean, logically, the purpose is to weaken existing power structures. For greatest efficacy, terrorists benefit from a desperate nation."

"Yeah." Cooper looked at the screens. "Well."

"However," Epstein said, "we're no closer to John Smith than before. Perhaps we should use alternate methods."

"You mean start torturing Soren? No."

"Extreme interrogation doesn't fit your personality matrix. Understood. But there are people suited for it."

"You think I'm squeamish?" Cooper made a sound that wasn't a laugh. "After all that's happened?" He shook his head. "I hate everything about the notion of torture, and I'd take Soren apart a piece at a time if I thought it would work. But it won't."

"Expand."

"I offered Soren the one thing he's always dreamed of and never imagined he might actually have. I'm sure you were watching. I even lied and suggested that it might be made permanent. And he pulled the plug out of his own skull."

"Still, perhaps pain would—"

Cooper shook his head. "He's too strong. I'm sure you could break him. But it would be his *mind* you broke, not his will. There are only two people in the world he cares about. Only two he even believes exist. You could drive him mad, but there's no amount of pain that would make him betray . . ."

He trailed off.

Millie stared at him. "Wow. Are you serious?"

Cooper turned away from her accusing eyes. Looked at Erik Epstein, pale and powerful and surrounded by images of a world in crisis. "I need you to get someone for me."

"Who?"

"The other person Soren cares about," Cooper said. "His lover, Samantha."

CHAPTER 21

Hawk was reading volume six of a graphic novel series when someone knocked on his door.

He didn't really know if there was a difference between comic books and graphic novels, but the latter sounded better. A comic book might be some silly story of a rich duck and his nephews. What he was reading was a philosophical exploration of the devil's continuing war with heaven. This devil wasn't red and scaly, and he wasn't exactly evil, although he certainly wasn't good, either. More like doing his own thing, no matter what. He wanted free will, and heaven was all about predestination. Hawk knew on which side his mom would have fallen, and he was kind of falling the same way.

The knock was three soft raps, could be anyone, and so as he walked to the door, he let himself imagine it was Tabitha. Maybe asking for help with something. He was a better shot, maybe she wanted to practice—

John Smith stood in the hallway. "Hiya, Hawk."

It was John who had first given him the nickname, and while Aaron had always liked Aaron Hakowski okay, it was no match for being the Hawk. He straightened and brushed his hair back. John had never come to his room before. Why would he? He was in charge of everything, and Aaron was just a kid whose mom had . . .

"Can I come in?"

"Ah, yeah, sure, of course." He held the door open.

John stepped inside, took in the room, and Aaron suddenly saw it through his eyes, the crumpled blankets and piles of stuff all over the desk and, shit, a comic book propped open on his bed.

"What are you reading?"

"Nothing, just—"

"Ah." John picked up the book, held it with a smile. "I love this series."

"I—you do?"

"Great writing. Plus, I identify with him some. Plenty of people think I'm the devil, too. Risks of forging your own path." John put it back on the pillow. "You mind if I smoke?"

"No, no, go ahead."

"Thanks." He slid a cigarette from the pack, snapped a silver Zippo. "Bad habit, but it helps me think."

"Aren't you worried about . . ."

"It killing me?"

Aaron nodded.

"Tell you the truth?" John shrugged. "I would be, if there was any chance I'd live long enough. Okay if I sit down?"

"Yeah." Aaron took the chair from the desk, dumped a pile of books off of it. "So what do you mean about living—"

"I'm playing a game against the whole world, Hawk. I have been since I was eight years old. Do you know what happened to me then?"

Aaron shook his head.

"I took a test. It was new then, the Treffert-Down. Everyone was very excited about it, this scale for measuring brilliance. I'd been taught to do well on tests, so I did. I did so well, in fact"—John dug a Coke can from the garbage and ashed his cigarette into it—"that government agents came and took me away from my mom. They put me in an academy. They changed my name and started trying to break me. I spent ten years there. I watched them destroy my friends. Brainwash them, or worse. Sometimes much worse."

"Mom told me about the academies," Aaron said. "I'm really sorry."

"I'm not." John looked straight at him. "That made me. I realized when I was eight years old that that wasn't a world I could live in. I decided to tear it down and build a better one. To pen a new history, one written in fire. And I'm going to succeed."

"I believe you," Aaron said.

"I'm going to succeed," John continued, "but I'm not going to live. They'll kill me." He took another drag off the cigarette. "It's pretty much guaranteed. So I can't get too worried about lung cancer, you know?"

"But—can't you run? Hide?"

"I ran for a long time. But now it's time to act. And I can't execute my plan and hide under a rock at the same time." He leaned forward. "The other day you asked me about it. Do you still want to know?"

"Yes, sir."

"You remember the man we brought in?"

"Dr. Abraham Couzen. You said he had discovered the most important thing in thousands of years."

John smiled. "That's right. Couzen discovered what makes people brilliant. More than that, he figured out a way to turn normals into abnorms. Non-coding RNA that alters gene expression."

This must be a dream. If he'd opened his door to find Tabitha wearing lingerie and waggling a condom, it would have seemed more real than John Freaking Smith sitting on his bed and talking about graphic novels and non-coding RNA, whatever that was. "Does it . . . it works?"

"Yes. But that's just the beginning. Do you know much about organic chemistry?"

From anyone else, the question would have been an insult, but Aaron realized that John meant it, face value. "No."

"Okay, well, it was obvious that someone would discover the root causes of brilliance. I won't bore you with the details, but there were indicators that it wasn't too far down the line. Some of the best abnorm scientists are part of our cause, and I could have put them to work on it. But that's a long-odds proposition. Better to let the world at large develop that, crowd-source it, if you will. Instead, we worked on a delivery mechanism. It started as a particularly nasty strain of flu, but that was a long time ago. Since then, we've refined and refined and refined it. We've created pretty much the most contagious cold the world has ever seen."

"I don't understand. How does making people sick help? Does it kill them?"

"I said contagious, not dangerous. The problem with biologicals as a strategic weapon is that they're hard to use, hard to contain, and if effective, tend to wipe out their hosts. This is different. It doesn't do much but give you the sniffles and a cough. But it's so incredibly communicable, and so long-lived, that if we release it properly, we can count on most of the world being infected."

"I don't understand. How does it help us?"

"Because influenza is an RNA virus. Like Ebola and SARS. Which means we can piggyback Dr. Couzen's non-coding RNA into it."

Hawk wanted to ask an intelligent question, wanted it badly, but he had a feeling that if he opened his mouth all that would come out was *ummmmm*, so instead he kept it shut.

"Which means that more or less everyone will get my flu," John continued. "And everyone who does will become gifted."

Aaron's mouth fell open. He hadn't realized that happened, not really, not in life. "You . . . you're going to turn the whole world . . ."

"Brilliant." John dropped his cigarette into the Coke can. "Yes."

"But that's . . . it would . . . I mean . . ."

"It will be humanity's biggest leap since the development of agriculture. Bigger. Because agriculture, like writing, and mathematics, and medicine, is just knowledge. Knowledge can be lost.

This is different. This is *evolution*. The changes to gene expression will be heritable. Do you get what that means?"

"I . . ."

"I'm not just turning everyone alive today brilliant. I'm turning the whole human race brilliant—forever."

Aaron had just managed to close his jaw, and now it fell open again. "My God."

"Think about it. A whole new world. A better one, with better people. Smarter, more capable, unafraid. Think what that could look like. Imagine what humanity could accomplish if everyone was brilliant."

"That's amazing." It felt like the bed was spinning beneath him. He had so many questions. But really, they all boiled down to one—*Can I have some?* He'd happily cut off a nut to be gifted. "What can I . . . what do you need from me?"

"Pardon?"

"Well . . ." Aaron paused. "I mean, there must be a reason you're telling me. Right?"

For a terrible second, he thought he'd offended John. But then his friend smiled. "Smart man. There is. We know everything about the pathology of our modified flu. Our virologists have been refining it for years. Now we've got Couzen's research, which we know works. And we've got detailed computer models of the two combined."

Suddenly it all clicked into place. "But you haven't actually tried it."

"I'd take it myself," John said, "but I'm already gifted."

"So it won't affect brilliants?"

"We'll still get the sniffles. And more importantly, the inheritance trait. But it won't change the way our gifts work."

"So you need a . . . a guinea pig?"

"No. I need a pioneer. We don't have time for clinical trials, Hawk. But I need to know how long this takes, and if there are side effects that we aren't anticipating, things like that. Because this is it. This is the masterstroke. We either win everything, or we lose everything. And I want to win."

It took all Aaron's willpower not to agree immediately. It was the thing he wanted more than anything. He had ever since Mom had explained the difference between her and him. She'd been so sad and self-conscious about it, had tried so hard to make it clear that she didn't think less of him because he was normal. And he knew she hadn't. But it didn't change the fact that he *was* less.

A thought hit him. "Dr. Couzen. You said he was going to die."

"Yes."

"Because he took his stuff?"

"The serum makes you brilliant, which means fundamentally changing the way the brain works. Couzen is too old for that not to have consequences. But you're fourteen. I'm not saying this will be a trip to Disney World, but you'll be fine. More than that. You'll be brilliant."

The phrase seemed to hang in the air. Aaron wondered what that might mean, specifically. Like turning into a superhero. "So old people who get this flu will die?"

"Some of them," John said. "But it was old people who shaped this world. If building a better one costs the lives of the people who designed the academies, well, I'd rather them than you."

Aaron bit at his thumbnail.

"Doing this," John continued quietly, "would be a huge help to the cause. A huge help to me. But it's up to you. It's always up to you."

He knew what Mom would want him to do. But she'd been his mom. It was her job to think he was perfect. Truth was, he knew better. Besides, this was his life, and his choice. He pointed at the cigarettes. "Can I have one?"

"You smoke, Aaron?"

"I don't know."

John looked at him appraisingly. Then held out the pack.

Aaron fumbled one free, put it between his lips. John Smith did the same, then snapped the Zippo again and lit both.

"Do me a favor?" Aaron held the cigarette. It felt weird between his fingers, but kind of good too. "Call me Hawk."

CHAPTER 22

When Natalie opened the door, her eyes, red and sunken, brightened with relief. "Oh thank God," she said, and then, "Come here," even as she opened her arms and came to him.

Cooper clutched at her, the familiar scent of her hair mingling with a faintly humid whiff of tears. Natalie always smelled different when she'd been crying. There was a permission in it, and he felt tears of his own close to the surface. When was the last time he'd cried? When Dad died?

"I was watching the news," she said into his shoulder. "I knew you weren't there, but I couldn't help it, when I saw that building, the same complex you went to work in every day, I just lost it."

"I'm okay," he said.

She heard the things he couldn't say, and stiffened. Leaned back without breaking the contact of their bodies, her eyes widening. "Bobby?"

"And Val, and Luisa."

Both her hands went to her open mouth, as if to contain the sound. But the cry made it through anyway. "Are they—are you sure?"

"I was talking to them when it happened. I . . . I saw . . ." He closed his eyes, sucked air in.

"Oh God, baby. Oh, Nick." She pressed herself against him, hands tightening around his back, strong fingers digging in. He heaved a gasping exhale that felt like it tore something. She held him, rocking slightly. "Come with me."

Cooper let her lead him into the apartment, through the kitchen, and down the hall to the bedroom. He was strangely aware that they'd made love the last time he'd been here, and then he realized he'd never get the chance to tell Bobby about that, to share his confusion and hear his old friend make an inappropriate joke, something funny and wrong that would get them laughing, and that was when he did start crying. Natalie climbed onto the bed and leaned against the wall and gestured him into her arms, and he crawled up after her and put his head in her lap and clutched her legs while she stroked his hair and knew better than to tell him it was all right.

It hadn't been all right for a very long time, and he was starting to doubt it ever would be again.

The tears didn't last long—he'd never had a problem with crying, he just didn't very much—but after they ceased he stayed where he was, head on her thighs, staring at her feet and the gauzy curtains beyond which the day died slowly. She ran her hands through his hair and waited, infinitely patient and present.

"It's wrong," he said at last. "It's just wrong. You know how many times Bobby and I were in danger? How many doors we kicked in, how many suspects we took down? Hell, the day of the stock exchange, he took a shotgun blast to the chest, broke two ribs. I was there, I knocked him down and . . ." He trailed off.

Natalie just ran her hands through his hair. After a moment, he said, "We were agents. We knew the risks. But . . . not like this. Not a bomb in the middle of the workday. No warning, no fighting back. Just boom, dead. He deserved better than that. A better death."

"There's no such thing as a better death, baby. There's just death."

"Yeah, but for Bobby Quinn it should have meant something. He should have been doing something that mattered."

"He was," Natalie said. "He was at work, trying to protect the country."

"It's not the same. He wasn't prepared."

"Who is?" She shrugged. "Bobby was a hero, and so were Luisa and Val and all the rest of them. But it's only in movies that heroes get to count on the big moment of glorious sacrifice. Real life is messier than that."

"I know, but . . . In a second. I mean, we were joking around when it happened. He said that beer was on me. Those were his last words. 'Just remember, the beer is on you.'"

Natalie made a sound that was almost a laugh. "Sorry, I just . . ." She paused, and this time she did laugh, though it was thick with sorrow. "If you asked Bobby, he'd have said those were pretty good last words."

The sentiment caught him off guard, and he found he could picture it, could picture his partner sitting at a bar, spinning a cigarette he didn't intend to light, and saying, *Hey, man, top that.*

"I don't mean to laugh."

"No, you're right. He'd have liked that." They lay quietly for a moment, his face mashed against her leg, his own pulse echoing in his ear.

"God," Natalie said. "His daughter."

"Shit." Bobby had been divorced, and not on the same terms with his ex that he and Natalie maintained. His daughter lived with her mom, and Cooper hadn't seen her in a while. "Maggie must be . . . eleven now?"

"Twelve," Natalie said. "Her birthday's in June."

"How do you remember that?"

"I loved him too, Nick. So do the kids."

Worse and worse. He'd have to tell them that Uncle Bobby was dead. Like they hadn't been through enough. "Kate and the academy. Todd in a coma. Maggie without her dad. All the way back to the kids in the Monocle restaurant. Why is it always children that suffer?" A thought struck him, and he turned his head. "Wait, where are—"

"Playing with friends. They're fine." She paused. "Was it John Smith?"

"Yes."

"He's never going to stop, is he?"

The words hit him with physical force. Something in his chest, not his biological heart but his metaphorical one, seemed to grow brittle and hard as cooling lava. "Yes," he said, and pushed himself up. "Yes he is."

"Nick—"

"I have to get going."

"Stay. There's no rush. I wasn't trying to . . ."

"No, I . . ." He wiped snot with the back of his hand. "Thank you. It's nothing you said."

"It's okay to let someone help, baby. To let me help."

"You have." He looked at her, the kind of long and naked stare that came with knowing someone so well it was hard to say where the boundaries between you lay. "Now it's my turn."

"To do what?"

Cooper thought about the preparations Epstein was making right this moment, about Samantha being kidnapped—a sudden motion and a hood over her head and the smell of chemicals before she lost consciousness. About a fist of smoke smashing a window and killing his friends and a thousand others. About a teenage corpse spinning at the end of a rope while Soren counted the holes of his cell. "What I have to."

She gazed back at him, her expression darkening. "You don't want to tell me."

"No."

"Why?"

"I'm not proud of it."

"Will it get you John Smith?"

"It has to."

"Then do it." Natalie's voice was steady. "Whatever it is."

For a long moment they stared at each other in the twilight room. Then he cupped her cheek and nodded.

NEW SONS OF LIBERTY NEARING TESLA

President Ramirez condemns NSOL, but "hands are tied."

Since breaching the New Canaan fence line on December 17th, the NSOL forces have traveled almost 80 miles, and are now nearing the capital city of Tesla. The civilian militia, which numbers approximately 17,000, suffered heavy casualties in a drone bombardment but has otherwise advanced without resistance. Under the direction of Erik Epstein, citizens of the Holdfast have been falling back to Tesla, long reputed to be protected by technological defenses.

In a brief prepared statement today, President Ramirez condemned the civilian militia, but said that due to the ongoing rollback of computer technology in US armed forces, the government could not directly intervene . . .

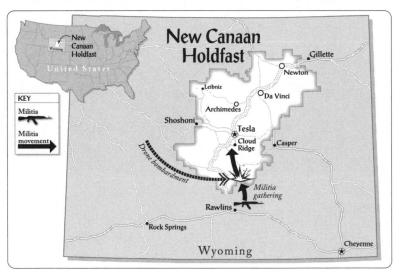

CHAPTER 23

The old man sat on the porch, fingerless gloves gripping the shotgun in his lap. He held it comfortably, like someone who considered it a tool. The kind of guy who would refer to it as a loaded burglar alarm.

Best Luke could tell, he was all that was left of the town of Cloud Ridge, the last outpost before Tesla.

Over the last days, the New Sons had traveled almost seventy miles, each one of them earned. Epstein may have run out of bombs, but he continued to harry the New Sons. Snipers dogged them at a distance, too far away and too poorly trained to score many kills, but every time there was the crack of distant gunfire, the whole army jumped. All day long, gliders kited silently above, their pilots dropping everything from bowling balls to Molotov cocktails. All night long, the abnorms used their audio projection trick, blaring taunts and sirens and loud music. None of it did much real damage, but it was wearing the men out. They were tired and radiated twitchy violence.

The horses, at least, had turned out to be a stroke of genius. Since the EMP disabled the vehicles, they pulled the bulk of the supplies. Miller had ordered hundreds of vans and SUVs gutted, the engines removed and seats discarded to transform them into makeshift wagons. The symbolism of the situation didn't escape Luke. A ragtag army leading a horse train against a small minority capable of projecting their voices from the heavens. It was the norm-abnorm conflict made a metaphor and underlined in blood.

Cloud Ridge was more a town than a city, with just over two thousand inhabitants. It was unlike any place Luke had ever seen. Instead of growing organically over decades, as most places did, it had been designed by urban planners and laid down as a unified whole in a matter of months. Everything was organized for function and efficiency, from the broad avenues surrounding the town park to the solar farm, hundreds of automated panels moving in perfect sync.

And all abandoned. Luke wasn't surprised, but he was disappointed. After the ass-kicking Epstein's drones had laid down and the constant harassment since, it would have been gratifying to face a battle. Even if every man, woman, and child in town had lined up against them, the New Sons could have smashed them. Which, of course, was why the place was empty. Their enemies weren't fools.

"Put it down, old man!" The militiaman was one of a dozen surrounding the porch, all clearly hoping for a fight. But the geezer just turned and spat.

Luke said, "Howdy."

"You the guy in charge?"

"One of them."

"Well, screw you, then."

"Why didn't you go on to Tesla yesterday with everybody else?" The timing was a guess, but one he was confident in. No doubt Epstein had tracked the militia's progress with drones, plotted it on radar, used computer simulations to project their progress. The order to clear out would have been given with exactly the right amount of time.

"This is my home."

"Son or daughter?"

"Huh?"

"You're too old to be an abnorm. Plenty of sympathizers came here, but I'm guessing at your age, it's something else."

"Aren't you the clever one." The man shifted, and a dozen fingers touched a dozen triggers. "Granddaughter."

"Your whole family came here?"

"My son, his wife, their kids. The youngest, Melissa, she's gifted, and none of us were gonna let her end up in an academy."

Luke nodded. He'd never put much thought into the academies before—they were only for the most powerful abnorms—but after the other night, he had a new appreciation of the dread they inspired.

"Your boys can relax, I'm not gonna fight. I don't have much food, but if you want to fill your canteens, be my guest."

Luke smiled. "Poisoned the supply, huh?"

"Worth a shot." The old man grinned back, fillings glinting in his teeth. "So now what?"

"Well, if you lay down that weapon and surrender, we'll let you go."

"Yeah? While you chase after my boy and his family?"

"You know," Luke said, "I had sons too. Your people burned them alive two weeks ago."

"Sorry for your loss," the guy said. The wind picked up off the high desert, whistling between the spindles of the porch rail. There was a gunshot from somewhere in the mid-distance. Another resident of Cloud Ridge, Luke supposed. "Last chance. Why don't you put the gun down and start walking?"

"Why don't you come on up here, unzip me, and—"

Luke pulled his sidearm and made a clean shot through the man's skull. The blast echoed off the gray belly of the sky. For a moment the grandfather remained sitting. Then as his muscles relaxed, his body slumped, slipping off the chair and thumping the boards of the porch. The shotgun clattered beside him.

One of the New Sons started to laugh. It was high-pitched and ragged, an edge of the hysterical in it.

"Pass it down that Miller's order not to drink the water stands," Luke said to no one in particular. "Check the houses as you move. No fresh food, just canned goods, ammunition, blankets."

The laughing soldier kept going, hinged at the knees and looking miserable. Luke glanced at him, then at the man standing beside him, a young guy with a patchy beard. "Then burn it."

"His house?"

"The town. Burn it to the ground."

CHAPTER 24

Soren woke.

Hips aching and back stiff from the metal bunk, he began the slow process of sitting up. As ever, his mind ranged ahead of his muscles, processing the sound that had awakened him. It was the door to his cage opening. Normally his captors just flooded the room with gas and did with his unconscious body as they liked.

So little changed in his tiny kingdom. Whatever this was, it would not be pleasant. He focused on calm, centering himself in nothingness.

The men who came had the broad shoulders and beefy necks of wrestlers. They wore dull uniforms marked with the rising blue sun of Epstein Industries, and leveled Tasers. In the leisure of his perception, Soren watched one squeeze the trigger, saw the pop of gas as the metal probes flew, cable looping through the air like a striking snake, and then the fangs hit his naked chest and tens of thousands of volts surged through him, washing away conscious thought and control. His muscles spasmed and a guttural sound wrenched from his throat.

The guards moved forward and wrestled his twitching body into a garment he was too scrambled to recognize at first. It wasn't until one of them used a length of steel chain to lash him to the wall that Soren realized he wore a straitjacket.

Torture, then. They evidently didn't understand him after all. He supposed they imagined his lingering perceptions of the agony would make it worse. From a certain perspective, they were right, but the results wouldn't be what they wished. He would simply retreat into nothingness and let them destroy him. Better than an eternity spent counting.

There was even room for victory of a sort, he realized. Simply not revealing the things they wanted to know would be the foundation. But the triumph would be in rising above. He would not scream. He had spent his whole life in pain. There was nothing they could do that he could not endure.

Once the guards had him bound to their satisfaction, they left. A stranger entered. Slender and unremarkable, with dark eyes and prominent cheekbones. He carried a chair in one hand and pushed a rolling tray laden with shiny instruments. Soren almost laughed at the theatricality of it.

Until Nick Cooper walked in, dragging a woman behind him, his fingers clenched around her arm. Pale and perfect. Samantha. She gasped when she saw him, then jerked free and ran to him, and he watched her come, slow, so slow, her brown eyes broad with horror, golden hair drifting behind, arms flung wide, and then she was on him, hugging him, her lips on his, the warmth and scent of her filling his world. Samantha was trembling, her mouth forming sounds more like whimpers than words.

"That's enough." Cooper yanked her away.

Soren lunged, but the straitjacket held his arms uselessly to his sides, and the chain snapped taut when he'd gone no more than an inch. He strained, the muscles of his legs knotting and locking fruitlessly as the only woman he'd ever loved, the only one who understood him, was forced into a chair, her arms and legs cuffed to it, a belt lashed around her narrow waist and duct tape stretched across her perfect mouth.

Cooper said, "I offered you a better way."

Soren stared, his nothingness shredding like a spiderweb in a hurricane. "I'll tell you. Everything."

"See, that's the problem." Cooper shrugged. "You're still nego-tiating. If you had just started telling me everything, maybe I'd feel different. But right now, I can't believe what you say."

Soren stared at him. Opened his mouth to share the things he knew. John wouldn't want Samantha hurt any more than he did. Besides, what could it matter? His friend planned for every contingency. He must have planned for this one.

But he might not have.

Then, *Cooper isn't the type to do this. It's a bluff.*

Soren hesitated.

"Yeah. What I thought." Cooper grimaced. "I wish I didn't have to do this, I really do. But today your friend killed two thou-sand of mine. And he's got worse planned for tomorrow." He nod-ded to the other man. "Go ahead, Rickard."

The dark-eyed torturer made a show of bending over the tray, fingering instruments. He lifted a scalpel to the light, brushed a bit of dust from the tip, then replaced it on the tray and chose another, a short, jagged blade curved like a grapefruit knife. Even from here, Soren could see the silver flicker of the edge.

Rickard stepped behind Samantha and trailed the point up her cheek, not quite touching. She moaned against the tape and strained at the handcuffs. Inside the straitjacket, Soren clenched his hands so hard his nails broke the skin of the palms, thinking, *A bluff, it's a bluff, they won't—*

With a smooth motion, the slim man pushed the blade through the lower lid of Samantha's left eye, slid it sideways to open a broad red ribbon, and then, with a deft scoop, popped the eyeball out of the socket, the optic nerve trailing behind, a mess of blood and fluid spattering her cheek as the gory thing dangled.

Soren screamed.

But Rickard wasn't finished.

Not even close.

■

Cooper clenched his fists, fought a rising in his stomach.

This has to be done.

He looked at the hologram, saw Soren twitch and jerk. The man's eyes were closed but moving frantically behind the lids as he lay on his bunk, the cable running up from the wall and to the interface in the back of his neck.

Beside him, Rickard typed frenetically. The terminal was layered with windows and wireframes that reacted as the programmer tweaked the controls. It was strangely chilling to stand in the control room outside Soren's cell, this bland computerized space, watching the holo of the man sweat and convulse.

"Pretty impressive, right?" Rickard's fingers danced. "No display as high-res as the one in our skull."

The audio of the virtual reality was turned low. The effect was like listening to a slasher film in the next room. Soren's screams were high-pitched and raw, skating on the edge of sanity. Samantha—*no, not her, just a digital construct, a program, nothing more*—moaned strangled sounds through the duct tape.

"Gotta hand it to you, never thought of this application. I designed the system as a game, you know, run around shooting aliens, get to feel the adrenaline and see the blood and stuff. We developed the personal scans so that people could do it together, save the universe with a buddy." Rickard smiled. "Not that I minded scanning her. I mean, damn, but that chick is *something.*"

One of the display windows showed Samantha the way Soren saw her, and when Cooper looked at it, he fought a gag, bile burning the back of his mouth.

"What?" Rickard looked up, his bland expression changing when he saw Cooper's. "We didn't actually hurt her. Just a multi-angle camera scan, skin scrapings, hair samples. Exactly like before your little trip to Rome. The subconscious does the heavy lifting. Same as when you have a dream, and you know someone is your wife, even when they look like your mom. It's not real. We're not torturing anybody."

"We're not torturing *her*. But look at that"—Cooper pointed at the quadrant of the display showing Soren's vitals, the indicators deep in the red line on heart rate, respiration, hormones—"and tell me we're not torturing him."

"Sure, but it's not real."

"He's still living it. As far as he knows, someone is cutting her up in front of him."

"Hold on," Rickard said, and tapped a command to trigger a subroutine. In another window, a digital version of Cooper said, "Are you ready to tell me where Smith is?"

In response, Soren wept and whimpered.

Digital Cooper said, "Rickard. Continue."

Cooper made himself watch as he said, "Why use yourself as the torturer?"

"Just easier, I've got myself thoroughly scanned." He took one hand off the keyboard, brushed back his hair to show the interface implant in his neck. "Did it when I was developing this."

"And you're okay with it? Being a torturer?"

"Well, I mean . . . it's not real."

"So you keep saying."

The programmer looked up. "Didn't this guy kill you?"

"He also put my son in a coma and tried to murder an innocent family, including a baby. And those are just the ones I was around for." Cooper paused. "If a dog is rabid, you have to put him down. But you shouldn't enjoy it."

Rickard was about to reply when something on the display caught his attention. "His betas are shifting."

"Huh?"

"This monitors his brainwave activity. He's been high beta, which makes sense given the stress. But the pattern is shifting."

"Which means?"

"He's about to talk."

In his private virtual hell, Soren yelled, "Stop!" He hung his head.

Then, in a halting voice, he began to tell them what Smith planned.

Cooper said, "Holy shit." He leaned forward and thumbed a button. "Epstein. Are you watching?"

"Yes." Erik's voice came from the speaker. "Readying a strike team now."

"I'll lead them."

"The NCH tactical division—"

"Isn't as good as I am," Cooper said.

"Negative. Two previous opportunities. Both failures."

"That's why it has to be me. This is John Smith we're talking about. I've been chasing him for almost a decade. No one knows his tactics the way I do."

For long seconds there was only silence. Cooper could picture Epstein in his cave, his face lit by a mass of data. *That's the answer.* "Erik. Put aside personal concerns. What course offers the statistically highest probability of success?"

More silence. For a moment, Cooper wondered if the abnorm had already broken the line. Then the speaker sounded again. "What do you need?"

"Your best people. Transportation. Weapons. And schematics, not only for the building, but for the surrounding blocks, as well as all civic and maintenance structure diagrams."

"Yes."

"One more thing." Cooper paused, smiled. "Shannon is in Newton. How fast can you get her here?"

CHAPTER 25

"Okay," Cooper said. "On the surface this is a simple breach-and-clear. But you all know the stakes. It needs to be textbook."

The moving truck was dim and crowded, humid with the breath of thirty muscular men and women. Though Epstein had no standing army, his tactical operatives were hard core. Technically the Wardens were part of the corporate police force that provided security for the Holdfast, but to Cooper they most resembled US Army Rangers—flexible, elite forces constantly training in everything from search-and-rescue to urban warfare. They sat on benches hurriedly placed against the truck walls, automatic rifles between their knees, black body armor stretched over broad chests.

"As you know, our target is John Smith. He cannot be allowed to escape. Teams Alpha and Bravo will breach the front and rear doors at the same time, then push through, clearing room by room and meeting in the lab. Charlie Team will remain outside to secure the street and all possible exits. In addition, we have snipers already in position on nearby buildings . . ."

It had taken Epstein a bit more than an hour to fetch Shannon via helicopter. Her travel time had defined Cooper's window to review schematics for the building and make a plan. One hour to organize an operation to catch the most dangerous man alive.

Yet brief as that was, it was longer than comfortable. By hacking the feed of government spy satellites, Epstein's programmers had been able to confirm that Soren was telling the truth. John

Smith had arrived at the facility two days ago. According to the footage, he hadn't left yet. But for all Cooper knew he was packing his bags at that very moment. They couldn't risk more time, not now, when they were so close.

There's an ironic way to put it. "So close" is right. Was John Smith hiding in the Congo, or a cave in Afghanistan, or even a secret lair beneath New York?

No. The bastard has been in Tesla, not five miles from the house where your children sleep. He's been preparing a biological weapon right around the corner.

As grave as the situation was, it was funny, but there hadn't been time to laugh about it. This was his last shot. He had to be sure he thought of everything. For years Cooper had hunted Smith, tracked him, studied him. Pored over his chess matches, watched footage of his speeches. Twice he'd caught up with the man: a year ago, when Smith had fed him half-truths that aimed him like a warhead at his own government, and then again a few weeks ago, when he and Bobby Quinn—*Bobby*—had hijacked Smith only to decide executing him might turn him into a martyr.

Now everything he had learned in that time, every pattern he had built, every sense of the man's tactics was about to be tested.

"Shannon." He turned to stare at her. It had taken all his effort not to notice the smell of her, the warmth of the spot where her thigh pressed against his. "You're our ace."

She brushed her hair back behind her ear. "I don't like it."

"I know."

"Let me shift through the building, make sure there are no surprises. I can do it."

"I know," Cooper said. "I know how good you are. That's why I need you to play your part. No one else can."

"But—"

"Will you trust me?" He met her eyes. "Please?"

She looked up at him, sucked the corner of her lip between her teeth, and nodded. He had a sudden urge to lean over and mash her against him, lock her in a kiss that lasted until neither could breathe.

"What about me?" Ethan looked ridiculous in tactical gear, his shoulders and arms swimming in the uniform, a helmet strapped comically to his head.

"Once we've cleared the building, you're the man. Smith may already have modified his flu to include the serum. Securing that is second priority only to taking him down." Cooper paused, scanned the ranks of commandos. "Any questions?"

None of the soldiers said anything, but he could read the tension in each of them, the way they wanted to check ammunition loads or the fit of their armor, and the way they were not doing either. Skilled professionals, nerved up—only cowboys wouldn't be—but ready to go.

"I've got a question," Ethan said.

"What is it, Doc?"

"Why is this such a bad thing?"

Looks bounced around the inside of the truck. Ethan saw them, but while he might not be a warrior, he wasn't a coward, either. "I don't mean taking down Smith. I mean a virus that turns people brilliant."

Cooper said, "That's like suggesting a rape victim should be grateful she got laid."

"Whoa." Ethan held up his hands. "I agree that it should be a personal choice. I didn't make a weapon."

"No," Shannon said. "You just developed the technology for someone else to do it."

"I'm a scientist. Figuring things out is my job. And before your horse gets too high, think about how the rest of us feel."

Cooper raised an eyebrow.

"I get that it's not always easy to be gifted," Ethan said. "But try being normal. I mean, seriously, boo-hoo, you're a superhero. Waa-waa, you can do things the rest of us only dream of." He shook his head. "The way society treats abnorms, especially recently, it's hideous. But don't you get how much we all want what you have?"

"Neanderthals and *Homo sapiens*," Shannon said quietly.

"Well . . ." Ethan shrugged. "Kind of, yeah. Abnorms are objectively better than norms. Which was true of Neanderthals and *Homo sapiens*, too."

"So, what," Cooper said, "we should just wipe out norms like *Homo sapiens* wiped out the Neanderthals?"

"Actually," Ethan replied, "it wasn't like that. The two species had conflict, no doubt, but they also did some crossbreeding. The latest research shows they coexisted for something like five thousand years. In the end, *Homo sapiens* won out because we were better. We had longer nascency periods, bigger brains, better symbolic capabilities. In a world of finite space and resources, we got more, so we lived and they didn't."

"And you're okay with that?"

"It's not about being okay. It's not a moral issue. It's an evolutionary one. Evolution is an ugly, bloody process. But it's also the reason we're sitting here. And you might want to remember that in this example, I'm a Neanderthal, and so are my wife and my daughter." Ethan shrugged. "If Neanderthals had a choice to become *Homo sapiens*, you think they wouldn't have taken it? Wouldn't have wanted it?"

"Two problems with that, Doc." The truck turned a corner, and Cooper found himself leaning into the soldier beside him. "First, you just said 'choice,' which is exactly what Smith is *not* giving anyone."

"Okay, but—"

"And second, this isn't evolution. It's not happening over thousands of years in a natural setting. This is your science project. It subverts the system."

Ethan opened his mouth, but he was cut off by a loud buzz. Fingers tightened on assault weapons. Cooper's heart kicked up, and his palms went wet. The truck didn't slow—they were hitting hard and fast—but the sound signaled that they were a block away.

"Listen up," Cooper said to the commandos. "I know you've gone up against terrorists before. This is different." He looked down the line, meeting the eyes of each. "This is John Smith. Do. Not. Hesitate."

The tires squealed as the driver slammed on the brakes, the truck sliding and skewing. It hadn't quite stopped when the two soldiers nearest the back kicked the doors open in an explosion of pale sunlight, and then they were moving.

This is it. Your last chance. Win now, or lose everything.

I'm coming for you, John.

CHAPTER 26

"Will it hurt?"

They were in Hawk's room again. He'd cleaned it up. It just sort of felt right, like something he would do before leaving on a long trip, even though he wasn't going anywhere. He sat on the bed, John in the chair. His friend looked tired, but comfortable, too, as if he was okay to let down his guard in here, a notion that Hawk treasured.

"This is a jet injector." John held up a device that looked like a futuristic squirt gun. "Fires a high-pressure blast of fluid through the dermis into your bloodstream. Feels like a mosquito bite."

"What about . . ."

"The flu is just the flu," John said. "Sneezing, coughing, maybe a little nausea. But we modified it to be as minor as possible. That's part of the point—if people feel awful, they'll stay home, and we need them out spreading the virus. But the change, becoming brilliant, that's a little different."

"How?"

"Well, it's altering the way your brain works. It's going to be disorienting. Probably a little scary."

Hawk realized he was biting his lip, made himself stop. "What will it feel like?"

"I don't know exactly. You're only the second person in history to go through it."

"Dr. Couzen was the first." He took a breath. "His face was all scratched up. Did he—he did that to himself?"

"Yes," John said. "But remember, he's too old, too rigid. You're young and strong and malleable. It will be confusing. You'll start to see things differently, to be able to do things that you weren't able to before. My advice is to take it slow. Like going from a dirt bike to a ten-speed. You don't want to go as fast as you can right away. Get used to it, learn how the gears interact, how the brakes work. As you get more comfortable, then you can stretch yourself."

"Do you know what my gift will be?"

"That's the best part. Those who are born gifted, our gifts are set. But because this is pure, you're going to be able to do a lot of things."

"Like what?"

"Maybe everything." John smiled. "Once you have it under control, you're going to be more powerful than I am."

"Really?"

"Really."

Hawk tried to imagine that, what it would feel like. To be able to think like John, to have that thing he had, that power that made people want to help him. Or to be able to move like Haruto—*Sensei Yamato*, he corrected himself—who could control his body with perfect precision, who could fight blindfolded using only sound to guide him. How amazing would that be?

"Are you ready?"

Aaron took a deep breath, then blew it out. Nodded.

The metal barrel of the injector was cool against his arm. Before he could tense up, his friend pulled the trigger. There was a *pfff* sound and a tiny pinch. "That's it?"

"Yup."

"I . . ." Emotion inflated his chest like a balloon. Hawk wanted to hug John, to cry. This was everything he'd ever wanted. To be like his mom, like John, or Tabitha. How would she look at him now? "Thank you." His voice came out a little wobbly, and he wiped at his nose "Thank you."

"No, Hawk." John put a hand on his shoulder. "Thank *you*."

There was a muffled boom, like someone dropping heavy free weights in the gym. John's head jerked up, and he stared at the door. Hawk said, "What was—"

"*Shh.*"

For a second, nothing happened.

Then the shooting started.

■

From the outside, the building wasn't particularly notable. A warehouse on the outskirts of Tesla, tucked in amidst the others. The Holdfast had to import the vast majority of products, and they all had to be stored somewhere.

The Wardens moved with easy precision, every commando knowing exactly where to move and what to cover. There was no shouting, no hardened sergeant yelling, *Go go go!* That was for the movies. Here, in the bright sunlight of a Wyoming winter afternoon, the only sounds were the hustle of footfalls, the hum of traffic from a nearby artery, and the rumble of the truck engine.

Alpha Team hit the warehouse like a black wave. The point man slapped charges against the front door, stepped back, made a quick hand symbol. Cooper checked the safety on the assault rifle he carried, a Holdfast design of curved carbon fiber. His armpits were sweaty and his heart was loud, but his hands had the in-mission steadiness he'd always been able to count on. How many times had he been in a raid for the DAR? Hundreds, counting the drills.

But never one where you knew John Smith was on the other side of the door.

He muted the thought. The time for second-guessing was past. It was do or die.

The charges took the door right off the hinges, hurling the heavy metal inside with a roar of sound, quickly followed by an explosion of light from a flashbang. Two-man teams flowed in, and Cooper followed.

A lobby of some sort. Tall ceilings with exposed girders. A bench, a security camera, a guard doubled over and clutching his eyes. The teams swept past him, Cooper surfing their wave, leaving the guard for the tail of the column. On the schematics this broad entrance connected directly to the storage space, with a side hall leading to a series of offices. But in reality, walls had been built that framed the space out differently. No surprise. Schematics only showed the initial design. Smith's team would have customized the interior to their specifications, and they wouldn't have filed permits. Cooper was glad of it. He was counting on it.

The team stormed the hall and took up positions at a corner, then moved around it in neat synchronicity. Cooper heard yelling, a Warden ordering someone to get on the ground, and before that was even possible, the fast hard crack of automatic weapons fire, forward commandos dropping a target. He swung around behind them, saw two bad guys bleeding, one on his knees, the other staggering, both clean shots. Behind him someone yelled, "Flash!" as another stun grenade arced over Cooper's head.

A man stepped from an alcove with the precision of a ballet dancer. His features were bland, his expression mild. His eyes were closed. Without breaking stride, he reached up to pluck the flashbang from the air and toss it back with a flick of his wrist. Cooper barely had time to turn away before everything vanished in a swell of roaring white.

The flashbang hazed out his vision, but he'd recognized the man. Haruto Yamato, one of the lieutenants who had been with Smith in New York. He made himself focus as Yamato started forward, eyes still shut as he took out the first Warden with a neck chop that segued into a leg sweep on the second.

Yamato's gift is audiokinetic. He fights with his eyes closed and holds high-rank black belts in a dozen martial arts.

You can't win toe-to-toe, but this doesn't need to be a fair fight. All you need to do is tie him up long enough for the others to—

Wait a second.

You're carrying an assault rifle.

Cooper raised his weapon and fired.

Yamato danced and sidestepped his way around the first three bullets. But the fourth, fifth, and sixth tore open his chest, and he staggered into a wall, then slid down it with a red smear. His empty eyes opened.

I'm coming for you, John.

∎

Gunshots, lots of them, and yelling, and more explosions. Hawk was starting for the door before he realized he'd moved at all.

"Stop." John's voice was a whip, no warmth in it.

Hawk froze. More gunfire, this time from the other direction. A scream. Everyone had always said that enemy soldiers could storm the building, but he'd never really believed it, not in his bones.

Smith opened the door a crack and peered into the hall before stepping out. Aaron followed, trying to remember the drills, what to do if they were ever raided. Stay in their rooms? No, that didn't make sense. The armory. Everyone was supposed to fall back to the armory.

"Come on." John set off at a jog.

"Wait, the armory is the other way!" More shots, closer. His heart was going crazy, and he needed to pee desperately.

"We're not going to the armory. Move!"

∎

Cooper hadn't been in that many secret laboratories. Two, to be precise. But so far they seemed like very dangerous places.

Abe Couzen's facility in the Bronx had been a shiny wonderland of science toys, but by the time he and Ethan had found it, it had been redecorated via hand-to-hand combat—benches overturned, blood splashed on the wall.

This one was bigger, harshly lit, and filled with objects whose function he could only guess at. Blood spatter covered the sparkling surfaces and broken glass crunched underfoot. Commandos hustled between the tables, shouting and zip-tying captives.

The Wardens had shock-and-awed their way through the warehouse without significant incident. Plenty of Smith's people resisted, but taken by surprise in ones and twos, none of them had posed even half the threat Haruto Yamato had. A dozen fighters had fallen back to a cinderblock armory, which Cooper found very considerate. So much easier to gas them all at the same time.

He paced the lab, taking in the place. The gunfire had died down to occasional bursts. Cooper stepped over a wet spray of brain matter and crouched beside a body. Two holes had been punched through the man's face, but even so, it was obviously not Smith.

He keyed his earpiece, said, "Status."

"This is Bravo Leader. We've cleared the building through our checkpoint."

"Any sign of Smith?"

"That's a negative."

"Roger," Cooper said. "Exterior?"

"All quiet on the street. One in custody, two KIA. Neither is Smith."

"Sir." The commander of Alpha Team was a squat, hard-eyed woman who looked like she could bicep-curl Cooper's weight. Her face was grim. "He wasn't with the people in the armory, either."

"You're sure?"

"We're doing a thorough sweep of the building now. But unless John Smith is hiding under the floorboards, we've missed him."

Slowly, Cooper nodded.

Then smiled.

∎

The tunnel was choked with dust. In the dark, Hawk couldn't see the spiderwebs that brushed against his face, but each one made his skin crawl. The space was too tight to crawl. He had to wriggle like a worm, his elbows jammed in his sides.

While gunfire raged in both directions, John had led them to the closet near the lab, an ammonia-smelling room with mops and tools and a big plastic utility sink. One of the weird things about being in a resistance movement was that it wasn't like you could hire janitors, so when it came to cleaning, there was a duty roster. Hawk had wielded a mop in John Smith's service more times than he could count.

As Aaron stepped into the room, John had grabbed the sink and yanked. The metal feet grumbled across the concrete, revealing a hole in the wall about two feet square. Without a word, John had stuck his head in and started wriggling his way forward. For a moment Hawk had just stared, hoping John was going after weapons, but the shadow swallowed more and more of Smith's body until he was gone.

Hawk had taken a deep breath and followed.

The first few feet were just the space behind the wall, but then they hit a ring of concrete, and beyond that, hard-packed dirt. He wasn't normally claustrophobic, but the space was tight enough that his shoulders touched on both sides as he squirmed diagonally downward. With every forward inch, the darkness grew more complete, until there was nothing but the sound of his breath and cold dirt and the silky panic of spiderwebs brushing his face. In that womb-dark all he could think about was the weight above him. His imagination painted a picture of all that earth, the tonnage of soil and cement and building and street.

What would happen if he got stuck? Would someone come to save him? In the chaos, maybe he'd be forgotten, trapped here, buried alive. Panic twisted in his belly, a blind and toothy worm, like the worms moving through the dirt around them, and who knew what kind of pale, crawling nightmare lived down here—

Don't you quit in front of John. Don't you dare, you pussy.

Slowly the tunnel leveled out. He kept moving, his breath fast and humid. He really needed to pee. After an eternity, John's voice drifted back. "Here we are." There was a metal-on-metal squeal, and then a ringing thud, and a burst of light ahead.

Pulling himself out of the tunnel felt like being born again. He panted, bent over, hands on his knees until he trusted himself enough to straighten.

They were in a long hallway lit by widely spaced bulbs. The ceiling was about eight feet high, but the top third was crammed with a dense lattice of wire that forced them both to stoop. John fit a metal panel back into the wall to conceal the hole they'd just come through, glanced both ways, then started moving. "Come on."

"What is this place?"

"Maintenance shaft. Tesla was planned and executed as a whole, so the first thing the engineers dug was an infrastructure support system." John put a hand up, traced the cables above. "All the data in the city runs through these lines."

"Where are we going?"

"Out. The nearest access hub is a quarter mile up. There's a truck parked nearby."

"A truck?" Hawk straightened, banged his head on a metal brace, winced. "You knew they were coming?"

"You think we'd have been there if I knew?" John glanced over his shoulder. "The truck has been parked there for two years. That's how you win, Hawk. Never focus everything on just one route to attaining your goal. Develop as many contingencies as possible. Like you."

"What do you mean?"

"Most options never get used. But if you have them at the right moment, you can change defeat into victory. Like turning a pawn into a queen."

Hawk tried to imagine the effort that had gone into just this escape route. Locating the exact spot in the maintenance passage. Digging the tunnel. Hauling away the dirt. Dodging maintenance engineers. Buying the truck, finding a place to park it where it could sit for years, checking it regularly to make sure that the battery hadn't died and the tires hadn't gone flat. A huge amount of effort, and all just in case someday, someone attacked your home—*oh*.

"Wait." He froze. "What about the others?"

Ahead of him, John stopped. He sighed, rubbed at his face. Then he turned and came back. "These are bad people we're playing against, Hawk."

"Are they—will they be—"

"I don't know." John put a hand on his shoulder. "I don't know."

"Sensei Yamato. And Ms. Herr, and—oh my God. Tabitha. What about Tabitha?"

John cocked his head. "Were you and she . . ."

"No. I mean. No. Will she be okay?"

"Probably. As long as she doesn't do anything stupid. And Tabitha isn't stupid." John paused. Hawk could see that he was weighing something.

Finally, he said, "I need to tell you something, Hawk. Something important."

■

At this distance, the explosions sounded like firecrackers, but Shannon recognized them for what they were. Breaching charges.

The assault had begun. Seconds later, there were more firecrackers, fainter and faster, and she recognized those too.

You should be there. The Wardens are good, but John is better. If you were there, you could shift, scout, make sure that Cooper didn't walk into an ambush.

There was nothing for it now but to wait. Wait, and hope that Cooper knew what he was doing.

Waiting was frequently part of her job, and sometimes she'd even enjoyed it. Her ability to move unseen meant that very often she was someplace she absolutely shouldn't be, a place where one wrong move could kill her. To be honest, she enjoyed that too. Everything was brighter when it was at risk. The colors more vivid, the air sweeter.

This time, though. Lately, though. All the fun had been going out of it. What she'd once considered the great big adventure that was her life had soured. Turned grim. The decline had started with the explosion at the stock exchange this spring, when Cooper had stopped her before she could prevent it. He hadn't known what she was doing, of course, and in truth, she doubted she could have succeeded anyway. A thousand innocent people had died that day, and many more had died since.

And if this goes pear shaped, a lot more will join them. So pay attention.

She'd never spent any time in this part of Tesla; it was all warehouses and distribution centers. There were a surprising number of civilian cars, which struck her as strange until she remembered the New Sons of Liberty. As the militia pushed forward, a huge percentage of the Holdfast population was falling back to the safety of the Vogler Ring. Tesla must be full to bursting, every hotel room booked. People would end up sleeping in gymnasiums and churches.

This side street, though, was largely deserted. Few cars, no foot traffic. She stayed out of sight anyway, her mind processing every witness, the trucker a hundred yards away watching as a

team unloaded his semi, the cameras mounted on every corner—
nothing she could do about those—the electric car turning down
the block, the drab metal hut with a sign on the door that read,
Maint Trunk Hub N4W7—

A door that was swinging open.

Shannon put all her focus on it, subconsciously plotting the
vectors of sight, the increasing angle of the door, the human eye's
tendency to dart rather than scan, the blind spot created by the
parked truck that was actually a danger zone because it would
draw attention, the change of light from inside the hut to the
sunny Wyoming afternoon, and confirmed that she was in the
best position given what she could see now. She sent up a silent
prayer that Cooper had been right, and more important, that he
was okay.

Two figures stepped out. The first paused to look around, a
careful, professional gaze, but she read the intentions and the
directions and shifted right around it.

John Smith. Her onetime leader, her onetime friend. Behind
him was a kid she didn't recognize, thin and tall given his age.
They were both filthy, clothes smudged brown, cobwebs in their
hair. The boy had the clenched-leg gait of someone who really
needed to pee.

Shannon stepped from the shadows of the loading dock,
shouldered the shotgun, and said in a loud, clear voice, "Don't
move."

The kid jumped, and she could see that at least some of his
bladder problem had been resolved.

John, on the other hand, only stared. They were separated by
fifteen feet, and she could see he was deciding whether to run.

"Don't." She stared down the barrel. Her finger had pressure
on the trigger.

"Shannon. Of course."

"Put your hands on your head, take two steps forward, and
drop to your knees."

"Okay." John laced his fingers behind his head. In a conversational tone, he said, "Run, Hawk."

"Don't move!"

"*Run.*"

The kid hesitated for a second, and then spun on his heel.

She couldn't miss at this distance. But did she want to take the shot? It would mean murdering a fleeing teenager.

More than that. It means shifting your aim from John. How many people have died because they took their eyes off him for a fraction of a second?

The boy started back into the hut. She let him go. Without releasing pressure on the trigger, she circled to put John between her and the doorway in case the kid came back with a weapon. "Another of your holy warriors?"

"Hawk? He's a friend."

"You don't have friends."

"That's not true." His voice was mild. "What about you?"

"Last time we spoke, another of your teenage suicide bombers was about to blow me up. Along with a trainful of civilians."

"It wasn't personal, you know that." He smiled wryly. "I don't suppose there's any chance we could talk about this?"

"Sure there is," she said. "As soon as you take two steps forward and hit your knees."

■

Cooper hauled the wheel sideways without letting up on the gas, and the truck slewed and rocked. *Almost there.*

The moment it had been confirmed that Smith wasn't in the warehouse, Cooper had sprinted outside. As he'd ordered, a Warden was waiting in an SUV, the engine running. The commando hadn't seemed too happy to be kicked out of the vehicle, but one look at Cooper's face and he'd done as he was told.

There wasn't really any need to go this fast, but Shannon was out here alone, and that scared him, scared him more than he had expected. She was one of the most capable people he'd ever met, but so was John Smith, and Cooper's imagination was conjuring all kinds of unwanted ugliness.

Be okay, Shannon. If it comes down to you or him, please choose right.

He spun around the last corner, hoping for the best and fearing—well, everything.

Then he saw her, his Girl Who Walked Through Walls. Silhouetted against a burning sky with a shotgun braced on her shoulder and John Smith kneeling at her feet. His heart howled with joy. He screeched to a stop, snatched the assault rifle off the passenger seat, and climbed out to lock in a second line of fire.

The man Cooper had chased for most of a decade squinted up at him. "Hello, Nick."

"John. Game over."

"Looks like. Well played." Smith was trying for cool, but Cooper could see the tremble in his hands. "Mind if I smoke?"

"Why not? Gently."

The terrorist reached into his pocket very slowly. Cooper watched, ready to fire at the first hint of danger, but all Smith withdrew was a crumpled pack. He took one, lit it, inhaled deep. "How did you know?"

"I've been chasing you half my adult life, man. I've got you patterned. It's all options and fail-safes with you. As soon as I saw that fifty yards away there was a maintenance passage that *didn't* connect to the warehouse, I knew."

"That's funny. I purposefully didn't buy a warehouse above the passage for that reason, and it's what tipped you off. So now what?"

"Finish your cigarette."

"Hmm." Smith smiled. "It's like that, huh?"

"After all the blood you've spilled? Yeah."

"Only way to build a new world. Gotta burn the old one down. History is written in fire." He took a long drag at his cigarette, then looked at Shannon. "You're okay with this?"

"You once told me," Shannon said, "to decide who I really care about. I have."

A ghost of a smile flitted across Smith's lips. "Good for you." He turned to Cooper. "You're a lucky man."

"I know." The moment had a surreal heft to it. So much of life slipped by like a breeze: sweet, brief, gone. This would linger, the impressions sharper than the details. Pale light from a white sky. Attenuated shadows. The smell of gun oil. The smear of dirt on Smith's cheek. The cigarette in the hinge of his fingers, the crackle of tobacco as he took a final drag, then grimaced and flicked it away.

"Want another?"

"No. Thanks." Smith inhaled a short, fast breath and rolled his shoulders. "You should know. Killing me isn't the same as beating me."

Cooper said, "It's a step in the right direction."

Then he pressed the trigger and blew three holes through John Smith's heart.

The report echoed out across the plain to the distant mountains beyond. A bird startled from a nearby roof with a screech. A few blocks down, a trucker flung himself to the ground.

John Smith blinked. His head drooped as he looked at the wound. For a moment, his muscles held him in place, wobbling.

He fell over.

"Target located," Cooper said, triggering his earpiece. "Come get him. Bring a body bag."

Then he lowered the weapon and stared across the corpse at one of the women he loved. She stared back.

Neither spoke.

Not with words, anyway.

CHAPTER 27

Cooper didn't know what to feel.

Killing Smith had been the best option. Sure, he could have captured him, tried to interrogate him, but the man had been *the* game player. They wouldn't have been able to believe a word he said, couldn't have trusted any cage to hold him. Ending him was the safe, sane tactical decision.

It wasn't that he had regrets. There was no cop-who-came-to-understand-the-criminal RKO Pictures vibe, no sense that they could have been friends under other circumstances, no reluctant respect for John Smith. The man had had options, same as anybody, and the choices he'd made had left the world a darker place.

But still, there was a strange void in Cooper. He wasn't over-joyed, didn't feel victorious. And maybe it was just that. After years of fighting Smith, some part of him had expected more out of the moment. Like after he pulled the trigger the music should have swelled and the credits rolled.

In the absence of emotional or philosophical clarity, though, there was always the job. The same job as always, he'd joked with Quinn more than once: saving the world.

He imagined Bobby responding, saying, *Yeah? How's that going?*

Same as always, Bobby.

"Huh?" Shannon looked over at him; evidently, he'd spoken aloud.

"Nothing." Cooper realized he'd been staring blankly out the windshield. He turned the key and the SUV started with a rumble. A quick three-point turn, and the scene was behind them, a team of Wardens zipping John Smith's corpse into a body bag.

He glanced sideways, saw Shannon glancing in her side mirror. She was a slight woman, but looked especially so now, her shoulders tucked in, something in her diminished. Before he could decide if it was a good idea, Cooper reached across the space between them and touched her hand. For a moment, she hesitated, then laced her fingers in his.

The roads were packed, the sounds muted by bulletproof glass. He steered one-handed for a few silent blocks. Finally, he said, "Are you okay?"

She seemed to consider the question. "Yeah."

"I know he was your friend."

"Yes," she said. "He was." She looked like she was going to add more, but decided against it. "I heard about Quinn. I'm sorry."

He nodded.

"You want to talk about it?"

"Maybe later."

The street outside the warehouse had been transformed into a confusion of vehicles, the trucks they'd arrived in, plus Holdfast security vehicles with lights spinning, ambulances, prisoner transfer vans, all surrounded by a ring of gawkers. Cooper steered through the crowd and parked by the door. When he turned off the ignition, he could hear the ticking of the engine and the soft sounds of her breath.

He looked over, found her looking back. Her expression was complicated. He imagined his was too. They held the gaze. There was a moment when they could both lunge in, hands and lips and skin finding each other. Then it passed, and they were still sitting there.

"I should go check on Ethan," Cooper said.

She nodded.

He started to get out, paused, looked back. "Do you want to come?"

■

After-action, and the warehouse had that surreal filter that battle overlaid on the normal. Normal drywall, apart from the bullet holes; normal rooms, apart from the blood spray. The Wardens had cleared the building, found the last stragglers hiding in closets and cupboards. Most had surrendered and were awaiting transport, their arms and legs flex-tied, their eyes filled with hate and shock. Those who had fought back waited considerably more peacefully.

Cooper and Shannon walked to the lab in silence, found it busy with people in white coats. He asked one of them where to find Ethan, and she jerked a thumb over her shoulder without looking up from her terminal.

The door she pointed to led to what once might have been a supply closet. Ethan was standing in it, his back to them, facing a cage. It was made of metal lattice, seamless and strong. There was a man inside.

Strike that.

There was a body inside. It was so badly mangled that it took Cooper a moment to catalog details—he was white, older, thin. His flesh had been torn in a hundred places, some shallow red scratches, others deep gashes with pale flesh bulging through. His eye sockets were ragged and ruined. Cooper had seen him before, a few days ago, on the streets of Manhattan. Dr. Abraham Couzen.

Ethan didn't turn, but Cooper could tell by the tightening of his shoulder muscles and a quiver in his throat that the scientist knew they were there. Cooper auditioned a dozen statements, then another dozen, but couldn't find anything that sounded even remotely helpful.

"I'd say rest in peace"—Ethan's voice sounded flat—"only Abe believed the afterlife was a lie idiots told to make it past breakfast without killing themselves."

"John did this?" Shannon asked.

"No. Look closer."

Cooper squatted down. He could see what Ethan meant. The way the cuts were angled didn't seem right. And fingernails hadn't been ripped out, they were broken backward, the pads of the fingers worn to the bone. It was almost as if the man had been scrabbling at stone, trying to dig his way—oh. "He did this to *himself*? Why?"

"I don't know."

"The serum? The side effects Vincent told us about?"

"I don't know."

Cooper rose, positioned himself so that he was between Ethan and his old boss. "I'm sorry."

Ethan didn't respond. His eyes were wide and wouldn't meet Cooper's.

"Let's get out of here. You don't need to see this right now."

"What?"

Cooper put his hands on the other man's shoulders, shook gently. "I really am sorry. And I know what I'm going to say next makes me sound like an insensitive bastard, and I'm sorry for that too. But you can't go into shock right now."

"Why the hell not?"

"Because your wife and daughter are nearby." Cooper tried for a tone that was firm but not harsh. "For Amy and Violet."

The names seemed to do what his other words hadn't. Ethan blinked, swallowed. "Yeah. Yeah, all right."

"Come on. We need to secure that virus, Doc."

"Well. I've got bad news and bad news." Ethan started out of the closet. "There's a ton of information here, years' worth of clinical notes. But just looking through the last couple of days, it's clear that Smith's people were successful in mounting the serum onto a disease vector, a custom strain of the flu. A nasty one, best I can tell, something they've been working on for a long time. Influenza is an RNA virus and our serum is built around non-coding RNA, so they basically could just splice it into junk genes included for that purpose. They fast-bred it, used an aerosolized suspension medium, total volume about three hundred CF."

"In English?"

"They made what John Smith wanted. A lot of it."

"And the other bad news?"

"According to the lab notes, the virus was stored in standard high-pressure tanks. Two of them, each about four feet tall, probably fifty pounds apiece."

"So?"

"So," Ethan said, and gestured around the lab, "you see anything that looks like that?"

Cooper looked, but he already knew what he'd find. On some level, he had already known the moment before he shot John Smith. *Killing me isn't the same as beating me.*

"Oh," said Shannon. "Oh, shit."

"Yeah," Ethan replied drily. "That about sums it up."

Cooper wanted to scream. It was a feeling he'd had a lot lately. All of this. All he'd done. And even dead, John Smith was outplaying him.

"Okay," he said. "Focus on the job."

"What does that—"

"You're in charge here, Ethan. Run your team. See if you can figure out where those tanks went. Failing that, figure out how we can beat the virus."

"Cooper—"

"A vaccine. A shot. A fucking antidote. I don't care. But you dig in and you work until you find something, you hear me?" Cooper gripped the man's biceps, squeezed hard. "This was your project, Doc. You and Abe built this. Clean up the mess."

"But—"

"Just *do it.*" He stalked away, had to find a place to think, to reach out to Epstein, figure out the next move. Maybe together they could pattern John Smith well enough to guess what he intended. Everything had happened fast, Smith couldn't be that far ahead of them—

His phone rang, and he was about to silence it when he saw the name. He answered, said, "Natalie."

Across the lab, Shannon stiffened. He didn't blame her, but there wasn't time to worry about dating niceties right now.

"Nick? Are you okay? You don't sound good."

"Busy. John Smith is dead."

"Are you sure?"

"I killed him."

"Oh," Natalie said, her voice strange. Why? Natalie had never loved violence, but she had always known what he did. And after the way they had mourned Bobby Quinn, he would have expected, maybe not elation, but something other than the flat tone she used as she said, "That's great."

"What's wrong?"

"So you haven't seen the news."

"No."

"The militia, the New Sons of Liberty. They're approaching the Vogler Ring." She took a ragged breath. "And they're marching children in front of them."

CHAPTER 28

"—this footage, streaming live from a CNN newsdrone, shows the New Sons of Liberty approaching the farthest borders of Tesla, capital of the New Canaan Holdfast. Now, at this altitude it's a little hard to make out details, but when we zoom in, you can see that these smaller figures at the head of the column are children, approximately six hundred of them. Given current relations with the Holdfast, information is limited, but sources have confirmed that all of these children are abnorms captured by NSOL since their dramatic attack—"

The news was always playing in the Situation Room, and the Laurel Lodge conference room at Camp David was no different. What was unusual was that the volume was turned up, and the people around the table were silent.

It can't be considered a positive, Owen Leahy thought, *when the American president is watching the news to find out what's happening.*

Beside the tri-d was a larger screen showing a similar angle, although this one was far more distinct. Government satellite footage, dialed up high enough to make out individual faces. The video rotated through different perspectives, a montage of roughly edited abominations:

A ten-year-old girl weeping as she walked, tears carving clean streaks down her dirty face.

A teenage boy carrying a four-year-old child in one arm and a ratty stuffed bear in the other.

A kid stumbling, rising hurriedly, his pants torn and his knee stained with blood, fear in his eyes as he looked over his shoulder.

And behind them, a long line of men carrying rifles. The ones in the front had them aimed at the children. The column stretched for half a mile.

Leahy checked his phone for the fiftieth time. Still no response.

The newscaster continued, "The New Canaan Holdfast has long been rumored to have a defensive perimeter surrounding the city of Tesla, and we presume that the purpose of these children is to serve as a kind of human shield—"

"Enough," President Ramirez said, and an aide quickly cut the sound. "Owen, how quickly can we intervene?"

"Madam President, we can't."

"Bad enough when the New Sons were burning abandoned cities. Now they're using children as mine detectors. I want American troops in there—"

"Ma'am, *we can't.*" Leahy caught his tone, quickly reeled it back in. "The militia is only five miles out of Tesla. We simply cannot get a sizable enough military presence there in time."

"What about drone strikes, or tactical bombardment? Even just as a warning, to turn them around."

"Most of those capabilities have been disabled on your orders, ma'am."

"Re-enable them."

"That would take time. And it would be a terrible risk. The only way we could intervene would require using the same technologies Epstein's virus took advantage of. Simply put, if it's more advanced than a bayonet, it might be turned against us."

"Why would the Holdfast do that? We'd be coming to their aid."

"Frankly, ma'am, I doubt they'd believe that. I certainly wouldn't, in their position. You'd be asking a man who killed seventy-five thousand soldiers and blew up the White House to let you bring your deadliest weapons into his living room to 'protect' him. Besides"—he gestured at the tri-d—"they already have defenses. The Vogler Ring isn't a minefield, it's a microwave emplacement. Casualties won't weaken it."

"Meaning that even if the New Sons march children into it to burn alive, they still won't breach it."

"It's horrific, but it's not our defense grid, and it's not our army. Think of it like it's happening on the far side—" Leahy's phone vibrated. There was no name, but he recognized the number immediately. He should; it belonged to a radiation-shielded cell he'd delivered himself. "I'm sorry, ma'am, but I need to take this."

"Go. DAR, what's your view—"

Leahy rose swiftly and headed for the door. Leaving was a breach of protocol, but he was betting no one would call him on it under the circumstances. He kept his eyes down and his steps quick through the door, past the Secret Service agents, down the hall, and outside.

Camp David had a winter wonderland look, all evergreens and Christmas lights and fresh powder. The network of paved paths had been shoveled and salted, but there were too many people on them. Leahy stepped off the porch toward the woods, his leather oxfords sinking into the snow as he accepted the call and said, "Just what the hell do you think you're doing?"

"What we said we would."

Leahy froze. *That's not Sam Miller.* He checked the phone display; the number was correct. The voice was one he'd heard before. It took him a moment to place it—Luke Hammond, the lean soldier with the killer's eyes. "We never discussed taking children hostage. Or using them to try to break through the Vogler Ring."

"We're doing what's necessary."

"Necessary for what? I told you, genocide isn't the goal." *Why does no one get that?* There was a balance to be maintained, a utility to conflict, so long as it was held in check. The political scientist Thomas Schelling had pinpointed that back in 1966, when he'd written that the power to hurt—the unacquisitive, unproductive power to destroy things that somebody treasures, to inflict pain and grief—was a kind of bargaining power. Arguably the most foundational statement of geopolitics, and yet some days it seemed like Leahy was the only person to understand that the word was *hurt*, not *obliterate*. "We don't want to destroy the Holdfast. We just want to bring Epstein to—"

"That's your goal. The New Sons of Liberty aren't part of your army. We're patriots fighting for our nation's future."

"Come on. Wake up. Chest beating is for football games. 'Once more unto the breach, dear friends,' is not a real-world policy."

There was a long pause. "Mr. Secretary, you're talking to a career soldier with forty years of special operations experience. Do you realize how ridiculous you sound?"

Leahy leaned against a tree and rubbed his eyes so hard they hurt. "I'd like to talk to General Miller."

"He's busy."

"Put him on, please."

"He's busy."

Leahy imagined having the power to reach through the phone and wrap his hands around the man's neck and squeeze until his eyeballs bulged. What was Miller thinking, going off the reservation and then not even answering the phone? *You're losing control of the situation.* "Luke. May I call you Luke? We don't know each other well, but I was a soldier too."

"I know, Mr. Secretary. Four whole years, right?"

"Followed by decades in intelligence before serving as the secretary of defense to three presidents," Leahy snapped. He caught himself, took a breath. "It should go without saying that I respect your service. You're right, you are patriots. But now the patriotic thing to do is stop. You're risking civil war."

"We're not risking it. We're declaring it. And we're going to win."

"By burning civilian cities? Kidnapping children and marching them out to die?"

There was a pause. "That's war."

"Luke, listen to me. Even if you succeed, you think anyone will thank you? President Ramirez already wants to label you all criminals."

"Up to her."

"Hammond," Leahy said, using his command voice, "I am ordering you to stop. This isn't a discussion. You are acting against your country's interests. You are wounding America. Maybe mortally."

Luke laughed. "You know what the problem with politicians is? They always think they can control things they can't. The genie doesn't go back in the bottle, no matter what the story says."

"Goddammit, listen to me. You've made your point. Turn your men around. Please. I'm begging you."

Silence was the only response. A cold wind rattled the branches of the trees, dumping snow in a fine filigree like ashes. His socks were wet, his shoes ruined.

"Luke?"

More silence.

"Hello?"

And it was only then that it occurred to Owen Leahy that he'd been hung up on.

CHAPTER 29

The streets were jammed, cars and trucks everywhere, most filled to bursting, suitcases strapped to the roof, people piled in the back. Cooper had driven fast and disrespectfully, blasting through parking lots, jumping sidewalks, ignoring traffic lights. It was the way he used to drive when his car had a transponder identifying him as a DAR agent. Today he got away with it because the SUV belonged to the Holdfast Wardens. There was an irony to that juxtaposition, but he didn't have time or inclination to savor it.

The crowd grew worse as they neared Epstein's compound of mirrored buildings. It made sense; the pitchforks and torches were at the gates. The residents of New Canaan would feel safest close to their leader.

"You sure you want to be part of this?" Cooper spared a glance sideways as he squealed up to the door. "I'm not sure what kind of welcome we'll get."

"Are you kidding?" Shannon looked incredulous. "I rescued those kids. I planned the operation on the academy, I led it, I blew the damn thing up. You think I'm going to let a bunch of rednecks burn them alive?"

"Roger that."

The lobby to the central building was airy and flooded with late afternoon winter sunlight. One whole wall was given over to a massive tri-d, the projection field showing children three stories high and terrified. People stood in the lobby staring, pale lips biting shaking knuckles. Cooper ignored the receptionist, strode across the floor to the unmarked elevator. No doubt the guard standing by it was normally very good at his job, but at the moment his attention was absorbed by the footage. Shannon smiled and faded back.

Cooper said, "Hey."

"What?" The guard straightened. "Yes, sir?"

"I need to see Erik Epstein right now."

"I'm sorry, but he isn't seeing anyone at the moment."

"He'll see me. Nick Cooper."

"I know who you are, sir. But Mr. Epstein was explicit. No one in at all."

"Son, I'm sorry. But we don't have time for this."

The guard was about to reply when Shannon slid the sidearm from his holster, planted it in his back, and cocked it.

■

They left the guard cuffed to the elevator rail and sprinted down the hall, the thick carpet muffling their footsteps. He could hear the rush of the ventilation system, the air cold against his sweating skin, and then they were pushing through the door to Epstein's private world.

It was different than the other times Cooper had been here. It was bright, and instead of constellations of data hanging in all directions, there was just one simple vector animation, a stylized blob intersecting a series of three concentric rings. Without the dizzying backdrop, the room looked cheap, the mystery deflated. A movie theater with the house lights up.

Three men stood in the center, their heads snapping around at the sound of Cooper's entrance. The first was tan and wild-haired, with that skin-stretched-over-skeleton look. Slouching beside him, Erik Epstein looked paler than usual, his eyes haunted, his plump neck sweaty. In his usual five-thousand-dollar suit, Jakob looked like the adult guardian to a couple of precocious nerds. "Cooper? What are you doing here?"

"John Smith is dead."

"We know," Jakob said. "We watched the operation via the Wardens' bodycams. Good work. But if you'll excuse us—"

Cooper gestured at the animation. "Is that the Vogler Ring?"

The three men exchanged looks.

"Cooper," Jakob said, "we appreciate your help, but you aren't needed at the moment. This is an internal matter."

"Tell me that you've turned it off."

"Turned it off?" the third man said like he'd been slapped. "Of course not."

"Who are you?"

"Randall Vogler."

"Vogler? You're the genius who developed this system?"

"Well, of course my whole team gets credit, but—"

"Erik, what are you doing?"

Epstein's eyes darted to his, then away. "Protecting us. The data—"

"Cooper," Jakob said, "we understand your feelings, but this system is all that's standing between the city of Tesla and a lynch mob."

"A lynch mob that's marching children in front of it," Cooper said. "These aren't game pieces. They're kids, and you're killing them."

"Not all," Vogler said. "This is a completely defensive system. I'm a pacifist, sir."

"Tell that to their parents," Shannon said.

Erik flinched. "We don't have a choice."

"You do. You're making it, right now."

"This is a civilian city," Jakob said. "Just regular people, including thousands of children. This system is all that's protecting them. The men coming for us are ex–special forces, paramilitary survivalists, and armed killers. None of us are twirling our mustache here. If we drop our defenses, those kids might live. But how many people here will die? How many children?"

"You. Vogler." Cooper gestured at the animation. "There are three rings up there, and the militia is almost to the second. What does that mean?"

"The system is a directed-energy weapon, generating electromagnetic radiation in the 2.45 gigahertz range, but the effects are modulated by particulate disturbance, humidity, air currents. The first ring represents guaranteed safe distance. The second is the corollary to that, the line at which, no matter the range of conditions—presuming relative norms, of course—the effects will be felt."

"What are the effects?" Shannon's voice had a girlish lilt that caught Cooper's attention. When he glanced over, she didn't wink, but he could see that she thought about winking, with the tiny resulting muscular motion that entailed. God love her, she was playing them.

"The ring agitates electric dipoles like water and fat, and their motion generates heat."

"Sort of like a microwave oven?"

"Yes, exactly." Vogler beamed at her.

"So . . ." She paused theatrically. "It will burn them alive?"

"Well, the advantage of the system is that there is plenty of warning. It's not like one moment targets are fine and the next they drop dead. The only way it would be fatal is if—"

Cooper said, "Somebody marched you into it with a rifle at your back."

"In the absence of ideal options," Erik said, "the only rational choice is the best of the worst."

"Then why aren't you watching?"

"What?"

"It's easy to talk about the greater good," Cooper said, "when you're looking at a colored blob crossing a dotted line. But that's not what's happening."

"I . . . I like people. You know I do, that children—"

"Stop playing the saint, Cooper." Jakob's tone was sharp. "How many people have you killed? How many have you killed *today*?"

"Today? Two. And I looked them both in the eyes." His hands clenched and unclenched. "I'm not a saint, Jakob. Far from. But if you're going to decide who lives and dies, have the stones to watch."

Erik took a deep breath. "Computer. Quads one to fifteen, activate, drone and security footage, multiple perspectives, militia approaching Vogler Ring."

The air shimmered to life. What had been empty space was suddenly filled with people, a mob of them, a horde of humanity. Cooper had heard the number over and over, the headcount of the New Sons of Liberty, but it was one thing to hear the figure and another to see the mass, a crowd that could fill a midsize stadium. At that scale, individual features were lost in a shifting whole, and the dust-coated clothing, coupled with the beards and the dirt and the rifles, compounded the impression that it was a single creature, some thousand-legged insect out of a nightmare.

"Better?" Jakob's voice was cold. "You see what's coming for us?"

"The children, Erik."

Jakob said, "Don't—" as his brother said, "Computer, group quads, refocus, front ranks."

The hologram shifted vertiginously, the multiple angles replaced by a single stream of video.

According to the news, there were about six hundred children. A small number when compared to the militia twenty yards behind them, but seen altogether, it was about the same size as the school Todd attended. The youngest were four or five, the oldest in their late teens, the majority somewhere in the middle. They were dressed too lightly for the weather, and fear shone bright from their faces.

"Erik," Jakob said softly. "No one *wants* this. We don't have a choice. It's a horrible decision, one we'll have to bear for the rest of our lives, but it's the right one."

"The right one?" Cooper couldn't take his eyes off the screen. Six hundred *children*. His mind kept wanting to zoom out, to see them as a mass; to counter that, he made himself focus on one. A teenage girl walking a bit forward of the others, her head bowed, hair falling across her face. She was one of the academy kids, he could tell instantly; where others risked defiant glances and might resist when the pain got bad enough, she just walked. Bore up under horror not because she was brave or strong, but because horror was what the world had shown her so far. "It might be the decision that lets you win. But it's not the right one."

Shannon said, "They're crossing the second line."

She was referring to the animation, he knew, but it was easy to see in the video as well. An invisible wave of sensation washed across the children. Not a wind that tugged at clothes or hair, but a ripple of pain that twisted their features into grimaces and gritted teeth. What had been strange warmth was beginning to burn as they moved farther into the radiation field. Several of the kids hesitated. Behind them, men raised rifles, made soundless threats. Some of the New Sons were laughing. One boy froze, then turned around, his defiance clear even without audio, his arms pointing and head shaking. A dark-haired man in his fifties slung the rifle casually to his shoulder, aimed with practiced ease, and fired.

Shannon gasped.

The dirt inches from the boy's toes exploded upward.

He staggered backward, his face wild with disbelief. A friend grabbed his shoulder, pulled him along.

Randall Vogler looked like he wanted to vomit. Erik Epstein had his tongue between his teeth and was biting savagely. Jakob put a hand on his brother's shoulder. "You don't have to watch."

The children continued marching, their faces tight and shining.

"We're saving lives," Jakob said, his voice hollow. "This is the choice we have to make."

Cooper turned back to the video, his fists clenching and unclenching, heart pounding. He made himself look at the same girl. "Turn it off, Erik. Please." She was still walking, her pace steady, even as her shoulders shook and chest heaved. "Erik." Walking through agony because the choice was death, and she didn't want to die, not before she'd had a chance to live. "Erik!" Her fingers knotted, the knuckles twisting. Her face was turning pink and spotted, a sunburn happening at high speed. Tears streamed from her eyes. Her skin rippled and tightened. Discolored splotches rose on her cheeks and nose, pink blotches that turned angry red, then white. Like acid sprayed across her flesh, and yet she kept walking—

Enough.

Cooper stepped forward, grabbed the world's richest man by the sweatshirt with one hand, then wound up and slapped him with the other. "Look at her."

Jakob opened his mouth, but before he got a syllable out, Shannon had the gun jammed in the base of his skull. "Whatever security system you were about to engage," she said, "don't."

"Look at her," Cooper said. "Look at her. Look at her god-damn face!"

Erik did. The blood rushed from his cheeks, and his eyes went wobbly, and then he said, "Computer, power down Vogler Ring."

"Yes, Erik."

Cooper turned back to the video. The effects must have been immediate. The kids were staggering as if something they'd been leaning against had vanished. They stared at one another in relieved disbelief, gingerly touched themselves, wincing as they did.

And behind them, a barbarian army began to howl, whooping and raising their guns in the air, firing shots at heaven.

"My God," Jakob said. "What have you done?"

Cooper let go of Erik, clapped him on the shoulder. He sucked in a deep breath, let it out. "You know what I've learned over the last year? Doing the right thing doesn't protect you. But it does help you live with the consequences."

"You let an army of murderers in," Jakob said. Shannon released him, and he collapsed into a seat. "You've killed us all."

"Just because I wasn't willing to sacrifice innocent kids," Cooper said, "doesn't mean I intend to quit fighting."

"What are you suggesting, Cooper? We hand out rifles to accountants and housewives?"

Maybe it was relief, or a year-long surplus of adrenaline, or just the best thing to do at the end of the world, but Cooper found himself laughing. "You know what? That's exactly what I suggest." He turned to Erik. "I know how your mind works, and I'm betting there are bunkers within the city. Something underground, just in case."

"Yes," Erik said, "designed for brief bombardment or extreme weather. Not defensible long term. Dependant on external support for air recirculation and water supply. Limited waste facilities."

"Get the children there, and the elderly. Do it now. Break the rest of the population into groups around the perimeter of the city. Choose multistory buildings with good sight lines. If they're old enough to operate a rifle and young enough that the recoil won't break their shoulder, put them in a window and give them a gun."

He stepped away, walked closer to the video feed, still live. The militia had spread the children out across the breadth of the defunct Vogler Ring, guards keeping them in place while the rest of the mass moved through. Thousands on thousands of men. Not monsters; just men. Men who had lost loved ones or lost faith, who were too panicked to see beyond the animal side of themselves. Steeped in fear, hardened with pain, and released from bounds.

There's nothing more dangerous.

Shannon was suddenly beside him, her eyes on the video even as her fingers found his. "The Vogler Ring is about five miles out of the city."

Cooper nodded. "My bet, they'll surround Tesla."

"They've been marching for days. They'll rest. Wait for night to fall."

From behind them, Vogler's voice said, "And then what?"

"Then we do the thing I've been trying to avoid," Cooper said. "We go to war."

CHAPTER 30

Natalie stood in the kitchen and stared at the news on her d-pad. A headphone in one ear, the other maternally tuned in to the sounds of Todd and Kate watching a movie in the living room. She'd offered them a daytime double feature with popcorn and Coke, and while they were surprised, they'd been quick to seize the opportunity before she changed her mind.

Funny to think that there had been a time when what she'd worried about was making sure they didn't watch too much tri-d, that they ate their broccoli.

The news was limited, just live footage from one angle, a high-altitude drone aimed at the militia. A reporter babbled pointlessly, using a lot of words to say nothing specific. The existence of the Vogler Ring was an open secret, but the details weren't public, and the reporter was clearly being cautious. It was only as it became clear that the kids were suffering that she started to sound like a human being, her voice cracking and fear spilling out.

Literally the last thing Natalie wanted to watch was children burning alive, but as their hands knotted in agony, as furious boils bubbled on their faces, she made a vow that she would not look away. That she would watch every second, no matter how horrible, because if she couldn't do anything to save them, then by God she could at least stand witness.

Then, suddenly, it was over. Whatever force had been hurting the kids vanished, leaving them baffled and obviously fearful of its return. Her joy had been both overwhelming and short lived, because behind the kids, the endless column of armed men had started cheering.

That was Nick. Her certainty was based on nothing, but it was certainty nonetheless, and her chest swelled with pride for the man she loved.

She continued watching the news, staring hypnotized as the New Sons marched ever closer. The sea of men began to split into two groups that would spill around Tesla, enclosing it like pincers. Natalie watched and listened to the reporter's breathless string of nonsense, and waited for the knock at the door.

When it came, she plucked out the earbud and walked to the front window. They were still in the diplomatic quarters they'd been given three weeks ago. It was a lovely space, but it wasn't home, and as she drew aside the sheer curtain, it felt like she was staring out a hotel window. She'd never seen the street below so busy, electric cars and mini-trucks bumper-to-bumper, bicycles zipping between them, nervous people in the street pausing to watch the video feed projected from the opposite building, the same news footage she had just been watching.

The SUV was an old-fashioned gasoline behemoth, muscular and black, and though the windows were tinted, she could see that a woman sat in the passenger seat, looking up at the window she looked down from. For a moment they stared at each other. Then Shannon raised one hand, and Natalie followed suit.

The knock came again. She dropped the curtain and opened the door for her ex-husband.

Nick looked tired but resolved, dark circles under his eyes but his shoulders high. She recognized his expression; she'd seen it before. It never meant things were about to get better. For a moment they just looked at each other. Then she said, "Come on."

■

They'd skirted the living room, stepping lightly as the movie played loud. She could see Nick's urge to join his kids, to drop down on the sofa between them and grab a handful of popcorn and tuck Kate under one arm and Todd beneath the other. Instead, they'd gone into the kitchen, where she'd set about making coffee. It had felt surreal to go through the motions of measuring beans, grinding them coarse, letting them bloom in the French press, all while Nick explained what she had already guessed, that he had convinced Erik to turn off the Vogler Ring, that in so doing he had saved six hundred children but set the rest of the city up for a war. Then he told her about killing John Smith, how he had shot him three times through the heart. Her husband—ex—had killed fourteen times that she knew about, and probably more that she didn't, and while for most women that would be distinctly a turn-on or a turn-off, for her it had always been something apart. A piece of Nick that she would never fully understand, and yet was grateful for. She knew that every time cost him something. He paid that price because he believed that he was making a better world for their kids.

"I can't stay," he said, nodding thanks as he took the mug of coffee.

"I know."

"The New Sons will wait until dark. We'll have a couple of hours to get ready." A pause. "This is everything I didn't want to happen."

"I know."

"Epstein is appealing to the president now. Maybe, with John Smith dead, he can convince Ramirez to help."

"If the government wanted to stop the New Sons of Liberty," she said, "they would have done it days ago."

"Yeah." He sipped his coffee. "There's a bunker beneath Erik's complex. You and the kids will be safe there."

"No."

"You will," he said. "It's under forty feet of rock. The doors are solid steel. Erik built it to—"

"I saw the bulletin." It had flashed up on her d-pad only moments after the militia had passed the Vogler Ring. A brief message from the king of New Canaan, telling his subjects that the barbarians were at the gates. "Children fourteen and under, report to the bunker. The rest of you, get ready to fight."

Nick paused, with that look on his face, the one that meant he was skipping conversational steps because he'd read her intent. It had always driven her crazy. He couldn't help it, she understood that, and his intentions were good, she understood that too, but being married to someone who always knew where you were going—or thought they did—wasn't easy. He said, "Natalie."

"Nick."

"Nat, don't—"

"Nick, don't."

"Listen to me." He set the mug down. "You need to get our children to that bunker, and you need to stay with them."

"I'll get them there."

"This is bad. Those men out there, they aren't soldiers. They're a lynch mob. They're wounded and angry, and they don't see the people here as people. There is nothing they won't do."

"I know."

"I will fight with everything I have. But I can't be worrying about you and the kids while I do it."

"I know."

"So you'll stay in the bunker?"

"No."

"Natalie—"

"I love you," she said. "I have forever. I loved you when my parents disapproved of us. I loved you when you started killing other abnorms for the DAR. I loved you when you went undercover to find John Smith and left me alone for six months, scared every moment that someone would firebomb our house. I loved you as you were dying in my arms. I will always love you."

"I love you too. But—"

"But you are not the only one willing to die for our children. Or kill for them." She saw the impact her words had, how profane the notion was to him. The dying, sure, but more the killing. She understood. It was profane to her too. Natalie locked eyes with him and said, "I'm going to take the kids to the bunker. And then like every other parent in this city, I'm going to get in a window, pick up a rifle, and fight."

He opened his mouth. Nothing came out. Finally, he closed it.

"Now," she said. "Let's go tell our kids that they don't get to watch the end of the movie."

CHAPTER 31

"Mr. Secretary?"

It was still snowing, that fine stuff that looked more like fog whipping back and forth in the wind. Owen Leahy stared out the window of his Camp David office, a onetime guest room with a folding table in place of a bed, a tangle of cables running down from the back of it. Funny to see so many cords; in regular life, everything was wireless, meaning and message floating through the air. Here security had trumped that. *That could be your epitaph: "Security trumped it."*

"Sir, the call you've been waiting for."

Leahy spoke to the window. "You're sure?"

"Yes, sir."

In a career built on taking risks, the last hours had been the most brazen of them. After Luke Hammond had hung up on him, Leahy had called his chief of staff, still in DC, and told her what he wanted.

"Are you kidding?" She'd been nervous, but also exhilarated, he could tell. No surprise there. What he'd asked her to do was the stuff of spy movies, and who didn't want to be pulling the strings?

"This is direct from the president," Leahy had told her. "Screen all calls to any governmental office originating from New Canaan. No matter who it is, no matter what they say, they go to you. When it's him, you send it to me."

"Sir, that's . . ." She trailed off. "Do you mind if I ask why?"

"Deniability," he said. "Ramirez wants cover, and we're it."

"But, sir—"

"If the president asks me to take the fall, I'll do it with my head high and my mouth shut. I need the same from you, Jessica. It's time to serve our country."

"Yes, sir."

A huge risk. But what choice did he have? At this point, nothing would stop the New Sons from burning Tesla to the ground. It wasn't what Leahy wanted, but politics never worked out the way anyone planned. The trick was to maneuver circumstances as close as possible to the goal, then quietly redefine your goal. *"Quietly" being the operative word. If you can keep this quiet for a little while longer, no one ever need know you were involved.*

Leahy turned from the view, said, "Thank you," the dismissal clear in his tone. When the aide left, he walked to the mirror, adjusted his tie. He took a deep breath, then sat down and accepted the video call.

The air shimmered to life. Erik Epstein sat with his hands folded on the table in front of him. Beside him was another man, pudgy and pale, wearing a hooded sweatshirt. "Mr. Secretary?" Epstein sounded confused. "I'm sorry, I used my security code to access the president directly."

"I know," Leahy said. "She's asked that you speak to me."

"Mr. Secretary, I'm going to have to insist—"

"She has asked that you speak to me."

"I see." Epstein paused, looked at the man sitting beside him. The deferral was obvious.

"You," Leahy said to the silent one. "I presume you're the real Erik Epstein?"

"Yes. Hello."

"Nice to meet you. We've known for some time that he"—gesturing at the well-dressed man—"wasn't you."

"My brother. Jakob."

Leahy nodded. "What can I do for you, gentlemen?"

Again the two exchanged a look, then Erik said, "We surrender."

Of course you do. The irony was bitter. This was what he had been playing toward for years. For years he and a few other clear-eyed men had done what needed doing to bring about this exact moment. Not the destruction of the gifted, but the control of them. It was what the initiative to microchip the gifted had really been about; it was why the DAR had funding greater than the NSA, why more than a thousand civilians had died in Manhattan, why Leahy had snuck into Wyoming to meet with General Miller in the first place. It was victory—and it came just slightly too late. *No choice now. No choice but to stay the course.* "I'm sorry?"

"We surrender. Unconditionally. The Holdfast. We will open all borders. Share all technology. Join the government."

"It's a bit late for that, isn't it? You've already murdered seventy-five thousand soldiers. Destroyed the White House. Killed our president."

"Self-defense. Orders were given to attack, to bomb our city—"

"I know," Leahy said. "I gave them."

The silence that fell was so thick he could practically see Epstein's thoughts, could follow as he rebuilt the lattice of his history. Jakob started to speak, but his brother gave the merest hint of a sideways glance, and he shut his mouth.

"Mr. Secretary," Erik said, "the New Sons of Liberty have cleared the Vogler Ring. They've split up and surrounded Tesla. Completely encircled."

"I know."

"Strategic analysis yields only one reason to do that."

"Yes."

"Not an attempt to defeat. Not a military victory. They're trying to annihilate. To kill everyone here. Civilians."

Leahy thought of the moment, not a week ago, when he'd sat in a wind-whipped tent opposite Sam Miller and Luke Hammond and made a bargain with them. He would hold off the US military, and they would push into New Canaan. It had never been his intention to wipe out the gifted. True, there were tens of thousands of abnorms not in New Canaan. But nowhere on earth had so many collected in one place. They had helped secure American sovereignty the world over, had pushed technology forward faster than anyone imagined possible. He hadn't wanted to destroy them; he'd wanted to tame them.

Damn the New Sons for pushing it this far. Another ugly irony. For decades, American policy had wrought exactly this kind of result. Third parties invented and armed to fight monsters had ended up becoming monsters themselves. Pinochet in Chile. Noriega in Panama. Countless warlords in Africa and the Middle East. *That's the risk of summoning a demon; they don't tend to follow orders.*

On the other hand, better the demons consumed each other.

"There's nothing I can do for you."

"Mr. Secretary, please." Erik Epstein's face was pale and guileless. "There are thousands of children in this city."

Leahy hit a button and severed the call. Then he rose and went back to the window.

The snow continued to fall.

CHAPTER 32

"How many of you have fired a gun before?"

The soldier had a man's height and muscle but a boy's face, zits like bright stars burning through a cloud-wisp of beard. His uniform was brown, marked with a rising blue sun. Natalie wondered how old he was. Someone had told her that while the average age in the Holdfast was twenty-six, the median was closer to sixteen. He beat that, but not by a lot.

"None of you?" The soldier boy's eyes darted over the dozen civilians in front of him. They looked at one another, shrugged.

"I have," Natalie said. "With my husband. Ex."

"A rifle?"

"Pistols. And a shotgun." She remembered the day, more than a decade ago, before the kids were born. Camping near the Grand Tetons, vibrant green and birdsong, Cooper showing her how to brace the gun, how to press the trigger—not pull, press—and the roar and kick of the thing, the rough joy when she'd blown a clump of hurled dirt out of the air, the soil erupting into nothing. Afterward they'd made love as the pine trees whispered, and she'd thought life perfect in every detail.

"Close enough." He bent to a long canvas bag at his feet, came out with a rifle that looked like a movie prop, dull metal and rounded plastic curves. "This is an HSD-11. Designed and built here. Open-bolt, selective fire, thirty rounds. Magazine release is here, safety here. It's fully automatic if you hold down the trigger, but ammo is a problem, so don't. Single shots and short bursts."

He held it out, and she took it, shouldered it, keeping the barrel down.

"Good," he said, sounding surprised. "Good. There are seven more, and ammunition. Runners will bring extra ammo later. You teach them."

"What?"

"Teach the others. Be careful when you do, the round can be lethal to a mile."

"You're not staying?"

"No, ma'am." He spun on his heel and headed for the truck.

For a moment Natalie just stared. Then, careful to keep the rifle pointed down, she hurried after him and grabbed his arm. "Wait."

"I have a lot of rifles to hand out, and not a lot of time—"

"Listen," she said, glancing over her shoulder at the others. A pale man in a suit, his thin hair combed with great precision. A pudgy girl in a shapeless dress holding a squirming dog. A statuesque woman with strong cheekbones, her dreadlocks bound up in a brilliant headscarf. Turning back, Natalie said, "We're all a little scared."

"So?"

"So, there's an army headed here, a militia of survivalists and soldiers, none of whom need to be *taught* how to use a rifle. What are we supposed to do?"

"Same as the rest of us." He looked at her, and in that moment she saw that he was frightened too. A boy, just a boy, and like all boys he had played at war, but he had never faced one. "Fight for your lives."

Then he was swinging up into the open back of the truck and thumping on the side. It pulled away in a huff of warm exhaust.

For a moment, she imagined running after it. Then she turned and saw the others looking at her.

Natalie said, "Right."

■

It had seemed so clear in the kitchen, talking to Nick. Telling him that she would join the battle. She'd imagined herself with a line of soldiers, not boys like the one who brought the rifles, but warriors. Tested, calm, ripped. Like Nick's buddies from the army days. She'd pictured fighting beside them, though really, that had meant behind them.

It wasn't until the bunker that she realized this war would look very different.

The underground complex was a series of broad gymnasiums with rows of bunk beds, each room connected to the others, each accessible by multiple staircases. Like the air raid shelters she'd seen in old movies, only brighter and cleaner and filled mostly with kids. The walls were bare and the sound echoed, mothers and fathers cajoling and promising and putting on a brave face for children crying and clutching at them.

She'd been so proud of Todd and Kate for not going to pieces. In truth, they'd been stronger than she was. Natalie had started to waver the moment they arrived, and when she saw her son standing with a strained look of duty, hand on his little sister's shoulder, she'd almost broken. Surely others would fight. They were too young to leave. She would stay, would climb into one of the bunk beds and clutch her kids to her and keep them safe through sheer maternal will.

"No, Mommy," Kate had said. "You have to go."

Todd had nodded, straightened. "We'll be all right."

They were her children, her babies. She had borne them and nursed them and cut their grapes in half and read them whole libraries of books and applied crates' worth of Band-Aids. She had a mother's nearly psychic connection with them, would sometimes wake in the night moments before they called out, or hear their thoughts echoing in her own brain. Right now, her ten-year-old son was telling himself that he had to be a man, had to protect his little sister, and the horror of that thought had nuances that went on for days.

There is no choice here. There was only one way to defend her kids, and while it would indeed involve will, that began by finding the will to leave.

So she'd hugged and kissed them, promised everything would be okay, and made herself walk out the door and wait her turn to talk to one of the harried people giving assignments. A young man staring at a d-pad had told her which van to board, and she'd joined a pudgy girl with a squirming dog in her arms and a statuesque beauty whose hair was bound in brilliant cloth.

None of them had spoken on the drive over. Most had cried at some point. Natalie hadn't. She was remembering something Nick told her years ago, when she'd asked if he was ever frightened doing the things he did.

"Of course," he'd said. "Only very stupid people aren't. The trick is to make it work for you. Use it to make your thoughts clearer and your planning better, so that you get home again."

And so she had tried to do that. To prepare herself for the fact that she might—would—have to point a gun at a human being and pull the trigger. She made herself picture it, over and over and over, all while staring out the window as the city of mirrors transformed itself into a battlefield.

She watched as a crew hitched a bulldozer to a bus and toppled it, the bus drifting and hanging and then crunching down, blocking the width of a street.

Felt the gut-rumble of chainsaws cutting down the gene-modified trees so every window had a clear line of sight.

Watched bartenders nail tables across doors. Teenagers haul floodlights. Cyclists distribute ammunition.

Smelled the smoke as outlying buildings were burned to deny the invaders cover.

Listened to:

Jackhammers.

Siren wails.

Gunfire.

And when her van started to slow, she took in the battlefield, the patch of earth she would be defending with her life. A complex of low-rise buildings, perhaps ten in all. The corporate headquarters of a firm called Magellan Designs. Atop the tallest building was a wireframe globe thirty feet across and glowing, a pulse of light circling it slowly. Magellan made expensive electronics; she remembered Nick drooling over one of their tri-ds, a sleek projector with sound that made her rib cage rattle. They hadn't bought it, of course—it cost a month of his government salary—but now she wished they had. Wished they hadn't been practical. They should have taken it home and watched movies all day long, then made love on the floor in front of it.

A long time ago, in a lost world.

■

The man with thinning hair turned out to be named Kurt, and he was the one who suggested they use the basement as a shooting range.

"Won't the bullets ricochet?"

"We'll stand here"—he gestured to one side—"and shoot at an oblique."

"But—"

"Do you usually wear your hair back like that?"

"Huh?"

"Given gravity as a constant and variable values for flexibility and curl, I can generate a fourth-order nonlinear differential equation to describe the shape of your ponytail."

"Right," she said. "You're gifted."

"Aren't you?"

"Standing here, you said?" She handed him the rifle. "No, not sideways. Face forward. One foot a little in front of the other.

Brace the butt against your body, and press your cheek against the stock. Okay. Now—"

■

Five o'clock, and the sun was nearly touching the horizon. Cold whiskey light glinted on mirrored glass, battling with the pale glow of the corporate logo atop the neighboring building. The ring around it pulsed slowly, tracing, she assumed, Ferdinand Magellan's course circumnavigating the earth. Every time his "ship" was in the Pacific, it turned her whole world violet.

Natalie could see a dozen other defenders up in other buildings. Like hers, their windows had been broken out, with desks and filing cabinets piled up to block incoming bullets. In one of the neighboring buildings, a handsome man in his fifties was doing the same thing she was, and for a moment their eyes met. He smiled and raised a closed fist. She returned the salute.

The complex was near the edge of the city, but the buildings beyond were all squat things, single story. A charging station. A restaurant. An empty parking lot beside the last stop of the light rail train. Cars had been towed and stacked in rough barricades of jagged metal and broken glass.

In the distance, out of range of her rifle, the enemy moved. Thousands of them. At this distance, she couldn't make out any details, and that was somehow more menacing. Like it was a single formless creature out there, stretching across her entire field of view, a shapeless, ruthless beast waiting only for darkness to fall. Her belly spasmed and her hands shook.

Use the fear.

She tried to think what Nick would do if he were here. Plan his reaction when the attack started? Well, keep low. Aim carefully. Don't waste ammunition. She practiced releasing the magazine from her rifle, grabbing a fresh one from the bag at her feet, and slapping it in. Squatting, she raised the rifle and sighted on the edge of a drugstore down the block, imagined a man stepping out from behind it. Kept her breathing easy, paused between exhales, visualized steadily pressing the trigger.

"Damn, girl, you look fierce."

Natalie turned. "Hey, Jolene."

"Brought you some food. Some firebombs. And this." She held up a bucket.

"What's that for?"

"Well, gonna be a long night. Not like you can head off to the ladies'."

"Wonderful." The sky was saddening, the shadows growing deep. "Hey, you should probably take that off," she said, gesturing to the woman's gold-and-scarlet headscarf.

"Huh? Why?"

"Too easy to see."

Jolene laughed, a warm, throaty sound, then unwrapped the cloth. "How do you know all this stuff?"

"My husband. Ex. He's . . . he was an agent with the DAR."

"DAR? What you doing here, then?"

"Long story." She set the rifle in the corner, took the sandwich Jolene had brought. It was the kind from a gas station, tired-looking and wrapped in plastic, and the purple light wasn't flattering.

"He ever kill anyone? Your ex?"

"Yes."

"Think you can?"

Natalie hesitated. "I don't know. I've been trying to imagine that all day. But imagining isn't the same."

"You know, I've shot thousands of people. Maybe tens of thousands." She sat down heavily and smiled. "I play a lot of video games. Don't think it will help. You got people here?"

"My kids. Nick. You?"

"My niece. Her momma left her with me when she was three, never came back. Kaylee's nine and speaks eleven languages. Says she sees words as colors, so it doesn't matter which language, she just uses the colors. Isn't that something?"

"Yes," Natalie said. "It really is."

"And because of that, those men out there, they want to kill her." Her voice was suddenly cold. "Oh, I know, it isn't that simple. They lost people too, they're scared, hurting. But you know what? It *is* that simple. Get me?"

Natalie took a bite of her sandwich. The bread was stale, the meat indeterminate, the lettuce like Kleenex. It was maybe the best thing she'd ever tasted. She thought of Todd, standing with his arm around his little sister; of Kate's too-wise eyes.

It doesn't matter that you'll be aiming at human beings. It doesn't matter that they have thoughts and feelings and parents and children.

And it doesn't matter what happens to you. Not at all.

There are only two things that matter.

"Yeah," she said. "I get you."

CHAPTER 33

Hawk was trying very hard not to cry.

Could it really only have been this afternoon that he'd been sitting in his bedroom with John Smith, the two of them talking like confidants? There had been that perfect moment at the end, when John put a hand on his shoulder, and for a second he didn't feel like a little kid whose mom had been killed, he felt like a soldier, a revolutionary. The kind of man he'd always wanted to be. Strong, determined, important.

Then the soldiers, the gunfire and screams. Wriggling through that endless tunnel. The woman pointing a shotgun, the way his throat had closed up and warmth had run down his leg, soaking all the way into his sweat sock. For years he'd daydreamed about action, had kept his vigil, but the moment actual danger had presented itself, he'd peed himself and run away.

John told you to. He wanted you to get away.

There was some comfort in that, but not much. First they'd killed his mom, now John. He hated them, hated them all so much, and now here he was running down a tunnel, head held low so he didn't bang it into the pipes and wires above, jeans wet and cold, and the part of him that was still a little boy really wanted to cry, but he couldn't, he wouldn't let himself.

Eventually his legs and lungs gave out, and he had to stop. Hawk bent over and braced his hands on his knees, sucking in gasps of air, the taste of vomit in the back of his throat. He had to think, had to start acting like a man.

Step one was getting out of the tunnels. The dusty smell of them, the pale light and hum of cables were making him sick. He set off at a walk, and a quarter mile later he'd found another ladder. When he climbed up, he found himself in a maintenance hut just like the other one, a small space lined with tools and spare parts. No windows, no way to tell where he was except to open the door and step out.

It was chilly in wet jeans and a T-shirt. He wrapped his arms around himself, blinked at the late afternoon sun. After the subterranean dimness, it made his eyes water. There were honks and yells, a line of cars crawling east. The sidewalk was crowded with people with their arms full, their kids on their shoulders.

Hawk thought about asking what was going on, but couldn't figure out who to talk to, everyone seemed to be in such a hurry. And there were his pee-soaked jeans to consider. Better to figure it out himself.

He wasn't sure where he was exactly, but near the edge of town. Everyone else was headed the opposite direction of where he wanted to go. He needed to get out of Tesla, not deeper into it. He started walking, dodging between people, muttering, "Excuse me," without looking anyone in the eye. There was a big intersection ahead. When they'd gotten here, Mom had made him memorize all the major streets in Tesla. She'd said that the first rule of being a revolutionary was knowing the lay of the land. While a lot of the stuff she'd taught him had been fun, this one had felt more like homework. He'd never imagined he might actually need it.

The intersection confirmed what he already knew, that he was on the western outskirts of Tesla. The buildings were low and spread out. Hawk stood on the corner and thought for a moment. He didn't have his wallet or any money. Maybe he could sneak onto a bus, or the light rail? It was the kind of thing that worked on tri-d, but it seemed pretty dicey in real life. He could probably steal a bicycle, but what then? Wyoming was a big state.

Finally, he remembered the place he and Mom had crashed when they first got here. A safe house on the northwestern edge of the city. They'd stayed there for like two weeks, bored out of their minds. One day, Mom had said screw it, they needed some air. Wandering around town was too big a risk, but there was a Jeep in the garage, and they'd loaded up a picnic and taken it out into the desert. It had been a joyous, jolting day of loud music and off-roading. She'd even let him drive. Everything had seemed such an adventure back then, such fun.

The house was only about a mile away. A green one-story with an attached garage. He banged on the door, but there was no answer. All the neighboring houses were dark too, and the streets were empty. He went around back, figured screw it, and tossed a paving stone through the patio door.

The interior looked like he remembered, the same ugly carpet, the same outdated tri-d. The lights worked, but he left them off. The fridge was empty, but there were some beans in the cabinet. He ate from the can as he walked around the house, checking the closets and dressers, hoping to find something to change into. No luck. Best he could do was scrub at the pee stains with a wet towel.

The Jeep was in the garage. It was coated in dirt, sprays of it running back from the wheels. Maybe no one had used it since he and Mom. A full tank of gas, which was good news, but no keys in the ignition.

Hawk went back inside. This was a safe house. The keys had to be somewhere. No hooks hanging by the door, so he went into the kitchen, started opening drawers. He found a white envelope with a thick stack of weathered twenty-dollar bills. He tucked it in his pocket, kept looking. Bingo, a ring of three keys, one of them bearing the Jeep logo. He was only fourteen, and hadn't driven since that day, but he'd figure it out, and besides, the streets were empty—

Outside the kitchen windows a parade was passing.

Hawk froze, glad he'd left the lights off.

It wasn't a parade.

It was an army.

The men didn't wear uniforms, but the dust on their clothes and dirt on their faces made them all look the same. They carried guns, mostly rifles and shotguns, but some heavier stuff too, things he recognized from games. There were so many of them, a flood, like a concert letting out, only they walked in silence, their eyes hard. Not more than forty feet away.

One of them looked over, a long-haired scarecrow with an assault rifle in his arms and a huge bowie knife on his hip. The man stared right at him, and Hawk felt his heart bang in his throat and forehead, a wave of panic so hot he thought he'd wet himself again. He wanted to run, but he couldn't move, just stood rooted at the counter, the keys in one hand. After a moment, the guy's eyes flicked away and he kept moving. The house was dark, the windows transformed into mirrors. He hadn't seen Hawk after all. Slowly, he lowered himself to his knees.

The men kept coming. Hundreds. Thousands. The sky was turning red behind them, and he had a sudden flash of something from the graphic novel.

An army of demons marching out of hell.

CHAPTER 34

"Yes, we know, but they are still outside the perimeter defenses . . ."

"Floodlights. Of course they'll shoot them out. That's why . . ."

"We've got more people than guns, and not enough ammunition, so get a network of runners going to keep it . . ."

"They don't have vehicles. Horses."

The room was a cross between a meeting space and an amphitheater, and packed with people jabbering into phones, staring at terminals, bouncing data back and forth. Until recently it had served for corporate meetings and product demos, and in one of those little ironies Cooper was growing tired of, the plaque on the outside of the door labeled it the War Room. A cutesy touch that would have fit in a tech start-up—which, he supposed, the NCH was.

"How should I know when they'll attack? Sometime after the big bright spot in the sky goes away, and before it comes back . . ."

"Casualty projections are all over the board . . ."

"No, *horses* . . ."

Cooper imagined bulling through the room, fighting his way to Jakob at the head of the table, offering help. The prospect tired him in every way. This was already a too-many-cooks situation, and while in theory his tactical experience would be valuable, without being plugged into the Holdfast bureaucracy, what was the point?

He glanced over at Shannon. She had one arm crossed to support her elbow, the other hand at her face, the tip of her thumb just between her teeth. Her eyes drank the room. Funny—he'd seen her naked, seen her kill, seen her make herself invisible, but he couldn't recall if he'd ever seen her just stand somewhere. It struck him as oddly intimate.

She sensed him looking—her gift, he supposed—and glanced over.

He said, "Let's get out of here."

■

The location was her idea.

When Erik had activated his Proteus virus, the first casualties had been three state-of-the-art fighter jets that were buzzing Tesla. Two of the Wyverns had collided midair, the debris raining down. The pilot had ejected from the third, and her bird had done a backflip into the side of the central building, tearing a hole four floors high and forty yards across, the jet fuel starting a fire that had consumed most of the furnishings before the auto-suppression system got it under control. The bodies had been removed and the gaping rip in the building had been sealed with plastic sheeting that billowed and popped in the wind, but little else had been done to repair the damage.

They looked at each other, then at the torched interior, the blackened remnants of desks and chairs. Shattered solar glass sparkled amidst the ash. Shannon stepped gingerly through a pile of debris, bent to pick up a metal picture frame. The glass was cracked, the image burned away. "Can you imagine sitting at a desk, just doing your job, all of a sudden an airplane comes through the window?"

"Kind of."

"Yeah," she said, threw him a glance not easily parsed. "Me too."

Cooper picked his way across the ruined floor. The stink of scorched plastic hung in the air even now. Translucent sheeting reduced the world outside to blurry shapes backlit by the setting sun. "A couple of miles away, an army is waiting for darkness to fall." He shook his head. "How did we get here?"

"Gradually, I guess." Shannon's voice was soft. "One lie at a time."

"You and your whole truth fetish," Cooper said. "Ever since the first time we talked, in that shitty hotel after the El platform. I had been very heroic, saving your life—"

"Funny, I remember that differently."

"And you said something like, 'Maybe there wouldn't be a war if people didn't keep going on television and saying there was one.'" He shook his head. "And now here we are."

"Yeah." She tossed the picture frame. The remaining glass tinkled. "Here we are."

Gunfire sounded in the distance, steady and slow. *Going to hear a lot more of it tonight.* He sighed, rubbed at his face. "My kids are in a bunker right now. They must be so scared."

Somehow Shannon was beside him, then. One hand on his arm. "Hey," she said. "We've saved them before. We'll do it again."

Before he could reply, his phone vibrated. He glanced at the display. "It's Ethan."

She straightened. "You should answer."

Cooper nodded, hit a button. "Hey, Doc, you're on speaker."

"I . . . is it . . ."

"Just me and Shannon. Have you found the missing canisters?"

"What? No. I haven't been looking for them."

"Doc, come on, I need you to focus—"

"You're the detective," Ethan said. "What do you want me to do, go door to door? I've been working the epidemiology of the virus instead. It's a sonuvabitch, man, a real monster. A modification of the flu, airborne, long-lived, but with R-naught estimates in the *twenties*. That means each case could result in twenty or more secondary cases. And since there's no dependable influenza vaccine, if this gets out, pretty much everyone is going to catch it."

Cooper winced. "How bad is the illness?"

"It's not. Pretty much the sniffles. The flu isn't the problem. I've been reviewing the research notes, analyzing blood and tissue samples, trying to figure out why Abe died." Ethan's voice caught on that. "Cooper, it was the serum. Our work. Becoming brilliant killed him."

"I don't understand—"

"Abe vanished before we could do proper trials. And then he injected himself, which was crazy, you just don't do that, but he was so paranoid, so sure he was right . . . anyway, you saw how effective it was."

"And that killed him?"

"Not the serum itself, but his mind's reaction to it." Ethan took a breath. "You're tier one, right? And so is Shannon and Epstein and that Soren asshole. But you've had your gifts from the beginning. They were part of you as a child. Now imagine that suddenly you also saw the world the way Shannon does. *And* the way Epstein does. *And* the way Soren does. That it all happened at the same time, in a span of a couple of days."

"It would be confusing, but—"

"It wouldn't be confusing," Ethan said. "It would be shattering." He paused. "Okay, look. Imagine you were born underground. A pitch-black cave. You grew up there, connecting with the world by touch and sound and smell. Completely unaware of vision. That was your normal for sixty years.

"Then there was a rockslide, and light flooded in. You wouldn't have the first idea what was happening. I mean that literally—your brain wouldn't have developed neural pathways for processing vision. You'd have no concept of scale, motion, even color. No way of knowing if a shape was your wife or a boulder about to squash you flat."

"I get you, but—"

"Now imagine it's not just sight, it's also sound, and touch, and taste, all at once," Ethan said. "Christ, man, Soren *perceives time differently.*"

Cooper opened his mouth. Closed it. Said, "Okay. So you're saying this could be fatal?"

"I'm saying Abe clawed his own eyes out to stop his vision and scratched at his cage until his fingers were bone. And this was a man with a first-rate intellect who knew what was happening to him. The human mind cannot survive that level of change. There just isn't the neurological flexibility. Not once we're fully developed."

"Which is when?"

"The frontal lobe stops forming around age twenty-five." Ethan paused. "Best guess? It wouldn't be easy on anyone, but kids'd be fine, teenagers would be okay, people in their twenties would have a shot. Much past that . . . I don't know. I think you'd be looking at survival percentages in the single digits. And along the way you've got confusion, panic, delirium, uncontrollable rage, homicidal impulses—"

"All in the most powerful gifted ever born," Shannon said. "Jesus Christ."

A gust of wind shook the plastic sheeting. Beyond it, the world was losing focus. In December, in Wyoming, the sun went down fast, and in the time they'd been talking things had darkened considerably.

Ethan said, "You have to stop this. Somehow. Please. My daughter—"

Cooper hung up the phone. Thought about hurling it right through the fucking wall.

"He's right," Shannon said. "We have to stop this."

"I know."

"We got distracted. The militia, saving the kids, preparing for war. We took our eyes off the ball."

"That's what John Smith does." Cooper had that feeling, almost a tingle, that he'd learned to identify as his gift patterning furiously, nearing an answer. "This isn't an accident, a glitch of timing. He planned all of this to happen at the same time."

"Sweetie," Shannon said, "that's paranoia."

"It's true. He even told us, remember? 'Killing me isn't the same as beating me.' I've been chasing Smith forever." Cooper shook his head. "I should have known that was too easy. He may be dead, but he's still trying to win."

"But how could he have predicted the attack?"

"He didn't." A lattice of connections was starting to fall into place. Cooper could feel the truth bobbing just out of reach, like stretching for a beach ball in a swimming pool. *Press too hard and you'll only push it away. Just follow the logic, let the currents draw you in.* "He didn't predict it. He provoked it."

"That's crazy. The assassinations, bombings, the organization, the stock exchange, the Children of Darwin—are you saying that was all so the Holdfast was under attack at just the right moment to distract us?"

"Not specifically to distract us. But yes, this was his will."

Shannon started to argue, but he could see that she was considering it, reevaluating her past in light of new information. "The last time I saw John, before today I mean, I accused him of wanting war. And he told me I was right. That the normal world would attack, and that they would doom themselves. He said he didn't care how much blood was spilled, so long as it was their blood, not ours."

"Which fits his virus perfectly," Cooper said. "It only affects normals. It kills everyone over twenty-five, which means pretty much the whole power structure. And everyone who survives is left gifted."

"Elegant," she said, "but tricky. There are a lot of fail-safes against biological attacks."

"Yeah." Another node of the pattern revealed itself. "But remember, this is just the flu. Every year the flu affects millions, and no one panics. And superficially, this is a mild one. It's only Ethan's serum that makes it dangerous, and no one knows to look for that. Hell, no one knows it *exists*. Plus, those fail-safes depend on a functional world. We're on our third president in a year, there are lynchings in Manhattan, a civil war. The government already played the quarantine card with the Children of Darwin, badly. I think Cleveland is still burning. All of that orchestrated or at least nudged by John Smith. Not to mention today's attacks—" He froze. "Oh shit. Today's attacks."

She thought for a moment. When it hit, the blood drained from her face. "The CDC, in Atlanta. If there was a place equipped to realize what this flu really is, it was the Centers for Disease Control. So he burned it down. That was the real target. All the rest was a smoke screen."

"Even the bomb at the DAR that killed my best friends and about a thousand other people."

"Everything we've done the last years, all the stuff he claimed was for equality. It was just John pushing the world far enough into darkness that defenses are down." Shannon paused. "Even so. Even if he releases it in a city, in a couple of cities. Even if millions die. That won't spread it far enough, fast enough."

That was it. Suddenly, the whole pattern came clear to Cooper. Like a curtain had been yanked away.

The perfect, crystalline clarity he must have had.

The detail involved. Years of working toward the most complex series of dominos in history.

The horrifying, relentless discipline.

"It's not going to be released in just any city," he said slowly.

Shannon stared at him. He let her ponder, wanted her to check his math. Finally, she said, "You're thinking it's going to be released here. Against the New Sons. Because they're all normals, all vulnerable. But he couldn't count on them winning."

"It doesn't matter who wins. If the militia burns Tesla to the ground, their war is over. They'll scatter back to every corner of the country, as will refugees from Tesla, plenty of them normal. And if the militia loses—"

"The same thing happens," she says. "Thousands of survivors will run back home. My God. John provoked the attack—the *war*—for this. To infect the whole country."

"The whole world," Cooper said. "Maybe not as completely, but still, if this is as contagious as Ethan thinks, how many people are going to die? Hundreds of millions? Billions?"

"We have to call the president."

"And tell her what?" Cooper shrugged. "I mean, imagine we somehow convince her, and she sends in the marines. That's just more normals, more vectors. It plays into Smith's hands. The only way to stop this is to keep the virus from being released."

"*How?* We don't have any idea where it is. And the militia could attack any minute."

"I don't know," he said, and took her hand. "But we have to figure it out. Fast."

"This isn't what I do, Nick."

"It is now. It's all on us. Like it or not."

She pulled away, wound up, and kicked a blackened desk. The legs gave way, the whole thing collapsing in a cloud of ash. "Okay." She gritted her teeth. "If he's infecting the New Sons, the canisters have to be here, in Tesla."

"Plus, Smith is dead. We've got that going for us."

"Right," she said. "Right. So it would have to be something that would work without his involvement. Something he could trust."

"Not some*thing*," he said. "He wouldn't have planned all of this and then left it to a timer. It's going to be a person. Someone he could rely on completely, even in death. His last contingency."

"Someone who would do it. Who wouldn't be troubled by the catastrophe they were about to cause, the deaths of millions or billions."

"You know these people better than I do," Cooper said. "Who would that describe?"

"Jesus, I don't know. Soren, but he's . . ."

For a moment they stared at each other.

Then Cooper was running full tilt for the stairwell, Shannon right behind, her steps lighter but just as quick. He took flights in jumps, the floor numbers falling away, his hand trailing the railing as the impacts rang up his ankles and knees, his head spinning and heart racing and soul praying, thinking, *Please, please, just one piece of good luck, that's not too much to ask, is it?*

They hit the second basement, yanked open the door.

A body sprawled at their feet.

Another down the hall.

In the prison control room, Rickard, the programmer who'd played the virtual torturer, sat in a chair. A pool of crimson surrounded him, the overhead light reflecting off his blood like the moon in a pond. His throat had been ripped open, his tongue yanked through the wound.

Soren's cell was open.

CHAPTER 35

Luke Hammond tapped the flare pistol and checked the time on his borrowed watch.

5:57 p.m.

The watch was mechanical, unaffected by the EMP. An hour ago he had synced it with a dozen others. A dozen men with a dozen flare guns, all watching the seconds tick away.

It had been a long couple of days, but he wasn't tired. Or rather, his exhaustion felt like it belonged to someone else. Partly his experience, he supposed—he'd been a boy when he became a warrior, and it was war that had forged him into a man, war and fatherhood—but also a purity of purpose. Looking around at the others, he could see it in them too. See it as they ate canned soup cold, as they checked and rechecked their weapons, as they huddled in small groups and joked edgily.

They were ready. They may have started as thousands of rough men, wounded people who had lost things that could never be replaced. But in the past week, they had become, if not quite an army, at least a team. United in loss and pain and purpose.

The sun had set half an hour ago, and darkness had fallen like a dropped blanket. The air was cold and smelled of fire. As the New Sons had surrounded Tesla, they had watched the abnorms burn their own buildings to deny cover. A few spots glowed still, the flames given over to embers and smoke trailing up to the sky. There would be more fire tonight, more smoke. Smoke to blot out the stars.

5:58 p.m.

Luke took a deep breath, blew it out slow. His body felt loose and ready, and in his chest bloomed hints of the feeling to come. He wondered if his sons had ever known it, and felt sure they had. Josh and Zack had been warriors too. How fierce they had looked in their uniforms, how proud he had been of them. He had never pushed his sons toward the military, but they had understood the things he stood for. Had shared them.

Raising binoculars, he surveyed his army. Once they had broken through the ring, they had split the New Sons into two, Miller leading one wing, Luke the other. Hard men stretched the breadth of the horizon, clustered in groups of fifty or a hundred. Their clothes were stained, their faces shrouded in beards, but their weapons shone. Luke wondered how the abnorms had felt as they saw the militia enclose their city like pincers. As they realized what it meant.

If this had been a traditional battle aimed at taking the city, their army would focus strength in a few specific places and leave the enemy room to flee. *But we're not here to gain a point on a map. We're here to cut that point out like a cancer.* A brutal surgery, but necessary to save the body as a whole. Tomorrow the sun would rise on a nation that no longer needed to fear the terrorists in its midst. Tomorrow, the healing could begin.

Tonight would come the scarring.

5:59 p.m.

He swept the binoculars toward the city. Beyond the smoldering buildings, the city rose in low towers. The main streets had been barricaded with cars and trucks, with toppled buses and stacked pallets of cinderblocks. Spotlights danced across the earth, scanning, scanning. Snipers would take those out first; one of the benefits of commanding an army of gun show enthusiasts, they brought a surprising amount of firepower. Ammunition for the long rifles wasn't plentiful, but there was enough to ensure darkness.

We will come in darkness, and we will bring fire.

The defenders were using the terrain to their advantage. He could see men and women up in the windows of most of the buildings. They were jumpy as rabbits. Hit them hard and fast, shatter what confidence they'd mustered, send them scattering. Once the New Sons had broken into the city, there would be chaos, and civilians didn't handle chaos well.

Luke lingered on a ring of low-rise buildings, eight of them beneath a glowing corporate logo. There was a park in the center of the ring, a place the workers could relax on their lunch hours. On the day his sons died, it had probably been filled with abnorms staring upward. Joshua had been flying patrol when Epstein triggered his virus, and the footage of his son's murder had been replayed a thousand times. The Wyvern tipping into a nose-down kite. Seeming to float for a moment before it collided with his wingman's fighter. The two of them erupting in flames.

Had the abnorms in the office park cheered? Had they howled and pointed while his son fell burning from the sky?

Luke scanned the buildings, looked at the people in the windows. A man in his fifties with weathered good looks. A girl petting a dog. A black woman with the cheekbones of a queen. A pretty brunette with her hair pulled into a ponytail and a rifle in her hand. Atop one of the buildings stood a sculpture of a globe, a corporate logo wrought in strands of glowing light. A purple comet charting a wobbling orbit around it.

That was where they would hit. Climbing the barricades left them too exposed. The roads would channel them, leave them open to fire from every side. Better to attack directly. Push through the complex of buildings. Kill anyone who got in their way. Light the structures on fire.

He looked at the watch. The second hand ticked once, twice, three times. The minute hand moved.

6:00 p.m.

Luke lowered the binoculars and raised the flare pistol.

CHAPTER 36

Soren trembled.

Thoughts whirling and wild.

A vision of Samantha, one eyeball dangling, half the skin of her face flayed away, screaming into her gag as the torturer leaned in again—

A voice called to him, pulled him from sleep. It sounded like John's voice, but Soren didn't want to obey it. Waking meant remembering. Remembering what they had done to his love, his pale and perfect love, who wanted only to be wanted.

But the thought of her, of what they had done, banished unconsciousness. How had he fallen asleep in the first place? He'd wanted to pass out while they hurt her, had wanted to die, but could do neither. So how could he have fallen asleep after watching what they'd done, right there in his cell, watching her blood arc slowly through the air—

There was no blood on the floor, no blood on the wall.

No straitjacket, no chain.

No bruises on his arms, no fingernail wounds in his palms.

And in that moment he realized the truth. He'd been tricked. They hadn't harmed Samantha. It had all happened in his head, in a virtual hell Cooper had constructed. Relief flooded him like warm water. Samantha was okay. She hadn't been destroyed, hadn't suffered, hadn't even really *been* here. It was just a computer program, a construct, just like the Roman choir. None of it had been real—

Except his betrayal of John.

Warmth calcified into the deepest cutting cold. His oldest friend. The man who had been the boy who had saved him at Hawkesdown Academy, who had brought him the only relief he had ever known, who had seen him when no one else could, who had helped him when no one else would, and Soren had failed him.

Not failed. Betrayed.

John spoke again, impossibly, in the cell. Saying, "Soren. Myfriend."

Saying, "Getready. Getfree."

Saying, "Thenlookformymessage."

He had risen from the steel bunk he'd lain on. No sign of his friend. Of course. A speaker system, some sort of intercom. John must have taken control of it. One of his hackers. The movement had moles everywhere, even in Epstein's organization.

Soren had stretched. Cracked his knuckles. A moment later, the door to his cell had swung open of its own accord.

The room beyond was an octagon, doors on each face, banks of terminals. And the torturer sitting in a chair. Rickard's mouth fell open. He started to rise. Slowly. So slowly.

Soren had crossed the room like a god, one hand lashing out in a nerve chop that dropped the torturer back into his chair.

The man's throat tasted of sweat as Soren closed his teeth on it and ripped it open.

Blood slashed his face, coppery on his lips as he reached inside to grip Rickard's living flesh and yank it through the wound he had made.

It wasn't enough.

Not the torturer. Not the guards outside. It would never be enough. Cracking the world would barely be a start.

Soren sat on a bench and trembled. Staring at his hands, the blood crusted on them.

"Are you all right?" A teenage girl with a rifle stood before him, a pack slung over her shoulders. Her face was twisted, lips screwed up in a grimace of concern. Soren rose, took her head in his hands, and snapped her neck. Her body went limp instantly. So fragile, life. It could be taken with little more than will.

And it was only then that he remembered John's last sentence. *Look for my message.*

He took ten of his seconds to think. Then rolled the corpse over and looked in her bag. Water, a flashlight, a jacket, a hunting knife, a d-pad. Yes. He lifted the girl onto the bench, her warm body heavy and smelling of urine. Sat down alongside and let her head fall on his shoulder as he used her thumbprint to access the d-pad.

The message was in a private mail account established years ago and never used. A number of files, and a video.

John's face filled the d-pad. "Myfriend. Forgivethecliché, butifyou'reseeingthis, I'mdead."

A howl rose in Soren's chest. He had a flash of John's smile as a boy. His charm, his smile, were weapons he'd used against their enemies. But for his friends, John's smile had been a true and precious gift that had made Soren proud to be the recipient.

In the video, his dead friend did not smile. He said, "I'msorrytoaskthisofyou."

He said, "Youaremylastcontingency. Readthesefiles."

He said, "Ineedyourhelp. Willyouhelpme?"

I betrayed you, John.

If you're dead, it's my fault.

There is nothing I will not do.

In the distance, a burning flare of light angled into the sky. Another followed, and another. Like fireworks. Like the soul of his friend, streaking brilliant and finally free.

And sitting on the bench beneath star-smeared skies, a dead girl leaning against him like a lover, Soren read the dying wish of the friend he had murdered.

CHAPTER 37

Natalie watched the flare carve a red scar in the night sky. Higher and higher it arced, burning as it went. Consuming itself.

She felt a sudden desperate urge to pee. What was she doing here? She was a lawyer, a mother, not a soldier. She hadn't been in a fight since Molly McCormick had taken her Twinkie in the second grade and the two of them had ended up rolling around pulling each other's hair.

In the distance, a white spark flared. A second or two later she heard the bang. It was a gun. Someone was shooting at them. Another spark flashed in the same place, but this time, before she heard the report, something shattered, like a champagne flute hurled at concrete. Out her window, the world grew suddenly darker.

They're shooting the floodlights.

In the twilight, the New Sons of Liberty had moved closer to town. It was hard to gauge, but she guessed that muzzle flare had been maybe half a mile away. Which was scary for another reason; she'd been married to a soldier and had some idea of the kind of weaponry and skill required to shoot at that range.

Another flash, and another spotlight died. She set down her the rifle and wiped her hands on her jeans, breathing fast and shallow. She should be used to fear by now. As a girl, she'd been effortlessly bold, but once she became a mom, worry had entered her life, a subsonic buzz that never went away. Worry that a cough was meningitis, that a tumble down the stairs could break a neck.

Then, later, worry that Kate was gifted, and once that was confirmed, worry that she would be taken away, sent to an academy. Worry that Nick would get careless and one day she would find Bobby Quinn on her front porch with pain for eyes.

When Nick had gone undercover, worry became fear. For six months fear had marked her every moment, sometimes a nagging ache, sometimes an open wound. No, that was wrong; it hadn't ended with his return. She and her children had been kidnapped at gunpoint. They had watched cities burn. Seen Todd attacked by a killer, suffered the endless hours of his surgery. Held Nick as he bled out on a restaurant floor.

She was no stranger to fear. But this. This was something different.

Why? Are you so frightened of dying?

She didn't think so. She wasn't eager or anything, but death was just leaving the party, and everybody did that eventually. No, it wasn't for herself.

It was for them. For Todd and Kate. The fear had less to do with dying and more to do with failing them.

Realizing that made the difference. She forced a deep breath, and then another. Held her fingers out in front of her face and willed them to stop shaking. After a moment, they obeyed.

Then she picked up the rifle, flipped off the safety, and looked out the window.

One by one, the floodlights died. And with each, the darkness crept closer, until the only light came from the glowing globe and from the embers of buildings. Slowly her vision acclimated enough for her to make out shapes.

Some of them were moving.

Use the fear.

"Jolene."

Twenty feet away, the woman sat at the base of a file cabinet, those cheekbones making her eyes seem even bigger than they were. Natalie pointed to the logo, then spun her finger in a circle to suggest the orbit of the purple light. For a moment, Jolene just stared, then she got it. Nodded, shouldered her own rifle, pointed it out the window.

Natalie stared into the darkness. Hard to tell what was a moving shadow and what was just a speck in her eyes. She made herself take steady yoga breaths, in through the nose, out through the mouth. Waited with the rifle braced on a filing cabinet, the metal cold on her forearm, finger soft on the trigger.

As the star swung around the front of the logo, her world washed purple, and then it passed, the purple light spilling out across the ground and the men creeping along the edge of a building thirty yards away.

Natalie stared down the barrel. Tried to line the sights upon the nearest man. The luminous dots swung and bobbed with the beat of her heart and the whistle of her breath. The man was moving at a crouch, a weapon in his hands. She inhaled. Let it out steadily.

Pressed the trigger.

The crack of the rifle was like God clapping. Her ears rang. The flare of light stole her vision.

But not before she saw the man fall.

There were answering flashes from the street, and the roar of guns. Glass shattered somewhere. A ricochet whined. Natalie aimed at the flashes, pressed the trigger. Again, and again, and again.

CHAPTER 38

Staring at the d-pad, Shannon said, "Got him."

Cooper nodded, eyes locked forward. The last thing they could afford was an accident. There weren't many other vehicles on the road, but no one was obeying stoplights or speed limits. All the buildings were dark too, although he caught flickers of motion behind the windows. No sign of the attackers here yet, but gunfire cracked from every direction, like being in the center of a storm. Epstein had concentrated the defenders at the edges of Tesla, but no one believed they would be able to contain the militia. Every block would be a battlefield. "Where is he?"

"On the outskirts of town." Shannon's fingers danced on the screen. "Looks like he's past the line."

Twenty minutes ago in the prison control room, Cooper had stepped through the pool of blood to touch Rickard's forehead. Still warm. That meant Soren had broken out only moments before, probably while he and Shannon had stood in the ruined upper floor putting John Smith's plan together.

They were being outplayed by a dead man.

Their shoes leaving blood prints behind them, they had sprinted to Epstein's inner sanctum. Erik stood in the center surrounded by 360 degrees of video. The outskirts of Tesla as seen from the center, the view an angel might have atop Epstein Industries. Above the street scenes ran a row of aerial footage taken by drones circling high above. The computer stitched all the pieces together as well as it could, but the video came from hundreds of sources, none of them aligned quite the same, and the result was a world turned to facets, something like the way insects saw. Bright flashes lit the night in every direction. The New Sons of Liberty were pushing in from all sides. Erik spoke in a high-speed monotone, giving orders to his computer and his commanders in a steady, unpunctuated stream. Jakob paced, running his hands through his hair. Millie sat in a chair, her legs tucked up and arms wrapped around them.

"Soren escaped," Cooper had announced, when it was clear Erik had no intention of acknowledging them.

Jakob said, "We're a little busy here."

"Trust me, you care."

"Cooper, at this point I wouldn't trust you to wipe my—"

"Jakob," Millie said. "It's important."

He squinted at her, then sighed and nodded. "Talk fast."

Cooper did. By the time he was done, Erik had stopped his monologue to listen. The brothers looked at each other. The abnorm nodded a confirmation, then went back to his low babble of command. Jakob said, "I'm not sure what you think we can do about that."

"We have to stop him. If Soren is able to infect the militia, none of this matters."

"The people who live here might feel differently."

"Jakob—"

"Cooper, look at those screens." He gestured. "We're matching housewives against soldiers. The New Sons have more men than we have *guns*. If you hadn't convinced Erik to drop the Vogler Ring, the militia would still be miles away—and not at risk of infection. So if you think that we're going to abandon our defenses to chase after Soren, you're dreaming."

"Shannon and I can take care of Soren. But we need your help finding him. If Erik can just run a video search—"

"We don't need to."

"Hundreds of millions of people could die—"

"We don't need to search for him," Jakob continued, "because you can just use the tracker." He saw Cooper's face. "We implanted a subdermal transmitter when he arrived. Soren is unbelievably dangerous, not to mention John Smith's best friend. What kind of assholes do you think we are?"

Finally, something goes right. "Jakob, I could kiss you right now."

"Glad you approve." He gave them the access information. "Now you just have to get to him."

"On it." Cooper turned and started for the door. Paused. "One more thing."

The idea had started forming while talking to Shannon; something had sparked when she'd said that they had built this world one lie at a time. But then Ethan had called, and he'd back-burnered it. *And the way things are looking, that may be where it stays.* Still. He told Jakob what he would need if everything went right. "Could you do that? Technically, I mean?"

"I think so." Jakob looked to his brother. "We had a call with the SecDef earlier that might be worth including." He paused. "Interesting idea, Cooper. Why not just do it now?"

"Won't work unless we stop Soren."

"Then why are you still standing here?"

They'd lingered only long enough to gear up. A shotgun for her and ammunition for his assault rifle, a couple of flashbangs. He'd considered a vest, decided against it. Light as they were these days, they would limit his mobility, and against Soren that would be fatal.

Shannon said, "Go right," and Cooper yanked the wheel, tapping the brakes just enough to keep the SUV upright as they squealed around a corner. The streetlights were on, but the avenues were abandoned, and the result was an eerie middle-of-the-night feeling, heightened by the sense that they were being watched, that behind those windows, people tracked their motion with guns. *Natalie is out here somewhere. A rifle in her hand.*

"What does it look like?"

"Pitched battle," she said. "Every direction." Her d-pad was wired into a tactical heat map, the city laid out from above, blue in the center, a rippled ring of red and orange around the outskirts. Live intel gathered by drones, allowing regional commanders to assess weak points and direct reinforcements and supplies. "Soren is past the line."

"He make it there before it started?"

She shook her head. "Looks like he cut his way through."

He remembered the way the man had moved, the lethal grace and precision afforded by his time sense. Cooper had hoped that the militia might at least slow him down, but it had been an idle sort of hope. No normal would stand a chance against Soren. Cooper wasn't sure he and Shannon did, either.

The gunfire was growing louder, not the steady *crack-crack-crack* of a firing range, but the clustered, hectic overlap of thousands of human beings trying to kill one another. He had a flash of memory from earlier this year, running down an abnorm hacker who had created a computer virus for John Smith. What had her name been? Velasquez? Vasquez. Alex Vasquez. Just before she put her hands in her pocket and hurled herself headfirst off a roof, she had told him that war was their future. That there was no stopping it, you just had to pick a side.

He'd been a DAR agent then, and filled with certainty. Certainty that humanity was too sane to get to this point. That cooler heads, heads like his, would prevent open conflict.

And now here we are. An army ready to slaughter the greatest concentration of brilliants in America—and an abnorm terrorist poised to wipe out everyone else.

Vasquez had been wrong. This wasn't war. It wasn't about picking a side. There was no winning a genocide—only measures of loss.

Shannon said, "Left."

They turned the corner to find a wall of fire.

The barricade spanned the width of the street a block ahead. The base was pallets of bricks, but atop them lumber and furniture had been piled, gasoline poured, a match struck. Flames leapt twenty feet in the air. A couch burned blue-green, and tires guttered thick black smoke. Cooper could feel the heat through the windshield. Sourceless gunfire cracked back and forth beyond it. "Can you find a hole?"

Shannon shook her head. "Nothing we can get the truck through. Tesla was built to be barricaded."

"The hard way, then." He pulled the SUV to the curb and killed the engine. As he swung out of the seat, a wave of battle noise crashed into him, screams and gun blasts and the roar of fire. Cooper opened the back, took his rifle and spare magazines. Shannon crumpled her d-pad, then tucked handfuls of shotgun shells in her jacket pockets

For a moment, they looked at each other. Her face was lit orange, infernos reflecting in her eyes. The heat washed in waves, like the whole world was burning. "Don't hold back out there," she said. "Don't hesitate, and don't play fair."

"They're here for my children." Cooper shook his head. "Fair's got nothing to do with it."

"Good. Let's go kill some assholes."

He leaned forward, grabbed a handful of her hair, and pulled her close. Their lips mashed together, tongues dancing, her teeth nipping at him, a kiss as fierce and raw as any he'd known. After far too brief a moment, she broke it. Grinned at him.

Together they headed into hell.

CHAPTER 39

Soren didn't wait for the man to finish dying. He just wiped the blade on his sleeve and kept walking.

It hadn't taken long to read John's plan, even as the signal flares rose into the sky and the militia attacked. One of the few benefits to his curse, he could easily digest ten pages a minute. And while John had included all the technical detail necessary, he'd understood how fluid the situation would be and hadn't tried to micromanage.

According to the date stamps, the files had been prepared several days ago. That was the way his friend worked, the way he saw—had seen—the world. A multilayered series of branching paths, options to options and contingencies to contingencies. This one had clearly been a last resort; John would never have opted for it if he'd had a choice. No doubt he had intended something far simpler and far more elegant.

But he had been betrayed before he could put it into motion.

Had John suspected Soren would fail him? It seemed unlikely. *He had a protocol in place to free me in case of his death. Why do that if he believed I would cause it?* No, far likelier, John had known that he was a prisoner, and had intended to rescue him later, after his plan was complete. He had believed Soren could hold out. Trusted him to.

Behind him, the man whose throat he'd opened with the knife made a liquid gurgling sound, fingers twitching. Soren continued walking. Not far now.

After rising from the bench, he had hitched up the guard uniform he had taken from a locker in the prison control room, unbuckled the belt, and threaded the knife's sheath through it. Then he'd pocketed the d-pad and left the rest of the detritus—rifle, pack, girl—on the bench.

Two blocks away he waved down a pickup loaded with ammunition, put his knife through the driver's eye, pulled her body to the street, and drove toward the edge of town. There was gunfire from all directions. In his prison of white, he hadn't even known that an army was descending on Tesla. Soren drove as far as the streets would allow, then abandoned the car and started walking. The low, slow thunder of gunshots rolled around him. Defenders leaned out windows, each trigger pull a flashbulb that made them glow.

The burning barricades had slowed him down, but not very much. In the end, he'd simply gone through a building. A man had stared at him, called him a fool. When he broke a window on the outside and started to climb through, the man had tried to stop him. Briefly.

Then he was out, beyond the line of defense, in the night.

The attacking army seemed more reapers than soldiers. A hundred or more were moving from darkness to darkness ahead of him. They howled and screamed as they loosed bursts of automatic fire at the buildings. Rather than waste time, he spun away, took a lateral route. Wended his way past a smoldering structure, heat still washing over it. The man he had just killed had been standing at the corner; staying out of his sight had been easy, and then the knife had finished the job.

Though the line of battle was behind him, he was still in town, amidst a loose sprawl of low buildings, many of them burned out. It made sense; the most defensible buildings would be the taller ones. At one point they might have marked the edge of Tesla, but towns continued to grow. Soren stepped lightly through shadows and smoke. In an alley, three men stood talking. Their eyes fell on him. One of them cocked his head, nudged another. They turned, rifles moving in slow motion.

He cut the brachial artery of the first, buried his knife in the ribs of the next. It caught and he left it there, spinning back to point the dead man's gun and pull the trigger. Guns were clumsy and loud, and the recoil was graceless, but the bullet worked. The three men fell at the same time. Soren gripped the knife and planted his foot against the man's head for leverage as he yanked the blade free.

A hundred yards farther, he found the restaurant. A diner, clean enough but not fancy, the kind of place no one made an effort to visit. He broke the front window with the pommel of the knife, chipped the glass from the frame, and climbed into the dark interior.

The air smelled of bacon and burnt coffee. He found a flashlight in the cabinet by the register and took it with him to the basement supply room. The walls were lined with shelves and stocked with canned goods. A safe as tall as he was sat in the back corner, a curved metal dolly resting against it. Soren opened the d-pad, found the combination, spun the safe dials, and tugged the heavy door open.

Inside stood the culmination of his friend's dream. Two aluminum tanks, each four feet high and fitted with a simple valve.

I won't fail you again, John.

■

Shannon led the way at a low dash, and Cooper followed, trying to step where she stepped, move as she moved. Her ability to shift wasn't operating at full potential—she had to be able to see people to know where they would be looking—but he trusted her instincts for stealth. Shots rang out around them, from the windows above, from darkness beyond the barricade. Bullets screamed into brick and glass and flesh. Someone wailed in pain, though in the chaos he couldn't tell from which direction, or even if it was a man or a woman. The heat of the burning barricade seemed to blister his face as they ran toward it. He held the rifle low, his finger outside the trigger guard, and had a flash of basic training, the endless drills, mud and sore muscles. A lifetime ago, before he'd met Natalie, before Todd and Kate, before the DAR, before the world had driven so intently toward its own destruction.

Shannon dodged to the right, swung around the corner of a building, running on the balls of her feet. As he followed, a bullet splintered the concrete cornice above him, a rain of dust falling, and then they were blitzing through a narrow alley, fire escapes and loading doors, the sour smell of trash. At the end, she slowed, peered around the corner. He moved alongside her, their arms touching. "Blocked," she yelled in his ear, the words barely audible over the constant fusillade. "A row of cars."

"On fire?"

"No."

He nodded. "Targets?"

"Can't tell. Probably."

"Can you shift past?"

"If they're looking at something else."

Roger that. He took a deep breath, then swung around the corner, rifle up. A minor street with buildings close on either side. Fifteen steps away a double line of cars were parked perpendicular to the street, their tires slashed. There was motion on the other side, and he fired two quick bursts without bothering to aim, then sprinted to the barricade, keeping low and dropping behind the engine block of an electric coupe. Shots pinged and sparked off the hood. Without sitting up, he laid the barrel of the rifle on the hood of the car and fired full auto until the magazine emptied. He slapped in a new one and glanced back to the alley, but Shannon was no longer there; she'd moved across the street, into a pocket of black beneath a broken streetlight. She held up three fingers, then pointed. Cooper took a flashbang from his pocket, made sure she saw it, then pulled the firing pin, counted Mississippis, and tossed it over the cars in a blind underhand arc.

He'd been looking at Shannon as he did it, and even facing away, the blast of light left afterimages of her floating on his retina. Cooper blinked, rolled, then leapt up onto the trunk of the car, the weapon at his shoulder. He saw a man behind a toppled trash can clawing at his eyes and put quick bursts into him, then ran along the trunk, jumped to the next car, and slid on his butt to land on the other side, weapon up. A second Son lay on his belly in the middle of the street forty yards away. Cooper aimed ahead of him, fired a strafing burst, the recoil of the weapon driving it upward, the bullets marching through the man.

Cooper couldn't see any other targets—

She said three.

Could the third have faded back into the darkness?

Not if he was blinded by the flash . . .

Oops.

—and realized his mistake. He whirled, spotted the third shooter ten feet away and behind him. He'd been up against the cars, nearly opposite Cooper, and hadn't been hit with the flash. A scrawny guy with bad teeth and a submachine gun coming to bear. Cooper told his muscles to spin, his arms to aim, but the other guy had the drop on him—

Until Shannon appeared on the cars above, shotgun braced against her slender shoulder. Fire burst from the barrel, the light framing her snarling face. The man's head collapsed like smashed fruit.

If he hadn't already, he would have fallen in love with her right then.

Shannon leapt off the car, landing like a cat, and pointed. Cooper set off in the direction she'd indicated, dropping the magazine from his rifle as he went and slamming in a new one. Better to waste a few rounds than run dry in a firefight.

Muzzle flashes lit the darkness ahead, dozens of them. A car window shattered, pavement chipped with the whine of a bullet. He took shelter behind the corner of a ruined building and covered her approach, firing full auto at the place where he'd seen the muzzle flashes. The three they'd faced had been scouts for a larger group, men revealed to him in brief strobe flashes that he chased with his weapon. He heard a man scream, and then she was past him. He followed, pausing only long enough to toss the second flashbang. Gratifying as it might be to stay and kill these men, there wasn't time.

They were on the outskirts of town. Most of the buildings here had been bulldozed or burned, and smoke still rose from the embers. They darted across the ruined landscape in a dancing zigzag, his gift intuiting her moves, her sliding and shifting unpredictable to everyone else, and for a moment he forgot the stakes, forgot the desperation of time, forgot that the world balanced on the head of a pin, and just relished the way they moved together, like one of those kung fu films where everyone was on wires and every move choreographed, the two of them covering each other without words, sharing a simple certainty that, succeed or fail, they would do it together.

A moment later they were on the edge of the combat zone, gunfire still constant but mostly behind them, when Cooper's foot caught on a body splayed out in a pool of blood. He hit the ground, the impact banging up his knee. *So much for kung fu.*

"You okay?"

He nodded. As he pushed himself up to a crouch, he noticed the man's throat had been slit wide.

Not two blocks later they found three more bodies, clustered in a circle. Two had knife wounds, the third was missing part of his face. Shannon grimaced as she pulled out the d-pad.

"Turns out we hardly need the tracker to find Soren. We could just follow the corpses." Cooper laced his hands on his head, sucked in breath. Then he looked at Shannon's face, saw her expression. "What is it?"

She glanced up from the screen, the pale light of the d-pad hollowing her eyes like a corpse. "I know where he's going."

■

The canisters were awkward, and each weighed about fifty pounds. Soren spent ten of his seconds considering taking just one of them; he'd move faster, and knowing how John's mind worked, if success had required two tanks, there would have been four here. His friend had never aimed for good odds—he sought certain victory. That was how he could win even in death.

In the end, the dolly made up his mind. It was heavy-gauged and wide-wheeled, but designed for two tanks. Loading just one would leave it off-balance. It took him less than a minute to strap them in and be on his way.

His body felt strong and limber, and even pushing the dolly he could keep up a swift pace. Captivity had afforded him ample time to exercise, and here at the city's edge, the streets were smooth and the buildings undisturbed. The battle raged on, but he hadn't seen any militia since the three he left in the alley. It made sense. They weren't here to hold territory, weren't interested in establishing a base camp.

They had come to burn.

Soren didn't care. Let them. Let them raze and rape and ruin. Let blood flow in the gutters. He'd never felt any particular loyalty to brilliants in general. The boys who had tormented him at the academy had been brilliants; Epstein and Nick Cooper and Rickard the torturer had been brilliants.

All that mattered now was that he finish what his friend had started. Not for the cause, but for John. Then find Samantha, the real one, and keep her safe while the world fell to ruin.

As he rounded the corner, he saw his goal ahead of him. A broad space hundreds of yards across, bounded by a chain-link fence. Red and white lights marked the edges, and a windsock hung limp. The gates were unguarded, but on the runway, a pilot had pushed a carbon-fiber glider out and was hurriedly attaching the cable that would fling it into the sky. The Tesla airfield.

Let this barbarian militia have their little massacre.

He would burn the whole world.

CHAPTER 40

Life had been reduced to extremes.

There was silence; and there was the thunder of gunfire. Cold, clean air; and the reek of smoke and gasoline. December chill; and the sudden sharp burn of an ejected casing pinging off Natalie's skin. Strangest of all was the darkness broken only by flares of brilliant light. Each muzzle flash revealed a living photograph, lovingly composed and yet vanishing almost too quickly to absorb, like a piece of conceptual art.

Flash: Here is a man in a puffy black ski jacket with a pistol in each hand, his mouth contorted in a howl as he pulls both triggers at the same time.

Flash: Here is the kind-faced older man in the neighboring building, tongue caught boyishly between his lips as he fires into a crowd.

Flash: Here is a teenager with a buzz cut hauling his bleeding body across broken ground as he shoots blindly.

Flash: Here is your hand on the barrel of a rifle, pale with cold and carved with the lines of your history.

Flash: Here is gentle Jolene screaming obscenities, lips curled back, hair swinging like snakes.

Earlier, when Natalie had tried to imagine the assault, she had mentally screened old movies, columns of men goose-stepping like Nazis down the center of the street. She had wondered if she would be able to frame the sights up on a living target and pull the trigger, send a hunk of metal screaming through space to tear the flesh of another.

That turned out not to be the problem. Any reluctance had vanished when they started shooting floodlights—when, like the beast that had lived in her childhood closet, they drew their strength from darkness. She had gone through five magazines of ammunition already, and although she couldn't say for sure how many people she had hit—how many she had killed—she knew the number was far from zero.

No, the problem was that the militia didn't goose-step down the middle of the street. Instead they sprinted, zigzagging. They hid behind every scrap of cover. They stormed the barricade and leapt from the top and hit the ground at a roll and came up running. They dashed along the paths that ran between the buildings. There were so many of them, an endless stream, and all desperate to live, and even as she lined up and fired and lined up and fired, even as she knew that her rounds found targets, there was always another, and another. It was like trying to poke holes in the ocean, only this ocean was clothed in black and howling and shooting back.

The slide of the rifle locked open. Natalie dropped to her knees, spun so her shoulders were against the filing cabinet. She spared a moment to look at her d-pad, where the battlefield map glowed faintly. Drones circling above tracked heat signatures, motion, and gunfire to build an interactive picture of war as a living organism. It looked like a ring of fire squeezing inward. The colors shifted and flowed as she watched, vortices of furious red spinning against blue as the New Sons broke the city defenses.

And there in the center are the bunkers where your children huddle.

Natalie released the magazine from her rifle and slapped in a new one, then poked her head up. A bullet snapped above, close enough that she could sense its passage. She dropped back down as more rounds blew through the shattered window and tore holes in the ceiling.

I think they've figured out where you are.

She grabbed a couple of spare magazines from the bag and crawled on hands and knees to the next window. Earlier she and Jolene had dragged a heavy desk from the corner office of some executive and tipped it up in front of the window. Her ear to the wood, she slowly eased her head up enough for one eye to clear.

Flashes and cracks echoed from all directions, but the area in front of her window, the space she felt responsible for, seemed quiet. She squinted, trying to separate darkness from darkness. The purple light was on the far side of the globe and helped not at all. Was something moving? She thought so. But the shape was wrong, motion here and here and there. How could one person—*oh.*

Natalie dropped the rifle, stood, and ran back to her window, ignoring the blasts that came from the street, the splintering of the walls, the wood spraying off the desk, just focused on making it to the filing cabinet, at the base of which stood five glass bottles. She grabbed one and the lighter, white plastic, the same Bic available in ten million checkout lines, but this one she was using to light a rag soaked in gasoline, the chemical smell ringing in her nostrils. One spin of the wheel, two, three, and then the lighter flared, and the flame leapt eagerly to the cloth tucked into the bottle. She risked standing up long enough to hurl it out the window as bullets blew in at her. She dropped too quickly to see it break, but she could hear the *whoomp* of gasoline and the sudden crackle of hair and cloth, and right on the heels of that, screams.

The sound tore at her. Instinctively, she wanted to call a time-out. To rush down and help whoever was hurt, as she might if one of Todd's friends were hurt roughhousing—put on a Band-Aid and call his mother. Instead, she returned to the other window, picked up the rifle, and made herself look out.

While shooters farther back had tried to pin her down, a group of ten or so had been crawling through her field of vision. The firebomb had landed amidst them, the glass shattering and gasoline flinging out, and now they writhed and screamed and flailed furiously at the flames. In the sudden glow of light, she could see not only the men she had lit on fire, but also many beyond, eyes glinting in the darkness, indiscernible shapes, a horde of them stretching into the horizon, a monster that wouldn't quit coming, and instead of bandaging the wounds she lined up her rifle and started shooting them, taking advantage of the light from their burning brothers.

CHAPTER 41

Soren worked.

He'd never mounted a canister of biological weaponry on a drone before, but John's notes were straightforward, and with the leisure of his perception he had time to review them twice before he even picked up a socket wrench.

The airfield had two hangars. One was for civilian gliders. The other was marked with Epstein Industries logos and warnings of dire consequences for trespassing. There had been no guards; no doubt they were back on the front lines, defending the city. The only people he'd seen were the glider pilot and a middle-aged mechanic with a broad gut. Neither had slowed him down.

He worked steadily, carefully. He had failed John when Cooper tricked him, and the mistake had cost his friend's life. He wouldn't let a mistake destroy John's dream, too.

The drones had a sort of alien grace to them that he admired. Streamlined and to the purpose, they resembled dull dragonflies with sixteen-foot wingspans. The schematics showed him exactly what to do, and the process was mechanical. Detach a dozen bolts to remove the modular payload—in this case, a camera package three feet long and dotted with lenses and sensors. Secure the high-pressure tank in its place, valve pointing downward. Push the drone to the open hangar door—it rolled surprisingly easily—and move to the next.

Earlier, searching the toolbox, he had come across a knife with a short, curved blade, and Samantha shrieked in his memory as a similar blade cut away her lower lid and popped the eyeball from its socket. He jammed the drawer shut so hard he almost took a finger off.

Not real, he had reminded himself. *She wasn't hurt. She wasn't even there.*

The thought didn't bring relief. It brought disgust. Self-loathing that he had been fooled, and a faint contempt for the methodology. Just before the cutting had begun, Soren had thought that Cooper had been bluffing, that he wasn't strong enough to do what was necessary. He had been right. Cooper's will was not the equal of his, or of John's.

Soren would teach him that tonight. He would finish what his friend had started and destroy everything Cooper had fought for. *And when that's done, find him, and repay the suffering. Let him die alone and screaming.*

He had recoded the girl's d-pad to his own thumbprint, and he activated it now. One of the files John had sent was a program to hack the drone controls. He executed it. A graphic of a radar ping appeared, the sensor line sweeping the circle once, twice, searching for signal recipients. When it found them, it gave way to a command screen.

The drones could be flown manually, and he considered it. There was a certain poetry to steering the engine of the world's death and rebirth. But he knew nothing of flying, and in the end, chose to upload the autopilot patterns John had provided. Simple inward spirals, one clockwise, the other counter. They would circle Tesla until the liquid hydrogen fuel cells gave out. Hours, he assumed. Maybe days.

He stepped back to examine his work. The tanks detracted from the aesthetic. Unlike the camera package, they hadn't been designed for this purpose, and they bulged like tumors on the bellies of the sleek machines. No doubt the drones' efficiency would suffer as well, but they didn't have far to go. As he had worked, the slow-motion thunder of the battle had, if anything, intensified.

Soren found the valve of the first tank and twisted it until he heard a faint hiss.

Then he pressed a button on the d-pad, and the engine spun to life.

Seconds later, the drone began to roll.

■

Cooper's veins pumped fire and his head ached. Adrenaline made his hands tremble. They had been running at a full sprint since Shannon figured out where Soren was headed, slowing down only when they just-shy-of-literally collided with a group of militiamen. It had been a fast and brutal fight, five Sons to the two of them, but at close range the men's weapons were useless, and he and Shannon had fought together with calm synchronicity, her spinning and sliding, never where they thought she would be, throwing high kicks and sword strikes with the edge of her palm, his approach more about churning through them, bulling right into one before stomping the heel of a second, twisting his arm back, and breaking it at the elbow. The third, a monster who looked like he could bench a truck, had gotten him in a bear hug, and it had taken a knee to the groin and two head-butts to the man's nose to break the grip.

By that time the one he'd first knocked over had started to rise, but Shannon's shotgun had put a stop to that. They had looked at each other, then leapt back into a sprint. The streets were dark, the buildings deserted, but behind them the battle raged on. The smell of smoke was in the air, and the sounds of dying men and women.

When they reached the airfield, his first thought was that she must have been mistaken. The runway lights were on, but there was no one around, no guards at the gate, no planes streaking down the field. Then he saw the glider at one end, already wheeled into position, the cable attached to the nose of it, the left-hand door open, and, crumpled beside the front wheel, the body of the pilot. Too far away to make out many details—other than a reflection of the moon in the pool of blood. Soren's signature.

Too late? Fear skewered him; if Soren had already taken off, it was all over. Not just this battle, but the whole of the world he knew. John Smith's virus would consume everything. It would destroy the government and bring ruin upon America, and perhaps the whole world. It would kill Natalie and corrupt his son and lead to the deaths of—

A small light danced in one hangar, the one marked with the Epstein Industries logos. Beneath the gunfire and growing louder was a sound. A hum, like a turbine, or . . .

An engine. "Shannon!" He didn't wait to see if she would follow, just ran toward the hangar with everything he had, his heart ripping his chest and breath burning.

A shape rolled from the open hangar, low and predatory. It was a third the size of the Seraphim the military used, but he recognized the UAV easily enough, and, as it began to pick up speed, he saw something slung on its belly. A cylinder perhaps four feet long.

He weighed options—

It's thirty yards away on a perpendicular path, and the engine is accelerating.

You don't know that an explosion will destroy the virus.

But once it's in the air, it will take less than a minute to reach the front and infect tens of thousands of people.

And you know for certain what will happen then.

—and had only one.

Cooper shouldered the assault rifle, standing in a bladed stance, the stock braced against his shoulder. The weapon had no scope, but the sights were luminous. He fired three quick bursts.

Two things happened. Sparks flickered off one of the wings where his rounds had hit.

And the slide of his rifle locked back. The magazine was empty.

Beside him, Shannon fired and racked again and again, but Cooper wasn't surprised to see the drone still rolling, rapidly picking up speed. If his bullets had ricocheted off the skin of the thing, shells would be useless. He thumbed the release and let the magazine fall from his weapon as he reached for his last one. The drone was hauling now, the distance growing rapidly, forty yards, fifty. He considered the fuel tank, but if the wing could take hits, there was no way in hell the fuel tank couldn't, which left what? The drone wasn't military, but it was newtech, obviously built to survive small arms under battle conditions.

Battle conditions. Not takeoff.

He primed the rifle and toggled it to full auto, trusting to muscle memory, to basic training. Seventeen years old, allowed to join up with Dad's consent, a heady, hard time, and he'd done well, this was just another drill, practicing against a moving target, moving fast, he let the sights lead the drone as it gathered speed and he stared down the barrel, unblinking as he aimed at the strut of the rear wheel and fired half the magazine in a go, set up again and loosed the rest.

The retractable strut tore away, the bottom two feet spinning and bouncing ahead of the drone as it rocked back on its hindquarters, the material shearing and tearing, surfing a trail of sparks, and friction took the fuel tank and the liquid hydrogen blew in a dazzling fireball of pale blue flame.

For a moment he just stared at it. Then Cooper threw his head back and roared. Beside him, Shannon was laughing, one hand cupped to her mouth, the shotgun dangling from the other. They had made it, pulled it off, and even as the battle raged behind them, even though the world was far from safe, it would keep turning, there was still time . . .

Is what he was thinking as the second drone left the hangar.

He and Shannon looked at each other. Then she glanced down the runway.

Cooper saw what she was looking at, said, "No."

"Yes." She threw him the shotgun. "Get Soren."
Then she sprinted for the abandoned glider.

CHAPTER 42

Luke Hammond stood in the darkness and watched men burn alive.

He had been a warrior his whole life, and long ago he'd recognized that no good man could have been the places he had been, seen the things he had seen, done the things he had done. It didn't matter that he had fought for his country, for his children. It didn't matter that he possessed discipline and restraint. There was a beast, a slavering, rotting, smiling thing that smelled of sex and sweat and shit. Every man sensed it. Most lived and died without spending time in the beast's company, without tasting that terrible freedom or knowing the beauty that grows in horror. There were no words to convey it, because it came from a place beyond words, before words.

Good men would never acknowledge that fire is most seductive when it is out of control.

But the people in those windows knew that now. Win or lose, live or die, that knowledge would never desert them. It could be ignored, forced down, loathed, but that wouldn't change its essential truth. The men screaming as they burned knew it too.

It was not romantic. It was not moral. It simply was.

Luke had expected that as soon as the line was broken, as soon as some of the Sons had made it past the defenses and into the city, the will of the defenders would snap. He'd been wrong. Even as scores of his men broke the lines, as the militia penetrated the city and the sounds of battle rose from every block, the people in the windows fought. They fought with the will of people protecting their homes and their children, and Luke honored that in them.

The Sons continued to charge, firing as they ran, leaping the bodies of their comrades. In the windows, rifles flashed, bottles rained down. The street was bright now, and the beast lurched from flame to flame, slavering and laughing.

Discipline and restraint did not make him a good man. But they had allowed him to live with the beast for decades. As chaos flared around him, Luke was calm. He moved in a low crouch, choosing his steps carefully, the rifle held low. As his heart screamed to rage, he kept his finger off the trigger. He moved to the edge of the light cast by the gasoline fires and knelt down. He ignored the bullets snapping off the concrete around him, the smoke that brought tears to his eyes, the smell of cooking meat, and he watched.

The defenders had set up barriers in the windows and fired from behind them. But not every barrier concealed a target. It might be a shortage of manpower, but he suspected instead a shortage of weapons. The abnorms had put too much faith in their technology, taken too much comfort in their invisible wall. Once it was breached, they were vulnerable.

He watched and saw that though there were many windows, many barriers, the number of defenders was quite limited. Their strength was an illusion. They would fire from one window, stop as soon as they drew attention, and move to a different one. He doubted there were more than a handful of snipers in each building. The only reason they had held on as long as they had was that they weren't facing an organized army—they were battling a horde.

Luke raised the rifle to his shoulder. He watched a man in his fifties empty a magazine, then drop from sight as bullets streamed upward. Luke waited.

When a muzzle flashed at a different window, he exhaled, sighted, and fired once.

The man jerked. Staggered. Fell across the barrier.

Luke waited.

From the neighboring building, another Molotov flew, the glass sparkling. He ignored it, ignored the blast of fire and the screams. Waited.

A woman rose like a cobra, a rifle in her arms. He recognized her. He had seen her earlier through the binoculars. She was even prettier up close. Or perhaps it wasn't the distance; perhaps it was that since then she had experienced a facet of life she'd never suspected. Had embodied a savagery that had no place in her parenting or her parties.

Like Luke, she had seen the beast. Like him, she had made her offerings to it. Were she to live, no doubt she would be horrified at what she had done; the screams of burning men would haunt her midnight hours. But there would be a part of her that missed it. A secret, unacknowledged quarter that would revel in the moment she had held the raw stuff of life in her hands.

Were she to live. But having seen the beast granted you no protection from it.

Luke framed her face in the sights of his rifle and pressed the trigger.

The round took her through the forehead.

CHAPTER 43

Shannon could feel the heat from the burning drone even from here, the flames so pale they were nearly invisible, and even as she sprinted down the runway, she couldn't quite believe what she was doing.

Behind her, Nick yelled something, but she couldn't hear it and she couldn't stop, not while the other UAV was already picking up speed, the engine whine loud enough to penetrate the gunfire and the crackle of melting composites.

She'd flown gliders hundreds of times, loved the feeling of them, the dance with wind and gravity, larking across the desert. Loved the knowledge that even though they were reasonably safe if you knew what you were doing, they were not merciful. Lose focus, lose the wind, misread a situation, and the ground was a hard teacher. It was the same thing she liked about going on mission, that feeling of hundred-proof life, and it couldn't exist without risk, without gambling against fate. She had always known that one day she'd lose. She just hoped it wasn't today.

The pilot crumpled under the wing wore a leather jacket and an astonished expression. There were bags near his feet. He'd probably been hoping for a last-second save against the militia and had waited too long. Soren's knife had opened his throat so cleanly and so deep she could see the white of vertebrae. She hoped he had been a better pilot than fighter; there wasn't time to check the body of the plane, to confirm that the wheels were unblocked, to ensure that the cable was properly attached and the release well-maintained. She just leapt his corpse, hauled herself into the cabin, and started flicking switches. The battery worked, the indicator lights snapped on, and then there was a streak of motion out the side window, the drone already barreling past, picking up speed rapidly. No time for niceties like safety, then. Time to do or die.

More like do and *die, sweetie.*

There's only one way to bring down that drone.

Shannon buckled her seat belt and, with a prayer that the automatic systems were online, reached for the button marked CABLE RETRACT.

There was the familiar jolt of the winch engaging, and then she was thrown back in her seat as the glider jerked forward.

■

Cooper dropped his empty assault rifle and caught the shotgun in the air, then yelled, "Wait!" Couldn't think what to add after that, and it didn't matter, because Shannon didn't.

He was about to start after her when a figure stepped from the hangar. Lean and graceful and filled with menace. Cold fingers seemed to wrap around Cooper's torso. As though his heart had a memory, knew what it faced. The man who had only weeks ago slid a knife into his chest. Who had put his son in a coma and killed Cooper without breaking a sweat. The fear that gripped him was primal. Brain stem stuff, deep and certain, and with every step Soren took, it magnified.

Then a thought occurred to him.

They had to stop that drone. Neither his life nor Shannon's meant anything compared to that. She would realize that. He knew his warrior woman, knew that she wouldn't hesitate.

But maybe he could spare her the choice. Soren had launched the drone; he might be able to stop it. To bring it down before Shannon was forced into the only course of action available to her.

Cooper raised the shotgun. The stock was still warm from her cheek. Soren was twenty feet away. He stopped when he saw the gun come up. He had no intention to read, no plan Cooper's gift could use. Calm as unmoving water.

Yeah? Make some waves.

Cooper aimed, exhaled, and pressed the trigger. The gun bucked in his hand.

In the instant his finger began to squeeze the trigger, Soren spun like a dancer, took two quick twisting steps and stood smiling and unscathed.

Fear's talons dug in. Soren's T-naught was 11.2. Even the fraction of a second it took Cooper to pull the trigger stretched out to full Mississippis for him, seconds during which he could see the angle of the gun, gauge Cooper's aim.

It wasn't dodging bullets, but it was—

This is a pump-action Remington tactical shotgun. Seven shells. If you fire rapidly and wide, you can catch him.

But she was shooting at the drone. How many times? Five?

Assume you have one shot left. Two if you're very lucky indeed.

—close enough. Cooper took a step left himself, aimed, faked a trigger pull. Soren didn't budge. The time dilation again. Trying to fake him out would be like a man on crutches trying to juke Muhammad Ali.

Behind him, he heard a snap and a whir, and knew what it was. The gliders were launched via massive winches that yanked them a mile in seconds. Shannon had just taken off. He had at most a minute before she sacrificed herself. And that was assuming she could make it at all; if not, the drone would loose its payload and everything they had done would be moot. The militia would kill Natalie and their children, and the virus would kill the country he had fought for his whole life.

Can't dodge, can't plan, what can you do?

Get reckless.

Cooper yelled through gritted teeth and charged at Soren, the shotgun held in one hand at waist height. He could see the man's confusion flicker quickly, and for just an instant Cooper's gift had a hold. There was no time to aim, just hope, and so he pulled the trigger as he ran, the recoil ripping his wrist back, pain shooting up it.

The blast jerked Soren halfway around. When the man turned back to face him, there were deep gouges across his right cheek. His ear had been shorn away. Blood flowed slick and dark down his face. His smile had vanished.

Cooper considered gambling on another shell in the gun, but if it was empty everything was over, so he just kept going, bringing the shotgun up to hold it by the barrel, the heat of it scorching his hands as he swung it like a club.

Soren stepped aside and jammed two locked fingers into Cooper's shoulder. His hand tingled and his fingers opened automatically and the gun flew off to skitter across the tarmac. He tried to use the momentum to crash into Soren, get him on the ground and land on top of him, but his opponent just wasn't there, he'd slid sideways and kept one foot out and braced to catch Cooper's, and now it was him falling, one arm numb, the other unable to get up in time to keep his face from colliding with the concrete, an electric shock through his teeth and a flash of white in his skull. Everything jumped, became two worlds that didn't line up. Before he could process the stereoscopic images, Soren grabbed Cooper's hair, yanked his head back, then slammed it into the concrete again. Fireworks exploded behind his retinas.

His body was distant and trembling, nothing working quite right, but he tried to rise, had to get off the ground, the ground was death in a fight, but there was a pressure against his shoulder, Soren's foot, he realized, pushing him so that instead of rising to a crouch he flipped over onto his back.

For a moment, Soren just stood looking down at him, a black silhouette against a burning city.

Then he reached down and drew a hunting knife.

"Do you remember," Soren said, "what you did to Samantha?"

■

The cable stretched taut ahead of her glider, the carbon fiber body racing down the tarmac, air whistling beneath the wings, that sense of yearning in it to take to the sky, bouncing less and less, and then the easy smoothness as wheels left runway, the cable still tugging. She'd blown past the drone, and there was the final yank and then release as the cable uncoupled, hurling her upward like a child throwing a paper airplane. As always, it felt like her stomach remained behind.

Normally, the thing to do would be to use the momentum of the launch to gain as much elevation as possible. Gliders loved the rocky desert, the howl of wind and the bounce of updraft, and with care and skill, could soar for hours. But this wasn't a pleasure trip, and she didn't have hours. Shannon grasped the stick with steady hands and pulled into a hard starboard roll, barely three hundred feet above the ground.

Still high enough for a marvelous view of hell.

Tesla wasn't her home, but the Holdfast was, and watching the capital city under siege was like being a Chicagoan watching enemies overwhelm DC. The battle lines were easy to see from up here; it was a real-life view of the battle map on her d-pad, only instead of using colors to represent the action, she could see the flicker of gunfire, a constant back-and-forth crackle like grains of gunpowder strewn in a circle and lit ablaze. At this height the attackers and defenders looked the same, ants locked in battle, fighting with weapons and hand-to-hand in the streets, their bodies lit by a thousand fires, Molotov cocktails and burning barricades and, she saw, quite a few of the buildings. Countless columns of greasy black smoke rose and smeared the view with a blanket of ash. The city looked like a Bosch painting, all smoky black and bloody red and writhing agony.

Shannon tore her eyes from it, focused on the runway. Somewhere down there Nick was facing Soren, and she threw a prayer his direction and then forced herself to scan for the drone. They were built for stealth, so there were no running lights, no shining surfaces, but its motion gave it away; there it was, in the air now and climbing. The glider took to the sky faster because of the winch, but that was the only advantage she had and it was fading fast. Unlike her craft, the drone was powered, which meant both more maneuverability and, soon, greater speed. If she was going to catch it, she had to do it now.

Not to mention that it doesn't have far to go.

She pitched downward in a hard spiral. The move built her speed at the cost of elevation, and while common enough as a soaring tactic, she didn't have much altitude to waste. If this were a fighter jet with roaring engines and mounted cannons and a targeting system, she could lock onto the drone and wipe it from the sky. But it wasn't. And besides, she didn't know how to fly a fighter jet.

Shannon lined up on the drone below her, plotting the vector of its motion against her own as she dove, the distance between them narrowing fast. Wind roared over the thin body of the glider, the material humming with it as she dove.

She'd have one try. If she missed, she might have time to pull up and regain altitude, but by then the UAV would be out of range. Her hands moved fluidly, the glider an extension of her body; she maneuvered it with the same precision she moved her limbs, the drone growing rapidly. It banked steadily, and she matched the motion, aligning the trajectories to intersect neatly.

Ten seconds.

Soren had launched the drone; he must have a way to control it. Cooper would have figured that out, and would be trying to bring it down.

Shannon stared at the drone. Barely blinking. It loomed larger and larger. She could see details now, the vapor trail from the engines, the registration number on the tail, the seams of its wide wing. She imagined it sputtering, the engines dying. Willed it to pitch downward into a fatal dive. Pictured it simply exploding, the self-destruct triggering the fuel tanks.

Five seconds.

It did not sputter.

Four.

It did not dive.

Three.

It did not blow up.

Two.

Come on, Nick. Don't make me do this.

One.

■

Cooper's vision was hazy, black gauze creeping in from the edges. His brain was trapped in a vise, like the worst hangover of all time, every beat of his heart ringing crystalline agony. His mouth was full of copper, and one of his teeth had broken, the exposed nerve shrieking. The sounds of battle had faded away, replaced by the thin thunder of breathing. He threw an awkward punch as Soren knelt to straddle him, but there was no power in it, and the man brushed it aside as he dropped down, knees pinning shoulders. The victory maneuver of a childhood brawl, and normally something Cooper could have countered easily, but his body was weak, he couldn't get any leverage. Every move he made, his enemy had time to read and counter.

Soren was lean, his kneecaps bony as he drove them into Cooper's shoulders. Half his face was coated in blood, a trickle that oozed down his neck and soaked his shirt. His cheekbone was visible in the worst of the gashes, the meat of muscle laid bare.

Reflected flames danced in his eyes and glinted off the edge of the knife, making it seem alive. Cooper tried to buck, but Soren could feel the play of muscles, had all the time in the world to redistribute his weight.

"You started," Soren said, "with her eye."

The knife slid down, the move slow, theatrical, giving Cooper time to see it coming, to anticipate the burning tear as it cut his flesh open, to imagine it plucking his eye from his skull. He wondered morbidly whether he would be able to see it happen through that eye. The drone was away, the militia was winning, Natalie would die in the battle, his children would be yanked from bunkers and murdered as the city burned around them and the world fell to darkness, and there was nothing Cooper could do about any of it. Soren had beaten him again, just as easily as before, but it would not be quick this time. Cooper could see the relish in the man's face, the madness whirling within him, the pleasure he would find in dispensing agony as civilization cracked and collapsed.

The knife drifted downward. The tip caressed his cheek. Penetrated. Scraped against the bone of his eye socket. The pain was sharpened by terror. He knew what would happen next, could imagine the blade digging, the agony, the permanence.

A blast of blue radiance flared like a lightning strike.

For a moment Cooper thought it was his eye going, but no, Soren saw it too, he was staring at the sky, his features carved in electric blue and darkness, a word forming—

That light is the same as when the other drone blew, liquid hydrogen burning explosively.

And Soren is staring, but it's not surprise or distraction that really has him.

It's despair.

Shannon took out the drone. She gave her life to do it.

And gave you an opportunity.

Are you going to waste her sacrifice?

—"No," he and Soren said at the same time, but where the other man was lost in his own time, staring upward in the slow revelation of his defeat, Cooper forced all thoughts of Shannon from his mind, knew what she would want him to do, that she hadn't thrown her life away, she had given it, and it was up to him to honor that, and Cooper put everything into a fast buck of his hips, throwing his arms up to lock Soren's wrist as he kept the momentum going, the two of them rolling, Soren's back hitting the ground as Cooper rolled atop him and twisted his arm, the man fighting back now, but inertia and strength were on Cooper's side and he used them, bending Soren's wrist back and driving the knife through the soft underside of his chin, the flesh stretching and then parting as Cooper slammed the heel of his hand into the pommel, driving the blade through the tongue and the palate and into his brain. Soren spasmed once, twice, and then Cooper got a firm grip and twisted the handle with everything he had and it was over.

He collapsed atop the monster's chest. Limbs weak and trembling. A shriek ripped from his lungs, a sound that wasn't a word. Was barely human. An animal howl of rage and pain and dominance.

Then he pushed himself to his feet, wobbling.

At the end of the airfield, blue flames danced like demons as pieces of metal and plastic rained from the sky.

He took a breath, made his feet move, a fall that became a step that became an awkward loping jog. Everything hurt. Blackness throbbed at his vision even as the fire grew brighter, hotter. He reached the UAV first, a twisted sculpture of flame, a licking inferno that forced him aside, but it wasn't the drone he was interested in. He kept moving, passing pieces of her plane, a teardrop wing bent awkwardly, the tail intact and upright, a rubber wheel belching smoke. The fuselage had snapped, the forward portion ahead and inverted. He ran to it, grabbed the handle, jerked his hands back from the heat, then took a breath and reached again, flesh scorching as he ripped the door open.

Shannon hung upside down, still belted to the seat, her torso packed hard in a white substance like Styrofoam but already melting, the impact foam dissolving to run thick and soapy to the tarmac, and something inside him gave the same way, a wash of warmth.

She opened her eyes. Met his. "Oww."

"You fucking nutcase," he said, laughing and gasping. "I thought you were dead."

"No," she groaned. "Not quite."

His burned fingers were clumsy, but he managed to undo her seat belt, her weight sliding into his arms, the two of them collapsing amidst the bubbling remains of the safety foam. She lay in his arms, both of them panting, lit in blue. Finally, he said, "A parachute was too much trouble?"

"Old-world thinking, Cooper." She smiled, and he bent down to kiss her, never mind the agony from his ribs, the shock from his splintered tooth.

There was another explosion, the UAV jumping and then crashing down again. They startled apart. Shannon said, "Soren?"

"Done."

"Good. That's good." She shifted, then winced. "I think my leg is broken."

"That'll teach you." He smiled, stood up, bringing her body with him, one arm draped around his shoulder, her body soft and warm against his.

"We won," she said.

"Almost. One more thing to do."

"What's that?"

"What you've been bugging me about since we met." He tried a wobbling step, found it okay, took another. He kissed the side of her hair, her hair smelling of smoke and sweat. "Tell the truth."

CHAPTER 44

In the flare of light from his rifle, the man kneeling in the street looked different from the others. For one thing he was older, fifty or even a very fit sixty. But there was more to it. It seemed to Natalie that he had a serenity about him. He had fired just a single shot, not a screaming burst, and where the others were lit by ferocity or pain, he had a killer's calm. As if this scene of horror was his home.

It scared her. And so when she lined up her sights on the place he had knelt, she didn't hold back. She held down the trigger and unloaded the rest of the magazine at him. The bullets ricocheted off the concrete, sparked off his rifle, and though she couldn't say for sure, she thought she saw his body fall.

She dropped to the floor, removed the magazine from her rifle, and reached for a new one. The bag was empty. She grimaced, said, "Jolene?"

As she looked over, she saw Jolene on the floor, arms outstretched and a strangely placid expression on her face. Staying low, Natalie hurried over. No point in checking for a pulse. There was a neat hole in her forehead.

Something tore in her then. She hadn't known the woman long, had really only had the one conversation, but they had fought side by side, and that had connected them in a way she'd never understood before. Like her, Jolene wasn't here for ideology, or Tesla, or even her own survival. She'd fought for a child. Natalie took a trembling breath. Laid a hand on Jolene's eyes and closed them. Then she grabbed her dead friend's spare ammunition and moved to the next window.

The moment she popped her head up, there was a fusillade of fire from the street below, flashes from a dozen spots. She dropped, fought the shake in her hands. The street had been filled with attackers, men sprinting across with impunity. For the first time in a long time, Natalie let herself look around.

When the attack started, there had been eight of them spread out across the floor. Eight men and women, including Jolene and Kurt and the pudgy girl with the dog. Jolene was down, Kurt was nowhere to be seen, and the dog was whimpering and pawing at the girl's body. Best Natalie could tell, she was the only one left.

Their line had failed. The Sons had broken past the building. It was over.

You don't know that. They'd been hit hard here, but maybe the rest of the city hadn't taken as much fire. She had to believe that, because otherwise it meant the militia was streaming in everywhere, and how long could it be before they reached the city center and the bunker where her children hid?

She didn't dare even crouch, instead crawled across the floor, pushing aside broken glass and spent shell casings. Her file cabinet was shredded, the metal punched with scores of holes through which paper scraps bled. The d-pad was already active; she'd left it up so that she could glance at the map as she reloaded, although she had been too focused to actually do it very often.

The city glowed in swirling colors like fire. It wasn't just their position that had broken. The Sons had gotten in through a dozen spots, and pitched battles raged all over the city. Epstein's towers still held, but the colors showed the militia drawing closer from every direction.

They'd failed. Somehow everything hadn't been enough.

Natalie stared. Tried to think what to do. She was low on ammunition and wildly outnumbered. The situation had flip-flopped, and now she was on the outside, and the killers were between her and her children. There was no way she could get through town.

She imagined Nick in this position and knew what he would think. *Fight until they kill you.* She loaded a fresh magazine, readied herself to face that fire again.

As she was about to stand, the battle map disappeared from her screen. There was a flash of an image, and not only from her d-pad, she saw, but from Jolene's. Others across the floor lit up too, casting bright lights against the ceiling. A ten-foot wall screen mounted on the opposite building glowed to life. And on all of them, the same image. A surreal, impossible picture.

Her ex-husband.

CHAPTER 45

When he'd thought of the idea earlier, Cooper had imagined a tri-d studio—lights, makeup, and more importantly, a professional. A newscaster, maybe, or Jakob Epstein. Someone who talked into cameras for a living.

"Time is a factor," Erik said over their video link. "And credibility."

"Exactly. That's why it should be someone who knows what they're doing—"

"They will not listen to us."

"What makes you think they'll listen to me?"

"Statistically also unlikely. Odds of success are—"

"Okay," Shannon cut in. "That's enough confidence-boosting, Erik. Is the link ready?"

"Yes. We've activated dormant Trojan horse software. Estimated efficiency puts the message on 96.4 percent of screens in America."

"Jesus Christ," Cooper said.

Shannon lowered the d-pad. "Give us a second."

They were still at the airfield, in the drone hangar. The lights were on, and Cooper felt strangely exposed under them, their sodium glare blasting out against the darkness of the city outskirts. The steady *pop-pop-pop* of gunfire continued in the distance, although it seemed quieter than before, which he was having a hard time imagining was a good thing. Shannon sat on a stool with her broken leg extended. His gift could read her pain in the sheen of neck sweat and the too-wide pupils. She said, "You okay?"

"I know this was my idea." He rubbed at his eyes. "But all of a sudden I don't know what to say."

"Just open your mouth and let the truth come out. I believe in you." She quirked her crooked smile at him. "So don't blow it, okay?"

Before he could respond, she pointed the d-pad camera at him, said, "Now, Erik."

"Activating."

Cooper swallowed his retort. Stared at the lens. Tried to imagine his face suddenly appearing on every d-pad, every phone, every tri-d in the country. Quickly decided that was a bad idea. Panic seized his belly. What was he supposed to say that could change the world?

Don't talk to the world.

Talk to Todd and Kate.

"My name is Nick Cooper," he said. "I am . . . I was a soldier, then an agent at the Department of Analysis and Response, an advisor to President Clay, and an ambassador to New Canaan. I'm an abnorm, I'm a patriot, and above all, I'm a father fighting for his children."

He took a breath, let it out. The air rushing past his broken tooth sparked electric. "Tesla is under attack by an illegal militia. The sound you hear is gunfire. Right now people on both sides are dying. Normals and gifted, men and women.

"Thirty years ago the world changed. We didn't ask for it. We didn't expect it. Since 1980 we've been trying to deal with it. We're doing a lousy job. And lately, both sides seem to think that war is the only way to make things right.

"But the words *right* and *war* don't belong together. War may sometimes be necessary, but it's never ethical. There is no such thing as a moral war." He thought of his children, huddled in a bunker. Of jets falling from the sky and a missile destroying the White House. Of Soren, trapped in a virtual hell Cooper had imagined. "It makes monsters of us all.

"Worst of all, war is never contained. It has no rules, no boundaries. We tell ourselves that we are fighting for our children. But it's our children who suffer the most."

■

Todd sat on the bunk with Kate and stared at the screen. The bunker was bright and had been noisy, thousands of kids all talking at the same time. But now all of them were quiet as they stared at the screens in their hands or those mounted on the wall.

He could barely breathe. Dad. Dad was alive. He looked terrible, his lips swollen and face dirty and a gash beneath his eye and blood between his teeth, but he was *alive*.

"A smart woman once told me," his father continued, "that there wouldn't be a war if people didn't keep going on television and saying there was. That the problem wasn't in our differences. It was in our lies.

"I have to believe that. I have to believe that by telling the truth, we can stop this. Not the politicians' truth, or the terrorists', not the part of the truth that we find convenient. The whole truth, even the stuff that stings.

"We are different, and dealing with those differences isn't easy. We're all scared. We're all hurting. And most of us just want to live our lives. We don't want to take to the streets, we want to put in a day and then have a beer and play with our kids."

Kate squirmed against him, and Todd looked down, saw her eyes were wide and wet. She said, "I told you he'd protect us."

"Shh." He wiped snot from her nose, put his arm around her, and tilted the d-pad so she could see better.

Dad said, "But this isn't happening far away, to people we'll never meet. It's happening to our children. We know it's wrong, and we've been letting ourselves ignore that.

"And there are people who are taking advantage. Extremists on both sides doing it for power. Some think they know better than you. Some are just scared. In the end, it doesn't matter. The fanatics don't care about you, and if you let them, they will push us into war for their own benefit.

"I'm talking about people like John Smith. And Secretary of Defense Owen Leahy."

■

Standing at the men's room sink, Leahy stiffened, his stomach filling with acid. He'd been using the toilet when the tri-d on the wall switched suddenly to video of Nick Cooper. He'd hurriedly wiped and flushed and now stood rooted.

"Both of these men," Cooper continued, "would tell you that they are fighting for their country. They may even believe it. But what they really want is war. The only weapon we have against fanatics is the truth, so here it is."

It's impossible, Leahy thought. *An abnorm trick. Cooper is dead. He was assassinated weeks ago.*

"Several months ago, a team of researchers discovered the biological source of brilliance. Not only that, but they figured out how to replicate it.

"That's been a goal for thirty years. It could change humanity's future forever. It's a triumph that belongs to all of us, that should have been screamed to the heavens.

"Instead, it was concealed. The scientists were chased by the government and terrorists alike. The work ended up in John Smith's hands. The greatest discovery in human history, and he immediately weaponized it. He used it to develop a virus that would have cost hundreds of millions of lives if he'd been able to release it.

"That's the truth. But there's more. Today, as an army of killers swept toward his city, Erik Epstein tried to beg the president for mercy. He couldn't get through."

The image cut away from Cooper, replaced by a split screen. On one side sat Erik and Jakob Epstein. On the other, Leahy found himself staring at himself. *The call from earlier. No. Oh, no . . .*

Erik: We surrender. Unconditionally.

Leahy: It's a bit late for that, isn't it? You've already murdered seventy-five thousand soldiers. Destroyed the White House. Killed our president.

Erik: Self-defense. Orders were given to attack, to bomb our city—

Leahy: I know. I gave them.

The video froze on him, an unflattering pause, a cold smile on his face.

Then Cooper was back. "That's the truth too. These people use our lives as poker chips. They did it in the Monocle. In the bombing of the stock exchange. Right now, a mob is burning a city of innocents. And all for lies.

"Both normals and gifted are staring into the abyss. But there is still time, barely, to make a choice. We can find a way to move forward together." He paused. "Or we can keep fighting. All of you watching can sit quietly while Tesla is destroyed, while thousands of brilliants are massacred with their families. But make no mistake, that won't be a victory. Someone will survive, and they will strike back harder. Blood will lead to blood. In the end, we'll annihilate each other."

Cooper stopped talking, and the video held on his face for a moment, blue flames burning behind him, the faint firecracker pop of gunfire. Finally, he said, "We are better than this. We have to be."

A moment later the video disappeared, and the screen returned to a newsfeed, the anchors confusedly blinking at one another.

Leahy stared. His hands shook. They looked so old. Part of him wanted to run, but where would he go? There was no window to crawl out of, no getaway car waiting to whisk him to safety.

You'll have to bluff it through. You can do that. You've done it before.

He took a deep breath and stepped out of the bathroom.

Camp David's largest conference room had been converted to serve as the Situation Room. Ranged around the table sat the chief advisors, the surviving cabinet, the commanders of the armed forces. Twenty pairs of eyes stared at him. On a dozen screens, the battle for Tesla raged.

President Ramirez rose from the head of the table. She pressed a button on the intercom. "Could we get some agents in here please?"

"Madam President, I can explain—"

The door to the conference room banged open and four men in dark suits rushed in, eyes sweeping for threats, their coats open and hands inside.

Ramirez said, "Detain Secretary Leahy for treason."

The Secret Service agents glanced at one another, then drew their sidearms and moved toward him. Leahy said, "Madam President, this is foolish—"

"If he resists," Ramirez said, "shoot him."

Then she turned to the people around the table. "Get me Epstein."

CHAPTER 46

"We are better than this." Cooper's face was ten feet high. "We have to be."

The video cut back to the anchor, a warm-eyed woman in severe glasses. "In the three days since former DAR agent Nicholas Cooper made an impassioned plea to the American public, round-the-clock negotiations between the United States and the New Canaan Holdfast have been ongoing, with sources close to the president saying they are confident that this marks, quote, a new era of communication and friendship, end quote. While no agreement has been formalized, the expected provisions will include sharing the technical details of the so-called Couzen-Park Therapy, the process by which abnorm gifts can be replicated in—"

Erik Epstein changed the channel with a gesture.

"—arrival of the prisoner transport carrying retired two-star General Samuel Miller. Miller, who incited and led the militia group known as the New Sons of Liberty, will be tried as a war criminal. His arrest is controversial, as is the general amnesty granted to all members of the militia who lay down their arms—"

Another gesture, another channel.

"—forty-five minutes later there were jet fighters over Tesla. The whole nation had been told that military intervention was impossible. The official story is that Secretary of Defense Owen Leahy exaggerated the effects of the military retrograde in order to allow the New Sons of Liberty to attack the Holdfast. But how far beyond him did the conspiracy go? How do we know that

President Ramirez herself was not part of that decision, and only forced to act because of the pirate broadcast?"

Gesture.

"—I agree that Mr. Cooper's speech was moving. But what people seem to be ignoring is that abnorms hijacked every device in America. It wasn't just a massive privacy violation, it was a criminal act employing the same methodology as the computer virus that murdered seventy-five thousand soldiers and destroyed the White House."

"Yes, but isn't that the point? Their technological superiority has to be taken into consideration. If NSOL hadn't been stopped, the Holdfast could have used that same technology aggressively—"

Gesture.

"—media is painting Nick Cooper like he's some kind of hero. The man is an assassin. He killed people for the DAR. He openly admits to murdering activist and author John Smith. But because he claims Smith was a terrorist, we're supposed to cheer—"

Cooper said, "I'm getting tired of myself. Mind switching me off?"

Erik smiled and muted the stream, then turned, tucking his hands in the pockets of his sweatshirt. Behind and above and around him, video kept playing in a dozen quadrants. Footage of helicopters buzzing the Tesla streets. Thousands of protesters packed around the Lincoln Memorial Reflecting Pool, waving placards. Owen Leahy in handcuffs. Ethan Park wearing a sharp suit and talking with his hands as diagrams of DNA helixes spun. Workers picking through the rubble of the DAR offices. The brothers Epstein lit in strobes of flashbulbs, Jakob suave as ever, Erik looking like he'd been balled up and slept in. And always, everywhere, the video of Cooper beat to shit, pleading to the camera as blue flames burned behind him.

That night, after Shannon turned off the d-pad, they had just stared at each other. Bone-weary, wrung dry, and out of moves. It had been a terrible feeling. Half a mile away, the battle had continued, the gunfire raging. Natalie was out there somewhere, his children were still in danger, and there was literally nothing more he could do. Nothing but wait and hope.

It had only been a few minutes before his phone rang, but they were the longest few minutes of his life. Millie had been on the other end, her voice filled with a lightness he'd never heard as she said that Erik and the president were speaking, and that they were agreeing to trust each other.

"Can they?"

She'd paused, then said, "Yes. I think they can."

Not long after that, the cavalry had arrived on a roar of afterburners and the whapping of helicopter blades. Mounted loudspeakers ordered both sides to put down their weapons, stern voices assuring the armies on the ground that the one in the sky was fully armed and ready to fire.

A bluff. The military retrograde had gone so far that it had taken a direct order from the president to the commander of Ellsworth Air Force Base to even get craft in the air, and they didn't have a bomb between them. But the New Sons didn't know that. And whatever else the militiamen were, by and large they were patriots. That was how General Miller had motivated them in the first place, selling them the idea that they were the rough men America needed. There were certainly a few psychos too, but faced with direct orders from their president, not to mention the seeming might of the United States Air Force, they had stood down.

President Ramirez had granted a full amnesty for every person on both sides—other than Miller, who would likely hang alongside Owen Leahy—assuming they laid down their weapons. That part stuck in Cooper's throat, the idea that these men who had marched children in front of them, who had tried to kill Natalie and Todd and Kate, would just go back to their homes. But he was the one who'd called for compromise, and the nature of compromise was that no one was happy. That's how you knew a fair deal had been reached.

"The tests at the airfield turned out okay?"

"Viral influenza is destroyed between seventy-five and one hundred degrees Celsius. Liquid hydrogen burns above two thousand degrees."

"But no traces were found? Nothing spattered in the explosions, survived on the ground?"

"The airfield was quarantined and incinerated. No evidence the virus escaped."

It was a relief. In the moment, there had been nothing to do but take the chance, but Cooper had been haunted since by the idea that they might have accidentally done Smith's work for him. "And now you're a celebrity, on your way to a summit with the president. How does it feel to be a public figure?"

The abnorm grimaced. "I like people."

"I know, Erik. I know." He smiled. "What's your take on Ramirez?"

"She operates with significant efficiency."

"Wow," Cooper said. "High praise. Is the deal finalized?"

"Broad strokes. Dotting and crossing remain." The terms of it were all over the newsfeeds. Besides sharing Ethan's work, the NCH agreed to remove all software backdoors from all computer systems, to obey laws both state and federal, and to relinquish all attempts at sovereignty. The Holdfast was American territory, and would remain so. In addition, Epstein had pledged half his fortune to reparations for the families of those killed by his Proteus virus.

For her part, the president had agreed to dismantle the Monitoring Oversight Initiative to microchip brilliants. The "abnorm refuges" like Haven in Madison Square Garden were dissolved, all residents free to go. Ramirez was also expected to issue executive orders extending nondiscrimination coverage to the gifted. Technically the Fourteenth Amendment covered that already, but given the last few years, the reminder was welcome.

There were a thousand questions yet to be answered—the functioning of the academies, the future of the DAR, war crimes trials, questions of copyright violation and cybercrime, access to Ethan's work, on and on and on. Each of them was a potential public policy nightmare, a flashpoint for civil unrest. No battle, no speech, kept the world from turning. But in theory, gifted and normals would have to deal with one another as American citizens, equal in the eyes of the law. It was something.

"What about December 1st? The troops, and the White House?"

Erik looked down. "I had no choice."

"You could have surrendered then."

"Statistically—" He broke off. "Perhaps."

"Those were American soldiers. Our president. Our history. It's nice that you're giving a couple hundred billion dollars, and forgive and forget is a pleasant sales pitch. But no one is buying. Me included."

"Each side bears blame. 'Both normals and gifted are staring into the abyss.' Your words. The abyss is frightening. It might be enough. To bring change."

"I hope so," Cooper said. He rose from his seat. Held out his hand. "To change."

Epstein took it. "To change."

"You're heading to DC tomorrow?"

"Yes."

"Good luck."

"Luck is an imprecise idiom. And you? Where are you going?"

"Long term? I'm not sure," Cooper said. "But right now, I'm going to go see my kids. And have a conversation I'm dreading."

Erik smiled. "Good luck."

CHAPTER 47

"Daddy!" Kate squealed as she threw herself at him. Cooper hoisted her up, her little-girl bottom resting on his forearm, her face jammed into his shoulder, her arms wrapped around his neck and squeezing. She smelled like shampoo and cereal bars, and immediately began a nonstop monologue, how she'd missed him, even though he'd been here yesterday, how all the kids wanted to be her friends now that he was famous and how she was staying friends with the ones who had been her friends before and . . .

"Hey, Dad," Todd said. He was trying a grown-up voice that didn't match his goofy grin. He held out a hand to shake, and Cooper grabbed it, yanked his son into the embrace.

This is what you fought for. Not ideals, not compromise, not some vague notion of tomorrow. These two people right here.

"Hey, you," Natalie said. There were dark circles under her eyes, but her smile was warm.

Three people.

"Hey, you," he said, and gestured her to join them in a family hug. They all held on for a long time. Finally, he said, "This is probably a long shot."

"What?"

"No, I feel silly."

"Daddy, what?"

"Well, I was just wondering, is there any chance, and it's okay to say no, but is there any chance that you guys would be interested in burgers and milkshakes?"

The kids ran about gathering their stuff, Todd's coat and hat and d-pad, Kate's worn lovey and new book and wasn't her scarf cool? Cooper let them go, lapping up the warmth of it, answering questions, rifling their hair. Natalie seemed far away, and he glanced sideways at her, almost asked if she was okay, decided against it. Reached out for her hand instead and squeezed it.

The morning after the attack, the two of them had put on a brave face for the kids, saying that things hadn't been that bad, never mind the burned-out buildings, the uniformed soldiers arriving in heavy trucks, the bodies still being collected, the smell of smoke and blood. It wasn't until after the kids were in bed that they'd gotten a chance to talk.

Natalie had told him about the siege, calmly at first, then her eyes drifting away, her fingers tracing coffee rings on the table, her voice growing hollow as she described the day and the night. The things she had seen. The things she had done. That she wasn't sure how many people she had killed but knew it was quite a few. That she had aimed her rifle and pressed the trigger and then done it again and again and again and again and again. That she had thrown flaming gasoline on living men, had heard their screams, smelled their hair scorching away, and then shot their comrades by the light of their burning flesh.

When she had cried, he had held her and whispered that it was okay, though they both knew that was a lie. He was a soldier, always had been, and it wasn't the killing that wounded him so deeply, it was the idea of Natalie doing it.

"You didn't have a choice," he'd said, and she had nodded into his chest.

"I know."

She wasn't going to have a nervous breakdown, wasn't going to question the reasons for her actions. She was fully aware of them. But he could see the change in her, see that her world had become a darker place, and he knew that she would probably carry that forever. Not every moment, not even most. But the weight would never really vanish.

You owe her everything. Every pure thing in your life has flowed from Natalie.

And you have given her nothing but fear and pain. You owe her more.

The things we do for our children, he thought. She had said that to him almost a year ago. He squeezed her hand again, and she blinked and smiled at him.

The diner was a madhouse, full to bursting with construction crews and research scientists and United States marines. But when the hostess saw him, she lit up like a forest fire, said, "Right this way, Mr. Cooper. We'll *make* space." Her voice was louder than he would have liked, and half the restaurant turned to look, pointing and shooting him nods and thumbs-up.

"Ohmygawwwd," Natalie said. "Is that really you, Mr. Cooper? Can I have your autograph? Please, please, oh pretty please?"

He gave her the finger.

The food was greasy goodness, fries cooked crisp, burgers that tasted the way he remembered from when he was a kid, washed down by rich chocolate milkshakes. The four of them laughed and joked, falling easily into the long-held rhythms of a happy family. It was good; it was more than good.

Afterward, they went for a walk. Columns of dust rose into the cold blue sky in all directions as construction crews demoed damaged buildings. Pillars of dust were an improvement on pillars of smoke, he figured. They stayed near the city center, which was largely undamaged. When they happened on a playground, both kids flashed questioning looks, then raced off to join the other children in a free-form game of tag that operated under elaborate rules he couldn't parse. Cooper and Natalie took a bench in the sun, sitting close.

"Would you look at that?" She smiled. "I know it's just a playground. But still. They're all playing together."

"Do you think it will last?"

"We can hope, right?"

They sat together, bellies full, watching children play. A simple pleasure, one of the everyday joys that Cooper rarely got enough of, and he could have sat there forever in pleasant, companionable silence. Instead he said, "I spoke to the president today."

"Ramirez? Really?"

He nodded. "She wants me to join the government."

"Savvy PR move."

"Yeah, but I get the sense she's sincere. Made it clear I could pretty much write my ticket, be an ambassador, an advisor. Though she did have a suggestion." He paused. "She asked me to come back to the DAR."

"As an agent?" Natalie's voice was incredulous.

"No," Cooper said. "As the director."

She whistled.

"I told her that I didn't think there was a place for the old DAR now. She agreed. She wants to completely re-envision it, change it from a monitoring agency to, well, something new. Ethan's formula is under wraps, but now that everyone knows it exists, there will need to be some sort of policy. Plus, there are still plenty of terrorist organizations out there, and hate groups on both sides. The president said she saw the new DAR not being solely about watching abnorms, but more about the intersection between . . ." He looked at her and trailed off.

Natalie's spine was tight, shoulders bunched, her hands folded in her lap. One of her surest tells, one his gift had patterned long ago. It meant that she was thinking about their relationship and was about to bring it up.

It was a moment he'd dreaded, because though he loved her, would always love her, he was going to have to tell her that he wanted to be with another woman.

"Listen," he said, at the same time that she said, "I'm sorry."

They stopped awkwardly. "Go ahead."

"I have to apologize. I don't think I . . ." Natalie sighed. Rubbed her hands together. "Look. I never liked what you did, even though I understood. But it just kept getting harder. While we were together, and even after we split up. I was scared all the time. I'd be sitting in a meeting, or, I don't know, folding Kate's pajamas, and my imagination would just serve up these pictures, these vivid little daymares of things that could be happening to you. Ways you could be getting hurt, or . . ."

She sighed. "Anyway. Then you left the department and started working for President Clay. You were still trying to make things better, but you were safe. And maybe it was the worry, or maybe it was that I thought the worry was over, but somewhere in there, I started to wonder if we'd given up too easily."

"Natalie, I—"

"Just let me do this, okay?" She stared straight ahead. "We've loved each other forever. And you're a great dad, and . . . We were good together. Really good."

He nodded.

"I thought I knew what your world was like. But I didn't, not really. I'd been a tourist. The other night I lived there. All on my own. I did what I had to do. To protect the kids, same as you. But I hated it. I can't live like that. I won't."

From the playfield, Kate waved, and Natalie waved back. "I know you've always thought your gift was our problem. But mostly it's the world you live in. When you joined Clay, I pretended that you were leaving that life. But you haven't. And now I understand that you can't." She turned to face him. "You can't, babe. You're too good at it. We need you. They need you. The next John Smith is out there somewhere."

"Natalie—"

"I know I made this messy. I reached out to you. I don't regret it. And I don't regret"—she almost-smiled—"making love again. But I'm sorry, Nick. I was wrong. I can't be with you. Not that way. I just can't."

He looked at her, at the face he had kissed a million times, the skin he knew every freckle and line of. The woman who had once been the first girl he'd fallen in love with. A woman who still managed to surprise him, despite his gift and their experience.

"Say something," she said.

"I was just thinking," he said, "that you're amazing."

"Oh, that." She shrugged, smiled. "That's true."

Her hand reached for his.

Together they watched the children play.

CHAPTER 48

"One second," her voice said through the wall. Then, "Stupid freaking lousy pieces of—" The door jerked open.

The device around Shannon's right thigh was clear plastic filled with glowing green gel, stretching from two inches above her knee to two inches below her groin and bound with weird centipede-looking straps that twitched and burrowed as she moved. No doubt it was the best the Holdfast could offer—he'd never seen anything like it—but the overall effect was a cross between steampunk jewelry and medieval torture device. She saw his expression, said, "What?"

Cooper tried not to laugh. He really did. But that only made it worse. What started as a muffled snort quickly threw off the reins. It was the exasperated, *you gotta be kidding me* look on her face, that and the notion of the Girl Who Walks Through Walls using crutches, her lissome grace reduced to bumps and lurches.

"Yeah, go ahead and laugh, asshole."

He made an effort to stop, found that he just couldn't.

"Enjoy yourself," she said. "Don't mind me."

"Sorry." He finally managed to lock it down. "Sorry. You look great."

"Ha-ha."

"No, really. Where can I get one of those?"

"Keep on like that, you're gonna find out."

He stepped in, took her head in his hands, and kissed her. They took their time, a dance of tongues and lips. When they finally broke it, he said, "Hi."

"Hi."

He glanced down. "Does it hurt?"

"Not with the pain pills. And according to Epstein's doc, two weeks wearing the monstrosity, two weeks of physio, I'm good as new. Not bad for a snapped femur."

"Yaa. Hearing 'snapped' and 'femur' in the same sentence sends shivers down my spine."

"Pretty heroic, huh?" She gestured him in. "You know, I survived a spectacular midair collision to save the world."

"Well, officially, *I* saved it. It says so on all the channels."

"Jesus." Shannon hobbled to the couch and lowered herself down. "You were already cocky. Now you're going to be insufferable. Beer?"

"Sure."

She winked. "In the fridge. Grab me one too."

The kitchen was tiny. There was nothing in the refrigerator but hot sauce, mustard, and beer. It looked a lot like his own. "Should you have this with the pain pills?"

"Definitely." She accepted it, took a long swallow. Cooper glanced around the apartment, cataloging the gun cleaning kit on the counter, the muted tri-d, the books propped facedown—she'd once told him that when she liked a book she snapped the spine so it could lie flat while she ate—the Murphy bed folded into the wall, the desk in the corner, stacks of junk spread out beneath the leaves of a plastic plant. A place for an un-life, a half-life. A way station for a life lived elsewhere. He smiled. "Remember when we were driving here? Before everything. Our fake passports had us married."

"Tom and Allison Cappello."

"Right. We were making up the backstory, how we'd worked together at some desk job. I asked if you'd ever actually had a desk, being a smartass, and you hit it back, said something like, 'Yeah, it does a good job holding my fake plant.'"

"True story," she said. "That desk is a team player."

"You didn't mention all the random crap on it."

"It's not random. I know where everything is. How'd your call with the prez go?"

"Kind of amazingly." He filled her in.

"Wow," she said. "Are you going to take the job?"

"I don't know yet. I told her I needed a vacation first."

"Oh? Where are you going?"

"We. Where are *we* going." Cooper sat beside her on the couch. "We never got that date. How about we do it somewhere warm? I'm thinking rum drinks and coconut oil and palm trees. No guns. No plots."

"No one trying to kill us?"

"For a week or two. Of course—" He glanced down at her cast, said, "I was also picturing you in a bikini."

She laughed, that good deep one he'd always liked. "As soon as I can move my leg, I'm going to kick your ass."

"I look forward to it, gimpy. In the meantime, there's something else we should do."

"Yeah? What?"

"Fold that bed out of the wall and carry you to it."

"Is that right? Got a thing for the handicapped, Cooper?" Her smile was slow and wicked. "I don't even know how we'd manage it."

"Nick," he said. "You call me Nick. And I bet we can figure it out."

They did.

EPILOGUE

For the third night in a row he'd gone to bed shivering, his mind on rails, racing on paths he didn't choose at speeds he didn't care for. There were sweats and a cough, too, but it wasn't the cold that was getting him.

When he woke, it was nearly noon, the sun pouring through the window. Some scout of his consciousness, ranging ahead of his waking self, warned him that he was about to feel awful again. He took a breath and lay still.

Nothing. He felt fine.

Hawk rolled out of the cot. The lodge was a two-room log cabin with lacquered walls and the smell of smoke from the woodstove. He staggered to the bathroom and took the longest leak in history. The toothbrush was someone else's but better than nothing, even though 532 of the bristles bent out in tired waves.

He was halfway through his bottom teeth when he realized that he knew how many bristles were bent. Without any effort or thought, he'd known it as certainly as he knew that if he dropped the toothbrush it would fall: 532 bristles, which represented 21.28 percent of the total number. He smiled. Finished brushing. Spat.

The night of the battle, after the militia had passed, he'd forced himself off the kitchen floor and into the garage. It took twenty minutes of alternately stalling out and grinding gears to get the hang of the Jeep, but by the time the gunfire started, he was out of town, riding west. Around midnight he'd let himself into the hunting cabin with a rock, intending to hit the road first thing. But he'd woken with his brain on fire, and everything since had been a blurry fugue.

In the kitchen he ate canned corn while the coffee dripped. When the machine hissed, he reached for a mug, but wasn't paying attention, and it slipped off the counter and tipped end over end.

It was beautiful.

Hawk didn't have the mathematics to describe it, but he could see the formula clearly, the way gravity and air resistance and momentum were dancing, and he found it so fascinating that he took a few seconds to watch, just made it spin slower and slower until he could examine every detail: the inside stained in distinct rings, a faint fingerprint on the handle, the way dust swirled around it and sunlight gleamed off the rim as the mug drifted slowly to the floor.

When it hit, it burst into fragments that vectored predictably, and he could hear the sound of each piece as it clicked against the tile, and for some reason they made him think of John.

In the maintenance tunnel, lecturing on the importance of contingencies, John had been paying only a small fraction of attention to the boy behind him. But then he'd stopped and stared full focus. "I need to tell you something, Hawk. Something important. There's a very good chance I won't make it out of this. If that happens, just remember that you're the future."

"I don't understand."

"You will," John had said, and then they had climbed up the ladder and a few minutes later he was dead.

He was right, Hawk thought. *There wouldn't have been any point in explaining then. But you understand now.*

He understood other things, too. That John had been using him, that when he'd referred to turning a pawn into a queen, this was what he'd meant. It was okay. He'd still cared about Hawk, had treated him like a man, given him a name and a purpose and his heart's desire. The reasons might matter, but not as much as the facts.

Hawk took a new mug and poured a cup of coffee, drank it slowly, thinking. Then he went outside and climbed into the Jeep. As he reached for his seat belt, a fit of coughing racked him, and he leaned against the steering wheel until it passed. When he could breathe again, he took a tissue from his pocket.

Then stopped.

Wadded up the tissue.

Wiped his nose with his hands, and rubbed them together.

The gas tank was three-quarters full. Figure it held sixteen gallons, with a fuel efficiency of roughly twenty-two miles per, call it three hundred and fifty miles per full tank. With the money he'd found in the safe house, he could fill the Jeep eight, maybe ten times. He'd need food too, and cash for contingencies—*thank you, John*—so assume twenty-five hundred miles.

Hawk called up a mental map, the image as crisp as if he were looking at the real thing, right down to the scale in the corner.

First, Salt Lake City.

Then Reno.

Sacramento.

San Francisco.

Los Angeles.

Northeast to Las Vegas, southeast to Phoenix.

Spin back to end the trip in San Diego.

Total distance, 2440 miles.

Forty hours if he did it straight. But he'd want to eat in restaurants, go to church, ride buses. Given the latency he'd experienced, though, he couldn't dawdle too much. So spend, say, four days shaking hands and sneezing his way through metropolitan areas encompassing a population of, let's see . . .

Nine million people.

Hawk coughed, smiled, and started the Jeep.

There was a long way to go.

END OF THE BRILLIANCE TRILOGY

ACKNOWLEDGMENTS

In 2010, on a climbing trip with my buddy Blake Crouch, I fell in love with an idea. We were camping at fourteen thousand feet, bullshitting and sipping bourbon when it happened. Like most love affairs, it started with a sense of intrigue, swiftly progressed to flirting, and before either of us knew it, we were both gaga over reckless notions. Blake's became the wildly successful *Wayward Pines* trilogy. Mine culminates in the book you're now holding.

It's been a long, wonderful journey, spanning five years, three books, and three hundred thousand words—and those are just the ones I kept. In that time my wife and I sold a condo, bought a house, had a daughter, laughed and cooked and traveled. That journey is now at an end, and like most experiences that change you, its ending brings both joy and regret.

It's been such a pleasure to live in this world, to hang out with Cooper and Shannon and Natalie and Ethan and Quinn—sorry, Bobby, really I am—and John Smith and Erik Epstein and Hawk, and the notion of that time being behind me is a melancholy one indeed. But while I may return to this world at some point, I think that those stories are done; everyone got their shining moments and their blackest midnights, and I am grateful to them for letting me hitch a ride.

There are a number of other people I'm grateful to as well, and while few of them have a body count, like my imaginary friends, they are all badasses.

My literary agent, Scott Miller, is a fine man and a good friend, a believer from the beginning. Jon Cassir whips Hollywood into line and looks suave doing it. Thank you both, gentlemen.

It remains an honor to work with Thomas & Mercer, publishers extraordinaire. No power in the 'verse can stop my editor and FF, Alison Dasho. Jacque Ben-Zekry bends the world to her will, and it thanks her and asks her for another. Gracie Doyle kicks ass and chews bubblegum. Additional huge thanks to Tiffany Pokorny, Alan Turkus, Mikyla Bruder, Daphne Durham, and Jeff Belle, brilliant and dedicated folks whose love for story burns like a star.

Shasti O'Leary Soudant did an amazing job re-envisioning the covers of the whole series. Jessica Fogleman caught approximately one million errors I'd made. Caitlin Alexander brought vision and style to her edit, and did it crazy-fast.

My old friend Dr. Yuval Raz was incredibly generous with his time and knowledge. Both the biological basis for brilliance and the methodology to burn down the world belong to him, a juxtaposition that tickles me.

When I was stuck, when I was insomniacal, when I was rocking back and forth sobbing and picking at my skin, my boys Blake Crouch and Sean Chercover were always there to get me through. The words are all mine, but plenty of the solutions are theirs.

As always, boundless thanks to my parents, Tony and Sally, and my brother, Matt. I love you all.

My girls are my life. Thank you to my grown-up love g.g. and our little love, the brilliant, fearless, and very silly Jocelyn Sally Sakey.

Finally, dear reader, thank you. This is what I have wanted to do since I was four years old, and I am grateful for every moment of it. And so I say again: thank you.

ABOUT THE AUTHOR

Photo by Jay Franco

Marcus Sakey's thrillers have been nominated for more than fifteen awards. They've been named *New York Times* Editors' Choice picks and have been selected among *Esquire*'s top five books of the year. His novel *Good People* was made into a movie starring James Franco and Kate Hudson, and *Brilliance* is currently in development. Sakey lives in Chicago with his wife and daughter.

For more information, visit MarcusSakey.com.